ghost warning

Caitlin Press Inc.
8100 Alderwood Road,
Halfmoon Bay, BC V0N 1Y1
www.caitlin-press.com

Text design and cover design by Vici Johnstone
Printed in Canada
Cover image Tom Chitty, www.drawnbytom.com

Caitlin Press Inc. acknowledges financial support from the Government
of Canada and the Canada Council for the Arts, and the Province of
British Columbia through the British Columbia Arts Council and the
Book Publisher's Tax Credit.

Library and Archives Canada Cataloguing in Publication

Stanley, Kara, author
        Ghost warning / Kara Stanley.

ISBN 978-1-987915-54-9 (softcover)

        I. Title.

PS8637.T352G56 2017   C813'.6   C2017-904598-9

ghost warning

kara stanley

For Simon and for Eli.

part 1

1

Linden, October 1988

I found Dad this morning when I went to the garage to pull out the box with our winter scarves, toques and mismatched mittens. October's bright autumn skies had been replaced overnight with a morning that dawned grey and cruelly cold, the sky low and dense with coming snow. Is that why I missed it? Him, his coldness? I felt it as soon as I opened the garage door and saw him, a different kind of coldness that surged through me with the force of an electrical current, a coldness that emanated from the stillness of his body and that filled the low-ceilinged room. The way, when you are near someone who is sick with the flu, say, and they have a fever and you can sense that fever in the air as both a disturbance and a smell, an overcrowded riot of breath that careens off corners with a sulfurous tang. It's like that when someone dies, only in reverse. You try to call their name but all breath, all sound, turns to stone in the cold air.

Dad and I keep very different schedules. Kept. We kept very different schedules, which is why —

I don't finish the sentence but everyone understands, at least I think they do, they all nod at me, yes, yes, their faces dumb and blurry at the edges. How could they understand? The early morning is when I am most alive and Dad never liked to wake before eleven or twelve. Almost always I was in bed, reading or asleep, when he came home. He was a night owl. When I was little I believed he could see in the dark. I explain that to the police. I explain it to the paramedics. I explain it to our next door neighbour, Mrs. Turner, and all the neighbours that follow. I explain it so many times I start to doubt myself.

I didn't worry when he didn't come home last night, I say. I didn't expect to see him. I was reading a book. A good book about a half-man, half-cyborg that travels through history collecting animals destined to become extinct in order to send them all to an island in the future. It is critical they understand, this parade of nodding faces, that it was a good book. I repeat myself. I can't, at the moment, remember the name of it, but it was a really good book. Yes, yes, they nod. Maybe they think I'm lying? Maybe I am lying. How could I not have known? That his car pulled up sometime after dinner. That between the car door and the garage door he had slumped and fallen, his heart choking or drowning or otherwise refusing to beat. That around the time I got out of my hot bath and into my pyjamas, he closed his eyes against the cold concrete of the garage floor and died.

"Sit down, dear," Mrs. Turner says. Kindness oozes out of her eyes as she pats the chair beside her, so much kindness it is as though I am permanently wrapped in a suffocating hug. The whole room is crammed full of kindness. And pity. It radiates from the gathered neighbours like a sickly sweet sweat and makes me want to scream. Inside I am screaming. If I open my mouth perhaps my scream will shatter the kindness that is posing as normalcy and everything can go back to being as strangely unreal as it was before they came. "Lou, sit down. Would you like some water?" Mrs. Turner uses both hands to push herself up from the table but I shake my head no and turn away, retreating to the small alcove midway between the kitchen and the garage door to Dad's phone desk. It's where he makes calls and hangs his calendar (Renoir, this year) and sorts mail. I call Jonah, but get his answering machine. *Jonah here. You know what to do.* I call again and again, dialling his number six or seven times in a row, just to hear his voice. I imagine him sitting by the phone, ignoring it the way Dad did when he was engrossed in work, and I silently beg Jonah to hear the desperation in my rings. *Please, Jonah. Pick up. I don't know what to do.* Nothing. On the tenth dial I listen all the way through to the end of his message, waiting for the long beep. "Jonah — " I squeak, not able to go on. What can I say? I can't start crying into the answering machine, it would freak Jonah right out. I take a deep breath. "Don't worry. I'll talk to you later."

I hang up but keep my hand on the top of the receiver, in case Jonah calls back. To my right, Mrs. Turner moves to the sink, filling the kettle. She rummages in the coffee cupboard and is rewarded with a partially crushed box of Red Rose. To my left, through the garage door, the paramedics lift Dad's body — cocooned in a black zipped-up bag, the kind you see on TV — onto a stretcher. When they first arrived, they rushed into the garage and bent over Dad. "What's happening?" I asked on repeat, a stupid question that implied there was something going on that could be stopped or altered, when all along it was clear that what was happening had already happened. Was over. One of the paramedics took me into the kitchen and sat me down on a chair. He said Dad's heart had stopped, there was nothing they could do but that it had been quick. Dad wouldn't have felt any pain.

The last remaining officer, Officer Wood, steps through the garage door and joins me in the alcove, blocking my view. I look out the round window beside the phone desk for the ambulance but it too is hidden. When I was little, Dad told me he stole that round window from a pirate ship and I believed him until the day I wised up and realized that every house on our block had a small round window that looked out onto the driveway. Outside the sky is so heavy with snow the midday light is the colour of a day-old bruise.

"Well." Officer Wood spreads his fingers in front of him, like a pianist about to tackle a particularly challenging concerto. His hands are large and covered in red scaly patches that look as though they must itch and sting in hot water. He has a comfortable face. You can tell he smiles easily and often, although he isn't smiling now. His forehead is crinkled with worry lines and his lips are pressed together. I imagine I'm a problem. At sixteen, I'm too old to be treated like a kid and not old enough to be treated like an adult. He scratches the back of his left hand. "What are we going to do with you?"

"I'll wait with Mrs. Turner," I say. "Until I get a hold of my brother. He's in Toronto. I can stay with him."

His hand scratching becomes more vigorous, and he chews on his bottom lip. He doesn't say anything, but like the ladies in the kitchen, his eyes are laser beams of kindness and pity, along with a good dose of doubt. Would this cop *not* let me go to Jonah? He couldn't, I don't think, but suddenly my heart is thumping so loudly I'm certain he must be able to hear it.

"He's twenty-one," I say. My voice is shaky but I press on. "My brother. He's twenty-one. He's responsible. I can stay with him."

"Hmmm," he says and hands me a card with his phone number. "Okay. You call if you need anything. Any time."

I pocket the card and maybe I nod, or shake my head. It's difficult to look him in the eyes.

"Well," he says again, left hand scratching right hand now. "You take care. I'm sorry for your loss." The door leading into the garage clicks shut behind him. Closed, it looks like any regular door.

Mrs. Turner has disappeared. I can't see, but can hear, the assembled ladies at the kitchen table, issuing forth a benevolent hum, a rhubarb rhubarb of troubled concern. Rhubarb rhubarb is what big crowds are directed to mutter on stage to mimic realistic chatter. Dad told me that. Dad also said that the power of kindness and civility should never be underestimated. According to him, if simple kindness and civility were human beings' default setting, many of history's horrors could have been avoided. *Kindness is not the worst thing in the world, Lou*. It's Dad's voice, so clear in my head that I crane my neck to see if he's coming down the stairs, still in his pyjamas, smiling his crooked left-sided smile. But he's not there. I take another deep breath and head back into the kitchen.

"Tea, Louise?" Mrs. Turner asks as I step into the fug of unusual lady smells: perfume, hairspray, baked goods. "Come, dear. Sit down."

All the faces at the table turn to me, nodding a little. I've grown up with these faces but I've never seen them like this all in one room and I have no idea what to say. An air of tense and expectant celebration hovers over the table, as if we are staging a grim but necessary tea party. Everyone has a part to play but I have been cast, unwillingly, as the guest of honour. A leading role.

Strange, there is even an array of food spread on the countertop. Two casseroles, a pan of brownies, a plate of oatmeal cookies. It's almost like they knew this was coming. Or maybe they keep extra casseroles in their freezer in case of unexpected deaths? Dad and I eat a lot of baked potatoes and scrambled eggs, meals of cheese, toast and various condiments: chutneys, jams, dipping sauces. Dad loves condiments. Loved. "I can't eat all of this," I say suddenly, out loud, too loud. I point at the counter of foreign food. Mrs. Turner stands and squeezes my shoulder.

"Of course not, dear." Squeezing, patting, leading me to a chair, sitting me down. "You take your time, Lou."

Time? Time for what? Mrs. Turner wears too much makeup and her hair flares up like a crazy troll's. Mr. Turner has a red nose and yellow eyes and when he drinks, which is all the time, he stands on the street and calls for their cat, a fat grey old thing named Whiskers — of course. "Piss, piss, piss," he says. Meaning "puss, puss, puss." They have three grown sons who never come home to visit. Last Sunday afternoon Dad and I heard them fighting. Mrs. Turner shouted, Mr. Turner bellowed, furniture crashed. Dad sighed, folded up his newspaper, said, Maybe it's time for us to go. This street is getting depressing.

"Excuse me," I say, and stand. "I have to go see my brother."

Mrs. Turner looks out the window at the bloated belly of the sky and I see her thinking, Snow. It's unusual this early in the year but we all know the signs. Once it starts, this snow could fall for days, covering up dry leaves and dog shit, hiding abandoned toys till spring, drifting as high as second-storey windows.

"I need — " The chorus of neighbourly faces fixes me with an expectant gaze but I don't know how to proceed. Dizzy, I lean into the countertop, knocking a pan of shepherd's pie. Dad loves shepherd's pie. So does
Jonah. I'm just so-so. I'd never eat a whole pan without them. I clear my
throat, which is tight and suddenly very sore, and try again: "I need to see
Jonah."

"The thing is — " Mrs. Turner hesitates, twisting in her kitchen chair. I
sense she is going to reach out to take my two hands in hers and so, carefully, I angle away. "Isn't there *anybody* we can call? Maybe you should spend
the night with one of us? You know, Mr. Turner and I have lots of room."

I shake my head no. Mrs. Turner was here earlier when I told the police, there is no one to call. It's just Jonah, me, Dad. If I say it again I will do
something totally inappropriate like start to cry in front of these friendly,
familiar women. There is no one. I have friends at school, of course, but no
one I want to call right now. My best friend, Julie Withers, moved to California two years ago. Last time we spoke, her words were slurry because
her tongue was sore and swollen from being pierced. She spoke of body
modifications, tats, incisions, cutting, scarring, of one day turning herself
into a cat. I love Julie but we are growing apart.

I walk to the sink, run water until it is cold. My water glass is on the
left side of the dish rack where I always leave it. That it is still there strikes
me as odd and terrifying. Taunting. As if suddenly everything in this room
belongs to the past. As if I'm drinking water in a museum. On display: the
area of counter Dad leaned against when he told dumb jokes (What do
you call a clam travelling to the moon? An oysternaut. Baahahaha), the
spatula Jonah flipped pancakes with, the whisk to froth cocoa when we
embarked on week-long diets of hot chocolate, buttery bagels and apple
slices, and the list of emergency numbers attached to the fridge with a
MADD magnet. Until today there never was an emergency. We managed
okay. I gulp down a few mouthfuls of cold water and empty the rest into
the sink, suppressing an urge to smash the glass on the kitchen tiles. Instead,
with care and precision, I return it to the left side of the dish rack.

"I'll call the police when I'm ready to leave," I say from my spot at the
sink. Mrs. Turner slowly nods her head and, sensing a turning point, I improvise a sort-of lie. "They said they would help me get to Jonah." I finger
the edge of Officer Wood's card in my pocket. He did say I could call for
anything, any time. I don't think I'll call but these ladies aren't going to
leave until they are sure I have a plan and all I want right now, all I need,

is for them to leave. "But … " I stumble. How do you say go away, get the hell out, and take your stupid casseroles with you, without offending? *Civility, Lou*, my father whispers in my ear. *It's not that hard*. The words come to me as if they are lines in a script: "Thank you so much for coming but, if you don't mind, I'd like to be alone for a bit."

Relief, worry, more kindness. I hear it in their voices as they agree to leave. They write their phone numbers, say: Sorry for your loss. Give Jonah our love. Call if you need anything. Yes, I say, over and over, mindlessly reciting my lines. Thank you. *Thank you*. I won't call. I know it, they know it. But we all need to stick to the script and this predictable exchange seems to plump us, buoy us through goodbye.

"I'm right next door, sweetheart," Mrs. Turner says. She touches my hair, squeezes my shoulder again. "We'll keep an eye on the house. You and Jonah — "

"It's okay," I say. She's crying and her tears make me feel distant and stupid. I want to ask her if she remembers when I was little and was sent home sick with a sore throat. Dad was at work and so I went to her house where I lay on the couch in her basement and watched game shows and soap operas and she brought me a piece of pumpkin pie and said, Eat up, there's lots more where that came from. But I am too tired to string together all those words. Instead I reach out, all clumsy elbows, and hug her. She hugs back, too tight, and I cry a bit but the tears aren't very real.

The door clicks shut behind her and the house, after all the commotion, is absolutely, totally silent. There are dirty snow prints from the boots of the cops and the paramedics in the hallway, and the temperature, after the many openings and closings of the garage door, verges on arctic. If I exhale from the bottom of my lungs, I can see my breath. The thermostat is at Dad's preferred setting but, reckless, I crank it as high as it will go, the soothing hum of heat rattling against the silence as I settle on the vent in the hallway, puffs of warm air billowing up my shirt. This is where I waited in the morning when I was a kid, nightie ballooned out around my bare feet, waiting for Dad to wake up.

But Dad's not asleep. And I'm not a little girl. There is no time to waste sitting on heaters. I need to leave the house and go to Toronto. What would Dad want me to do before leaving? Take out the garbage. Turn down the heat. Check every room: close the windows, switch off the lights. In the kitchen, I move the casseroles into the fridge, check the stove is turned off, open the faucet to a little dribble so the pipes don't freeze, then check the stove again, panic pushing my stomach up into my chest. If I'm not here, and Dad's not here, who will take care of the house?

I pause by the window at the foot of the stairs, watching the Turners in their living room. This is the first time I've gone back upstairs all day. When I came down the stairs this morning, everything was normal. Now everything is changed, and the house already feels as if it is less and less mine. But Mrs. Turner said she'd keep an eye on it. Maybe Nancy will come too. Every other Monday while I am at school, Nancy arrives at our house to sweep, vacuum and wash the floors. Nancy, Dad says, My One Extravagance, as if that is her proper title. She dusts the light fixtures and polishes the faucets and when I arrive home it is as though a magic trick has been performed and the whole world is fresh and clean again. I have chores, too, more now that Jonah doesn't live at home. I do dishes and laundry and take out the garbage on Wednesday mornings. Occasionally I even make my bed. But it is Nancy, invisible, magical, extravagant Nancy, who keeps the house from falling into utter disaster. The only room Nancy does not clean, is not allowed to enter, is Dad's home office at the top of the stairs, past the landing with the gold wingback chair that no one ever sits in.

Free from Nancy's purifying influence, the room represents Dad in his preferred natural environment: messy, chaotic, interesting. Coated in a floating mobile skin of dust, splashed with coffee. It is how the whole house would look if he hadn't been burdened with the job of raising two kids. But that's silly. He never would have ended up here, on this street, in this house, without us.

His work desk is covered, every square inch. It looks disorganized but I know better. Dad has an internal logic that orders the stacks of books and photocopied articles and sheets of looseleaf paper and he has specific pens for specific notepads and specific notepads for specific ideas. He would show me sometimes, grabbing this sheet or that, demonstrating how he was making connections between seemingly unrelated facts, or drawing relationships between apparently random events, and he could, with ridiculous ease, sift through the baffling stacks of papers to pinpoint a quote, or a statistic, to support any argument. There is precision and meaning to the mishmash of his desk. I just have no way of knowing what it is. His blue sweatshirt, the one he wears when he is working, is draped over the back of the office chair. I pull it over my head and, wriggling for armholes, am caught for a moment inside a darkness that smells strongly

of him: Pears soap and sweat. Cigarette smoke, even though he was supposed to have quit.

In the bottom right-hand drawer of his desk is an almost empty mickey of Scotch, a full ashtray, a silver Zippo lighter, a Swiss Army knife and a
slightly crushed pack of Player's with three cigarettes in it. The day before
Julie moved away, we raided that drawer to steal sips of the Scotch. At
first they were wimpy touch-the-liquid-to-our-lips sips, but the sadder
we became, the more we drank until we were semi-drunk and crying and
promising never to forget one another. I was in trouble for that, but not
too much. Now I only periodically check to see if the cigarettes are still
there. I've been trying to get him to quit forever. "I'm sorry, kiddo," he said
to me once after I complained loudly over the state of his lungs, my lungs,
and what he personally was doing to the planet. "Smoking is a prerequisite
to being a writer, didn't you know?" He pulled me onto his lap, razzing my
hair with the palm of his hand, smiling sidewise. Dad has nerve damage on
the right side of his mouth from bad dental work when he was a kid, so his
whole face is charmingly lopsided. When he smiles, he is very forgivable.

I light one of the cigarettes, the smoke in my mouth ashy and unpleasant. I don't inhale again, just hold it in my hand the way Dad did when he
was deep in thought, the familiar, bitter smell drifting toward the ceiling,
and I look across the expanse of his notes, trying to see them the way he
would. It's hard to decipher his handwriting. *Parkdale area, significant increase
in multiple assaults. Nine? Ten?* It's his next big story. Tell the truth; serve the
public: according to Dad this is the job of a journalist. He writes for the
local newspaper but also for the bigger ones in Toronto, and for different
magazines too. Before I was born, before my mother died, he travelled the
world and Jonah says he was barely ever home. I worried a lot that Dad
missed digging up stories in Asia or Europe or Africa, and that it was my
fault, but he always swore he didn't mind settling down. There's news everywhere, he said, if you know how to ask the right questions. He taught
Jonah and me how to form strong thesis statements long before most of
our classmates would recognize the word thesis, and every year either Jonah or I have won the high school's essay writing contest. Not that that
means anything — nobody else had a professional writer helping to edit
their essays. It wasn't even fair.

The next big story was a kind of family joke. "Hey Dad," Jonah or I
would say, "What's the next big story?" When we were little we'd ask, like,
fifty times a day, just to bug him. "Parkdale," he said, last time I asked, which

was about a week ago. It was Sunday, the day of the Turners' fight, and I was making toast and he was reading the newspaper. "Parkdale, in the west end of Toronto. A big story brewing. People getting beat up or disappearing and the OPP not doing a damn thing. Now, there's a story," he said, coughing into his housecoat sleeve. The flu was going around town and though he wasn't sick that day he was a sweaty, hacking mess by the next morning. "There's a story someone needs to break."

Two framed pictures sit at the back of Dad's desk, one of Jonah and my mom and one of me and Jonah, and in front of them, to the right of the electric typewriter, is the stack of blue index cards. The blue cards, too, are a kind of family joke. Dad used the cards to write down interesting words, odd scraps of information, ideas or inspirations and Jonah and I made a game of randomly choosing one and using it as a message or fortune for the day. The tarot of Dad's magpie mind. There may be no practical purpose to knowing that the cellular structure of pigeon's eyes allows them to perceive fluctuations in the earth's magnetic field or that during the Middle Ages glamour was synonymous with grammar, implying a thinking process that was associated with magical forces, an ability to shift reality — to glamorize it — with a carefully worded spell, but the blue card messages infused everyday life with special meaning. At least for me they did. I shouldn't speak for Jonah.

Jonah. I have to talk to Jonah. I dial the phone in Dad's office but it's still the stupid answering machine on the other end of the line. I surprise myself by slamming the receiver back in the cradle, suddenly furious with Jonah for not telepathically knowing I need to talk to him. The cigarette, burned down to the filter, is a long cylinder of ash perfectly formed in the ashtray. It makes me think of David Bowie's song "Rock 'n' Roll Suicide," the line about time and cigarettes. That album, *Ziggy Stardust*, was our album, Dad's and mine. Sometimes, after Jonah left home and Julie moved away and I was often at loose ends, we'd put it on and sing-shout the lyrics at the top of our lungs.

The blue card on the top of the pile, likely the last one he wrote, reads: *Death hath its seat close to the entrance of delight.*

A little too on point, no? It's Dad's voice again. Clear, but distant. I spin around but he's not in the room, not down the hall.

"I don't know, honey." That's what he said last weekend when I said he should be the one to break the Parkdale story. "I don't know, honey, I don't think I've got the heart."

I was listening but had no idea what he was saying. No idea what he meant. Did he mean he couldn't face yet another story that featured a violent psychopath bully attacking the vulnerable? Or did he know his heart, his actual heart, was stuttering, slowing down to a standstill?

Later that day I saw him standing in the bathroom counting out pills into his hand, flushing them down the toilet. "What are you doing?" I asked. He startled a little. "Prescriptions out of date," he said, and emptied the remaining contents into the toilet, dropping the bottle into the trash can. What medication was it? An important one? And why am I asking that only now? Why didn't I ask it then?

The medicine cabinet in the bathroom is lined with a baffling row of pill jars: beta blockers, anticoagulants, pills to bring down blood pressure. I don't know which is which. Dad explained it all to me when I was younger. He drew a picture of a heart and explained how arteries carried oxygen-rich blood from the heart to the body and veins returned the oxygen-poor blood back to the heart. The in, the out, of the heartbeat. He said his heart was weak. As a child, he had almost died from an infection in the lining of his heart. He explained using words like atria and ventricle and valve, words I didn't know. Words I didn't want to know. I didn't like to think about him sick. The prescription dates on the pill jars in the medicine cabinet are all about a month old and the jars almost empty. I took the trash out, so the only thing in the can now is a crumpled-up tissue. No empty pill jars. Everything seems to be in order. Dad wanted it to look that way. He stopped taking his meds but he didn't want anyone to know.

One minute I know this fact; the next I don't. What do I know? Nothing. Nothing, except I need to talk to Jonah. Outside snow is falling. It's time to go.

It's harder to leave than I imagined. I am okay choosing a few pairs of socks, underwear, jeans and T-shirts to shove in a knapsack, but I am confounded by the decision to pack, or not to pack, my really good book. *Indium's Ark* it's called, and it is ludicrous that I couldn't remember the title an hour ago. I want to read more about that island of the future, the one where all the extinct animals are restored, and I want to know what happens in the end. Equally, I am scared to pack it, struck by the thought that if I continue to read, more bad things will happen. This is silly and superstitious, but maybe also desperately true. Maybe, my thought continues (it's a renegade thought, haphazard and dangerously loose), maybe if I un-read the book, Dad won't be dead at all. There are so many potential versions of yesterday afternoon: I call Dad after school and suggest we go to the Troubadour Cafe for dinner or Dad calls to tell me he's coming home early and I suggest he bring a pizza or I hear his car pull into the garage and go check on him in time to call an ambulance. I did a first aid course last year. I'm sure I could do CPR. All these scenarios end with him being alive right now. Maybe in the hospital, sure, but alive. I want a redo. A do-over. A rewind. Crazy, I know, but yesterday night is still close enough, it feels possible. It's a good thing the posse of neighbours is gone. Excuse me, ladies. I need to be alone so I can undo time. That would really start them nodding their heads. No casserole can fix a kid that far gone.

I don't pack the book. Instead, I take the bottle of Scotch, the crushed pack of Player's, the Zippo lighter, the Swiss Army knife and Dad's stack of blue index cards. Also the photos of me and Jonah and my mom. They almost don't fit in the knapsack but I squeeze them in.

The car is in the garage. Dad took me out to practise in the spring and I tested, and passed, for my licence in the summer. I could drive to Toronto. But the snow has started to fall and I've never driven in snow and the car is in the garage and I don't want to go back into the garage. Fuck the car. Fuck the garage.

Outside snow pours from the sky in silent streams, curtaining the world. The house door closes with a small click. The temperature has continued to drop and the lock is stiff. I strain to turn the key, twisting hard, but the lock won't budge. My hands are thick and numb, clumsy with cold, fishwife hands, stupid and useless. A hot sparkle of tears fill my eyes as I lean into the door and the key finally makes its quarter turn with a small weighted thud. Done.

I walk. The soundtrack in my head plays "Rock 'n' Roll Suicide." The street is snow-silent but I hear the operatic swells of David Bowie's song, as sung, slightly out of tune, by Dad. It's something he'd want to say right now: *It's okay, Lou, you're not alone.* But I am alone as I walk to Becker's convenience store, which is also the closest bus depot, and buy a ticket to Toronto and a cup of coffee, double cream, double sugar. I sip slowly, aim to think of nothing and wait for the bus to come. And I am alone, one of only six people on the bus, as we slowly pull out of town and onto the highway. There's not much to Linden, not much to say goodbye to, and what is there is blotted out behind a blank wall of swirling snow, gone before I've even left.

At Bloor and Bathurst, where I get off, the world is a shaken snow globe, more snow than air, the bright marquee lights of Honest Ed's across the street barely visible. Snow accumulates along the thin collar of my fall jacket, melting in cold, stinging trails down the back of my neck and shoulder blades. Snow up to my knees drenches my jeans and Converse sneakers as though I am wading through a river. There is not a single person on the street and only a few cars pass, slowly, with the loud sound of crunching and compacting snow, engines revving to an agitated whine when the wheels swerve and lose traction. I head west, in the general direction of Jonah's, but can't shake the feeling that I am lost. And late. Lost and late, late and lost, twin tidal waves of barely suppressed panic rolling me forward until I reach Northwood and turn south, two blocks to Rosalind, Jonah's street, the narrow brick houses appearing crooked and tilted behind the kaleidoscopic eddies of falling snow.

I bang on Jonah's door but no one answers. His salt-stained Kodiak boots are lying on the other side of the door, one tallowy sole flipped on its side. They look perfectly dry and unworn. Jonah must be out in the snowstorm wearing sneakers, like me. I bang again, but this time with no expectation.

A key. Jonah must have a hidden key. But the underside of the rubber mat yields nothing, nor does the inside of a cracked clay pot. As I turn to his small patch of a front yard to find a rock to smash a window to let myself in, I see a girl. She's about my age and she's standing on the sidewalk looking up at me.

"Did you get locked out?"

"No. Well, yeah." I try to smile, a hungry, stray-dog attempt at a smile but I am breathless and so blown through with cold, my lips refuse to come apart.

"Are you — " She pauses, tilting her head. She's very pretty. Gold-y locks tumble out of a black angora beret that fluffs around her face, snowflakes catching in her eyelashes and melting on the pink flush of her cheeks. A thin red scar travels from her lip down across her chin, transforming into a crooked dimple when she smiles. "Are you a friend of Jonah's?"

So. She likes my brother. "No. I'm Lou. His sister. He wasn't expecting me."

"Ohhh." She nods her head, crooked dimple revealed. "Do you want to go to my house until he gets home?"

It's tempting. I am cold and have to pee but I shove my mitten-less hands back in my pockets, undecided.

"Or I could take you to him. He's working at the Falafel Hut on Bloor, for probably another hour or so."

"Yes, please. Thanks," I say, my head bobbing up and down in uncontrolled assent. "Thanks. I really need to see Jonah."

"No problem. I'm Isabelle." She pulls off a mitten and shakes my hand. "Oh good gravy, you are cold."

"I'm fine," I say, as we walk back down the street. It seems wrong to tell such a monumental lie when we've only just met but if I tell her the truth there is no way I can make it, no way I can go somewhere else, do something else, before I see Jonah. My only hope is pretending to be normal. I take a deep breath and attempt conversation. "You're a friend of Jonah's?"

"Ha!" she says. "More like a stalker." She jerks to a stop and puts her mittened hands over her mouth. "Oh my God, I can't believe I said that. I don't mean it like that. I mean, we *are* friends. We're neighbours. I live right here — " She points to a house across the street. A garland of multi-coloured lanterns hangs across the porch and a bright blue woman's bicycle with a wicker basket full of snow is padlocked to the banister. "Jonah and me, we met at the summer street party, last summer, and we both really like the same kind of music and … and stuff," she continues. "It's just, I mean, I like him, you know? I don't know, I mean, he's older than me and he's busy with school and stuff and … oh my God. I'm not really a stalker at all. You're his sister. I can't believe I said that."

Her face is scarlet. It's cute. "Don't worry about it," I say, and we start walking again. "Jonah can be kind of oblivious."

"Yeah," she says, still scarlet.

"He's a dreamer," I say. I don't mean it. I'm trying to make her feel better. We've reached Bloor and as we turn the corner, he's there, walking toward us, thick mop of dark hair crusted with the fast-falling snow.

It's Isabelle he sees first. Out of context, I am invisible next to her. "Hey Iz!" He points at the sky. "Snow day! I'm off early." There is a stutter to his step as his eyes focus on me. "Lou? What — "

"Jonah," I manage before words leave me and the small frantic animal of panic, the one tearing up my guts, claws its way free, howling out my throat, leaving me shaking and hollow inside. Jonah's hands, rough and worried, grab at my coat and upper arms, and I lean into his bony shoulders, his tight embrace, there on the snowy street corner, and I hold on.

2

Bright shafts of sun through stained glass window stream red and gold, glorying the air in the church, as if God were directing his late-afternoon thoughts directly on us. As if the sun were setting right on cue in the middle of the day, in the middle of the service, fierce in its dying. Dad would like this light. He'd hate the minister though, picked by Mrs. Turner. The man drones on and on, like a lost bee. Dad hated churchy stuff. Devout atheist. That's what he said when I asked him what religion he was, what religion we were. I was about eleven or twelve and had high hopes of cleaning him up, physically and spiritually. I agitated for him to quit drinking and smoking and take me to a church service. What the hell, he said, am I raising a Quaker?

It's pretty, this church, but in a simple, no budget, small town kind of a way. There's nothing fancy. It's tiny and wooden and painted white, unadorned except for the stained-glass windows encircling the room, each pane depicting the same design, a sharply pointed star on a backdrop of celestial blue. The pews are long, scratched-up wood benches that can be pushed to the sides of the room. The one and only other time I came here was after I successfully convinced Dad that he was denying me a well-rounded education by not ever going to a church service. But it was horrible: the sermon was long-winded and the singing a bitter disappointment. Timid and thin, the voices wavered as if, despite the clutched hymn books open in their hands, no one in the congregation knew the next lines. Mid-hymn Dad looked down at me and mouthed, *You asked for it.* Afterwards we drove to a nearby well fed by an underground spring and filled a big glass jar with clear fresh water. Holy, Dad said, swigging from the water bottle, then passing it to me. *This* is holy. I swigged from the bottle the way he did, gulping cold mouthfuls, splashing water onto my face. It was satisfying. After that we went to Dairy Queen and thoroughly debased ourselves with hot fudge sundaes covered in roasted peanuts. Holy, I said, mimicking him as we sat in the car, the engine idling, my mouth full of the salty sweetness, *this* is holy. Dad licked his thumb, then reached over to rub a smudge of chocolate off my face, and said, Fun too.

I don't know where Jonah was that day. Busy, I guess. He would have been about sixteen and he was always busy then. He pretty much disowned me when he was thirteen. He talked to me the way you'd talk to a mangy, unwanted dog following you down the street: Get lost, buzz off, beat it. Leave me alone! If Dad wouldn't have killed him, he probably would have thrown stones. In my fury, I tried to punish him with my fists (useless and embarrassing), and with the silent treatment (equally useless and worse for me than for him). His attention, or inattention, has always been far more potent than my fury. It was only after he moved to Toronto that he started to talk to me again. He sent me postcards with short stories about the houses he was living in, his classes at university and his crazy roommates, written in neat block letters on the back. There was this one roommate, the craziest, whose idea of a joke was farting into a beer can. I loved that. But Jonah's hard to read today. He is sitting beside me, staring straight ahead, self-contained and remote.

Comfort, the minister says, can be found in our memories, in thinking good thoughts. Comfort, he continues, can be found in God's love, and I snort-laugh out loud. Like a donkey. Totally inappropriate. Jonah leans into me and I anticipate a *ssshh* and a big-brother glare but instead he smiles and lightly knocks his head against mine.

The minister invites people to speak. A lot of the people here I don't know, strangers who apparently felt close to Dad, but for a long, still second I am certain no one will stand up. Then Mrs. Turner is on her feet and making her way to the front. Mrs. Turner? It's too absurd. If Dad were here, he'd be laughing.

Mrs. Turner isn't laughing. She's practically foamy with tears. Ugly crying, Dad would say. It's infectious, her crying, her tears, and I dig my nails into my palms to stop blubbering away too. He was a good man, Mrs. Turner says, a good neighbour, a devoted father. Another guy gets up, says he and Dad worked together in the early seventies. That Dad was a natural reporter, that he was compassionate. That he had a rare intelligence and integrity. All nice, sure, but you'd only say this sort of stuff about someone after they're dead.

Directly behind me someone is snuffly crying, louder and louder, the long inhales turning into full-on sobs. It seems wrong to turn and look but I do anyway. It's a woman, blonde, and she's clutching a linen handkerchief to her face. Pretty, beneath the smeared mascara and red puffiness, in a strained, trying-too-hard sort of way. I've never met her before. Who are these people?

No one mentions Dad's crooked smile, his bizarre obsession with sauerkraut or how he slurped coffee in the morning. No one mentions his beloved vinyl collection, how he stacked his Bob Dylan and Beatles records in strategic piles around the living room. No one talks about the day he punched out a window, angry at how a major story of his had been edited. No one talks about how he strummed silly made-up songs to me on his old, permanently out-of-tune guitar. Or how he paced at night, listening to Tom Waits' *Rain Dogs,* and sometimes played the piano, also out of tune, late, when he thought no one was listening, and it always sounded like someone crying. No one talks about the day he and I made doughnuts and got grease everywhere. No one talks about his heart, his hot, sad heart. His tired heart. His heart that gave up, gave out. Stopped. Why did it stop? I glance over at Sal, who is sitting on the other side of Jonah. Sal came with us from Toronto on the bus and he should be the one up there talking. Sal knows. He's Dad's best friend from when they were kids and the closest thing Jonah and I have to an uncle. Last time Sal came to our house in Linden, he and Dad got drunk and almost had a fist fight over which was a better Beatles album: *Revolver* or *Sgt. Pepper's?* But Sal's not saying anything. He's staring straight ahead, his face grey and contorted, a mute gargoyle. Someone starts playing the organ and we all sing "I Shall Be Released," Jonah's idea. I sing loud, for Dad. Then it's time to go.

Mr. and Mrs. Turner drive us back to their house, Jonah, then me, then Sal, all crammed in the back of their brown station wagon. Up close, Sal smells bad, like cat food and mildew and those disgusting rum-tipped cigarillos and I turn my head and press it into Jonah's shoulder, breathing through my nose, out more than in, so I can avoid all contact with Sal's gross weirdness. Jonah doesn't punch me, or inch away. He doesn't move at all, his heart thumping against my ear, strong and steady. Different than Dad's, whose heart made a swooshing flourish with every beat.

"Oh dear," Mrs. Turner says, as if that sums up everything, and there is nothing else for anyone to say for the rest of the drive.

Mr. Turner has a shop downtown where he refinishes and sells wood furniture and their house is a kind of messy warehouse where he stores (or hoards) an outrageous number of desks (small and big), tables (bedside to dining room), chairs, cabinets, armoires and hutches, and there are several spots, in the living room or walking toward the kitchen, where you have to sidle sideways to avoid sharp corners. The neighbourhood ladies have congregated in the kitchen, filling the countertops with spreads of cold cuts and cheeses and small sandwiches and cupcakes, and all the strangers from the service stuff into the already overcrowded house and walk around with napkins, licking mustard or frosting off their fingertips and drinking small cups of fruit punch. Spiked, if Mr. Turner had anything to do with it. It's an after-party for a funeral. I'm impressed that there are so many people here and so much food. It's seems generous and strange, both. Dad and me, we always kept to ourselves. I have no idea what to say to any of these adults.

Sal perches on the edge of an ornate couch crammed into the alcove where Dad's phone desk is at home, and he looks more awkward and out of place, more mute gargoyle, than he did at the service.

"You should have said something," I say, from the edge of the hallway arch, keeping my distance. Luckily the smell of furniture polish is so strong at the Turners, you can't smell anything else. "You should have said something at the service."

Sal nods his head without looking at me. After a long pause, he says, "I know. I let Danny down." He rubs the heels of both hands into his eyes. "I was always letting Danny down."

It's wrong, I know, but I feel a sense of satisfaction seeing Sal cry. Dad would be pissed at me. He always said Sal was fragile. Sal is crazy, like really mentally ill. He was hospitalized and everything. I sit down beside him on the couch.

"I've never done this before," he says. "Been alive, without Danny. He's always been there."

"Yeah. No kidding."

Sal looks at me and does an exaggerated double take, bushy eyebrows hiked up, mouth so widely ajar I can spot the fillings in the back of his teeth, a look that is cartoonish in its extravagance, as if only now he's seeing me, *really* seeing me, for the first time. It's the kind of look that demands a response but I don't know what to say.

Sal cups his face in his hands and directs his words at the floor. "Danny loved the Blue Jays. We'd listen to the games on the radio when we were kids and if they lost he'd get so upset he'd either fight me or start bawling." I can see the punch, but not the tears. There is, however, no time to ask a question as Sal, King of the Non Sequitur, is rambling on. "We found a baby robin once. Stayed up all night feeding it drops of sugar water. It died anyway and Danny cried then too."

It's funny hearing Sal call Dad Danny. I always think of him as Dad, or Dan. Danny makes him sound like a real kid. The blonde woman from the church nods her head at Sal as she passes by on her way to the kitchen.

"Did he ever tell you about the time we fed chocolate-covered soap to Jack Brightman — "

"Who is that woman, Sal? The fake blonde? The one that kept crying all over the place at the service?"

Long pause. "Jillian Nash," Sal says finally. Long pause, again.

"And … "

"She was your dad's high school sweetheart. They got in touch after your mom died and they've been seeing each other, off and on, ever since."

"What do you mean, seeing each other?"

"You know," Sal says, shifting in his seat. "Going on dates, weekends away. That kind of thing."

"What the fuck!" Heads turn in the kitchen. "Excuse me," I say and get up, squeezing past Sal's knees, bumping down the hallway, bruising my hip and jabbing my ribs on furniture corners, until I am out the front door and in the fresh air. I cross the driveway to our house and sit on the front step of the porch. The sun, small and wintery, burns white and the sky is the colour of tin. It has been warm all day, the soft edges of snow dripping and disappearing into fast-flowing rivulets, but now, as the sun begins to drop so does the temperature. The cement under my bum is perilously cold. *Perilous.* A word Dad loved. Adjectives and adverbs had to be picked carefully, according to him, but *perilous* was solid, a good one. He was away a lot this past year. Working a story, I thought, while I did laundry and homework and ate frozen pizza by myself. Meanwhile he had a secret life. I put my hands over my face and curl my head down to my knees, wishing I could be somewhere else.

"Hey! Lou!"

It's Rufus, on a bike, wearing a black hat and black-and-white striped scarf over a big grey sweater. His cheeks are rosy, like he's been biking all day. Rufus was in my elementary school, we used to fingerpaint in kindergarten class, but it is only in the last few years, since Julie moved away, that I've got to know him. We have math and French and homeroom together. I see him practically every day but seeing him here now seems as strange as all the strange things that have happened over the last week.

"Hey." I wave my hand and shrug my shoulders all at the same time. "What are you doing here?"

"My mom is over there," he points at the Turners. "She knew your dad. They went to school together."

This is news to me. A sudden, awful thought occurs. "Her name's not Jillian, is it?"

"No," he shakes his head. He leans the bike against the house and sits down on the porch beside me. "It's Sam."

I know who he is talking about. She introduced herself. Nice smile, dark hair and green eyes, like Rufus. "Long hair?" I say, tapping the small of my back.

"That's her," he says, handing me a mixed tape. "I wanted to bring you this."

"Cool." The inside cover is scrawled with his handwriting, which is small and surprisingly neat. He's put some Bowie on it — the first track is "Five Years." That's how I got to know him at school, talking about Bowie. Unlike most kids, he knows all of Bowie's earlier records, not just the stuff that is popular right now like "Let's Dance" or "Modern Love." We both love the album *Hunky Dory*.

"My mom says you're moving to Toronto."

The door behind us opens and Jonah steps onto the porch. I didn't realize he was in the house and, in my shock, he seems less than real, a ghost of himself. I jump to my feet. His eyes are spacey, unfocussed. Maybe he's the one who's seen a ghost.

"Have you been in there all this time?" I don't intend, but can't hide, the shrill accusation in my voice. Jonah nods, frowning. "Did you find anything?"

"Like what?" he says. "What would I find?"

I don't have an answer. Rufus is on his feet, moving toward his bike. "I'll see you," he says as he rides off and all I do is wave. I don't even say goodbye. Jonah opens the garage door.

"Can you go get Sal?" he asks, dangling the car keys. "We're going to drive back to TO."

As we drive out of town, the evening side of the sky lengthens, quickly outpacing the modest setting of the sun. Linden is prettiest at dusk, when the street lamps switch on. Dad liked to turn off the lights in the house and sit in the backyard waiting for it to be fully dark, waiting for the stars to freckle across the sky. Sometimes we'd sit together, not talking, and eat our dinner and listen to all the night sounds: the tree and wind noise, people shouting, dogs barking, car doors slamming, the surrounding houses like little bubbles of light in a great sea of darkness.

The moon is bright tonight and the sky is clear, and it is very cold, which might mean more snow tomorrow. We pass the water tower and the turnoff to Julie's old street. We pass through downtown, past Mr. Turner's store and the Troubadour Cafe, where Dad and I liked to go on Cajun night. We drive down First Street, lined on both sides by the bare branches of huge oak trees, but instead of turning right toward my school, we go left and out to the highway. Sal is in the front seat with Jonah and the radio is turned to CBC, some jazz program. I'm in the back, which always makes me carsick. I would have called the front seat but it took so long for us to say goodbye to everyone, all the people we did and didn't know, and Mrs. Turner made a big production of giving us an envelope that everyone had contributed to and that had over $500 in it, which was great, but by the time I got to the car Sal was firmly ensconced in the front seat.

I don't dare read Rufus' set list as that will really make me want to puke but, as we drive, I roll the square corners of the cassette in my mittened hands and think about the songs that might be on it. No one talks, except for a few times when Jonah or Sal says something in response to the radio. When we reach the city, Jonah lets me off at the top of Rosalind and I walk to the apartment while he drives Sal home.

I have my own key now, two keys, one that opens the front door into the little vestibule and a second one that opens the door on the left, that leads up a flight of stairs into the apartment. The door on the right leads to the downstairs apartment. A man who works for Air Canada lives there but Jonah says he's never, ever home. I make a rookie mistake, closing the second door behind me before I find the light switch, lurching into pitch dark. The small landing at the foot of the stairs is a minefield of shoes and boots and umbrellas and a hanging wall rack draped with coats and hoodies and sweaters. The light switch is not where you expect it would be and I spend a long time inching my hands up and down the walls, cursing Jonah for not leaving a light on. Finally, after hitting my shin on the bottom stair, I find and flip the switch and the overhead sconce illuminates the landing and stairwell in a soft orange glow.

It's not a large apartment, but it's all relative. While it's cramped by Linden standards, Jonah says it's *huge* for the city. Plus, it's got its own washer and dryer. The stairs are narrow and steep, and several of the steps are slanted underfoot, tilting like a funhouse floor. Wind seeps through the poorly insulated windows, none of the doors are hung quite square, and the corners of rooms dip and pitch at unexpected angles. Compared to our house in Linden, which was solid and grounded, the apartment is cobbled together, crooked corners put together with white glue and bent nails, barely tethered to its spot on the street. It might, at any moment, blow away. There are mice in the walls too.

Jonah's room is to the left of the stairs, and he always keeps his door shut. To the right, across the hallway, is his self-importantly titled "office," which is only a large cupboard where he has a desk and a computer with a printer. There's a bathroom with a shower that Jonah uses mostly, and then a kitchen and a living room that are open to each other through arches in the walls of the hallway, as if they were mirrors to one another. There's a big window in the kitchen but it only looks out at a brick wall. The laundry area is across the hall from a second bathroom with a small claw-foot bathtub and a toilet with no lid on the back tank, so you see that the chain part of the lever system inside has been replaced by a grody-looking shoelace. The hallway ends here, at the door to my new room.

Giorgio, Jonah's roommate, was on the verge of giving his one-month notice, so he could move in with his girlfriend, and he was happy to be able to leave early. Jonah hustled up a bunch of their friends so they could move Giorgio out right away, and I only ended up sleeping on the couch in the living room for two nights. Isabelle came over with cans of leftover paint and while Jonah was preoccupied with endless phone calls and forms to fill in, she and I painted over the ancient and vomitous shade of green on the walls. While we worked, Isabelle chatted effortlessly, freely offering up details about the high school I will start next week, and about life in Toronto in general. Apparently, my new school has a killer athletics program and kids come from all over the city to attend, but Isabelle isn't into sports; she is part of the drama club, Studio B. Most of the teachers are decent, except for Mr. DeSilva, the history teacher, who moonlights as an evangelical preacher on a Sunday cable TV show. Mr. Bernier, the French teacher, is a playwright and he wears outlandish socks. His first name is Charles and he is married to a woman named Charlie, who owns an art gallery on Queen Street, and sometimes Mr. Bernier, Charles, invites students to the openings of his plays. Charlie's art gallery is not too far from the bakery that Isabelle works at, which is the best job she has ever had, and they serve, at the bakery, the best cheesecake in the city. Isabelle knows all the *bests:* the best place to shop second-hand, the best place for used books and albums, the best discount shoe store, the best place for ice cream. Her chatter was warming, welcoming, and I wanted all those things that make up Isabelle's *best* of all possible worlds: cheesecake, work, second-hand treasures, reliable footwear. It's easy to imagine having all those things in Isabelle's easy and generous presence. But now, returning to an empty apartment that is not yet home, it hits me that no matter what I want, the person I am right now is the person I am always going to be. At the core, a hard pith of panic. Everything else *me* blurs at the edges and dissolves. Nothing but bruised flesh and salt water.

My room is painted a seaside shade of blue. Isabelle suggested we paint the door and window frames white, and somehow the tidiness of this trim next to the fluid blue is soothing. Truth is, my room is a comfort. There are more windows here than anywhere else in the apartment. They run along the entire back wall and look out onto a small fenced-in mound of snow, the boughs of a naked cherry tree black against the white, and beyond the fence, a small laneway running parallel to Rosalind. The windows let in a lot of light but the wind also blows strongest here, straight off Lake Ontario, wet drafts that gust from the south, and then the west, then all directions at once. I inherited a futon bed, left behind from a previous inhabitant, as well as a chest of drawers painted turquoise and purple, also abandoned, and an old table, made from a wooden door, that serves as a desk. The window closest to my bed is big, with a sill wide enough to sit on. Isabelle donated a few pillows that she made out of old floral printed dresses to prop in the corners, and that gives the window, despite the serpentine wind that whistles through the cracks in the frame, an inviting, cozy look. I am a little ashamed by how much I like this room. It seems a betrayal of my father and our life in Linden, but I know he would like it too. It has character, he'd say.

And what about his betrayals? A hidden life? A secret girlfriend? Like a coward, I avoided Jillian Nash during goodbyes at the Turners but now I wish I had confronted her and asked some of the questions stampeding through my brain. Where did he take her on those weekends away? What did they do? Why did he never tell me? Did she think he was depressed? I do. The more I revisit the moment I caught him in the bathroom, the more I am certain he was intentionally messing with his meds. Did he know that not taking that particular med might kill him? And if he did know that, why would he do it? Why would he leave Jonah and me alone?

Maybe he was depressed. His work had been slowing down and he was home more often, some days never getting out of his sweatpants and T-shirt that doubled as pyjamas. He said he was thinking about a new direction, but he wouldn't tell me what it was yet. "It's a surprise," he said. Two days before he died I came home late from school. I had watched half a basketball game with Rochelle Sanders and Jenn Abrahms and then we had shared two slices of raspberry cheesecake at the Dutch deli downtown and when I got home it was already dark. There wasn't a single lamp on in the house and when I flicked on the overhead light in the hall, I nearly jumped out of my skin because Dad was there, sitting on the couch in the living room. "What are you doing?" I asked. "You scared the bejeesus out of me!"

"Just enjoying the darkness," he said. It didn't seem like a strange answer at the time: he was fighting off the flu and his eyes were sparkly with fever. But now it is an answer both strange and telling. Who enjoys the darkness? A depressed person, that's who.

The flu hit him hard and he should never have gone to work the day he died. Before I left for school I told him to stay home but he waved me off, said there was a story breaking. Too big for him to miss. I don't know the details of the story — some cokehead tried to rob a bank or a politician was up on corruption charges or some kid brought an assault rifle into a high school in the States — but I blame it, that stupid story, whatever it was, for killing Dad that day.

The bottle of Scotch, the pack of Player's, the lighter, the knife and the stack of blue cards are on the desk, along with the framed photos I took from Dad's office, my Walkman and some of my school books. The top card hasn't changed: *Death hath its seat close to the entrance of delight.* What does that even mean? Why would Dad write that down? I pull his sweatshirt overtop my dressy churchy clothes, shuffle the cards, making certain to hide the perturbing message deep inside the stack and then randomly pick a new one. *John Lennon's first girlfriend was named Thelma Pickles.* Hmmm. As far as messages from beyond the grave go, this one is useless. Funny, but useless.

It's too cold to get undressed. I crawl into bed with my Walkman and Rufus' cassette, pulling the sweatshirt hood over my head. The first song is "Five Years." I know it off by heart. Dad used to sing it to me in a fake opera voice that always produced a kind of pleasurable anxiety, a sense of inevitable and beautiful doom. Why five years? I asked him. Why not three? Fifteen? Fifty-two? Don't ask it to make sense, Dad said, it's a song for the nuclear age. I rewind the tape over and over, replaying that song until finally, after my fifth or sixth listen, I switch off the Walkman and fall asleep.

3

I dream about Indium, the main character in the book I left behind. In my dream, I am sometimes Indium, or sometimes myself travelling with him, and he looks a little like me and a little like David Bowie, which is to say he is a scrawny girl with a crooked smile, disconcerting eyes and hair blonder, shorter and straighter than mine that swoops over his forehead. We are preoccupied with a small, dead bird that is curled into a question mark in the palm of my hand. We should bury the bird but we're waiting to see if it comes back alive. I lay the bird on a table beside a vase of lilacs in a beam of sunlight and wait. A dog comes over to lick the bird and I wonder if that will revive him and then I wake up.

When I poke my head out of the covers my breath billows, little dragon puffs of cold in the washed-out morning light. Snowflakes float in the frame of the window, soaking up the colour of the sky. I can hear Jonah in the kitchen moving about. The tap runs, the kettle boils, a cupboard door shuts. It is the smell of toast, faint and heavenly, that coaxes me from the warmth of bed. Armed with a clean pair of jeans and T-shirt, I scoot into the bathroom where there is a pocket of warmth, a continual whoosh of furnace heat, that makes early-morning dressing almost bearable, switching my church clothes for the new ones, before pulling Dad's sweatshirt back overtop. I splash my face with warm water, then cold water, brush my teeth, and briefly run a wide-tooth comb through the tangles in my hair, a standard morning routine.

Jonah, in his blue plaid pyjamas that Dad gave him last year for Christmas, is at the kitchen table reading an essay. He eats a piece of peanut butter and banana toast and slurps from a cup of coffee with one hand, while the other takes notes and marks up the page with a neon yellow highlighter. His hair is all bed-head messy and he slurps noisily, like Dad, totally lost in his focus. It's been three years since we lived in the same house and it's been so busy since the day I showed up we haven't talked much, not really. We've just circled each other, politely desolate strangers.

"Morning." I pour a half a cup of milk in a pan and whisk it while warming it on the stove. It was one of Dad's rules that I could only have a half a cup of coffee in the morning. He didn't have many rules, barely any, and this was one of the most stupid and random. I argued with him about it all the time but, on my second morning at Jonah's, I tried a full cup of coffee with a small sploosh of milk and found I didn't like it all.

"Morning," Jonah sighs, barely looking up. I grab the newspaper and sit on the opposite side of the table, scanning the headlines. They are mostly what Dad would call filler animal stories: An escape-artist gorilla stumps experts at a Texas zoo; an East Coast man is ordered to pay $200 a month in dog support to his former girlfriend; squirrels in Alberta speed onto the fairway and steal golf balls. Then there is a story about a Québec woman who is getting married to the man who abducted her and another on the general and lasting appeal of the Vietnamese leader Ho Chi Minh. Hospitals in Iraq are in terrible conditions and yet another family is devastated by a drunk driver. Nothing much holds my interest until the local page where a brief article about sexual assault catches my eye: four attacks in seven months, all occurring around Dundas down to Queen Street, west of Bathurst. The OPP recommend that any woman who feels threatened should immediately make for a house or place of safety and dial 911, and they warn that all women should carefully plan the routes they take after dark. I grunt, the way Dad does when he disapproves of the way a story is being reported, and slam the paper down. He'd say the article implies that being safe is the responsibility of potential victims, which is absurd. "Next they'll be setting a curfew and telling us not to wear skirts above the knee."

"What?" Jonah looks up from his article. Finally, I've piqued his interest. I pass him the folded-up newspaper and point to the article, which he reads quickly, wrinkling his brow and scrunching his nose as he hands the paper back. "That's not what they are saying at all. It's common sense. They don't want people to get hurt."

"Common sense? First, they imply it's the women's responsibility to change their behaviour to avoid being attacked. Second, why recommend that women get paranoid about their usual route home? Why not recommend they learn some self-defence? Or at least carry pepper spray?"

"Well, maybe fighting back increases the risk the attack will be more serious."

"Well, maybe not fighting back increases the risk of being a loser."

"C'mon, Lou. You've never thrown a punch in your life. It's not that easy. Especially if someone has a knife, or outweighs you by a hundred pounds."

It's true. Jonah's got a point. I acknowledge this with curt silence and turn to the crossword, which is in section D, page 8, safely surrounded by a recipe for Hungarian goulash and an article on the importance of sleep when trying to lose weight.

"Blank fatale. Five letters," I say. "That's too easy. Can you pass me a pen?"

Jonah rolls over a leaky ballpoint, then pours himself another coffee. He leans against the counter and takes a long slurp, watching as I fill in the blanks with big block letters. He reminds me of Dad right now with his messy hair, his thoughtful slurps, his otherworldly focus, and for some reason I find this irritating. Enraging almost.

I put down the pen. "Why are you looking at me?"

"Sorry." He sits down. "I sold the car last night — "

"What?!" I can't keep the screech out of my voice. "That was going to be my car. Dad said so. Next summer, when I graduate." The doorbell rings. "Shit. That's probably Isabelle."

"I'm sorry, Lou, but we need the money."

"Are things really *that* bad?" Jonah shrugs, but doesn't say anything, turning back to his article. Avoiding me. He has been on the phone every day trying to sort out our finances. Dad had some savings but no will, and Jonah says it will likely be at least six months before we see any money. Even then it will only be half of it, Jonah's half, because my half will be held back until I am nineteen. We have to sell the house in Linden, which I also don't want to do, but we have to, and Jonah says he can maybe get some of my money released to put toward my schooling if he makes a court application, whatever that entails. Thinking about it makes my head ache. Jonah's too, by the look of him. He rubs the heel of his hand across his temple, mussing up his hair even more, another gesture of Dad's. "You look like Dad." This comes out like an accusation. The doorbell rings again as Jonah exhales with force, slapping the article onto the table. "Look. We need money, Lou. We can't fuck things up. They're going to be watching us. You."

"They, who? Who's watching me?"

"Social workers, I guess, I don't know. Family and Children Services. They called to check in on us."

"I'm almost seventeen." This I hiss at Jonah as I get up to answer the door. In point of fact, my birthday is less than a week away. Jonah has totally forgotten about it, which is fine with me. I'm not in a mood to celebrate anything. Downstairs, the open door reveals Isabelle, smiling and stamping her feet, radiating the scent of fruity shampoo and cold air. She'd love any excuse to go upstairs and hang out with mussy Jonah in his pyjamas but I don't give her the chance. "Let's go," I say, buttoning up my coat and pushing out the door.

Isabelle lets me stomp down the street in silence, our footsteps making a muffled crunch on the compacted snow. A bareheaded man shovels his sidewalk and walkway with military precision, shaping snowy corners into sharp points. "Morning," Isabelle says as we pass and he nods his head, smiling quickly. His face is old but his dark eyes are bright and his brown hair barely greyed. "Mr. Baptiste," Isabelle says when we are out of earshot. "He's always in his yard. And he never says anything. Barely a word." We head south to College and then turn left, walking east. I have been repeating the names of streets and my corresponding orientations, north, south, east, west, like a litany. Dad and I had visited Jonah plenty, so it's not like I've never been to the city, but our visits usually consisted of running a few errands and then taking Jonah out for dinner, and the city had swirled around me too big and colourful and amorphous to really know. As long as I was with Dad and Jonah, I didn't mind feeling pleasantly lost and overwhelmed. Now, living here, I need to know the city in a different way and Isabelle is a stellar guide. All-night diners, bars that don't ask for ID, rep theatres, she points them out as we walk.

"Rep theatres?" I ask.

"Repertory," she says. "They show old movies, foreign films. Nothing mainstream. It's usually pretty cheap, cheaper if you get a membership."

I have sixty dollars in my pocket, taken from the money the neighbours gave us. Sixty dollars felt like hitting the jackpot but, I realize, out in the city, wandering streets filled with storefronts of things to buy buy buy, it is nothing at all. There is so much of everything, it is almost impossible to decide. But I trust Isabelle and follow her lead. I pick up some notebooks, pens and pencils at a stationery store on Spadina, and both Isabelle and I buy cheap woollen socks and bars of rose soap in Chinatown from a wizened Mao-era granny in black silk. We walk down a narrow street, crowded with parked cars, into Kensington Market. It is even more crowded here, filled with people having to walk single file between the piles of snow and the storefronts lined with bins of bulk food or hanging displays of knapsacks and sports jerseys. Isabelle has a tip for almost every store we pass. "Great dumplings," she says, pointing to a Chinese bakery across the street and, as we pass a tiny storefront with a hand-scribbled poster advertising saffron and turmeric, adds, "This place has the best price for almonds and pistachios." A few storefronts later, she points again. "We'll come here in spring. Best sandals in the city." I am distracted by a woman, sitting on a duffel bag on the curb, crying. Her hair is short and cut in a sharp geometric angle, dyed an impenetrable shade of black. Her eyes are hidden by big black sunglasses, and her bare hands cover the rest of her face, but she huffs out a wet gurgling sob as Isabelle and I walk by. It is overwhelming, all these people, all the food, all the stuff, and my head is buzzing by the time Isabelle leads me into a cheese store, the long display cabinet stacked with rounds and bricks of cheese piled into staggeringly high towers. It's a wall of cheese.

"We've come for samples," Isabelle announces and the guy behind the counter smiles at her.

"Sure," he says, winking at me. "What'll you have?"

Isabelle moves purposefully from soft to hard cheeses, requesting a bite of this, a bite of that, the counter guy handing over a square of each for both of us. Stinky cheese, sweet cheese, crumbly cheese, salty cheese, tangy cheese, smoky cheese, we taste it all. I am certain buddy's flirtations will fizzle out when he realizes we aren't planning on buying anything but he continues to smile and wink right up until the moment when, bellies pleasantly full, we say thanks and leave. He even waves as we exit and I wave back, immediately feeling silly, but I can't help it. I am a little in love. With the counter guy, with Isabelle, with Kensington Market.

The street widens slightly as Isabelle leads me past a strip of old residential houses transformed into funky-looking used-clothing stores, paisley shirts, black turtlenecks and striped pants hanging off the porch banisters. Racks of winter coats line the narrow, snow-filled yard of one store, all impossibly stylish and cool looking. Jonah grabbed some of my winter stuff out of the garage so my coat is plenty warm and I have my matching mitts and hat and scarf, all fine winter wear for Linden, but here in the city, next to the impossibly cool, I am impossibly dowdy. Isabelle sees my look of longing and says, "Don't even think about it. They are outrageously overpriced. We can go coat shopping sometime at the Sally Ann on Dundas. They have great deals there."

Isabelle leads me into Dolce di Carne, the door to the small café opening with a welcoming blast of warmth and good smells into a loud, crowded room. A guy in the corner with a pink mohawk bobs his head energetically to the Clash's "Rudie Can't Fail" and the tables are filled with clusters of people, most of them about Jonah's age, drinking beer or coffee and eating some kind of large pastry. Like the winter coats, they all seem impossibly cool. They talk loudly and laugh loudly and I wonder what kind of currency it would take to possess the almost magical quality of lightheartedness the room exudes. I mentally calculate the remaining cash in my wallet, hoping I have enough for whatever snack Isabelle has planned.

"I always get the house empanada and a café con leche," Isabelle says as we line up behind a big sign that reads Order at Cashier. I don't know what an empanada is or a café con leche but I nod my head, looking up the prices on the chalkboard. All together it'll be under ten dollars, so I'm good. "Sounds great. I'll get that too."

The air is heavy with strong spices, paprika and pepper, and a meaty richness, like the way our house smelled when Dad made his slow cooker stew. The display shelves are filled with various semicircle-shaped pastries. Empanadas, I assume, are a type of meat pastry.

We settle into a cramped corner table and I am pleased my deduction is correct: the house empanada is a pastry filled with spicy beef, onion, peas, grated carrot and black olives. And a café con leche is strong coffee with warm milk. I like the way the vowels roll up and down and off the tongue, *café con leche*, and think: Dad will love it too. This has happened all day long, all week long. I see something interesting and think, Dad will love it. I can't wait to tell Dad. And then I remember his white lips and white tip of his nose and blind eyes all over again.

"You okay?" Isabelle asks. I nod my head. Isabelle has an uncanny ability to read my thoughts. She knows the instant when they drift away to some place other than the immediate moment of wanting things: cheese, counter guys, new coats. She would like me to let her in. I know this, and I've tried. But I have no out-loud words to explain how strange being in Toronto feels. Like a holiday, or an aberration or an elaborate, tasteless joke, certainly none of it real, or permanent. There's a ghost story in my thoughts that goes like this: Dad is away on work, in South Africa or Iraq, maybe. It's a big story. *The* big story. Or perhaps he's off on a holiday with his secret girlfriend, Jillian Nash, enjoying the life he never shared with me. Either scenario, he hasn't called for a long time and I miss him but he'll call soon and then things will get back to normal. The subtext to the story, Dad would say, is that I still can't face the facts. It's still impossible he's gone, impossible I won't see him again. *You've got to face the facts, kiddo.* That's what he'd tell me.

"This is good," I say, taking a big bite. "I've never had an empanada before. There's a spice? I like it, but I don't know what it is."

"Cumin, likely," Isabelle smiles. "It looks a little like a caraway seed. It's good for digestion."

Food is Isabelle's favourite topic and she can reliably be distracted with a foodie question. She loves to talk about spices and marinades and the best way to make a pie crust and can do so at great length with only the slightest encouragement. She's wonderful. My brother is an idiot. If I were him, I'd ask her out in a heartbeat. Even if she is just trying to impress Jonah, it still seems too good to be true, the way she has taken me under her golden wing. If I could, I'd like to tell her everything. I'd like to tell her about *Indium's Ark* and Dad's marble face and the casseroles and the heart medicine and Rufus coming to say goodbye and the strangeness of having one kind of life one day and having it gone the next. But I can't.

It's dusk when we leave the café and the power lines and streetcar cables spool ahead of us, a long black web against the dark blue sky. We turn west on Queen Street, heading toward WildFlour, the bakery that Isabelle works at. She's arranged a meeting with the owners. Business is good and they need extra help. Even though I told Isabelle the closest I've come to bakery experience is making mac'n cheese for the kids I babysat, she still thinks they might consider hiring me.

There are fewer and fewer occupied buildings the farther west we walk and every abandoned storefront adds a little more to the sense of grungy squalor. We pass a grizzled old guy who lurches down the street clutching a raggedy wool blanket. Give him a mule, a metal pan and a pickaxe and he'd be a perfect prospector, driven mad by his search for gold. The sole of one of his shoes is split open, flashing a reddened patch of skin. Skin like a scar, skin burned by the cold. A few blocks too late, I realize I should have given him my woollen socks.

"Here we are," Isabelle gestures grandly. "WildFlour." Unlike it's dingy neighbours, the bakery has been freshly painted white, a bright sunflower bursting through the *o* of Flour. It's the last building on the block and so the windows wrap around two sides. The lights inside are dim and the sign on the front door reads Closed. I follow Isabelle around the corner to the alley and the back entrance where an old woman sits hunched against the cold, clutching a cup of coffee. There is a pale wildness about her face and when we pass, she turns her gaze away with a look of tragic alarm.

"Hey, Stella," Isabelle says as we climb the steps.

"Flowers!" the woman says, followed by a string of indecipherable ashy-mouthed mutters. Pinch 'em, I think I hear her say. Crush 'em.

Inside, we hang our coats on a rack and Isabelle taps a stack of hanging aprons on the last hook. "Our uniform." We pass through a narrow storage room and into a large, bright kitchen that smells like fresh bread and burnt sugar and cinnamon. God's farts. That's what Dad said when a kitchen smelled especially good. God must've farted. A man and a woman lean over a long wooden work table, eating and talking with their mouths full, and beyond them is a large open window that looks into the front of the bakery.

"Leo," Isabelle gestures to the man, then to the woman, "Anna, this is Lou."

"Come," Leo says, waving us over to the table. "You must try. Spanakopita. Here, dip it in this." He hands me a small triangle of flaky pastry and, following his orders, I plunge a corner into the dip bowl and take a big bite: warm spinach, cheese, onion, yogurt. Lots of garlic. "Delicious," I say, swiping the dip from the corner of my mouth.

"This girl," Anna says. She puts a hand on my shoulder as she turns to Isabelle. "I like this girl."

Leo is tall and pale, his fading-to-grey hair cut in a straggly mullet, knobby bones jutting through his skin in all directions. The best thing about his skinny face: his eyes, droopy and kind. Anna is a study in rounds and curves. Her long black hair is thick and wavy, and she moves silkily, like a dancer. It's hard not to be reminded of the Jack Sprat rhyme in their presence. Jack Sprat could eat no fat, his wife could eat no lean. And so between them both, you see, they licked the platter clean. Another thing I'd like to tell Dad.

After a few questions and a quick tour, Leo pencils me in to the schedule to work with Isabelle Saturdays during the day and on Wednesday and Friday evening after school. Before we leave, they package up a bag of day-old muffins and croissants, and a loaf of French bread. Anna apologizes, says Leo's loaves are always crooked and that, if I find it inedible, I can always feed it to the squirrels. Leo calls her a witch and a shrew and then they kiss. I like them. It seems entirely possible that they love one another.

Back outside the temperature has dropped along with the sun and an icy, prickly snow has begun to fall. The back steps are vacant except for an abandoned Styrofoam cup. Did that old troll have a place to go? Or the sock-less prospector? It's too cold to be outside. I shiver into my scarf as

Isabelle checks her watch. She's meeting her father and his family tonight. We walk along Queen, farther west, and stop in front of a park. "This is Trinity Bellwoods. It's a shortcut," Isabelle says, pointing north. "You can take this path all the way up to Dundas. I've got to keep going this way." She reaches her arms around me in a big bear hug. "Bye. I'll see you to-morrow?"

"Sure." She moves down the street away from me as I remain standing, stranded, resisting the urge to trail behind, like a lost puppy. I turn to face the park, which looms, darkly shadowed, into an unseeable distance. An ornate wrought iron gate hangs between two white pillars and forms an entrance, except there is no fence on either side, and so no need of a gate. I find this troublesome and skirt around the imposing iron bars with the de-tailed crest featuring a crown, a key, a heavily antlered stag and some kind of a bird. Tall black lampposts spill silvery pools of light onto the curving path and the snow glints like diamonds, but behind the small circles of light the shadows deepen to an expansive darkness. I head north. Or north-ish. The path is winding, not straight, and as I move deeper into the park, the light from Queen Street fading behind me, I lose my sense of direction, uncertain if my sense of true north has somehow now veered east. The warning in the newspaper that all women should plan their routes after dark pops unwanted, but forcefully, into my mind. That this is an ill-advised route is a fact I know with an abrupt but absolute certainty, knowledge that courses up from the electrified soles of my feet, tingles the hair on the back of my neck and tunes my ears to every sound. Spiders, needles, the highest point on a roller coaster, some things you can't help but feel with your whole body even if you're not exactly scared. I'm not exactly scared but I'm not relaxed either. I am an idiot for not paying attention to the police warning, or to Jonah, and ending up lost in the middle of a dark and winding park that is the stomping ground of a serial sexual predator. Dad would be incensed. Somewhere he is waiting for me, vibrating with a potent combination of anger mixed with worry, face whitening and hard-ening, voice ready to rocket to a shout. Rarely did I do anything to warrant that reaction from Dad but the few times I did were memorable. If he were here, I would tell him, in my defence, that the quietness and stillness of the park is impossible. Shocking. After a day of walking with Isabelle along streets stuffed with all of humanity, rich and poor and everything in between, through a babel of Russian, Korean, Portuguese, French, the dancing lilt of a Jamaican patois, to suddenly find myself so alone is absurd.

The pools of lamplight leave me vulnerable and exposed, visible to anyone or anything hiding in the shadows. My left bootlace dangles loose, a potential liability, but I don't bend down to tie it. Once, Dad told me never to kneel down and tie your shoe if you thought you were being followed by a cougar. We were on the main drag of Linden, killing time while the vacuum repair guy fixed the old Hoover. Downtown Linden: not exactly cougar country. I was irritated Dad kept changing the subject from a set of Prismacolors I coveted and was trying to convince him to buy. Don't stop to tie your shoes and don't run, he said, because that's when they will get you. It's instinct, he said. They see you vulnerable and they *have* to attack. You must be a smart animal.

What would a smart animal do now? Breathe. Slow down. I measure my steps into smooth loping strides and force my shoulders open and down my back. Despite the cold, I lift my head high, out of the warmth of my scarf, the icy needles of snow sharpening my senses. I keep moving. The park is endless and just as I swear I will never find my way out, the path opens and I am back on a main street, turning right. Up ahead is an ambulance, paramedics lifting a body onto a stretcher. There is a dense city smell as I pass by, something old and toxic.

I keep moving, crossing the street. At the next corner, I plan to take a left, north, and as I turn I am almost knocked down by a stampede of boys. Men. Boy-men. Well dressed in peacoats and varsity jackets, they run in a noxious cloud of alcohol and aggression, one of the middle runners slamming into my shoulder and knocking me into someone else.

"Sorry," the second runner calls back. He breaks stride long enough to make a quarter turn, to check me out. Not, I'm certain, to see if I'm okay. He laughs, waves and turns to catch up with his friends.

My heart races like a dumb, scared animal. A taxi passes and I consider flagging it down. But it's expensive and I don't know if I have enough money left. I could catch a bus, but I'm not sure which goes where. I keep moving, heading north, waiting until something looks familiar. As soon as I can I move onto residential streets where there are houses to run to and hedges to hide behind when the occasional car passes. I dart and scurry like a scared bunny. It's not pretty but I make it eventually to Northwood and then Rosalind. Back at Jonah's, I keep both hands on the wall to steady myself as I climb the seasick stairs. Jonah is at the kitchen table, overhead light casting a bright ring in the otherwise dark apartment. He drags his eyes away from the page as I barge in but, when he sees me, he springs to his feet.

"What's the matter? Are you okay?"

"Yeah," I say, sitting down. I am okay. It hits me that there was never any real danger out on the street. I imagined it all. "Just a little out of breath. But you know what? You were right: I would be lousy at self-defence."

"I never said that," Jonah says, sitting back down. "Why? Did somebody threaten you? I thought you were with Isabelle."

"I was with Isabelle for most of the day. And, no, I wasn't threatened. It's the city, you know? It's … bigger, a lot bigger, than Linden."

"No shit, Sherlock." Jonah chews on his bottom lip and glares at me. "You have to be careful, Lou. I swear, if anyone touches you, I'd kill them."

His voice is so serious and fierce, I can't help but laugh. "Right. Have *you* ever punched anybody?"

"I mean it, Lou."

"Give me a break, Jonah. I may be a country bumpkin but I don't need you to look after me. Look." I plop the bag of day-olds on the table and sit down beside him. "I got a job at Isabelle's bakery. Extra money and extra food. *They* will be happy to hear I'm gainfully employed."

"They?" Jonah lays his pen down and brings the heel of his hand to his temple, then grabs a handful of hair and gives it a pull. "What are you talking about?"

"*They*. Social services or whatever. The ones who are watching me."

"Oh that. I'm sorry I was so dramatic. It'll be fine. We have to meet with someone, sometime. Maybe next week." He opens the bag and grabs a croissant, stuffing half of it in his mouth in one bite. He's a wreck. Bluish ink stains smear across his right temple and aside from the fact that he's changed his clothes — blue plaid pyjamas exchanged for a bright red one-piece woollen long underwear set overlaid with baggy jeans and a "Freddie and Eddie Shreddie" T-shirt — he might not have moved from the table all day. His black waves of bed-head hair have flattened but are still unbrushed and his bleary eyes blink, mole-like, as he focusses on my face. "That's great, about the job. Congratulations."

It's chilly in the kitchen and I pull my arms into the sleeves of Dad's sweatshirt and hug my knees to my chest.

"That's Dad's, right?"

Jonah knows the answer so I don't respond. The sweatshirt is more his size and he probably wants me to give it to him. I'm not going to but he could borrow it sometime. Instead I ask him about the fake blonde who was crying at the funeral. "Did you know about this Jillian Nash that Dad was dating?"

Jonah nods. There's another blue ink stain, below his lip next to a few croissant flakes. "Sort of. He kept it pretty private."

I hate this answer. Dad was all about telling the truth and I didn't think we had any secrets but maybe there's a whole bunch of things I don't know about him. And will never know now. I want to ask Jonah if he thinks Dad was depressed and wanted to die but this doesn't seem a fair question. So, instead: "Why do you think Dad's heart stopped?"

Jonah's thick eyebrows lift, then lower, creasing together in a comical waggle but he isn't laughing. "Cardiac arrest. It's like an electrical malfunction where the heart doesn't beat properly and blood doesn't get to the body. The heart stops."

"I know. I get that. I'm not an idiot. Cardiac arrest, arrest as in stop. But why? Why does it stop?"

"It happens sometimes during a heart attack."

"So Dad was having a heart attack?"

"Maybe. Likely." Jonah shrugs. "There's no way to know without an autopsy. But given Dad's medical history, it makes the most sense. He had an irregular heartbeat and that can increase your risk for a heart attack or cardiac arrest."

I nod. "So, if I had been there to do CPR and call an ambulance and they arrived and did that emergency shock thing with the paddles they could have got his heart started?"

"Maybe." Jonah shrugs again. "But it's not your fault, Lou. You know that, right?" It's my turn to shrug. He reaches over and razzes my hair, the way Dad always did, and then clears his throat, horking into a crumpled-up tissue he pulls from his jean pocket. "The cremation is tomorrow. Do you want to go?"

"Oh." Talk about unfair questions. "No. Yes. I don't know. Do you? What do they do? Is it, like, a ceremony or something?"

"No, I don't think so. It would only be us. Maybe Sal. I think it's at a warehouse, near the funeral home, some place with a big incinerator. We would watch."

"Watch? What?" I picture four guys in overalls, work boots and plaid jackets picking up Dad's body, swinging it back and forth, and on the count of three, jettisoning him into a pit of flames. "No thanks," I say. "I don't want to go."

"Good. Me too." Jonah sighs and leans his head into the heels of both hands, elbows on the table. "Are you okay with meeting Sal tomorrow instead? For a drink. A toast. To Dad." His voice cracks and he slides his hands down his face. When he looks up there is more ink, streaking down his cheek.

"Ink," I say, circling my face with my finger. "You look like you went ten rounds with a ballpoint pen."

"Bah," he says, grabbing another croissant. "Means I'm working hard." He stretches, bent arms drawing behind his head. "I should get back at it," he says. "I have a few more hours left."

"I don't know what it is you're working on."

"Can I explain later? Tomorrow? When we're going to meet Sal?" He smiles. It's a tired smile, but, unlike Dad's lopsided grin, it's wide and symmetrical. "If I stop now, I'm done for." I take his hint and head off to my room. On an impulse, I shuffle the deck of blue index cards, picking one from the middle. It is filled completely with Dad's handwriting, the letters compressed so everything fits: *The only people for me are the mad ones, the ones who are mad to live, mad to talk, mad to be saved, desirous of everything at the same time, the ones who never yawn or say a commonplace thing but who burn, burn, burn like fabulous yellow Roman candles exploding like spiders across the stars, and in the middle you see the blue centerlight pop, and everybody goes "Awww!"* Kerouac.

It's hard for me to agree with Dad on this one. I saw madness on the streets today and there was no warmth or dazzle to it, just the cold ruin of an old woman on a back doorstep or an old man with no socks and only a wool blanket to protect him from the icy snow. It was a kind of madness that sent me scurrying through the streets. It wasn't fabulous. It was freaky.

I put my headphones on, pull the sweatshirt hood up over my head, switch off the lights and get into bed with Rufus' tape. I'm not tired, only cold and unable to think of anything productive to do. I wish I had some homework. Which is crazy, I know, but it would be good to have something to focus on. Even with all the lights off the room isn't pitch dark. The absence of inside light only makes space for the outside light, a ghostly white brilliance that is bright enough to read or write by. I pull the blankets up over my head, leaving a small space for my face, and the woollen weight and the lullaby softness of the flannel sheet is a comfort. The tape is cued to the Talking Heads' "Once in a Lifetime," followed by "Fisherman's Blues" by the Waterboys, and listening to it is a little like having a conversation with Rufus. The two of us danced to "Fisherman's Blues" at the start-of-the-year field party. Not seriously, just skipping around the bonfire, faking a country reel. By the end we were breathless and hanging off of each other's arms. Next on the tape is another Bowie, "Bewlay Brothers," a song Rufus and I both agreed was a masterpiece although the absurd ending didn't fit and should have been different, and for some reason the seriousness, and then the silliness, of it makes me want to cry.

4

At Jonah's request, Dad's body was taken to the Lasting Sands Funeral Chapel Cremation and Reception Centre in Toronto. All this time I've been gallivanting around, unpacking, eating pastries, buying soap and settling into my new room, he's been stored in some cold metallic fridge, absolutely and utterly alone. When Jonah and I talked to the man at Lasting Sands, he said this time of year was too cold for a burial and if we wanted one, we would have to wait until spring, and I immediately thought Dad would hate that. He hated having to wait for anything. Jonah and I agreed cremation was the best way to go.

The air in my room is so cold it makes me want to get back into bed and never get up. The incredible effort it is taking to be a normal, lively human being hardly seems worth it. This cold, it's easy to imagine how a heart could say, No. No more of this. And just refuse to beat. I'd like to see Rufus again. "Hello, human." That's what he'd say to me if we met unexpectedly in the halls or downtown, which I found dorky and endearing. He left his phone number and address on the inside flap of the tape, so I could call or write him a letter.

That night, at the field party, after Rufus and I danced to the Waterboys, we panted for a minute or two afterwards, staring at each other and smiling until the silence was awkward and then we started talking about our favourite Bowie songs, which is what we always talked about. Rufus said, "I love how David Bowie makes me feel like, if I wanted, I could put on a dress and wear lipstick and mascara."

"Do you want to wear mascara?" I asked. I owned neither mascara nor lipstick, just a Bonne Bell lip gloss, and it was hard to imagine what kind of dress Rufus might wear. He's tall and broad shouldered, more lumberjack than debutante. He laughed and said, no, he just liked that it was an option. I told him if he dressed like a lady for Halloween, I'd dress like a man and we could go to the school dance. "Like a date?" he said, raising his eyebrows suggestively. "Like you'd be my boyfriend?" Then we both laughed, a little too long. We were drinking red wine. He'd had a lot and his cheeks were flushed. I hadn't had so much, just enough that when we spun around to "Fisherman's Blues" the whole world went a-kilter and blurred. Except for Rufus' face. He stayed in focus.

I pull on a second pair of socks and settle into my desk with a cup of coffee and bakery muffin, tearing a sheet out of one of my new school notebooks. I write *Dear Rufus,* but can't think of anything else to say. Back at school, after the party, we were shy and reserved with each other and now Halloween has passed and I wasn't there and he probably went with someone else anyway. I'd like to tell him that Dad is being cremated today but it seems like a weird thing to put in a letter. Dad's lighter is on my desk. It's nothing fancy, a plain metal Zippo, but it's old. It was his father's before and Dad always had it with him. I flip it open and light it. The base of the flame is watery blue and the dancing tip, apricot. Such pretty colours to do such harm. Dad used to have a picture in his office of a monk who had set himself on fire in protest but he took it down when I told him it gave me nightmares. Sometimes I can't stop the pictures in my head. Last night it was the workman in overalls tossing Dad through some civilized portal into the underworld, all hellfire and brimstone. Now, it's more like a big industrial oven and Dad is sliding in like a pizza off a pizza paddle. And then Dad's body, his big calloused hands, the spot on his chest where he would let me lean my head, the swooshy beat of his heart, his whiskery cheek and his sometimes bad breath, all that would be ash. I glance at my watch. It's past three o'clock. It may be all over already.

I have the rest of Dad's stuff on my desk: his almost empty bottle of Scotch, the last two cigarettes in his pack of Player's, his Swiss Army knife and his two framed pictures. The knife might come in handy. Like the lighter, it's old and belonged to his father. The handle is made of walnut, smoothed and shaped to fit the curve of a hand. There is a knife to flip out, a nasty steel blade that could cut through wire, and a pair of sharp scissors, a corkscrew and a nail file, but Dad only ever used the knife and, occasionally, the scissors to cut things when we were camping. In the framed picture of my mom, Jonah is about three and a half and Mom is pregnant with me. She died when I was born so I never knew her, but when I was little I would stare at this picture and imagine so clearly what she was like, it almost feels like memory now. She's reading to Jonah, her eyes lowered to the page, and her long hair, which is like mine, same woody black, same tousle of shaggy curls, falls forward over her face. Jonah is looking up at her like she has all the answers in the world. I imagine Dad, the eye behind the camera, gazing at her with the same unfettered adoration. In the other picture, Jonah is about eight and I am about four and we are on a Lake Huron beach. Jonah is lounging on his side, cool guy, smoking a twig cigarette, and I am sitting on one bent knee, face smeared with chocolate popsicle, arms stretched to the sky, shouting ta-da! Dad said he loved that picture because it was the one and only time he captured a ta-da mid-pose. He took us camping every year on Lake Huron and we would spend a month hiking and canoeing and swimming and reading on the beach. Dad never thought of things like sunscreen and so Jonah and me, both fair skinned like our mother, would burn to a crisp in the first few days. The burns would keep us up at night, tossing in our sleeping bags, and then we would get insanely itchy and all our skin would flake off. It was a game to see who could peel the biggest strip of unbroken skin.

There is a knock on the door and Jonah pops his head into my room. "You ready to go?" I'm in my jeans and Dad's sweatshirt, which is starting to get a little grimy, but what the hell. "Sure, I'm ready." I ball up the piece of looseleaf paper with its lonely *Dear Rufus* at the top, and throw it in the bathroom garbage as we pass by.

We're meeting Sal at a bar named Zane's. "Crummy," Jonah says as we backtrack through a route similar to the one I took last night, moving south toward Queen. "And sleazy."

"The two dwarfs you never hear about," I say.

"It's pretty infamous, though. Leonard Cohen played there before he was famous, and so did Etta James. She called herself 'Miss Peaches.' And a few years ago, Neil Young showed up after a stadium gig and jammed with the house band."

"For real?" I ask. When we were kids Jonah would lie to me all the time and I always believed him. "It's not like the time you told me that Elvis Presley was, for sure, showing up to kindergarten open house?"

Jonah shrugs. "That's what I heard."

"I should have invited Isabelle."

"Yeah, well. This is for Dad. She didn't know him."

"She likes you."

"She's a kid."

"She's my age. Almost a year older, in fact." Dad started me in junior kindergarten a year early so I've always been younger than everyone else.

"My point," Jonah says. "She's a kid."

I consider reminding Jonah about my upcoming birthday, but don't. He doesn't need anything else to worry about. As we turn off Dundas into the lamplit park, I recognize the spot where I saw the ambulance last night.

"Don't you find these lamps spooky?" I ask Jonah. "They belong in a Victorian novel. The kind of lighting that transforms responsible Dr. Jekyll into bloodthirsty Mr. Hyde."

Jonah laughs. "You'd love my comparative literature course, Lou. The prof is always talking about stories being *fabula*."

"Sounds like a vampire. A disco vampire. Count Fabula."

"I've come to funk your blood."

"Ew."

There's a dog up ahead, trotting along, peeing on bushes, a long-legged mutt, with short curly hair speckled black and white. He looks tough and smart and he pays no attention to us.

"Dad said I could get a dog." This isn't exactly true. Our dog Jude died when I was about six and Dad was gutted. For the past ten years I've been asking if we could get a dog, and he always said no, a dog is just a heart-break waiting to happen. He said that every time, except for the very last time, which was on the Sunday afternoon when the Turners were fighting. Dad said it might be time to move. I said, If we move, I want to get a dog, and he said, We'll see.

"I don't know, Lou. I can barely take care of myself, let alone you. A dog's too much."

"You don't have to take care of me."

"Well. We have to take care of each other, right?"

I don't agree or disagree. I've never taken care of Jonah. And when he hit puberty he disappeared from my life. But before that, when I was a kid, I depended on him for everything. I could ask him any question and he'd have an answer, although it took me years to realize that most of it he was making up. Up ahead, the mutt pees on a chain-link fence and then dis-appears behind the tennis courts. "I don't know how to take care of you." I lower my voice and talk into my scarf, not sure if I want Jonah to hear what I'm saying. "I barely know you anymore."

"What? What do you mean? That's crazy, Lou." He swivels to face me as we walk but I keep my eyes facing forward.

"Well. What have you been working on this whole week? You've barely spoken to me." I sound childish but I can't stop talking now. Plus, it's true.

"It's an essay, Lou. It's fifty percent of my mark! I *have* to work on it." Jonah steps off to the left to kick an abandoned pop can a few feet down the path, and when we reach it, I take a turn. We alternate kicking the can in silence until we reach Queen, where we turn right. Jonah gestures behind us. "Sal runs a bookstore down there. He lives above it."

"Cool," I say. "The bakery is a few blocks that way too." I turn and point. "The white building, with the red brick above? Sal and I'll be work neighbours. What's it like? The bookstore?"

"Uh, dusty. Lots of books he scavenged from church sales and thrift stores. A few rare ones. He likes the old beatnik stuff. Ginsberg, Kerouac, Ferlinghetti."

I wince at the name Kerouac, remembering the stack of cards. "I didn't tell you yet, but I brought Dad's index cards." Jonah nods, but doesn't say anything. "I've been reading them every day. It's kind of like talking to him." Jonah's head is down, his hands shoved in his pockets, and he still doesn't say anything. "Does that sound crazy?"

Jonah shakes his head no and reaches up to brush his eyes. He's not crying but his eyelashes are wet. I don't know what to say. It is both important and impossible to tell Jonah that Dad was depressed, that he was screwing around with his meds, that he sat alone in a pitch-black house enjoying the darkness. I keep my mouth shut.

"I'm taking media studies. You know that, right?" Jonah says. He sounds cross, and he's still staring at the ground.

"Yeah, I know that."

"Well, my focus is on understanding the relationship between technology and culture. The essay I'm working on is looking at the difference between print media and radio and TV. How those different mediums affect perception, imagination and the relationship of the individual to society. In fact that is pretty much going to be the title of my essay. Eventually I'd like to be a journalist but maybe not exclusively print, like Dad. I'd like to make documentaries."

"Cool," I say again. "Sorry."

"What for?"

I shrug. I am sorry for just about everything. Sorry for acting like Jonah was a stranger. Sorry for not making Dad stay home sick. Sorry for not being there to do CPR. Sorry for knowing that Dad thought that death was close to the entrance of delight and not telling Jonah. A sudden crazy image fills my mind: Jonah and I camping as kids, building a big bonfire, sharpening sticks for hot dogs and marshmallows and being chased in circles by windblown streams of smoke. In the fire, Dad, sitting cross-legged like the burning monk, smiling and waving to us. And now that the image is there, imprinted into my brain, I am sorry for it too. Before I can figure out what to say, Jonah nods toward the opposite side of the street.

"Sal was a patient over there."

We pass a long stone wall that runs perpendicular to Queen. Past the wall is a long institutional-style building set far back from the road by a gently rolling, treed lawn. Rows of park benches run parallel to the sidewalk like squat sentries standing guard.

"That's the mental hospital, right?"

"Yeah, Nine Ninety-Nine. The actual address is 1001 Queen Street but everyone calls it Nine Ninety-Nine. I don't know why." Jonah stuffs his hands in his coat pocket. "I remember visiting Sal at the bookstore and Dad was trying to convince him to leave. Move out of the city. That hospital was the worst thing for you, he said. Time to leave it behind. Sal said Dad was an ignorant, self-entitled boob who didn't know what he was talking about. Then we made sandwiches. With hot mustard and sauerkraut and pastrami. Dad always brought a big bag of deli food when he visited Sal."

"Always the sauerkraut with Dad," I say. "Where was I?"

"I don't know. Off doing girlie things with Julie. Ice Capades, maybe." Jonah looks up and laughs, then grimaces, his face contorting as if he suddenly smelled something bad. "He has cats. Sal has cats. Here it is." He turns and opens a heavy wood door into a wide dark room.

"Sal's an old cat lady?"

"Sssshh." Jonah knocks his shoulder into mine. "There he is."

"Where?" The room is so dark and smoky it is as if I am trying to see underwater, my eyes sticky in the thick air so that when I blink it happens in slow motion, the room disappearing for a beat and then reappearing, still murky and warbly in the orange-tinted cast of the overhead lights. Sal is seated at a red leather bar stool but he stands and waves when he sees us, moving through the centre of the room to settle in an empty corner.

The tables are arranged in straight rows and are the kind you'd find in a mess hall or a bingo parlour. At the far right, in the back, is a small platform stage with a drum kit and at the front of the room is a shabby pool table. To the room's left of centre is a large, ornate but aging horseshoe-shaped bar, which interrupts the symmetry of the tables in a way I find disturbing. "It would be better if these tables were round," I say. "And smaller. Or the bar was moved to the centre of the room."

Jonah and Sal look at me as if I am off my rocker.

"Sorry," I say. "Just saying."

"Beer?" Jonah asks, pulling his wallet out and moving toward the bar.

"Sure." I hate the taste of beer but drinking in a public place is a totally new experience for me. I'm going to ride it out. Best case scenario, if I get picky and ask for a wine spritzer, Jonah and Sal will razz me horribly for ordering such a girlie drink. Worst case, the bartender will card me, then kick me out. Plus, Zane's? Not so much a wine spritzer kind of establishment.

Sal's gaze is intent on his beer. It is the most intriguing, the most fascinating glass of beer in the history of beer. He rolls the glass in his hands, fingering a dab of foam. When I was little, I used to think Sal was handsome, a cross between Buddy Holly and Elvis Presley, but now he reminds me of a chubby man-owl, puffy, with dark brown hair and dark brown eyes framed with dark glasses that rise to an owlish horn-rimmed tip. "Hi," he says, glancing up and then back to his beer, lips forming a non-smile.

"Hi." I mirror his non-smile, staring him down. He lifts his gaze to somewhere over my left shoulder.

"If your dad wasn't dead, he'd kill me for inviting you to a bar of such ill repute."

"Cool," I say as Jonah sits down with two glasses and a pitcher of beer. He pours for himself and then passes the pitcher to me. But I'm an idiot and don't tip the glass, so the foam bubbles up and cascades over the edge. I sop it up with cocktail napkins, hoping I'm not making too much of a fool of myself.

"We should have met somewhere else," Sal says, nodding in my direction. "Someplace more civilized."

"I'm fine with uncivilized," I say, sliding my elbow through the remaining puddle. Dad's sweatshirt will smell like beer now.

"Lou's going to be working a few blocks from here," Jonah says. "At a bakery."

There's an old couple seated behind Jonah, a few tables away. The man is short and weedy, wearing tight blue jeans and enormous cowboy boots, and the woman, also in jeans, sports a frilly peach-coloured blouse. They lean into each other all smoochy, both drinking caesars through a straw, the leaves of an uneaten celery stalk fanning the woman's heavily rouged cheek. I wish I had invited Isabelle, although this might not be her kind of place. Zane's hardly seems the best of anything. I'm not sure what Rufus would make of a place like this. The only person from Linden I can picture frequenting this bar is Freddy, my lab partner in science. Freddy's last name was Robbins but I always thought of him as Freddy Fender because he looked a little like that old-timey singer. He was short and stocky and had a coarse, puffy halo of black pubic-y hair and the ghost of a moustache that you just knew was going to grow in all bushy and disgusting in a few years. Freddy is the crudest person I know. He was always telling me the gory details of what he did with his girlfriends while we were supposed to be mixing chemicals or dissecting a worm. Pretty much after *Where Did I Come From?* the sex-ed book Dad bought me to explain all the stuff he didn't want to talk about, everything I know about sex came from Freddy Fender. And Judy Blume books.

"Jonah," I say, interrupting Sal's long-winded rant on the horrors of yuppies and boomers and how they were coming to invade, and ruin, the neighbourhood any time now. "Do you remember how Dad used to sing that Freddy Fender song "Wasted Days and Wasted Nights," and you and I would do the back up lalalalaaa's?"

Jonah shrugs but doesn't say anything. Sal glances at his watch, then reaches for the pitcher and tops up each of our glasses. "It's time to toast your dad." He raises his glass and says, "To Danny boy."

Jonah raises his glass. "To Danny."

Suddenly light-headed, I raise my glass too. "To Dad," I say. Jonah and Sal start drinking but I keep going, reciting the last half of the quote from Dad's index card. "Burn, burn, burn like fabulous yellow Roman candles exploding like spiders across the stars. ..." I drink as much of my beer as I can in one go, almost two-thirds of the glass. I take a big breath and finish the last third, then lurch upward and teeter off into the darkest corner in hopes of finding a bathroom.

Propelled by a wave of nausea, I bang through the door and bounce off the sink into a stall where I throw up a vile mixture of beer and blueberry muffin, again and again and again, until my stomach is empty but still heaving. As the wave recedes, I sit back on my heels and lean into the wall. *Marie L is a total cunt*, someone has written in large childish letters along the bottom of the partition. *Call her for a good time.*

When it is over I am fine. Cool and detached. Hungry even. I rinse the puke with a gargle of cold water and head back to Jonah and Sal.

"Oh," Jonah says when he sees me. "I'll get some water."

"*On the Road*, right?" Sal says. "That quote?"

"It's Kerouac."

"Right, Kerouac is *On the Road*. Where'd you pull that from?"

"I read, you know."

Sal gives me a pinched, doubting look as if to say he thinks I am a liar and possibly too dumb to continue the conversation. Jonah returns with a pitcher of ice water and a fresh glass. He fills it and places it in front of me.

"It's something Dad used to say."

"Really?" Jonah says. "Drink some water."

"Really?" Sal says. "Danny wasn't much of a Kerouac fan. He preferred William Carlos Williams. Interplay of form and content. He thought Kerouac was a windbag."

"Williams was the doctor, right? The red wheelbarrow guy?" Dad read me one of his poems once. I can't remember the exact words but the image it left is still clear: a red wheelbarrow, half filled with rainwater, surrounded by bedraggled chickens pecking the muddy ground.

"Yeah," Sal snorts in an unbecoming way. "The red wheelbarrow guy." I can tell he's impressed. He waves the waitress over and introduces us as Dan's kids. She's tiny and plain and at least as old as Sal, much too old to be working in a crappy joint like this, but, somehow, she is sparkly too. There's an unfashionable gap between the bottom of her pants and her sneakers and her anklet socks are blue with a pattern of tiny red hearts.

"Whom, I assume, are both," she turns to me, "of legal drinking age?"

"Absolutely," I say and raise my glass of water in a cheers. She winks at me.

"Shelley, you old tart, bring us another pitcher of beer. And Scotch." Sal's voice is inching toward a roar. "Danny would want a toast with something more than this piss water."

"Lou?" Jonah asks. "You okay for another round?"

I shrug my shoulders, meaning no. No, Dad wouldn't want us to stay for another round. He would want me to go home and get ready for my first day at a new school. Jonah doesn't read my meaning though and he nods okay to Shelley.

The front door opens and one guy, then another, then another, all carrying instruments, push through. The first one props the door open with a wedge of wood and cold air infiltrates the haze of the bar. They are young and laughing, aware, I am certain, of the hungry eyes watching them as they go in and out, weighed down with various pieces of equipment, an amp, a snare drum, a second mike stand. Shelley hands out shot glasses to our table as one of the trio kicks the doorstop out and the glow of lamplight and the cold night disappear.

"No ideas but in things!" Sal shouts, raising his glass.

One whiff of the amber liquid sets my stomach rolling and I return my glass to the table, pushing it away, untouched. Jonah slugs his back like a champ and then asks Sal if the line is from a Williams poem. Sal says it's bad luck not to drink during a toast so I dip my finger in the Scotch and stick it in my mouth.

"Why don't they play poker in the jungle?" I ask. I look from Jonah to Sal to Jonah, drawing the moment out. Wait for it, wait for it. "Too many cheetahs!"

"What did the Buddhist say to the hot dog vendor?" Jonah counters. I know the answer but I let him have it. "Make me one with everything!" We both turn to Sal.

"Uh, okay. What did the shellfish... no wait. Uh, why did the shrimp hoard his lunch?"

Jonah and I shout the answer in unison: "He was a little shellfish!"

"I can never remember jokes. Not like your dad. He knew hundreds. Thousands," Sal says, pouring more beer. The mike in the back corner crackles into life.

"Check one, check one," the guitarist says, then, "One-two-three-four — " and the band erupts into a fast and fierce version of a vaguely familiar song. It's not until the gravelly-voiced guitarist leans into the mike and sings the first few lines that I place it: Bob Dylan's "Subterranean Home-sick Blues." The guitarist is short and slight, pale with inky black hair and he's wearing a black T-shirt and baggy jeans with rolled-up cuffs. The bass player is tall and skinny with a red plaid flannel shirt and a spiky mullet. He reminds me of a younger, hipper version of my new boss, Leo. The drummer is the most gorgeous: curly brown hair, cocoa complexion, kiss-able lips. I'm in love with all of them. The song sputters to an end midway through the third verse and the guitarist asks the room if the sound is okay.

"Not bad," Jonah shouts and gives a thumbs-up.

"We'll be back," the lead guy says, glancing at his watch. "First set is in about an hour." They file out through a small door to the left of the stage. I don't feel so bad about sticking around anymore. But I'm hungry.

"I'll be back," I say and pass my shot glass to Jonah.

It's cold outside but not crisp and cold. It's wet and cold and the sky is a distant muddy black, no visible stars. The bright lights of Legacy Variety beckon, but I pass in hopes of finding a friendly pizza place farther on.

Or someplace selling french fries, hot and salty, with a good dousing of malt vinegar. But aside from the convenience store, nothing is open. Past the hospital on the south side of the street looms a huge building, the Ce De Candy Company, although nothing in its sinister air suggests candy-making fun. The Seedy Candy Company is a better name, the kind of place that manufactures lollipops and jujubes to sell to pervy men in white vans. Several storefronts have paper taped to the windows and flashes of light glint in the cracks, giving the impression of being both abandoned and occupied. A coin laundromat on the next block is open, but empty, and that's it. Not a single slice of pizza or salty fry in sight. I return to the fluorescent aisles of Legacy Variety where I settle for a bag of salt and vinegar chips and four licorice pipes, two red, two black, and a small Styrofoam cup of coffee.

The girl behind the till is about my age or a little older, and she hunches over the counter reading a magazine, cornrows dividing the crown of her head into tight, black stripes. Her name tag says Irene.

"What you tink?" She speaks with a musical lilt, pushing her magazine, a *Playboy*, toward me and tapping a page with a picture of a couple fucking doggy-style on the lawn of the White House. "Real? Or fake?"

"That man," I say, "he looks Swedish to me."

She shrugs and nods as if this is an appropriate response to her question. Why do I say the things I do? What are you supposed to say when discussing the contents of *Playboy* with a total stranger? I've never even seen inside a *Playboy*. I pocket my change and leave, cheeks prickling with an irritating heat.

The phone booth out front of Zane's smells like pee; there are swooping stains along the back bottom of the booth. Despite the outhouse vibe, I eat chips while I dial Isabelle's number. A woman answers, her mom, and she hollers off the phone for Isabelle to pick up. From my vantage point in the phone booth I can read the graffiti on the white brick side of Legacy Variety. *ILL KIDD*, written in black block letters and in bright orange: *No Parking SCUMBAGS*.

"Hello?" Isabelle's voice sounds warm and cozy, far away from this cold street corner.

"Hey, it's Lou," I say.

"Hey, where are you? I tried to call earlier."

"We're — Jonah and me — we're at this bar. Zane's — "

"The place Neil Young played at? I know it. What are you doing there?"

"Meeting a friend of my dad's, Sal, for a thing. A drink. But there's this band playing now and Jonah and I are going to stick around. You want to come down?"

"Ahhh. I don't know. I'm already in my pyjamas. Maybe — "

Indecision quivers Isabelle's voice. I can picture her at home: her flannel pyjamas have cupcakes on them. My third night in Toronto, I stayed over at her house. She lent me pyjamas (cotton with a pattern of Eiffel Towers and high-heeled shoes and broad-brimmed French chapeaux) and we ate a whole package of Arrowroot cookies dipped in hot Nestlé Quik. Pierced with a sudden longing to be curled in the window seat of her rose-coloured room instead of out in this bone-shivering cold, I interrupt her mid-sentence. "Isabelle. Don't worry about it. It's cold as a witch's teat out here."

"A what?" Isabelle laughs. "What did you say?"

"A witch's teat, it's something my dad used to — " A sudden light across the street catches my eye, something bright and random flaring in the dark treed lawn of the hospital. Flames dart and flash along the underside of the canopy of a tree. A bonfire? But it is moving between the dark shapes of trees and bushes. Moving closer. I lean out of the phone booth for a clearer view, the smell of smoke thick in the damp air. Somewhere close by the grumble of a car engine climbs in pitch as it accelerates down a side street. For a moment, I lose sight of the fire but then it returns: a streak of red behind a tree, then darkness, then a flare. Then I see it's a person, a human, outlined by flame, limbs jerking like a marionette pulled by invisible strings. I crouch back into the booth, the phone still pressed ridiculously to my ear. Isabelle is still talking. "Lou? Are you there? Lou?"

"Holy fuck, Iz. There's something on fire across the street. I have to go." I drop the phone and my bag of chips, pressing both hands against the glass. I don't know what to do. The person lurches and tumbles down a small incline, a moving pinwheel of flame, falling directly across the street from me at the edge of the road. The door to Zane's is only about twenty feet away but my knees have turned to Jell-O. I don't know if I can make it to the door. My arms, too, have turned into a quivering mess and it takes a colossal effort to open the glass door. The smell is brutal: gasoline, burnt hair, acrid smoke. I want to move but can't, am totally unable. Even if I were to start running and screaming I would still be stuck in this same spot, going nowhere, the way it sometimes happens in a bad dream. A car drives by, momentarily blocking the view across the street, and I am able to reset my sights on Zane's. I stumble forward, gagging on undigested chips, and push blindly through the swinging doors. Shelley is the first person I see.

"Call an ambulance," I say. "The police. There's a man, burning — "

Several things happen at once. When the blur of motion has settled, I am seated on one of the red stools at the bar beside Sal. Jonah and several other patrons and the guys from the band are outside. The sound of sirens draws closer.

"I don't know if it was a man," I tell Sal. "It could have been a woman."

"It could have been anyone," Sal says, staring at his hands. He sounds dreamy and distant, as if he was talking about any old thing. It could have been anyone who won the lotto jackpot. It could have been anyone who was hit with lightning. It could have been anyone who burst into flame. He shakes his head, a horse shivering off flies. "Here," he says, pushing a glass of ice water toward me. "Drink."

But I can't. I'm cold. I'm freezing. My shoulders shake and my teeth chatter, loud and uncontrollable, clacking as if I am a character in a cartoon. "They can't do anything. Outside," I tell Sal. "It's too late."

"Here, sweetie." Shelley moves the ice water away, replacing it with a mug of milky tea. "Sal!" She snaps her fingers in his face. "Get her your jacket, man. The girl's in shock."

Sal's jacket smells of a sickly sweet smoke and as he wraps it around my shoulders my stomach once again rolls upward, bile souring the back of my throat. Retreating to the bathroom is tempting but I am too dizzy to stand. Both hands hold the cup of tea, elbows resting on the bar, and slowly the dizziness recedes enough that I can take tentative sips. It is very good: hot and sweet, warming from the inside out. Around me people appear to be moving in slow motion, their movements exaggerated and extra loud. Sal lights a purple cigarillo, inhaling, the cloying smoke disappearing inside his body, then issuing forth through his nose with force, white plumes of jet stream streaking over the bar counter toward the large bottles of vodka and Scotch lined up against the wall. Shelley punches in a bar tab and the register bangs open. Behind me, the talking and laughing and shouting of the bar has turned feral, like hyenas gathered around a carcass. I slip my arms into the armholes of Sal's jacket. It doesn't smell any different than Zane's, no better or worse, and its heavy weight is comforting, especially now as the door to the bar opens and closes with increased frequency as the crowd of people who rushed outside slowly return. Among them is a new group of patrons, all guys, most of them older than Jonah, and dressed like investment bankers and smelling strongly of men's cologne. As they pass, I recognize the face of the boy who ran into me the other night. He recognizes me too.

"Hey!" He raises an arm, veering in my direction. "I've seen you around. You live in the neighbourhood?"

"Yeah. Sort of," I say, standing, so I am closer to his eye level. He's tall. Behind him, the swinging doors open, cool air lightening the smoky haze, and I wrap Sal's jacket more tightly across my chest. "I just moved."

"Cool. I'm Donnie."

"Lou," I say.

"What school — " he says as two older guys join us, the first punching Donnie's shoulder hard enough to make him take a half-step forward. The puncher resembles Donnie, but with the beginnings of a shifty-looking moustache. The second guy is shorter, dirty-brown hair styled like a Sears model.

"C'mon, dickwad," Shifty Moustache says, yanking Donnie's arm, "we got business still. No time for pussy." He glances back over his shoulder with a look of smug appraisal. "No matter how sweet."

"My brother and his friend. Assholes," Donnie says as he turns to follow. "They're assholes. See you around, Lou."

I jump as a hand lands on my shoulder from behind.

"You okay?" It's the dreamy lead singer. Up close I can see tiny scars on his skin. From acne likely, maybe chicken pox, but still, he's gorgeous. He's standing so close and his eyes are so kind, it's possible we're old friends.

"I'm okay," I say.

"There's a cop wants to talk to you. Said he'd be in any minute." His hand pats my shoulder, rests for a moment, and then withdraws. He nods in the direction of the stage. "Time to get to work."

"Show must go on," I say and immediately regret it. But he smiles as he walks away.

Sal is looking at me again and when I return his gaze he does his dramatic double-take move, wagging his head in exaggerated disbelief. As if I am some unknown creature he can't possibly figure out.

"What?" I say. Or shout, my voice pitchy, out of control. "What is it, Sal?"

"Easy, Lou." It's Jonah and his arm is around my shoulder. The cop is there too, with a card, Detective Rory Phillips, an extra phone number printed below the office one, and Jonah is arranging for questions to be asked while the cop drives us home. The band begins to play as Jonah leads me out the door, following the cop to his car. I wish briefly we could stay and hear the music but then wonder if we're in trouble for being in the bar. Maybe we've fucked up and the cop will tell social services I was at a bar, drinking and barfing and falling in love and watching a man burn. Maybe this is exactly the kind of thing *they* are looking out for. It's not until the cop car turns onto Ossington that I realize I still have Sal's jacket. It's cold in the car and I lean into Jonah's shoulder. There's a Snickers wrapper on the floor, caught under the heel of his Kodiak boot. I want to ask the cop if that's what he eats on stakeouts but don't.

The cop parks out front of the apartment and lets the engine idle while he turns in his seat to ask me a few questions. I try to re-create the scene: the potato chips, the phone booth, the pee stains. Then the flash of light, the stumbling figure, the sound of the car peeling away, the smell of gasoline and burnt hair.

"Anything else?" he asks. My teeth have started to chatter again and I shake my head no. "Call me, if you think of anything else." He hands me a second card, the same hand-printed number below the first. I slide it into my wallet next to the card from the cop in Linden. "Take it easy," he says, as Jonah opens the door and we climb out of the car.

Anything else? I lie in bed not able to sleep, thinking, Anything else? I have this crazy notion of calling up the cop and telling him everything about Dad's death, his cremation and how I kept thinking about a burning monk all day long. How Dad's blue card last night read *Burn, burn, burn,* words that looped through my mind all day like a silent incantation. Like some kind of premonition, or prayer. Like somehow I made it happen. When sleep finally comes there is no peace, only a kind of blank claustrophobic darkness for a few hours.

At quarter after four, I am awake again. Curled into a tight ball, I crouch deep inside the blankets, hoarding warmth and trying but failing to keep the soft, muted edges of sleep from completely dissolving. The wind that buffets the windowpanes is an audible moan, and my breath is a visible puff of air. Blankets wrapped round me like a heavy shawl, I grab Dad's blue cards and settle in the moonlit seat of the bay window. The branches of the trees outside are blue with frost. A cat walks down the centre of the alleyway with tiny, elegant, sashaying steps, too far away to see the true colours of its coat.

The first card I pick reads, *A Rubik's cube has 43 quintillion possible configurations.* The second is a recipe for spaghetti bolognese and the third, written in a wider, more sprawling script, says, *Owls are the only birds that can see the colour blue.* None of it is relevant. I reshuffle the pack and return it to the desk on my way to the bathroom. Scalding hot water drizzles from the shower head — the pressure is always low — and I twist and contort like a child acrobat to get as much of my body under the thin stream as possible, working up a comforting lather of Pears soap before towelling off and returning to bed to huddle under the blankets, trying to dry the chilling film of dampness left on my skin. When it is too cold to stay still any longer, I get dressed in my first-day-of-school clothes and return to the window seat with a coffee to wait for the dawn.

5

The new school is three storeys high, a giant square with four sets of staircases leading inside. Jonah and I visited last week so I could register, but it was late in the afternoon and empty of people. Now kids line the sides of the steps, talking, laughing, some even smoking cigarettes. This is something that would not be allowed at my school in Linden. There, the smoking area was hidden behind the school and enclosed with chain-link fence, a place where it was not uncommon for fights to break out.

"It's nice, right?" Jonah asks, as Isabelle leads us around the building to the main entrance. He insisted on walking with us, as though I am a kid embarking on the first day of kindergarten and need someone to hold my hand. It is a gesture both reassuring and annoying, Jonah's specialty. "It looks like the set for a John Hughes movie."

I shrug. Yes, the well-dressed students exude a kind of movieland quality. There's not a single guy in sight wearing a lumberjacket, which was practically a required uniform in Linden. But unlike Linden, or a white-washed John Hughes movie, the faces here are more varied and colourful. I attempt to formulate a comeback, something about Ferris Bueller's Day at the UN, but am out of my depth. Instead, like an idiot, I blurt out: "I've never been the new kid before."

Jonah and Isabelle talk over one another as we walk through the main entrance, both assuring me that everything will be fine.

"Of course it will," I snap as we arrive at the door to the principal's office, the glass window coated in a frosted glaze so it is impossible to see inside. A steady stream of kids moves through the brightly lit hall. Everyone knows where they are going. The buzzing ring of an electronic bell, close by and very loud, startles me and my palms and pits start to sweat.

"First homeroom bell," Isabelle says. "But don't worry, I can skip it."

"Go," I say. "You too, Jonah. You'll be late for work. I'm fine."

"Okay." Jonah punches my shoulder, his klutzy attempt at upbeat and chummy. "Have a good first day."

Isabelle manages a bit better. She winks, says, "I'll see you soon."

They turn to go and I am gutted. How can they leave me? Isabelle turns back to wave and I have to push through the principal's door so she doesn't see how close I am to running after them, begging them not to go.

I am *exactly* like a kid going to kindergarten. It's embarrassing.

Seated in a small plastic chair, I wait, while the secretary, face crinkled in lines of permanent irritation, speaks into a small microphone mounted on her desk. Announcements done, she hands me a class timetable and a map of the school, and then turns back to her typing.

"That's it?" I say.

"That's it," she says, gaze never leaving the keyboard.

I step back into the empty hall. My first class is math, on the second floor. As I attempt to locate it on the map, the bell, sounding like a hive of electrocuted bees, rings again and the halls are suddenly swarming with people, all of them shoulder to shoulder moving in one direction. A stampede. It's tempting to be swept up but I'm certain my class is in the other direction. Isabelle materializes out of the throng on the far side of the hall and I push through the flow of students to reach her.

"I'm so glad to see you. Five minutes in and I'm totally lost," I say. "I have math first. Second floor?"

"Either direction will get you there," she says, grabbing my elbow. "C'mon."

Isabelle leads me up a flight of stairs and drops me off at room 212. "Wait for me at the end of class. I'll meet you back here," she says before racing down the hall.

The math teacher, Mr. Vernon, is friendly. He hands me a dilapidated textbook, points to an empty desk at the front of the room and explains that the class is starting chapter 9: trigonometric functions. My math class in Linden finished the first trig chapter, so I am a little ahead. I wipe the sweat from my palms, pull out a new notebook and freshly sharpened pencil and begin the satisfying process of figuring out the cosine. Math has always made sense to me. It is a relief to focus on a single, small, solvable problem.

When classes are finished, Isabelle takes me to the library on the first floor. "Tomorrow? Eight fifteen, your place?" she says before racing off to her drama rehearsal. They're starting to build sets so she'll be at the school until late. I wanted to acquaint myself with the library and do a little research before walking to Sal's bookstore to return his jacket. Unlike Linden, this library doesn't have a computer although the book-y smell and hushed vibe is the same. I flip through the card catalogue and then search the chaotically misfiled bookshelves until I find *The Cardiovascular System: The Heart*, an academic booklet that somehow ended up in the poetry section.

What the book tells me: Your heart is about the same size as your closed fist and beats roughly a hundred thousand times a day. *Atrium* means "entry hall" and *ventricle* means "little belly." The right atrium and ventricle form the pulmonary pump, blood travelling to and from the lungs, while the left atrium and ventricle form the stronger, systemic pump of the body. In the hand-drawn pictures the heart is coloured bright red on the left side, pale blue on the right. There are also pictures of real-life dissected hearts, both whole and bisected, the flesh a lifeless beige. I skim the chapter entitled "Diseases of the Heart," each description of a disease followed by a standard list of predictable lifestyle choices. Don't smoke, limit your alcohol intake. Eat a low-cholesterol diet, exercise regularly. Dad knew all this, but he loved eggs. And his idea of exercise was walking upstairs to his office to have a shot of Scotch and smoke a Player's. That, or watching baseball on TV. After introducing myself to the librarian, a big-boned, fleshy woman with grey hair, Birkenstocks and red apple cheeks, I check the book out for further study.

"More tea?" Sal holds up a china teapot.

"Please." Turns out Sal is a meticulous brewer of tea. My visit has been full of surprises. The store, a half a block east of the bakery, is called Black Cat Books. I didn't notice it the first time Isabelle and I walked past, which is odd because it is distinctly stylish. Elegant even. The window frames are painted black against a polished rust-coloured brick, and the front door, six rectangular panes of glass topped with a brilliant semicircle of a sunburst stained glass, is painted a dark forest green. The first thing you see when you enter is a large Toulouse-Lautrec *Chat Noir* poster framed behind the cash register. The shelves are crammed with books but they are neat and organized into various sections: poetry, non-fiction, fiction, drama. The windows hum and rattle when a streetcar passes, the air smells of dust and dry paper, and the winter sun that filters through the shuttered panes lights up the dust motes so they dance in the air. In front of the cash register are two display cases filled with rare editions and a collection of early pulp magazines with names like *Famous Crime Cases* and *Thrilling Wonder Stories*.

All this is pleasant and unexpected but earlier, when Sal pushed firmly on a section of wall behind the cash register and a small handle-less door underneath the *Chat Noir* poster sprang open, I was blown away. Closed, the door blends into the wall invisibly. Open, it looks like an entranceway for hobbits. We both had to crouch to enter, and he showed me the real surprise, a hidden tunnel, barely wide enough for Sal to walk through, that runs along two sides of the bookstore. This is where he stores his most valuable books. The dusty smell was stronger there and I found it claustrophobic, though cool. Back in the bookstore, Sal reached into the pocket of his oversized, shapeless smock shirt and pulled out an orange-and-white kitten, smaller than the palm of his hand, her triangle face looking this way and that and mewling until he fed her from a dropper.

Belly full, the kitten curled into a tiny puffy ball and Sal placed her on the table and then proceeded to pull out an electric kettle and a china tea set, white with gold leaf and hand-painted flowers, delicate little posies and violets. He warmed the teapot with hot water while the kettle boiled, used a tiny hourglass to time how long it steeped and placed a small plate with six shortbread fingers on the table beside the sleepy kitten. This might be the most surprising thing: Sal is a considerate host. Now, after refilling my teacup, he asks how school was.

"Terrifying at first, and then okay," I say. "It's school. It'll be fine."

On the table, the kitten wobbles upright, sniffing the shortbread. Sal scoops her up, holding her aloft in his chubby hand and she circles once, then settles into a tight orange tuft in the centre of his palm. "She seems like a Courtney. What do you think?"

"Courtney is a lovely name." The tea, a creamy Earl Grey, is fragrant and delicious. The shortbread is stale but fine when dipped in the hot liquid. Sal makes moo moo faces at the kitten as I pick up a square of folded newspaper stashed at the cash register. "Hey Sal? Do you think Dad was depressed?" As soon as the words are out of my mouth I regret asking and can't look him in the face. My eyes blur staring at the newsprint.

"Well, I don't know." A long silence stretches between us. Sal sips his tea noisily while I pretend to read the lead article, my face burning. He clears his throat, says, "After Danny got sick his heart had to work extra hard, all the time. It wore him down sometimes. It would wear anybody down. Do you think he was depressed?"

I shrug and hold up the newspaper, wanting to change the subject. "Anything in there about last night?" Sal snorts and wags his head no.

"Dad would be outraged."

"Outraged, yeah." Sal tucks Courtney back in his pocket. "What are they going to write? What's the story? Three people burned to death in the past year? It'll take a couple more bodies and then they'll start writing about a suicide trend or some other bullshit. 'Crazy poor,' they'll say, 'crazy poor and their suicide trends.'"

"Dad would write the real story," I say. This is the Sal I'm used to, all sweaty and puffed up, pointing fingers, his voice on the edge of a shout. "Dad would try to get the truth. And what's with this *they* all the time. You and Jonah, with the big bad *They*. Who are — "

"They," Sal spat, pushing his glasses up his nose. "Consolidated Man, the big fat cat with the swivel chair and the subsidies, with the billy clubs, the tanks, the tear gas, the seed patents, the printing presses, the pipelines, the arms deals and the hair shirts." Sal's up now and pacing. Waving his arms. "*They*, with the RRS-frigging-Ps and stocks and bonds and all of their godforsaken nepotistic family around the world, the sons and daughters, the nieces and nephews. They," he says, pausing to light a cigarette, "the ones who truly appreciate someone with the balls to splash a little fossil fuel around. Your dad knew all about them."

"Whoa," I say. Sal's a train rolling off the tracks. I don't understand half the things he's talking about. Hair shirts? Seed patents? RRSP stands for a kind of retirement savings plan, I think. Dad had some, it's part of the money we're waiting to get.

"Don't 'whoa' me, missy." Sal is all-out shouting now. He stops mid-pace and points a finger at me. "I'll tell you something. For the better part of a century they've been rounding up people with the outrageous character defect of being poor and throwing them in that hospital. Some people too dumb for their own good, some too smart. Some lost, some ill, some mad. Crazy mad, furious mad. Pissed-fucking-off mad."

"That's you, right? Pissed fucking off," I say to lighten the mood but it backfires. Sal doesn't smile. He picks up his cigarette and takes a long drag, his hand shaking slightly. Dad always said it was a travesty that Sal was put in the hospital. I don't know why he was there, or how he got out, but it must have been a nightmare.

"It's not a joke, Lou."

"I know, I know. I'm sorry. But, it can't just all be poor people in there."

"Yeah, but, poor people got nobody to fight for them. They are at the mercy of a system that wants to beat and medicate and electrocute them into submission until the time that same system decides it's not cost efficient to lock people up in rooms and then they dump all that craziness back into the streets, barefoot and hungry and whacked out and nobody knows what to do with them. Until some crazed fucker decides it's time to clean up. That it's his civic fucking duty to deal with all the disposable people and someone somewhere in the chain of command has decided we should all shush up about it. Say something — anything approaching the truth — and good people will panic."

"Sounds like a bit too much TV," I say. I swill down the last of my tea. When Sal starts talking conspiracy theories, it's time to head. If some of his drunken late-night rants and rambles with Dad are anything to gauge by, he could go on for hours.

"That's it?" Sal's voice is thick with accusation. "That's what the youth of today has got to say. Too much TV?"

"I've got stuff to say — " I want to tell Sal that I did think it might be a suicide but that I couldn't understand how someone could choose to die. How could life be so bad that you would choose that? I want to say, too, that if you did decide to die, fire, though shocking and violent, is also fast and decisive. For those too poor to kill themselves with slower indulgences, with booze, or pills, or cigarettes, fire provides its own sharp accusation. Its own final resolution. But the words are clumsy in my mouth and I stumble to the end of my sentence lamely, " — like, stuff."

"Stuff. Like stuff." Sal's voice is quiet but harsh. He sits back down and leans over the table toward me. "That's precious, sweetheart, precious. Penetrating and articulate. You are the future."

"Don't call me sweetheart," I say, standing. Leaving. But I stop at the door and turn back, adjusting my knapsack. "You know what? You can be very mean, Sal."

He sighs and stubs out his cigarette. "True. I am an asshole. Sorry, kid."

"Whatever. You have opinions. But, have you even considered that maybe it was a suicide?"

"Maybe." Sal shrugs and pulls another smoke from the pack. "Maybe the guy poured his own gasoline. Maybe he lit his own match. But I can guaran-fucking-tee someone started killing him long before that whole thing burst into flame."

It is so cold out the top layer of snow blows on wayward currents of wind, drifting here, then there, insubstantial as mist, lifting in small eddies and miniature cyclones. I can't help but think of the old prospector. If you were out on the streets with nowhere to go on a night like this, you might build a fire to get warm. Maybe it was all an accident. Some drunk, cold guy decided to build a fire and ended up lighting himself aflame. Or maybe Sal's right, maybe it's not suicide. Maybe it is part of the assaults-in-Parkdale story that Dad thought needed to be investigated. I wish I had read the notes on his desk more closely. I wish he was here. There are a lot of things I'd like to ask him. He believed it was important to fight for the truth. Inside, in yourself, first, he'd say. And then, outside, in the world. But how? The world inside and outside is contradictory and confusing. Even Dad himself had a secret, hidden life. So how do you go about finding the truth, let alone fighting for it? I saw the burning man with my own eyes, and I have no idea what the truth is.

When I reach the apartment, I stampede up the stairs in a sudden burst of energy but clatter to an inelegant halt when I see a woman seated at the kitchen table. She's older than Dad with silver-grey hair that falls past her shoulders. She must be the social worker but she wasn't supposed to be here until six thirty, a half-hour away.

Behind her, Jonah gestures a wide-eyed, shoulders-raised, open-palmed what the fuck, but his voice is calm when he asks where I've been.

"I had to drop Sal's jacket off," I say.

"Ellen Bisbey." She reaches out to me without standing, so I am forced to step in close to shake her hand. "I'm early. I had a change in schedule and have to leave shortly. I wanted to stop by and introduce myself and see how you are settling in." A blank silence follows before Jonah pipes up and says we're doing fine. Ms. Busybee looks pointedly at me. "Are you, Lou? Doing fine?"

This must be a trick question. Does she know that Dad was cremated yesterday? That, at about roughly the same time, a man burned alive in front of me on Queen Street? That I started a new school today? Suddenly more tired than I have ever been in my entire life, too tired to stay standing, I slide into the chair across from her. "Yes, of course. I'm doing fine."

"Well, that's good." Now she stands, releasing a perfumy billow, and pats my shoulder with a disinterested, mechanical precision. She reaches into her oversized purse and hands me a card. "Here's my phone number. You can call any time." It's the third card I've received in less than two weeks.

"I'll add it to my collection," I say.

She raises her eyebrows and forces a smile. "Well then. I'll check back in around Christmas."

Jonah escorts her to the top of the stairs and then returns to the kitchen, two hands rubbing his face. "Fuck," he says, collapsing into a chair. "I was scared she was going to ask to see in here." He turns in his seat and leans backwards, opening the fridge door. There's a half a jug of milk, a bottle of ketchup and some dried-up rice in a takeout container. As we gaze into this culinary abyss, my stomach rumbles and growls a perfectly timed complaint. Jonah laughs and reaches over to pull my earlobe the way he used to when I was kid. "I hear ya. Don't worry, I'm going to order two-for-one pizza. Then you can tell me about your first day."

We eat in the living room, the warmest room in the house, the room that most reminds me of home, both of us on the floor. Jonah leans against the nubbly beige couch and I brace myself against the oversized, lumpy, cherry-red chair. Next to Jonah are newspapers scattered in a big messy pile. Stacks of albums, propped so the front covers face out, line the walls, interrupted only by an ancient TV in a large oak cabinet. The TV is rarely turned on, and when it is, it takes a good fifteen minutes to warm up enough to get a picture. We don't have cable, so the only channel it picks up is CBC and neither of us watches hockey. Sometimes we check out *The National* or *The Nature of Things* but mostly the TV just sits, useless and mocking, like some kind of high-concept art installation. After the first piece of pizza, our conversation fades and Jonah returns to marking up yet another article with a neon yellow highlighter. After completing my small amount of homework, I attempt a new letter to Rufus in one of my notebooks. *Dear Rufus, I started my new school today* is as far as I get before stalling out. My ability to focus is pure crap. Unlike Jonah, who is still going strong. He has this way of holding both pen and highlighter in his right hand, switching like a pro between underlining and note taking.

When he left home I missed him, although he had been absent from my life long before he actually left. But the absence of his actual physical self allowed him to grow increasingly legendary in my imagining. All the irritating and mean-spirited things he did, the way he called me scarecrow when his friends were around or pinched me or ate three times his share of the chocolate-covered biscuits and never apologized, all those things disappeared. I remembered only how he always had an answer for any of my questions or how he chased Ronnie Jenkins down the street after Ronnie Jenkins threatened to cut me with his knife because I'd pushed him and told him to buzz off when he was throwing stones at the Turners' cat. I remembered how Jonah would lift me onto his shoulders and walk out into Lake Huron. If a wave knocked too hard and we both fell in the churning water, he always managed to get to his feet and pull me up. I loved this version of Jonah for a long time but this new version is better.

He is Jonah of the ink-stained face, rumpled hair and unperturbed concentration. Focussed Jonah. Considerate Jonah. He is so engrossed in his work I am certain he has forgotten I am in the room. We can comfortably occupy the same space and give no thought to one another at all. Alone together.

I turn to a fresh page of paper and write:

Dear Rufus,
I started my new school today. It seemed very different at first but by the end of the day it seemed very familiar. School is school, I guess. It was a strange experience being the new kid, but I have already made a good friend named Isabelle.
Life in the city is very unsettling. I feel a little like Alice falling down the rabbit hole, you know? Everything is strange. I'm glad I have your tape. It makes me feel a little less disconnected from home. How are you? Did you go to the Halloween dance? Did you wear mascara and a dress?
All the best,
Lou

It's not exactly all I want to say but I think it will do for a start.

Stashed under my bed is the booklet *The Cardiovascular System: The Heart,* hidden like some kind of porn that I pore over when Jonah is not around, learning the shapes and names of the heart so thoroughly that by day I fill the margin of my school notes with anatomical drawings, correctly labelling the arch of the aorta, the inferior vena cava, the left carotid artery. Arrhythmia, the disease section explains, is a problem with the rhythm of your heartbeat. Tachycardia means the heart beats too fast. Bradycardia is too slow. Atrial fibrillation is a fast, fluttery, irregular beat. When the heart's ability to rhythmically contract is reduced, when it quivers instead of pumps, blood clots can form and cause a stroke. Or the heart can just stop, blood pooling instead of moving, resulting in sudden cardiac arrest. Dad's heartbeat swished under my ear, a quivering kind of noise. Arrythmia is a possible explanation: Dad's heart was out of beat.

I think about Dad and the burning man often, the two of them melding so that sometimes I catch myself thinking that Dad *was* the burning man, a crazy idea, I know. But not any crazier than the fact that Dad is dead, and I won't ever see him again. It's like his cremation was made visible for a reason. Like he was trying to tell me something. What? I don't know. If I was smarter I could figure it out. Even though he's passed, kicked it, bought the farm, or any of those other stupid euphemisms, even though he was sneaking around with Jillian Nash and has lost significant credibility as an honest person, Dad would still want me to get to the truth, but every time I contemplate calling the police my stomach transforms into a mosh pit of anarchist butterflies. Still, I know contacting the police was usually step one for Dad when he began an investigation, so it's likely my best place to start. It takes two weeks of procrastination — the apartment is spotless and I am ahead in all my classwork — for me to finally get the gumption to call Detective Phillips' number. Blank silence swells on the other end of the line when I introduce myself. "Louise James?" I repeat into the empty air. "From Zane's? The night of the fire? You gave me your card and said I could call any time."

"Oh, yes, Louise. What can I do for you?"

"I was wondering if there's been any breakthroughs on the case?" On the other end of the line, he laughs as if I've said something funny, punctuated by another gap of silence.

"Uh, no," he says, clearing his throat. "No breakthroughs. And I can't share details of an ongoing investigation with you."

"Of course," I say, trying to sound professional. "It's just my dad was investigating a series of assaults in the Parkdale area and I was wondering if the two things were connected." But this stab at professionalism backfires. Detective Phillips wants to talk to Dad, and when he discovers that Dad is dead, his voice lowers with suspicion and he spends the next ten minutes grilling me. When I get off the phone my heart is racing, and I can't shake the sense that I am forgetting something, or not remembering it quite right. Somehow I keep missing the point. Dad's point. The butterflies pull on combat boots and arm themselves with rocks and baseball bats. The more I think about it, the more there's a full-on riot in my gut.

Routine helps. Jonah and I have regular pizza nights and regular falafel nights and most evenings we settle into the living room, an album playing, while we do our school work. After a month or so, the street names are familiar enough that I can stop tagging on a north, south, east or west to know what direction I'm heading. The Friday and Saturday nights that Isabelle doesn't have to visit her dad, we sleep over at her house because it's warmer there and her cushioned window seat is wide enough to double as a second bed. In the mornings, we walk to work or school together. Occasionally, Jonah meets us at Zane's as Isabelle and I experiment with the illicit pleasure of drinking in public like real adults. Jonah gets bossy, insisting on cutting us off at one or two drinks, and then scoffs at us for being amateurs, lightweights. It's fun. All these daily routines plaster over my old life in Linden, and Dad slips further and further away. I washed his beer-sopped, puke-scented sweatshirt after that first night at Zane's and that feels like a betrayal too.

It is Jonah, and Isabelle, who keep the bigness of Toronto manageable. There are so many faces, so many stories, it's a minefield of humanity per city block. Alone you have to watch where you walk, where you look, what you see, because if you do look, really look, the way you should, with curiosity and compassion, you can't help but see how singular each face is. How valiant or defeated or dissipated. How alone and lonely and ultimately unknowable. And all these faces, in their singularity and loneliness, in their tenacity and grit, each and every one claims a part of you so that you can return from a simple walk along Dundas and be shredded to your core, vaporized. But everything changes when you navigate a world this big with one other dependable person. Two together are strong, protected. Two can look out at the buffeting world of strange faces and then back at each other and laugh because there is a sturdy kind of courage in the fact that you can, and do, know somebody and that somebody knows you too.

One Sunday afternoon Isabelle took me to her favourite thrift store where clothes are sold by the pound. I scored a vintage black leather jacket, skinny jeans and a beautiful heather-green cashmere sweater that smelled of baby powder. On the way to the cash register I spotted a pair of men's boots that fit me if I doubled up my socks — an expensive item because of their weight. But, as Isabelle said, too awesome to pass up. "Wingtip brogues," the white-haired lady ringing us up said in a strong Irish accent, her r rolling like a cresting wave. "Did you know *brogue* is Gaelic for 'shoe'? But the English call an Irish accent a brogue because they say we all talk like we have a shoe in our mouth." She winked at us both. "Bloody English!" My total was under twenty dollars and Isabelle, who scored a stack of dresses and a black miniskirt, only paid twelve dollars.

After shopping Isabelle took me to her favourite burger place, then her favourite ice cream place, and then her favourite rep theatre. We watched a movie called *Down by Law* and it wasn't like any movie either of us had ever seen before. It was shot in grainy black and white and set to the swampiest soundtrack you could imagine. Dad would have loved it. There was a scene where drunk Zack, played by a skinny Tom Waits, is approached by a travelling Italian, Roberto Benigni. "It's a sad and beautiful world," Benigni says to open the conversation. "Yeah, sad and beautiful," Waits says, "that's a good one." Then he tells Benigni to buzz off. "Buzz off?" Benigni checks his book of English phrases. "Ahh, good evening," he says, "and buzza offa to you too."

It's what we say now, Isabelle and me, when crazy shit happens at the bakery. In the short time I've been there, a substantial amount of crazy shit has happened. Funny shit, creepy shit, sad shit, or some combination of all three. Once I asked this extremely normal-looking businesswoman standing in line if I could help her. "What!" she shrieked. "Do I look like I need help!?! Do I look like I have an eating disorder!?! What!! Do you think I have a banana in my vagina!?! You're crazy," she shouted as she left. "Loco!" And there it was: funny, creepy, sad. I've started taking notes so I can put some of the crazy shit in a letter to Rufus. If he writes me back.

Now that I'm working on Saturdays, Leo and Anna finish up their baking as Isabelle and I arrive, and then they leave for the day. "Be good," Leo said, the first morning they left us alone. "Stella's keeping an eye on you." He waved his hand across the street to the wide steps of the closed side door of the big brick church. Stella was sitting there then and she is sitting there now. She is almost always there, troll-shouldered and furious, glaring at us through the bakery window. Or me, she glares at me, to be specific. Apparently, Stella often comes into the bakery but won't when I'm working. It seems I've flunked some kind of test. Kind of like the time Julie's mom let me hold her happily cooing four-month-old baby and as soon as the kid was in my arms it bust out crying. I've tried with Stella but she won't have it. Once I carried over a bag of day-olds but before I reached her she moved off the steps, trundling down the street like a giant ladybug.

I watch her watch me as I wipe down the bakery tables. She's an indistinct blob in a lumpy blue coat, surrounded by shopping bags and a tall bottle of Pepsi, malignant evil eye turned in my direction. She's on the very top step, pressed into the corner, muttering away, a brisk wind lifting wisps of her thin white hair.

It worries me.

"What do you think?" I ask Isabelle, who is cleaning the display glass with Windex. "Is she cursing me?"

"What's she going to curse you with?" Isabelle laughs. "Poor posture? Bad breath?"

Isabelle is right. I know she's right, but still I work up my own steady muttered stream of curses, freaking-irate-asshole-gargoyle-loony-bat-witch, to ward off Stella's bad juju. Thankfully the December days are short, shortest days of the year, although they really aren't short, just dark, and by four in the afternoon the sky is lowering, the thin clotted grey light turns dusky and the wind sops up all the warmth before the light is even gone. Stella packs up her Pepsi and moves on. I note the time because she's only just left when Sal arrives. Sal has begun to frequent the bakery on Saturdays with curmudgeonly precision: ten-thirty muffin break; one o'clock lunch; four-fifteen pastries. I don't know why. It appears to cause him anxiety to have people prepare his food.

"Three minutes," Sal barks at Isabelle, who is making his tea. He sighs and wrings his pudgy hands and barks again: "Hey! Tea steeps for three minutes."

"Sal," Isabelle says, carrying over his cup. "You are one bossy bastard."

Tea in hand, he is more relaxed. "Ahhh, girls," he stretches his legs onto a neighbouring chair and nudges his glasses up the bridge of his nose, "the devil is in the details."

"It's God," I say. "'I'm pretty sure it's God who's in the details."

"Semantics!" he says. "Kid, stop wasting my time."

I don't take the bait. I deliver his warmed blueberry Danish without saying a thing. He grunts a thank you and opens his newspaper while Isabelle and I begin our nightly cleanup routine. I refill the drink cooler and start the pileup of dishes while Isabelle disassembles and cleans the meat slicer. Sal brings his feet to the floor with a bang and stabs at his newspaper with a stubby finger.

"Here it is! Exactly like I said: suicide trend. A trend! Like leg warmers, or aid concerts. Read it," he orders, standing and throwing the folded paper down on the table. "Rubik's fucking cube," he shouts on his way out the door. "That's a fucking trend!"

It's a small article, and it contains no real new information. "There is a possible alarming suicide trend among the ranks of Toronto's poor and disadvantaged," it says. "Self-immolation is one of the various suicide methods being employed."

Employed? It's a funny choice of words. I wonder what Dad would say about it. He would definitely want to grill the author on their sloppy sentence construction. Does "possible alarming suicide trend" mean it's possibly alarming? Or that it is a possible suicide trend?

"What do you think?" Isabelle asks. "You're the one that saw it, not Sal. Do you think it was a suicide?"

"Yes. No. I don't know," I say. "It's the kind of thing my dad would investigate."

"I don't know what's worse," Isabelle says. "If it's suicide, or if it isn't."

We return to our scrubbing and stocking and saran-wrapping. The bakery is empty for the first time all day and Anna and Leo's Robert Cray CD, which has been on constant rotation along with the Gipsy Kings and Tracy Chapman, is suddenly audible. Cray's singing the blues. His lady is working late on Wednesday night; she's promising to bring home double-time pay but he suspects foul play. That's the chorus and I sing along.

I don't like talking about that night. When Isabelle heard, she wanted all the gory details. She was aghast. She was horrified. She was dumbfounded, and utterly dissatisfied with my monosyllabic answers. But talking about what happened makes it seem surreal and rehearsed, as if it only happened in a fictional account, the movie version, of my life. But it happened. It was real. It is real. In a way, more real than everyday life. Every day, every moment, there are a thousand thoughts competing for space in your head: things you need, things you want, things you dream of. Things to remember, things to forget. But for those super-shocked hyper-real times, you are only and entirely in that present moment. A moment so big, time ceases to exist. It was like that when I found Dad. A moment so brief and endless and real I will carry it with me always, unaltered, as if it's imprinted into my skin. Like a birthmark or a scar. Or, a tattoo of a black hole in the shape of a human body. Cold as stone on the garage floor, or surrounded by a halo of bright flame.

The CD ends and I press the power off. Five minutes to closing. I turn the sign around, lock the door and open the till to tally the day's proceeds. I've counted all the bills and moved onto the quarters when Isabelle interrupts the quiet.

"Naked boys, naked boys," she says, singsongy. "Naked, naked, naked boys."

"Sheesh, you made me lose count."

Isabelle ignores me and continues to sing, shimmying her shoulders as she cleans the steam spout on the cappuccino machine with unusual verve, even for her. Earlier in the day she made a bitter, totally random remark about how all of Toronto had a date for Saturday night except for us. All of Toronto being, in this case, Jonah and her mother. She had pressed for details about Jonah's date but I had nothing to tell her. I was quite content to be as oblivious and uninformed as possible in matters of Jonah's love life. Last Sunday I witnessed a woman hitting on Jonah at Zane's and it was something that, one, I never wanted to witness again and, two, could not ever, ever speak of to Isabelle. The woman had been older, in her thirties at least, with dark brown hair streaked with a platinum-tinted widow's peak that fell forward onto her face like a horse's forelock. She kept dragging it back, behind her ear, with a long fingernail. Her nails were a colour I would call magenta, a shrill and violent lollipop colour. Jonah was fascinated. He had a funny look on his face, as if someone was threatening him with a spoonful of maple syrup. "I drive a bus for the city," she said, pursing her lips. "I can fix any engine, *any* engine, in this goddamned town." I could see her, in mechanic's overalls, her heavily made-up face streaked with oil, her killer nails holding a spark plug aloft, like a barbarian jewel or something severed. She told Jonah she was a widow and I couldn't help but laugh out loud.

"So, tell me about Jonah's date," Isabelle asks, as if she can read my mind.

"Jonah wouldn't tell me anything," I say, dumping streams of nickels and dimes into separate bags, finished with the count.

"Liar."

"He wouldn't, I swear. Thank God. Sometimes it is better not to know."

"Pfoof." Isabelle is less happy with my company tonight than I am with hers. I'm pleased with our evening plans. Iz and me, we're eating at Chez WildFlour. To start, we have an appetizer tray: the last slice of a delicious salmon mousse pâté, droopy with age but still edible, a mashed but otherwise also entirely edible blob of liver and black pepper pâté, and a generous wedge of Emmenthal, the veins of blue mould scraped off. Next, soup and salad, the last of today's special, not a full serving for both of us but that's okay, it's to be followed by a creamy mushroom tortellini pasta dish, the dryness of which should be unnoticeable once it's nuked and covered in the extra cream sauce Isabelle whipped up this afternoon. For dessert, there are hazelnut brownies, freshly baked, so in need of some taste-testing. Also, Isabelle thieved a three-quarters-full bottle of red wine from some party her mom threw and four extra long, extra thin, black cigarettes.

We sit at the back staff table and start with the wine and cigarettes. All the glasses are in the dishwasher so our only option for the wine is to use Anna's black mug that reads, *So many books, so little time,* and Leo's giant A&W soda glass, the one he constantly fills with cranberry juice and club soda.

"Libations," Isabelle says, as she attempts to pour an equal amount into the mismatched glassware. I light the cigarettes with Dad's Zippo and pass one to Isabelle. Neither of us knows how to smoke and we both take little sippy breaths, uncommitted to a full inhale. Dad would be aghast to see me smoking and would rightfully call me a hypocrite. But there is scandalous pleasure in the idea of Isabelle's long black cigarettes and the act of smoking allows us to mime a kind of boldness and sophistication. The reality, however, is not particularly enjoyable. The smoke makes me light-headed and woozy, my heart wobbling in my chest, and I worry that even one cigarette might do damage. Dad likely smoked hundreds, maybe thousands of cigarettes. No wonder his heart was weak.

The wine is called Gato Negro and the small plastic black cat tied to the neck of the bottle is easy to remove. "Rrreow." I make my best catcall noise, smoke sputtering out of my mouth, and march him across the table toward Leo's overfull ashtray. "Did you know that cats have thirty-two muscles in each ear?"

"I don't know where you find that stuff out. Both you and Jonah. Full of weird facts."

"*Fun* facts," I say. I explain about Dad and his blue index cards and she tells me how her dad left home when she was three and how he eventually started a new and better family that lives in a house that is practically a mansion in Roncesvalles and vacations at a time-share in the Canary Islands. She had an older stepsister for a while when this guy moved in with her mom but he and his daughter left a few years ago. More wine is poured after we stub out our cigarettes, and we begin eating our way through the appetizers and the soup and salad, slowing to linger over the tortellini. I tell her about Julie moving to California and her current obsession with body modifications and how she personally knows someone who implanted devil horns onto his own head. Isabelle tells me about being the odd man out of the group of friends she's had since elementary school and while it is a sad story, I am secretly pleased: Isabelle's previous social exclusion only cements our status as best buddies, soulmates, kindred spirits.

"They are all rich and we're poor," she says. "And we're not even poor poor, we're just not rich. No summer European vacations, no winter trips to Hawaii. We clip coupons and premake popcorn to sneak into the movie theatre. Very uncool."

I nod but don't say anything. I make a point of not saying anything bad about Isabelle's other friends, mainly because they are all polite and civil to me. Some are even friendly. But I can't relate. They all have expensive hair and wear designer clothes and jewellery to school. I'm not keen on their style but when I'm surrounded by them, it's me who feels impoverished, as if I'm a character out of a Dickens novel, some grimy street urchin, scrappy and forever hungry. And even though my marks are as good as theirs, even better, I would bet, they have a sense of purpose and direction I find baffling. Law, medicine, investment banking, broadcast journalism. They say those words and you can see their careers unfurling before them like a great red carpet. Even with Isabelle's friendship, I exist on the fringe of their world and it's the people on the fringes, sometimes embarrassingly so, who have befriended me at school.

"Hey, did I tell you Marilynne gave me a copy of her latest 'zine?"

"Marilynne? The chick in grade eleven who dresses like Cyndi Lauper?"

"Yeah," I say and reach under the counter for my knapsack, pulling out the hand-bound ten-page booklet. "Look." I open the 'zine to the middle page. "A pop-up dick."

"Oh good gravy!" Isabelle laughs. "Please tell me it's not scratch-and-sniff."

Now I laugh. We both laugh with a kind of hysterical glee. People over twenty-five never laugh like this. Jonah doesn't even laugh like this. Maybe there is a cut-off for laughing this hard? It's a thought that only makes me laugh harder. I laugh so hard I fart and this tips Isabelle over the edge of laughing insanity.

"Farter!" she sputters out. "Trouble starter!"

"Oh I farted, yes I farted," I sing, "I was broken-hearted."

"Ha ha ha, it's a song," Isabelle says. "Let's go to the studio and *cut* it."

Ha ha ha. On and on, like that, until a loud bang on the bakery's front door surprises us into sober silence. Technically we're not supposed to be in the bakery more than an hour or so after closing.

"Shit," I say, dropping down behind the dessert display case. "I knew we were going to get caught."

"Sssshh." Isabelle drops down beside me. "We're not doing anything wrong." She cranes her neck an inch or so around the counter to get a better look. "Oh. Don't sweat it." She scoots to the door and I creep around to the front of the display case. "It's only Stella. She pushed something under the door." From the front of the counter Stella is visible, her round back ambling away from the bakery. Isabelle returns with an envelope, obviously used before and brown with dirt. On the back is a large coffee ring stain and all the sealing glue is worn or licked away. Inside there is a folded napkin with a message written in black marker:

> I listen to Angus reid now
> so good
> love happy home stella LO

On the back of the napkin there is a colourful crayon picture: cookies and cupcakes, heavy with frosting, swirl around the head of two rosy-cheeked girls, along with the words *whoo whoo 2gurls an Dim Pels*. It looks like the drawing of a ten-year-old, something simple and unaffected, designed only to delight. Who knew Stella could be so sweet? Or artistic? Or even literate?

"Let's give her a brownie," I say, looking out the window, watching as Stella's tottering body slows to a stop in the middle of the cross street and then, with obscene speed, jerks downward, as if grabbed by an unseen hand reaching out of the cement, twisting and twitching with a horror movie violence.

"Shit," I say, again.

"Call an ambulance," Isabelle says, unlocking and out the front door before I'm even on my feet.

When I arrive, Stella is unmoving. I am cold with the certainty she is dead.

"She's breathing," Isabelle says. "Don't worry."

It isn't safe in the middle of the road but we are too scared to move her. Scared we might hurt her, but scared, too, of touching her. A car signals to make a turn off Queen but Isabelle waves it on as I stand guard by Stella, the driver giving us the finger before pulling away.

Stella's face is limp against the cement and filthy, her blue coat fallen open to reveal a dirty long-sleeved cotton sweatshirt with three tutu-wearing kittens on the front. It's not warm enough for the weather. A dark stain spreads down her pant leg, and the strong smell of urine carries in the cold air. I am suddenly ashamed of my string of curses. This is Stella. She is an old, old woman and she stinks.

"Did you use to run and jump into bed at night because there was a witch lurking under the bed?" Isabelle asks.

"Yeah," I say. "Witches, trolls, snaggle-toothed things."

"My witch looked like her." Isabelle nods in Stella's direction. "Who'd have thought the scariest thing about her is that she is totally defenceless?"

Sirens. Distant but coming closer. The cars on Queen slow, pulling over to the edge of the street.

"I hate sirens," I say.

Something in the sound rouses Stella and she lifts her head slightly.

"Seize her, seize her," she says.

I look at Isabelle, who shrugs her shoulders. "Maybe Stella's been drinking?" she whispers.

"Unlikely," I say. "Why do you think that?"

"Caesar, caesar," Isabelle says. Now it's my turn to shrug my shoulders.

Stella mumbles a bit more, then lays her head back down and closes her eyes. She is so deeply asleep when the ambulance arrives, she is snoring. Which is normal, the ambulance guy says, after a seizure.

Ah. Seize her. Seizure. "You're going to take her to the hospital, right?" I ask the driver.

"We take her to emergency," buddy says. "Hopefully there will be a bed and she can spend the night."

"Sad and beautiful world," I mutter to Isabelle as Stella is bundled into the back of the ambulance and the doors are shut.

"Good night," the ambulance guy says and waves.

"Good night," Isabelle says, "and buzza offa to you too."

On Monday afternoon, a letter arrives from Rufus. Small cartoon drawings decorate the back of the envelope and a larger picture falls out from the inside, accompanied by a short note.

Lou!
I'm glad you wrote. I would say that school is not the same without you but that isn't true. It is the same, it is exactly, excruciatingly, boringly the same. Now I just don't have anyone to copy my math homework from! (Just kidding!) But really, I miss you. I'm glad you didn't forget about us in boring old Linden now that you're in the Big Smoke. Have you seen any cool bands yet?

I did go to the school dance but not in a dress. I did my old standby costume, the one I've been doing since grade six: pirate. So there was some eyeliner and a fake parrot involved but no feathered boas or mascara, which is for the best. You are completely correct, mascara is gross. What did you dress up as? Do people dress up in the city?

I hope this isn't too boring as I don't have much practice letter writing. But please write me lots and let me know what you are doing and what you are seeing.

Your friend,

Rufus

The picture is titled *Bored kids in a boring class in a boring town* and it's good. I didn't know Rufus was so talented. In the picture, a handful of kids sit at desks staring off into a chalkboard distance. One of them is drooling, another is snoring, and another, the girl, is reading a book underneath the cover of the desk. That must be me. I always had a book hidden under my desk in public school. Beyond the profiles of the bored kids is a bank of windows and out the windows in the far distance is a blurry someone standing in the basket of a hot-air balloon, floating up into a blue sky, waving goodbye.

6

Stella isn't on the church steps Wednesday night but she shows up Friday at closing time. She trundles into the bakery, stopping briefly to stare accusingly at the tinkling chimes over the door. Her eyes, when they turn to us behind the counter, seem full of suspicion and hope, both at once, the crackling eyes of one eternally tormented by bolts of lightning, her hair sparking in all directions, refusing to settle.

"Here," she says in a croaky voice. She plops a bag of overripe grapes on the counter. Some of the grapes have split open, transparent green pulp squished out of purple skin. Puffs of white mould sprout at the juncture of fruit and stem.

"For us?" I say.

"Those look like winemaking grapes," Isabelle says.

"Yeah," I add, pouring Stella a cup of coffee. "We'll have to take off our socks and shoes and stomp ourselves some hooch."

Stella grabs for the coffee, a noise like a crow choking — *ca-ca-caw-wff* — erupting out of her. A laugh. She's laughing. She keeps laughing as she fills her coffee with several sugar packs and a stack of creamers. Then, with only a brief glare at the chimes, she's back out the door and off, weaving a crooked path down the street.

The next day she leaves a little nest of Hershey's Kisses in a torn and ketchup-stained napkin with *!!!STella!!!happy home* printed on one side in turquoise highlighter ink. On the back is a picture of two girl heads atop the body of birds and another message: *make yur GRINNER a WINNER.*

"I was wrong," I say. "She's not a gargoyle. She's an artist."

"Maybe she's fabulously wealthy," Isabelle speculates as she rings up Sal's lunch bill. "Maybe the whole bag lady thing is a wacky artistic tic or something."

"Or something." Sal pulls out his wallet. "That crazy old bird, she's as loony as they come."

"You're as loony as they come, Sal," I say as he leaves. It's not much of an insult but it's all I've got.

"Damn straight," he calls back over his shoulder. He always has to have the last word. He squeezes through the door as Irene, the girl who works at the convenience store, comes in.

"Good day, Irene," Isabelle sings to the tune of "Goodnight, Irene." Isabelle is always singing, it's one of the things I love best about her. Unlike me, she has a good strong voice and she is fearless, serenading just about anyone: bus drivers, customers, teachers at school. What might be considered eccentric and odd in some seems only open and generous in Isabelle. People don't roll their eyes and veer away, as I imagine they would do if I suddenly burst into song. No, when Isabelle sings people smile and seem to step out of themselves, for a moment exempt from having to rush through their day. This might be because she is young and pretty but I tend to think it is more because Isabelle has the easy gift of singing *to* people, not *at* people, the way some perpetual singers do.

Isabelle is always making up songs with silly rhymes or silly sounds; she can turn anything into a song. Plus, she also knows a whole ton of cool old standards and show tunes. Her dad had been a disc jockey on a golden oldies show when he was in college and he left behind boxes of old forty-five records that Isabelle now plays in her room on a red-and-white kid's record player and they sound all scratchy and crackly and amazing. And she's good at making up new words to the old songs, like now:

"Irene, good day,
Irene, good day,
Come in from the cold street."

"You crazy girl," Irene says, her voice, also musical, in sharp contrast to her guffaw-y, goofy, hee-haw laugh. She's about to place her order, which is always the same, a small macaroni salad and a mixed berry yogurt, when the cute front man from the band at Zane's walks in.

"Hey," he says when he sees me.

"Hey," I say. He's smiling, I'm smiling, but a long stupid silence stretches between us. Finally, he pulls off the fingerless glove on his right hand and stretches an open palm toward me.

"Finn," he says and we shake hands.

"Lou." Another pause, but this time I come to the rescue. "Can I get you anything?"

"Yeah," he says. "A coffee and — " he moves to the baked goods, "a muffin. Blueberry." He smiles the entire time I pack up the muffin and pour his coffee but doesn't say anything else until I'm ringing him in.

"That was a crazy night at Zane's."

"Yeah," I say, taking his money. "I'm sorry I missed you play. Sound check sounded good."

"I think you mean loud," he says and laughs.

"Loud is right," Irene says as she leaves. "I hear dem racket all night." Finn laughs again and Isabelle laughs too but then becomes very busy stocking takeout containers and plastic utensils.

"I go to Zane's all the time," I say, stretching the truth to a breaking point. A half-dozen visits or so hardly constitute all the time. "Will you play there again soon?" I am successful, I think, in achieving my desired tone of casual interest.

"New Year's," he says, nodding his head. "There's a really good band playing there next Thursday that I was thinking of checking out. The bass player and the drummer once toured with Sleepy LaBeef."

"Sleepy LaBeef?" I say, incredulous. My dad gave me a pretty good musical education but I've never heard of Sleepy LaBeef. "Is that a band name? Or the name of a dude?"

"Dude," he says and I blush. I don't know why. Finn holds up his left hand in a goodbye salute and walks to the door. "Maybe I'll see you there?"

"Yeah, maybe." I blow my cool by waving a big windshield wiper motion as he leaves. Jeez. It's so goofy, I might as well have blown him a kiss.

"*Who* is that?" Isabelle is on me as soon as the door closes. "Who is he? And what's with the sparks? You never said."

"Sparks," I say. "Bah."

"Bah indeed." Isabelle sticks her tongue out at me. "I know what we're doing next Thursday night."

Thursday afternoon the school halls are deserted. Everyone except for me is getting ready for the big assembly scheduled for tomorrow, the last day before Christmas vacation. The assembly will be a showcase of the various school clubs, of which there are a gazillion. My old school had a handful of clubs, the old regulars: drama, chess, debating, mathletes, that kind of thing. Here, not only are there clubs for every nation on earth, there are clubs for every sport and conceivable activity, however mundane or unexpected. The Thousand and One Cranes Origami Folding Club. The Toast Burners' Club. The Russian-English Translation Club. My favourite club so far is the Vietnamese Candle Dancers, but it's not one I could join. I checked to see if there was a swing dancing club, but there wasn't. It's, like, the only club the school doesn't have. I considered starting one, a club of only me, but since swing dancing is usually done with a partner, and, also, I don't know how to swing dance, it didn't seem worth the bother. I don't mind. I'm not a club kind of person. I sit in front of my locker in the quiet corner of the fourth floor, waiting, occasionally invaded by a herd of grade nine girls, all lip gloss, dimples, shrieks and bubbly laughter, who come at regular intervals to retrieve single items: juice box, hairbrush, paper, pen. What kind of logic animates such mono-focussed movement? They remind me of flitting moths, or sparrows, that turn and swerve in unison, that arc and wheel with no seeming purpose. Movement determined by a whim of the wind.

It's windy out. And wet without rain. It's more of an icy turbulence in the air that would be warmer if it turned to snow. A thin branch lashes the double-wide window at the end of the hallway, and beyond its spidery outline is a sky the hue and texture of soggy wool. While I wait for Isabelle, I work on a letter to Rufus.

Dear Rufus,

I remember your pirate costume. Isn't the parrot's name Hermione, like from the Bowie song? I didn't dress up this year. In the confusion of moving, not only did we ignore Halloween but we also totally forgot about my birthday, which is a week later. I didn't totally forget about it, but my brother did, and I didn't feel like celebrating anything so I didn't mention it. It didn't bum me out at the time, but now, it kind of bums me out. I had expectations for turning seventeen! And now Christmas is coming. I'd kind of like to ignore it, but you can't do that with Christmas. It's everywhere.

People did dress up for Halloween but sometimes I feel like every day is dress-up in the city. Every day people put on a costume, businessman, bus driver, unconventional artist, and pretend to be that. Sometimes walking down the street, the faces of the old buildings look so one-dimensional, as if they were stage sets, and if you ran behind them quickly enough you could see the angled wood propping it all up. I don't know if that's the city or if that's me. The night before I left Linden I was in the middle of this really good book about this time-travelling half-man, half-robot, named Indium, who I pictured looking a lot like David Bowie.

Anyways, I left the book there, lying on the floor beside my bed. I didn't want to take it with me and I didn't want to keep reading it but now, I worry about Indium all the time. Like I've left him interrupted, stranded, in the middle of his story. Does that sound crazy?!? I'm hanging around with a lot of crazy people so it could be some of it is wearing off on me.

Isabelle and I work at a bakery that is down the street from a big mental hospital. A LOT of crazy-maybe-homeless people come in to the bakery. Most of the time they want in out of the cold, or to use the bathroom. Leo and Anna, my bosses, have a strict policy to let people use the bathroom, which is the opposite of most businesses around here, so we tend to get a lot of activity and, on a pretty regular basis, there are also hijinks involved. Yesterday, for example, this guy comes in, walking wild, with fanatical eyes and fanatical hair, and he starts throwing shelled peanuts at Isabelle and me and the other customers. You're nuts! he's shouting. A bunch of Bible freaks! So Leo, who is really nice and really diplomatic, stops working right in the middle of making cinnamon buns, so he can pour this guy a coffee, and he sits with him at a corner table for forty-five minutes with this guy shouting scripture and Leo agreeing with every contradictory or crazy thing he says until buddy gets so fired up again he throws his entire bag of peanuts at Leo and storms out. The whole time I was wondering whether we should be calling the cops but Leo kept making this sign with his hand, a lowdown discreet little patting wave, that said, don't worry, this is all under control.

And then, at the end of the night, this old guy grabs my arm as I'm ringing in his potato salad and says, I'm onto you. I'm CIA and you better watch your step. You better watch that gap in your front teeth. Anything, he says, as he backs away holding the brown-bagged potato salad with two hands pressed up against his chest, anything could get in a hole like that.

It's four thirty when Isabelle bursts into the hallway. She is breathless and apple-cheeked, explaining that everything the drama department is doing has turned to shit and she can't possibly leave yet.

"I'm so sorry," she says, "but it's likely best if I meet you at Zane's."

To my credit, I don't mention the fact that I have been waiting for hours and that she promised to use her new flax gel to put big glamorous curls in my relentlessly unstylish mop of hair.

"Sure, whatever." Surly and brief is the best I can manage. Isabelle cringes but rallies quickly, waving and backing up down the hallway. "I'll see you at eight," she says, offering up a smile of apology, which I don't return. I sign my letter to Rufus although I'm not certain about that last paragraph. It seems like the kind of thing that a boy, even a nice one like Rufus, would interpret as overtly sexual, which is not how I meant it. But I don't want to write the whole letter over again and it is what happened, so I fold the sheet of paper and slide it into an addressed envelope. I'll mail it on the way home.

I bump into Donnie exiting the school. He is bunched into a black ski jacket and appears to share my mood of pathetic crankiness.

"Not part of the assembly?"

We both turn left and I pick up the pace to match Donnie's long stride, but he doesn't say anything as, apparently, my question is too stupid to warrant an answer. I see Donnie daily, he's in my English and biology classes, but aside from the occasional head nod in the halls, we haven't spoken since he introduced himself at Zane's. His style is super preppy, polo shirts in primary colours and crewcut hair, and he's one of those guys who parades around busting through the nervous clusters of grade nines and tens that are constantly forming and re-forming in the school hallways like agitated electrons looking for a nucleus. Outta my way, I'm coming through, and boom, the electrons scatter, coffee spilling, books falling. He's that kind of guy. Asshole kind. Isabelle has known Donnie since they were in grade school and she says his older brother bullied him and that his dad is a wealthy realtor but everyone says it's a front for drug dealing and maybe he's in jail right now. Even though Donnie's an asshole she feels sorry for him because she still remembers him crying during kindergarten games of duck, duck, goose. Donnie hated being the goose.

It's a wicked wind, the kind that bullies a body into mute survival, but still the silence stretching between me and Donnie is anything but comfortable. I am about to make an abrupt right and detour down a side street to avoid walking with him when he mutters something that gets lost in the wind.

"What?"

"I said, I'm quitting."

"Oh. Quitting what? School?"

"Everything," he says.

"Oh." I have no idea what he is talking about but I can relate to this general sentiment.

"There's a lot of work out west," he says. "Alberta or BC. Planting trees. Or cutting them down."

"Sure," I say.

He turns his face toward me. His skin is red and blotchy from the wind. He looks like he's been crying but that seems impossible. "I'd rather plant them," he says.

"Sure," I say.

"Trees," he says.

"Gotcha," I say.

"I had a dog when I was a kid. A rottie named Dasher," he says. Total non sequitur.

"Oh yeah?"

"Yeah. My brother killed it."

I don't know what to say.

"He and his friends made Dasher fight this other dog and when he lost they killed him."

"Dog fighting?"

"Yeah."

Silence for another half-block. This time I break it.

"You mean like real dog fighting?"

"What?" Donnie turns his head toward me again. His eyes are definitely red and glossy. Crying maybe, or dope. "What did you say?"

I reformat my sentence: "Was it a real dog fight? Like people taking bets and stuff? I thought that only happened on TV."

Now Donnie looks at me as if I'm the one who is high.

More silence. At the next street Donnie turns, raises a hand and half smiles. "This is me." He's off and running before I answer.

The wind doesn't let up. It blasts down the street creating a howling tunnel strong enough to snatch my toque off my head, animating my hair into a Medusa-worthy frenzy as I dart and lunge, hapless as Buster Keaton, until I recapture my runaway hat. Dad always complained there was too much wind in Canadian novels. "Canadians and their weather," he'd kvetch, brandishing some new novel with an endorsement from W.O. Mitchell on the back cover. "You can't have a literary tradition where the wind — the wind! — defines you." I didn't agree. I had a corner room in our house in

Linden, very windy, and nightly it was a defining, reassuring presence. I like all the descriptions, the summer breezes, the gentle rustling in the pines, the cold northern gales. This would be an Atlantic wind, full of cresting waves, overturned boats and the lost cries of fishermen. You could drown in a wind like this or, helpless, give up and quit everything. Like Donnie, the Christmas decorations, with Christmas still over a week away, have given up. Whipped and buffeted, the wreaths and Rudolphs and fake Marys tilt and hang at odd angles, abandoned in all their sodden squalor. The snow is gone too, washed away until all that remains are slippery, exhaust-riddled patches, the air of upcoming festive celebration replaced by the suggestion of an advanced state of fruit rot.

It has infiltrated the apartment too, this wind. I don't like being in the apartment alone, really. I never minded being alone at home but here the silence is unfamiliar and somehow sad. Still, I am getting used to the apartment and have come to appreciate its untidy, splayed-out coziness, my bed invitingly unmade, newspapers spread out across the living room floor, my mug waiting on the kitchen counter to be filled, as though Jonah and I had been in the midst of some pleasant home activity when we were suddenly called out to school, or work. But not today. Wind pours through every possible opening, doorknobs, window frames, even the drain in the sink, so that the air has a carved-out, hollow quality and all our measly possessions appear diminished in the grey light. I turn on every lamp in the house as well as the radio in the kitchen, which is tuned to CBC, boil a kettle, make mint tea and run a bath.

I sit Dad's blue cards on the window ledge beside the old claw-foot tub as I climb into the hot water. The first one I pull out is blank. The second has a series of point-form notes: *European starling (Sturnus vulgaris). Brought to North America by Eugene Schieffelin. Wanted New York to be alive with the sounds of the birds that populated Shakespeare's works. 60 pairs released in Central Park in 1890. Starlings ravage indigenous NA bird populations (bluebirds, flickers, tree swallows, great crested flycatchers). Starlings: are prolific breeders, beat up smaller birds, steal their nests and eat their eggs.* I find this card inexpressibly depressing and pull out a third one immediately. *ROBOT*, it reads, *Czech for "forced labour." Coined by Karel Capek in 1920 play "Rossum's Universal Robots."* Underneath this printed message is another, cursive and in different ink: *Stress is the force exerted on an object; how an object is changed is dependent upon the resistance it offers against that pressure. Order disorder reorder.* I have no idea what it is in reference to but it is so characteristic of Dad's stray turns of thought that I am comforted and a little less lonely.

I know, and yet choose to ignore, that any aesthetic attempts made on my part will be sabotaged by the wet and the wind. I comb my hair and twist it into long, hopeful ringlets, carefully applying eyeliner and lip balm. After chasing my mint tea with a strong cup of coffee, I am ready to brave the weather again. Outside, stinging pellets of rain aim themselves directly into my face so that the bit of exposed flesh between scarf and hat feels pulpy and raw. I am bedraggled and frozen before I reach the end of Rosalind, the sidewalks empty of pedestrians because no one aside from me is stupid enough to be out walking in this biting cold.

Inside my small leather purse is my wallet, Dad's lighter and his Swiss Army knife, these last two items being my protection against terrible things happening. Under scrutiny, neither of these items offers any real protection. The lighter is hardly threatening and it is quite difficult to open the knife part of the Swiss Army knife; first you pull out the corkscrew and then the nail file, and by the time you get to the knife almost any kind of terrible thing could have happened, but still there's some security in resting my hand on the wet leather of the purse and curving it around the walnut handle underneath. A poster stapled to a telephone pole on Dundas, just before the turnoff to the park, depicts the hypothetical face of the bus stop stalker underneath an ominous message: *To the person assaulting the women of our neighbourhood — we will stop you.* Plastered all over by a women's shelter fed up with supposed police inaction, the posters are a constant reminder that terrible things do happen regularly to women and girls. And it's not just the posters, it's newspapers, broadcasts, even in fiction. On Jonah's recommendation, I am reading *Lolita* and last week our English class started *The Handmaid's Tale*; both are super depressing. Point is, you don't have to look very far: it's everywhere. And here I am, in the wet and windy streets, where terrible things happen. It is absurd. I want to be home with Dad in a time before terrible things happened. It is childish and impossible, my wanting, because that time never existed. Still. Sometimes at night, if we hadn't seen each other, Dad would come into my room and sit on the edge of my bed and tell me about his day, or what story he was working on. I told him about whatever book I was reading because my days were mostly the same. Now, I am visited by a memory of something that never happened: Dad sits at the end of the bed, while I tell him all about Indium, how he was enhanced, meaning he didn't age and was immune to most diseases but, even with his enhancements, he was vulnerable to blunt-force trauma or fire, same as any other mortal being. Dad says it sounds like a good book, says even though it sounds sci-fi now, the idea of enhanced humans is prescient. This was a favourite topic of his — our imminent sci-fi future — and he could go on and on about how soon we would be able to clone animals, or build organs, hearts, livers, kidneys, in a lab. Rich people would be able to vacation on Mars and soon, very soon, we would all be able to video chat on our computers, like in *Star Trek*. He could go on for hours. That's the way that night should have gone: him talking while I drowsed in my cozy bed, winter wind singing on the other side of the window. I want that memory to be true and real, a want so strong it replaces all other thought, steals my breath. But instead of being there, safe, I am here, where terrible things happen. In place of breath, fear blossoms, unfurls, fans out, a fast-growing vine circling my bones.

Fear animates the shadows. As I pass through the park under the glow of the Victorian lanterns, I scour the dark corners for not one but two bogeymen: Sal's fire demon, some crazed fucker, lurking just beyond the edges of sight with his jerry can of gasoline and Bic lighter, and Mr. Everyman, the bland, wide-browed face of the suspected rapist. The shadowy margins glint with small movements and ripples of light, placeless and disembodied, as if I am seeing the world in a dream. Midway through the park, I see eyes, real animal eyes, reflective flashes low to the ground, following me. I am about to break into a run when the long-legged mutt I saw with Jonah trots into the light, his black-and-white curls slick and dripping. Wet as a wet dog can be. "Bubs," I say, holding out a tentative hand. "You should be home. Where's your home?" He ignores me and passes back into the shadows. Ahead the bright lights of Queen are a beacon of safety. Reaching the street, turning right, I pass two girls, younger than me, laughing and holding hands, their laughter immediately transforming my fearful thoughts into something ridiculous. These girls are untroubled by yet another concentration of stalker posters adorning every available surface along Queen. The face in the poster is so crudely drawn it resembles a caricature of a western wanted poster more than it could ever resemble any living person and the printed description — white, between the ages of twenty and thirty-five, brown hair, brown eyes — is so broad it is essentially useless. "Oh," Isabelle said, the first time we saw the poster, "I saw that guy. Like eight kajillion times since last Thursday. He could be anyone."

I stop at Legacy Variety to buy my new favourite food, chocolate icy squares, buying one for now and one for later. Irene isn't working tonight. It's a guy as round and big as Irene is straight and thin. He's older than

Irene, I'd say, but not much, and he's reading the Stephen King novel *Fire-starter*, a pudgy baby Drew Barrymore on the cover, hair electric, surrounded by a red and gold fiery light. *Firestarter.* My stomach lurches upward so hard it slams into the roof of my mouth. Maybe this is the guy. Maybe this is Sal's crazed fucker.

I take a small step back and take a good second look. Does pure evil leave any telltale signs? His name tag reads Desmond. His skin is dusky black but there is a large greyish-pink splotch the shape of Italy on his right hand where the skin lacks pigment. His eyes are small and dark and his tightly curled hair is cut in a round bowl shape, reminding me of Friar Tuck.

"Thirty-four cents." Soft-spoken, he avoids looking in my eyes.

"Good book?" I say, handing him a five.

"Oh. Yes." Now he looks up, puzzled, by me or the book, I can't say. "Do you want a paper bill?" He passes me three loonies and some coins and then holds up a paper dollar bill. "I don't see these too often anymore."

"Please," I say, derailed in my investigation. I leave without saying anything else, concerned our interaction is clouding my judgment. If I had to pick a single word to describe him, it would be gentle. Still, that's what people always say after the fact: he seemed so nice and normal. I pop an icy square in my mouth, the buttery chocolate dissolving on my tongue as I push the door open to Zane's.

It's busy. At least two-thirds of the tables are full although I don't see Finn or his bandmates at any of them. Sal is at his regular spot at the bar, leaning into his drink and watching a small TV mounted high on the wall, his extra-large butt lipping over the red leather edge of the stool. Isabelle and Jonah are already there too, seated at a table and so deep in conversation they don't notice me. Sal looks up and groans when I walk over.

"See that," he raises a hand, palm open, toward the TV as I sit down beside him. Two boxers, hair wet with sweat and bodies clenched, bob across the screen. "The world needs more heroes."

"Amen," I say.

"Gesundheit," Sal says. He's drunk and sweaty, nostrils flaring like a tormented bull's, a pointy tangle of nose hairs breaching their opening with each loud exhale. I've seen Sal drunk a few times, and it's never pretty. He'd come by the house in Linden for a long weekend, like Easter or Thanksgiving, and he and Dad would eat fried eggs, chain-smoke and argue while drinking bourbon or Scotch. They loved to argue. It usually started with big topics — politics and religion — but quickly disintegrat-ed into anything and everything: their favourite music, the best brand of toothpaste, who could take who in the wild. Grizzly versus wolf pack. Beaver versus raccoon. Anaconda versus alligator. It was work, hard work, to find things to argue about, because they mostly agreed on everything. Occasionally these weekend benders ended with Sal crying or throwing something at Dad, or both. Once he broke the shower door right off its hinges. He was a wreck, and when I complained to Dad, he apologized but said I should cut Sal some slack. The way Dad saw it, drinking for Sal was a form of self-medication and it was important that he had a safe space to cut loose, but I wonder if Dad was right. Safe or not, Sal's cutting loose tonight and there is nothing therapeutic about it.

"Hey Lou!" It's Isabelle, she's seen me and she's using her thousand-watt voice to reach across the room. "Don't you think they should have a house drink here? Call it an InZane? Quick!" She flaps her hands beside her face. "Gimme a drink, I'm going InZane!"

I flash a quick smile — Isabelle's chirpiness will not be denied — before turning back to Sal. "Hey, you know what you were saying about some crazed fuck — "

"Old Ben got beaten up last night. He's in a coma," Sal says.

"Old Ben?"

"You know, Ben, the guy with that little flea-bitten terrier, Mickey, and the recorder."

I shake my head no. I don't know him.

"Recorder, you know, it's like a flute, but different?" Sal's slurry voice arches with accusation, as if I am purposefully being dumb. Obviously he is too drunk to carry on a two-way conversation but like an idiot I press on.

"The guy next door?" I say. "At the Variety store? He's reading *Fire-starter.*"

"Desmond? Yeah, I sold it to him." Sal does one of his dramatic double takes, this time in a groggy, overemphasized slow motion. "Are you saying Desmond? That boy is a duck. A lamb. A goddamned bunny." Sal swallows the rest of his drink in one long gulp and bangs his glass down. "Shelley! Get me another!"

"Well, Sal, I was thinking — "

"Stop thinking, kid. You're not very good at it."

"Whoa there, cowboy." Shelley's dressed in red and green and her earrings are miniature Christmas tree lights. She smiles at me and wipes the bar in front of Sal where his drink sploshed over.

"Shelley, tell me this," Sal says, and there is a new quality to his voice. Mean, nasty even. "Do you *ever* feel like a woman?"

"Every time I do the dishes, asshole, every time I do the dishes." Shelley winks at me, unfazed, and places another drink in front of Sal. "Now slow it down, or this will be your last one."

"Witch," Sal says. The two of them square off to spar in what seems a practised routine; both know their lines and are happy to play their parts. But still. What would Dad say to this Sal? There's not a lot of slack to cut. Our conversation is going nowhere so I walk over to Isabelle and Jonah.

"Are you mad at me?" Isabelle asks as I reach the table. Direct and open, that's Isabelle. I am embarrassed by my surliness.

"No." I sit down. "Do you guys think Sal and Shelley are sweet on each other? Do you think they could ever be a couple?"

We all watch as Sal and Shelley fake-threaten one another. Sal raises a mock fist in her direction. Shelley whips her bar rag inches from his face.

"Maybe by Christmas," Jonah says.

"During an eggnog and rum-soaked moment, under the mistletoe," Isabelle adds, glancing in Jonah's direction.

"What are we talking about here?" I say.

"Smooches," Isabelle says.

"Those two will never realize their love until one of them is dying from a wasting disease," I say, "and by then it will be too late."

"Ever the romantic, Lou," Jonah says. "I see somebody's been reading their Brontës."

I don't have a comeback. Silent, the three of us watch as the band files into the room and onto the stage. They are old. Nothing against old people, but they're *really* old. Old, like they only just abandoned their walkers and canes and oxygen tanks at the door of the band room. They walk single file past the billboard sign that reads Red Randy and the Rockets onto the stage, bony arms and legs swimming underneath their matching grey suits. The drummer wears a jaunty cowboy hat and moves with a springy energy but judging by the liver spots and grey hair, he's easily as ancient as the other two. The guy who leans into the mike, Red Randy, has been at Zane's every time I've been there, seated a few stools down from where Sal usually sits.

I recognize some of the faces in the crowd too. There's the couple from the first night I was at Zane's, dressed in their fancy Duke-and-Daisy cowboy gear, still drinking caesars. They hoot and whistle during Red Randy's intro like a couple of overexcited teenagers and as soon as the music starts, a fast-paced blues full of rockabilly jitters and sounding anything but old, they jog to the space cleared in front of the band and start dancing. Real swing dancing. Kick-up-your-heels partner dancing. They know how to do it and people cheer and clap them on. More and more people are coming in: all the Zane's dusty and wrinkled regulars, plus a new crowd of younger, pretentiously dressed twenty- and thirtysomethings, the men in suit jackets and tailored shirts, their long hair slicked back into ponytails, the women all in tight black, their lips a slash of red. Some of the newbies I recognize as customers at the bakery but none of them is Finn.

"Dance?" I ask. Jonah shakes his head no, but Isabelle follows me to the increasingly crowded dance floor. Or patch, it's more of a dance patch. I don't know any proper dance steps but I love to dance. Julie and I used to spend whole days dancing, and Dad and I regularly did something called Crazy Dance, which was pretty much moving as weirdly as we could to very loud music. Dad always bobbed up and down, nodding his head, like a character from the Charlie Brown cartoons. He got tired fast, but I could dance for hours: eyes closed, everything good and uncomplicated and flowing. Just music and movement. It's even better with a live band.

At the end of the first set Isabelle and I lean into each other, smiling, too breathless to laugh.

"Thank you, Solid Gold dancers," Red Randy says to the crowd. "We do appreciate it."

Shelley delivers a pitcher of water and a pitcher of beer to our table as Isabelle and I return. I pour some beer but, as always, forget to tip the glass and the foam cascades over the side.

"Shoot, girl, you haven't started drinking and you're already spilling," Shelley says, swiping with her dishrag. "Don't make me cut you off."

"Shelley!" This barked by a heavy-set, red-faced man behind the bar. He holds a shot glass in one hand and with the other makes a vigorous circular motion, as if imitating a hamster on a wheel.

"Tony," Shelley mutters under her breath, turning her back on him. "Motherfucking cork-soaker bar owner." It is shocking to hear someone as old and skinny as Shelley be so foul-mouthed. She wags her head back and forth, a universal and weary *no*, lips pressing and puckering, as though acknowledging the presence somewhere in the room of a bad egg. "Welfare

Thursday. Busiest night of the month. Tony wants me to keep pushing drinks to them." She nods her head in the direction of two large tables that have been pushed together to accommodate a big group. "But they've had enough and, well," here she lowers her voice to an uncomfortable whisper, "they're *disabled.*"

"That's vile," Isabelle says and we all turn to take a second look at the table. Clearly one of the people has Down syndrome. Somebody else is dressed like Vegas Presley, complete with a sideburned wig.

"Shelley!" Tony, again.

As Shelley sighs and returns to the bar, the front door opens behind Isabelle. Ever hopeful, I check out the newcomers. It's not Finn; it's Donnie's older brother and his Sears model friend. The band returns and the music starts up. This time when Isabelle asks Jonah to dance, he looks tempted but still refuses. Wuss.

Red Randy sings about a train coming round the bend as we hit the dance floor. Eyes closed, I return to that state of pure movement. Occasionally I peek out and catch a quick glimpse of the two-stepping cowboy couple or Isabelle. At some point Vegas Elvis joins us on the dance floor, doing a spastic hip-shaking dance and grinning like a fiend, looking impossibly, even illegally, happy. But I don't fully leave my own blissful trance state until after the last song. When I do, buddy with the Sears model hair is standing close, too close. As I open my eyes, he leans over, says, "Do you fuck as good as you dance?"

I'm too shocked for even a basic fuck off and retreat to the washroom without saying anything. When I come out, he's standing at the end of the narrow hallway, blocking my path back to the table.

"Hey," he says. Smiles. "I'm sorry, you must think I'm really rude. I never know the right thing to say to a pretty girl."

Buddy's all tooth and lapel and wavy hair. About as sincere as the Big Bad Wolf crossed with Mussolini. The fascist in the fairy tale. I smile, which he misinterprets.

"Drink?" He holds out a glass.

"No." I wave the drink off but hesitate in pushing past him. My purse, with the lighter and the knife, is hanging over the back of my chair at our table. Jonah leans in to say something to Isabelle and Isabelle leans in to hear. She tugs a golden curl behind her ear and they both move a little closer.

"Vodka martini," the fascist says, pushing the drink into my hand. "I insist."

As he moves closer, I catch a strong whiff of men's cologne and something else. A car smell. Gasoline? I take a sip of the drink. It's light and tastes like lemonade. Not bad. "Thanks." I give him a half-hearted smile, worried as to what I have agreed to by accepting it, and he winks at me, smirking.

"Cheers," he says, raising his cocktail glass. I avoid his blue eyes by focussing on the hand holding the drink. Wide and thick, with an oversized gold ring on the fourth finger. Oily crescents underneath the nails. He could have been working on a car this afternoon, fixing the carburetor or rebuilding the engine, or whatever guys do with cars. "So, pretty girl, what's your name?"

"I'm Lou."

"What? You a foreman on a construction site? Or is that some kind of dyke name?"

"Louise," I say. "It's short for Louise." I attempt to hand him back the drink and make my escape but instead of taking the glass, he grabs my shoulder.

"Puh-leeeeze Louise, don't go yet."

I twist away from his hand but end up backing myself further into the corner.

"Hey." Donnie's brother appears, his moustache grown in thick and gross. He flanks his friend, completely blocking my route to Jonah and Isabelle.

"This is Louise," the fascist says, then turns to me. "Louise, do you like Michael Jackson?"

Be a smart animal, a voice in my head says, don't tie your shoe. I look at him but don't answer.

"David Bowie?"

"Yeah," I say. "I love David Bowie. And thanks," I hold up the drink, "but I have to get back to my friends now."

Neither of them moves. "You should come over some time," the fascist says. "We have an awesome apartment not far from here. Great record collection. What about tonight?"

"Sorry." I smile. "I don't know you guys."

"Well. We're businessmen," he says, shrugging as if this is the only logical occupation in the world. "But what might surprise you is that we are also exceptionally good cooks."

"Yeah," Donnie's brother chimes in. "I do dinners, he does desserts. We're rocking the Italian meals these days."

"C'mon on over, Louise. We'll have lasagna and garlic bread and ti-ramisu. And lots of red wine. Italian wine is the best. Magnifico!" The fascist presses his fingertips against his lips with a loud smacking kiss. Donnie's brother smiles widely with seemingly genuine enthusiasm. It is mind-boggling how quickly they have transformed from the douchiest guys in the world to a sweet and savoury version of Julia Child. I guess even Mussolini had his moments.

"It sounds good," I say. Beyond Donnie's brother's shoulder I see Sal lurch from his stool at the bar and start to move toward Jonah. "I have to go."

"All right, Cinderella. But before you split let me introduce myself: Mike Hunt." Donnie's brother holds out his hand. As we shake, I manage to angle myself into some clear space.

"And I'm Mike Hawk," the fascist says, laughing, as I walk away. "You can call me that any time, princess."

Sal and I converge on the table at the same time, Sal so drunk he can barely stand up. The band is back for a third set and I consider returning to the dance floor. But the energy has dissipated. The band looks tired, as if they'd rather be home watching *Miami Vice* or reruns of *The Love Boat*. And I'm not so comfortable going to my happy dancing place knowing the eyes of the two Mikes are watching.

"You guys ready to get out of here?"

"Yup," Isabelle says. She finishes the last chug of her beer and reaches for her coat.

"I saw him," Sal says to Jonah. "Outside my window. Like an angel. And he had the story but he wouldn't tell it to me. I wanted to know, but he wouldn't tell it!"

"What's he talking about?" I ask, pulling my own coat on. It's still clammy from the wet walk over and a wave of cold ripples down the back of my neck.

"Dad," Jonah says.

Sal's attempts to stand go horribly wrong and he ends up planting his face into the table.

"It's because you're drunk," I say as Isabelle helps Jonah to sit Sal up. "That's why he wouldn't tell you the story."

Sal's eyes are red and teary. "Witches!" he says, waving a wild hand. "Good witches? Or bad witches?"

"Sandwiches," Jonah says, helping Sal to stand and return to the bar.

"Goodnight, Sal. We're going to hit the road." Sal waves his hand again, a king dismissing his subjects.

"I better pee before we go," Isabelle says.

"Me too." Jonah follows her. At the bar, Sal folds over the counter crying, while Shelley awkwardly pats his head. I move to the door.

Outside the wind and rain have abated but the temperature has dropped and the air has turned glassy, sharp on the lungs, and so cold on the skin it's like being scalded. The wet wool of the daytime clouds has pulled back to reveal a silvery moon set against a dark blue sky.

A black Nissan pumping loud club music pulls up to the curb and the passenger window rolls down. Fascist Mike is in the driver's seat with Donnie's brother beside him.

"C'mon," Fascist Mike says. "If you don't want to come to our place, I'll drive you home."

"No thanks." I rest my hand on my purse and try to stand like someone who is holding a sharp knife. "I'm waiting for my brother."

"Fuck your brother. Help her out, Mike." The passenger door starts to open as Isabelle and Jonah bust through the doors, laughing, and the Nissan peals away.

"That was Mike Hunt," I say to Isabelle as we walk in the opposite direction. "Donnie Hunt's older brother."

"Hunter," she says. "Donnie Hunter."

"Oh," I say. "I thought he said his name was Hunt. Mike Hunt."

"Eeew," Isabelle says. Jonah gives me one of his patented older-brother looks: eyebrows arched, mouth pressed into a thin-lipped non-smile.

"What?"

"Mi-ke Hunt?" Isabelle says, slowly, enunciating clearly.

I shrug. I still don't get it.

"My cunt," Jonah says, a little louder than necessary. Clearly he is fed up with my stupidity.

"Oh." Understanding dawns rapidly. "His friend said his name was Mike Hawk. Ah. My cock. I get it now. Gross."

"Ew," Isabelle says again. "His friend's name is Kevin, I think. Keith? Kevin? Something like that. They live in a house, like, three blocks that way," she points. "It's nice, an old Victorian place, on a totally crap, run-down street. Donnie invited a bunch of people to a party at the end of the summer there. I went but didn't stay long. There were all these rumours the place was filled with hidden cameras. Like in the bathroom and stuff."

"I wouldn't put it past them. They are definitely creeps," I say. "They cornered me in Zane's. I thought I smelled gasoline." Jonah shakes his head and shudders. "What?"

"Nothing."

"*What?*"

"Nothing," he says. "*Nothing.* Just don't go getting all Nancy Drew on me. Stay away from those guys."

There's no sign of the black-and-white mutt as we cross the park. There is so much moonlight, it falls in waves and rumpled sheets, lightening the dark corners, casting the entire park, the picnic tables and benches, the swing sets and the slide and the tennis courts, in a grey half-light the colour of driftwood or polished beach stone. By contrast, the sky is a dark blue-black. "See the sky?" I say. "I've always thought of that colour as Nova Blue."

"Who blew?" Isabelle says.

"The sky," I say. "It's Nova Blue."

"It would make a good name for a rocket," Isabelle says.

"Or a popsicle," I say.

"Or a kid," Isabelle says. "They could grow up and drive race cars. Very fast, in big circles."

"She's always making up colours." Jonah directs his comments to Isabelle. "Dad thought she might have an illustrious career as a paint-chip namer."

"Red Randy would be a pretty good paint-chip name," I say.

"Or Randy Red," Isabelle says. She laughs, Jonah laughs. We spend the rest of our walk home speculating on Red Randy's name. Is Red his first name, Randy his last? Or if Red is a nickname and Randy his real name, then is Rocket his last name? Red Randy Rocket! It is the kind of pointless, cheerful conversation that makes the long walk back to the apartment seem to take no time at all.

7

On Saturday, about an hour before the bakery closes, it starts to snow. It's the day before the solstice, one of the darkest days of the year, and by the time we lock up, daylight has disappeared and the snow is about six inches deep and falling in fast fat flakes, as clearly formed as a kid's construction paper cut-out on a Christmas tree. Flakes that fall against your skin with the weight of butterfly wings. Snow kisses. Once Dad woke Jonah and me up in the middle of the night when it was snowing like this. He helped us pull on snowsuits over our pyjamas and we went outside and built two snowmen with a bench in between them, big enough for all three of us to sit on.

"Snow," Isabelle says, and I concur. We're making a small detour past Keith-whatever-his-name and Mike Hunter's house so I can get their address. Isabelle agreed to my request without asking any questions and she doesn't say anything now as we walk past 1407 Walker Street. The black Nissan is parked in a narrow driveway and the white gables and fading blue paint of the house look pretty in the falling snow. Aside from an overturned garbage pail on the front porch, there's not much else to see. We keep walking and I repeat the number, 1407, seven times in my head so I won't forget.

We are the first footsteps to make a trail down the sidewalk in the new snow and we trudge like pioneers, like Ma and Pa Ingalls trying not to get lost between the barn door and the house. Isabelle is lobbying for me to attend her lineup of Christmas parties when our footsteps join an earlier set. Not much earlier though; the snow has barely settled in the imprints. They are big. I place my boot squarely in the centre of one and there is space on all sides. A man's size twelve or thirteen, I'd guess.

"Clea's mom makes a jelly roll *and* a chocolate Christmas log," Isabelle says. Clea, a primary school friend, is holding her annual and apparently infamous Christmas tea tomorrow afternoon and I've been invited, in a roundabout way, as Isabelle's guest. "Also, these little almond cookies?" Isabelle presses on. She knows I'm a sucker for a free meal, especially if it ends with good cookies. "Dipped in chocolate? You have to come."

"Did you know," I say, jump-stepping from one oversized footprint to another, "that almonds are a member of the peach family?" We pass a bus stop and the footsteps veer suddenly to the right along a narrow laneway and disappear. A sudden combustion of ideas compels me to spin back toward the bus stop as Isabelle continues her litany of desserts. Inside the shelter the poster of the bus stop stalker is stuck with peeling tape over a milk ad, the moisture in the air defeating the adhesive. As I watch, the last of the tape gives way and the poster see-saws down, disappearing into a snowdrift. Beyond the circle of street-lamp light, there is nothing to see down the laneway but a velvety darkness drizzled with falling snow. Is someone hiding back there? Was I walking in the stalker's footsteps? Panic flares inside, then settles into something cold and hard but electric. I continue walking backwards, the sense of imminent danger so intense it tastes like blood, thick and metallic at the back of my tongue. Isabelle hasn't noticed a thing.

"The secret is, Clea's mom doesn't use cocoa. She buys Baker's chocolate, like we use at — hey! What are you doing?" She grabs my arm as I sprawl backward over a large drift of snow that's saved me from too hard a landing. "Walk much?" Isabelle laughs, her face hovering over mine, rosy-lit, haloed by her own soft, insulating nimbus, as if somewhere in the grey cotton of the sky a warm spotlight trains its beam directly on her. It reminds me of the first day we met, when she rescued me off Jonah's porch.

"You look like a milk commercial," I say, as she helps me to my feet.

"Are you okay?"

"Nope," I say. I glance over my shoulder. Nothing, nobody there. "Did you know that camel's milk doesn't curdle like cow's milk?" I brush the snow off my butt and turn my back on the dark laneway. "And a cow's udder can hold between twenty-five and fifty pounds of milk?"

"Milk," Isabelle says, imitating the ads. "It does a body good."

One last glance over my shoulder. The street, framed by tree branches heavy and low with snow, is empty behind us. I pack a loose and lumpy snowball and toss it at Isabelle. She yelps as it splats on her shoulder. I want to ask if she ever feels scared but instead tell her one of Dad's favourite jokes.

"Why were the dyslexic cow and the Buddhist monk such good friends?"

Isabelle shrugs, already laughing.

"They both like to oom."

She groans and returns the snowball fire.

"Two snowmen are standing in a field," I say and scoop an armful of snow in her direction. "Funny, the first one says to the other, I smell carrots too." Dad told Jonah and me that joke standing behind the snowman in our backyard in the middle of the night, all three of us in our pyjamas, in the fluttery falling snow. I was sitting on the newly made snow bench beside Jonah, and Dad was talking in his Groucho Marx voice, the one he used for stupid jokes, and none of us wanted to ever go back inside. There's a sudden catch in my breath and I start to cry as Isabelle's next volley plasters across my face and snow slides under my scarf and down my throat with an icy burn. The tears are more surprising than the snow, which, thankfully, camouflages the red and wet in my eyes.

"I'm sorry, I didn't mean to get you full face," Isabelle says, conciliatory mittened hand on my arm. She brushes bits of snow off my coat. "Are you okay?"

"Sure," I say, corralling my hiccupy breath. "Just cold." I scoop a finger full of melting slush from my neckline.

We walk on, silent, listening to the muffled sound of snow falling. When we are half a block away from the apartment she asks if I'll come to Clea's tea party tomorrow.

"Call me?" I say. "I'm not sure. I need to check with Jonah. We might have plans." I don't have to check with Jonah and I know we don't have plans. He's working a double at the Falafel Hut. No offence to Clea, but I don't have the heart to hang out at her perfect house, with her perfect mother and her perfect friends around a perfect Christmas tree, eating a perfect Christmas buffet. Isabelle knows I'm making excuses. When we reach my house, time to say goodbye, we are awkward with one another.

"Well, that was fun," Isabelle says. "I haven't had a snowball fight in, like, forever."

"Me too."

"We laughed, we cried."

"It was a blast," I say. "Well, see ya. Call me tomorrow?"

Isabelle waves and trudges down the sidewalk. I'm unlocking the door when she shouts again. "Hey! Lou! What's the difference between chopped beef and pea soup?" I shrug. "Anybody can chop beef. It takes someone special to pee soup."

Ha ha. She's no Groucho Marx, but Isabelle's not bad.

Jonah's left a note on the kitchen table saying he'll be late. Living with Jonah is not so different from living with Dad. In a certain light, or from the corner of my eye, or when he rubs the heel of his hand across his forehead or leans his face into his hand while reading, Jonah might be Dad. Or at least an echo or shadow come to life. I thought I knew Dad, and I think I know Jonah, but they both have secrets they keep from me.

A week after the cremation, Jonah picked up Dad's ashes. They are in a ceramic urn glazed opalescent white like the inside of a seashell. Inside, the ashes are coarse, like beach sand, and surprisingly heavy. We placed the urn on the oak cabinet of the unwatched TV. It's not a good spot but it's the best we have. Sometimes, when Jonah isn't home, I bring the blue cards and sit in front of the dead TV, letting myself sense Dad's presence fill the room. Tonight the card I pick reads, *"More light!" Goethe's final words on his deathbed.*

It's an interesting card but I have no idea what it means. Did Goethe intend it to be his legacy? A dying hope that his loved ones live on after him with more light, less darkness? Or was it what he saw as he approached death — more and more dazzlingly bright light? Maybe it was a description of how he felt, as the weight of the world and his body left him? Or, maybe, it was a simple request. In a darkened death room, Goethe simply wanted someone to bring a candle or unshutter the window and let in the sunlit air.

The next morning, I call Detective Phillips. His voice is familiar but I can't picture his face, that night at Zane's was such a blur. I can see the back of his car, the lone Snickers wrapper on the back-seat floor, but I can't remember if he had dark hair or was balding, if he was pale or olive skinned. I'm pretty sure he had kind eyes. "It's Sunday!" he says, when I ask him if he has any news on the case. I want to say, I didn't think detectives took days off, but Dad would say that was being saucy. Instead, I tell him how the Mikes were aggressively in my face and how they smelled like gasoline, only it was just the one Mike that smelled like gasoline and his name isn't actually Mike, it's Kevin or Keith. I'm midway through my sentence when I realize how pointless and absurd it sounds. What was I thinking? "They live at 1407 Walker Street." This is the only certain fact I know. "I'm sorry, Detective, I realize this sounds flaky but there's something not right about those guys."

"You do realize I need more than 'there's something not right' to launch an investigation," he says.

I tell him I do and that I won't bug him again unless I have something concrete.

"Listen," he says. "Don't go looking for trouble."

"I'm not," I say. I want to add, I can't help it if trouble comes looking for me, but don't. It sounds like something someone would say in a movie.

"Louise?"

"Yeah?"

"Merry Christmas."

I hang up and call Isabelle to tell her I'm not going to the tea party. "I'm going Christmas shopping and it's going to be tricky. I have to buy at least three presents with no money."

"You don't have to get me anything," Isabelle says. "We said no presents."

"Everybody says that and nobody means it. I have to get you something. You're the best friend I ever had." This comes out cornier than I intended and also sounds like a line from a movie but I hear in Isabelle's silence that she is not offended.

"Lou — "

"Don't sweat it," I say. "I'll call you tomorrow."

Outside, it's a bright day, everything covered in clean snow, the air squeaky with frost. Mr. Baptiste is out on the sidewalk, bareheaded and shovelling snow, and we both nod and smile as I walk past, heading south. I walk all the way to Front Street, to a flea market Isabelle and I went to a few weeks ago. It is a big open space crammed with vendors selling fancy china and old toys and costume jewellery. Stacks of old magazines and boxes of albums bookend the cluttered tables and the air smells of mothballs and the darkest corners of attics. It's the kind of place where if you look long enough, you'll find treasures. I have fifty dollars in my purse, the remnants of the five hundred dollars from Mrs. Turner and the neighbours.

My shopping spree is a stunning success. Three hours later when I emerge from the dusty hall, I have scored Paul Simon's *One-Trick Pony* album and a brown T-shirt with a turquoise drawing of a snare drum and the words Louisiana Music Factory for Jonah. At a table selling wool and knitting needles, I bought a beautiful thick heather-green scarf, knitted in a continuous circle, for Isabelle, as well as a baby-blue matching scarf, mitten and hat set for Stella. I wasn't planning on buying anything for Stella, but the knitting lady gave it to me dirt cheap. The set looks like something a great-aunt would make for you and is not nearly as elegant as Isabelle's scarf, but Stella will love it. For Sal, there's a tea tray decorated with the image of a cherry bough and a matching creamer and sugar boat. My big score, after the Paul Simon record, is a bag of old pulp magazines, the kind that Sal collects. There are twelve in the bag. I'm going to pick one out for Isabelle and one for Rufus and give the rest to Sal, in case they're worth some money. The last thing I bought was a postcard of Frank Zappa for Rufus. Zappa's hair is in two bushy ponytails, like he's an eight-year-old girl, and he has a bright pink rose over one ear. The card reads Happy Mother's Day. I think Rufus will appreciate the absurdity. All of that, and I still have almost thirteen dollars left.

I buy a mocha at a Second Cup and walk north on Yonge and then west on Queen. There's music playing at Nathan Phillips Square and skaters circling the ice rink. This part of Queen is busier and more upscale. I push through wave after wave of happy Christmas shoppers but the crowds thin, the street narrows, the snow dirties and the garbage bins overflow the farther west I go. This far west, there are so few people on the street that I can see the figure of Donnie approaching from almost a block away. He's not wearing his usual preppy peacoat but is radically underdressed in a thin hoodie and fingerless gloves. We both reach the cross street at the same time. "You heading this way?" he asks and I nod, both of us turning north and falling into an easy, loping stride. He points to the outline of the album in my shopping bag. "An album? That's, like, totally ghetto. There's these newfangled things, I don't know if you've ever heard of them, called compact discs, or as I like to call them, CDs."

"Ha," I say. "You're one to talk about being ghetto. What's with the getup?"

"Where I'm heading, a polo sweater and a peacoat doesn't go over well." He shoves his hands in his pockets. "I'm working for my brother."

"Your brother? And his friend? No offence, but they're assholes. Like date-rape-drug-in-the-drink assholes. Big-time assholes. You should stay away from them."

"Assholes," Donnie says, nodding in agreement, as we pass two goth kids. Pale skinned, dressed all in black, metal studs glinting round their necks. They lean against a bus stop making out with freakish abandon, two vampires caught in the thin December daylight. Donnie openly stares as we pass, then jostles his head as if trying to erase an etch-a-sketch image deep inside his brain. "They're assholes, yeah, but they're keeping me busy. I'm making money." At the edge of a parking lot lined with high banks of snow, Donnie slows to a stop. He nods down a small back laneway heading east. "This is me."

"Okay, see ya." I start to move on but he steps in and grabs my arm.

"Can I show you something?" Up close, Donnie's eyes are dark brown, long-lashed and surprisingly steady. He holds my gaze until I nod yes.

"Okay, but not here." His fingerless glove moves down my forearm and he grabs my mittened hand, pulling me up and over the snowbank. We cross the unlit parking lot, my hand still in his, small crystals of snow salting the air. He draws me behind a garage into a protected corner and pulls his backpack off, unzips it, and a rich, skunky perfume fills the air.

"You're selling weed?"

"Yep." His smile is proud, as though this was something he'd been working for and had finally achieved. "And anything else you might like."

"Anything?" I say. "Are you fucking high?"

"Actually," he winks at me, "yes. You want to smoke?"

"Ahh, no," I say. "I don't think so. Not out here. And I don't smoke. Not really. Plus, how do I know you're not the kind of guy who sprays his product with oven cleaner or some other chemical crap to make it more toxic and addictive?"

"Hey, I wouldn't do that." He looks hurt. "You should know me better than that."

"Donnie," I say. "I don't know you at all."

"Well, here." He rustles in the backpack and pulls out a small bag of weed and a tinfoil package. "This seems like your kind of thing. It's my Christmas present to you." He comes half a step closer, places the weed and the tinfoil pack in my hands and then holds them closed. "They're magic mushrooms. Psilocybin. It's all natural shit." And then he kisses me.

It's a long kiss and by the end of it I am angled up against the garage, breathless. Donnie backs away smiling and scoops up his backpack. "See you around, Lou," he says, before sprinting down the alley.

Drugs shoved in my shopping bag, lips tingling, I hustle the last few blocks home, certain that even if passing people can't tell that I have been in a back alleyway making out with a delinquent drug dealer, they can definitely smell the fumes of weed radiating off me, heady, muggy, illegal.

The next morning, I lie in bed listening to Jonah have breakfast and leave for work, the whole time trying to make sense of the kiss. I don't like Donnie, but the kiss was okay. If it wasn't long distance, I'd call Julie. She used to call me Late Bloomer Lou, because I had no experience with boys, and I used to call her Unruly Julie, because she had tons, and, for the most part, I was quite happy to live vicariously through her stories. The pawing around in back fields and broom closets and the smooshing of faces with somebody you've sat beside through grade school never sounded very appealing. That is, until the party when Rufus and I danced to the Waterboys beside the bonfire. At the end of the night he kissed me. It was a sweet kiss but short. I was biking home and Rufus was getting a ride with Sean Richards, and Sean's mother was in her car, honking the horn. I was holding onto the handlebars of my bike when he leaned in. Neither of us said anything afterwards, just smiled like goofballs, and then he left, and ever since then I've been thinking about kissing him again.

Just kissing. Basically, everything I know about all the other stuff that people do comes from Freddy Fender and his gory science lab stories of hand jobs and blow jobs and three-ways. He'd gross me out, describing the dirtiest of acts and ending with a mock-innocent shrug. It's just biology, he'd say. Yeah, I'd say, if latex gloves and lube grew on trees. Freddy Fender put some pretty dirty pictures in my head, although I could never picture any actual, real-life people doing the kinds of things he described. The people in Freddy's stories were all faceless, nameless accumulations of body parts, sharp edges and angles turning wavy and fluid. But I could imagine kissing Rufus. In fact, I could imagine kissing a lot of people. There was Finn and Monsieur Charles Bernier, our dashing French-teacher-slash-playwright, with his dark wavy hair. Also, his wife, Charlie, who owned an art gallery. Charlie frequented the bakery and, like her husband, was gorgeous and smelled like grapefruit body wash. There was also a kid in grade ten who sang Elvis Presley songs at the school assembly and Kiko, the elegant Japanese exchange student who didn't speak any English, and Dolph, the Danish exchange student whose English grammar was better than the teacher's. Even Isabelle. There was a world of kissable lips out there and the inevitability and anticipation of a next kiss was excruciatingly fine. But Donnie? I don't want to think about kissing Donnie. I don't want to *like* thinking about kissing Donnie. But still, despite my best intentions, the thought keeps returning. When I run my tongue over my lips, I can taste the not unpleasant combination of cinnamon gum and cigarette smoke, can press into the strength of his muscled arms, can feel the ticklish woollen edge of his gloves and his cold, dry fingertips on my neck.

When someone knocks on our front door, I spring out of bed and race down the hallway, down the stairs, as if I can outrun these thoughts.

Rumpled, bed-headed and pyjama'd, I open the door. It's Ellen Bisbey, a.k.a. the Busybee, from Family and Children Social Services.

"Uh," I say, "hi."

"Hi." She's not very tall and she's at least fifty-five. Even though she looks fit, I'm pretty sure I could take her in a fight. She clears her throat. "Can I come in?"

I don't move. What's the state of the kitchen and the living room? Is it a big mess? Did Jonah do the dishes last night? Is she going to do an inspection? The bag of weed is in my underwear drawer. If she goes in my room, she might smell it. "My brother's not here," I say. Vampires can't cross your threshold without an invitation. Maybe the same is true of social workers? I'm not inviting her in.

"That's okay." She inches closer. "I'm here to see you." She takes another step forward and I am forced to take one back. She sees her opening and pushes in.

"I have the flu," I say, as she pulls off her boots and hangs her navy wool coat on a hook.

"Oh dear," she says, sounding neither sympathetic nor concerned. "Here I thought you were lazing about because it's your Christmas holiday."

"No." I walk up the stairs and she follows. "I'm an early riser." This is true. Why do I feel like I'm lying? The kitchen is a mess, countertop covered in unwashed dishes, but a quick glance tells me the living room is worse. I clear away some of the newspapers from a chair and she sits down, plopping an oversized purse on the table.

"Tea?" she prompts.

I put the kettle on without saying a word. As I pull out the tea bags and cups she rummages in her purse, emerging with a bag of hard peppermints and a small tub of Blistex, which she opens and applies liberally to her lips.

"Mint?" She holds the bag out as I carry over our cups. I shake my head no. Maybe if I don't say anything she'll go away faster.

"Sorry to be a pain, dear, but … milk?"

I bristle at the *dear* but still don't say anything. Thankfully the container of milk is half full. Behind me, I sense her sizing up the contents of our fridge: jar of peanut butter, upside-down bottle of ketchup, loaf of bread, Styrofoam container filled with watery tzatziki, carton of milk. I decide to be direct. "Why are you here?"

"Follow-up visit," she says. She tilts her head the way dogs do when they are pretending to understand human speech. "I'm here to see how you are doing." She pauses. "How are you doing?"

"Fine," I say. "I'm seventeen now, you know."

"Christmas can be a hard time of year." She smiles and re-tilts her head. When I don't respond, she straightens up and clasps her hands together, pointer fingers forming an arrow, which she touches to her lips and adds: "It can be hard when you've lost someone."

Conversation stalls. She's waiting for me to say something and I have nothing to say. But she doesn't let it drop. Dog with a bone.

"Would you agree," she says, "that Christmas can be a difficult time?"

"Sure," I say. I almost add, Especially difficult when you have no money, but stop myself in time.

She backs up her attack. "How's school?"

"Fine."

"And work? Jonah said you got a job in a bakery."

"Fine," I say, surprised. Jonah's been talking to her?

She sees her advantage and goes for the kill. "You must miss your dad."

"Yes."

She presses on. "You must feel very sad sometimes. And scared."

Sad, yes. Scared, yes. But I don't like the way she says *must* and I'm tired of agreeing with her. This woman doesn't even know me. "Jonah and I are fine."

"Yes." She smiles primly. "I can see that. Well," she stands and picks up her bag. "I won't take up any more of your time."

I've offended her. Have I blown the visit? Do social workers have a checklist of warning signs to identify troubled teens? If so, general surliness must be a tipoff. To what, exactly, I don't know but I should have been chattier, asked her advice about something.

"We're doing our Christmas shopping tomorrow," I lie, following her back down the hallway. There is no money for extra Christmasy food. "Our turkey and yams and stuff. I'm not sure how long to cook a turkey." More lies. I'm a good cook and I always took care of the turkey back at home, but the lies work. Her smile softens.

"Twenty minutes a pound," she says, pulling on her coat. "And don't forget to baste it every hour."

"Thanks," I say, fake smile hardening into a mask.

"Like I said before, you can call any time, Lou." She grabs my right forearm, clasping it with two hands and squeezes tightly, a down-and-dirty play for intimacy and connection, before stepping out the door. "Merry Christmas," she says, pointed and emphatic. "And a happy new year."

I close the door, something small and mean inside me refusing to return her holiday cheer. And angry. I am angry but from a long way away, as if I am both a character in a play and someone watching it. I imagine myself trashing the apartment: breaking plates, kicking walls, smashing a chair into the TV screen. I imagine demanding answers from Dad. How could you leave me alone? How could you leave me alone at Christmas with the Busybee social-working vampire raised by inquisitive dogs? And after I finish the physical carnage, I'll fall to my knees and shake my fists at the heavens. How can Jonah and I have Christmas alone? Dad!? You're Santa Claus.

I don't do any of this, of course. I go back to bed. I'll wait until Jonah gets home, then I can pick a fight with him.

Despite being more than a month overdue, *The Cardiovascular System: The Heart* is still under my bed. I pull it out, turning to the section on valve disease, a section I have pretty much memorized. A healthy valve system ensures that blood flows freely in a forward direction through the four valves of the heart with no backward leakage, but when damaged, the valves either become thick and rigid, narrowing the valve opening and reducing blood flow causing the heart to work extra hard, or they don't close tightly enough and the blood seeps backward, pooling in the heart and potentially causing muscle damage. Valve disease, I deduce, is responsible for the swooshing beat of Dad's heart, a sound caused by "turbulent blood flow" through one or more of these valves. Some people are born with valve abnormalities but sometimes they can be caused or worsened by endocarditis, an infection of the inner lining of your heart. That's what happened to Dad when he was a kid. I flip forward searching for the section on endocarditis but end up in a chapter entitled "The Mind Body Connection" where the opening paragraph states that common phrases such as *sick at heart* or *heartbroken* might be more than romantic metaphors. Stress can cause heart disease, as can negative emotions such as fear, anger or chronic depression. It seems a little unfair. I stuff the book back under my bed wondering what Dad would say if I told him all he had to do was think positive to heal his heart.

I shuffle the blue index cards and pick one from the middle of the pack: *A Zen archer climbs to the top of a cliff overlooking the seemingly endless expanse of the sea. He has only one arrow to make his shot and when he takes it, the arrow arcs across the blue of the sky, landing in the blue of the water. Bull's Eye.* Jonah comes home while I'm pondering this one.

"Lou! There's a letter for you." It's from Rufus. I tuck it into the pocket of Dad's sweatshirt as Jonah gives me the once-over. "Did you stay in bed all day?"

"Yep." It's not a bad opening for a potential fight but I am deflated, no fight left. Really, I'm happy Jonah's home. "How was your day?"

"Busy, boring and long. I'm going out with friends from school tonight. Do you want to come?" He fills the fridge with mysterious cartons from Falafel Hut. Dinner, I assume. I'm still in my pyjamas but I have been waiting for an invite to meet Jonah's school friends since I arrived. I'm about to say, yeah, let me go get changed, when he adds, with a dorky forced nonchalance, "You can invite Isabelle, too."

Hmm. A sudden spark of fight stirs but I ignore it. "Naw. I'm going to stay home." I retreat to my room and close the door.

Rufus has drawn a picture on the back of the envelope: David Bowie, in a Santa hat, singing "Let's Dance" (LOU!) into a microphone shaped like a Christmas tree. It's goofy and heartbreaking and makes me feel far away from home. I unstick the flap carefully, so it doesn't tear. A bracelet falls free from the folded papers. It's similar in design to the friendship bracelets kids make at camp — one summer Julie and I made *thousands* — but this one is much cooler, with two strands of dark leather edging an inner metal track of tiny silver squares, linked point to point, a paler thread of leather braiding it all together and a vintage copper button for the clasp. I put it on my left wrist before I start to read.

> Lou!
> I am devastated about your birthday. This is a terrible thing and should be remedied. This is what I propose: we will have a big celebration for your 17th unbirthday. Maybe this summer? Did I tell you I am applying to the Ontario College of Art and Ryerson and maybe U of T? The plan is to move to the city. Then we can celebrate your birthday and anything else any time. We could celebrate Thursdays by going out dancing and Sundays by eating nachos. We could celebrate you getting a cold with chicken soup. We could celebrate your unbirthday with caketime and balloontime and gametime. What do you think?

The bracelet is NOT for your birthday. We're doing a leather and jewellery-making section in art and this was my first attempt at a bracelet. Don't laugh at it! I thought you might like the button though. I got it off a fuzzy old sweater I bought for a buck at the St. Mary's church sale. The sweater is butt ugly but the buttons are beautiful.

Merry Christmas, Happy New Year and all that holiday peace,

Rufus

The letter is only a page long but there are two more pages of unlined paper filled with a cartoon account of the story of the man who came into the bakery and threw unshelled peanuts at Isabelle and me. Rufus has titled it *The Adventures of Squirrelyman* and in the panels where Squirrelyman is shouting at Leo, Rufus has real scripture quotes. After storming out of the bakery, Squirrelyman retreats to the park and into his home in the treetops where he continues to ping unsuspecting pedestrians, stray cats and beady-eyed birds with twigs and acorns and peanut shells. It's brilliant. I make several attempts to start a return letter but each attempt is brutally sabotaged by the unwanted memory of Donnie's lips.

8

Dear Rufus,

It took me a few days to write a reply and now tomorrow is Christmas Eve and I wish I could come home and hand-deliver this letter to you in time for Christmas. Truthfully, I am homesick right now. It's funny because Christmas wasn't a huge thing at our house but it was so utterly predictable that I almost feel it is still happening. Like there is an alternate reality me and tomorrow afternoon she (I) will be at home alone in the kitchen, making Christmas cookies and listening to Q107. I will make chocolate macaroon, chocolate chip, shortbread and spice cookies. In the late afternoon, my brother Jonah will arrive home on the bus from Toronto loaded with bags of dirty laundry and presents and shortly after that my dad will follow, slightly late and flustered from work, with too much takeout Chinese that we will eat along with turkey leftovers for days. After dinner, Jonah and I will give each other our presents, most likely a book for me and a book or an album for him, then we will stay up late watching movies on CityTV. On Christmas we will open presents with coffee and cookies and read books and take long baths all day long. We will cook a turkey and potatoes and peas and the turkey will take a couple more hours to cook than we bargained for so by the time the food is ready we are all starving and on the verge of grouchy. As far as traditions go, it's not much, but I always loved it. I don't know what Jonah and I are going to do this year but I'm sure, at best, it will only feel like an imitation of that other, alternate reality. What are you doing?

There's lots of things I'd like to talk to you about but it's hard to get it all organized down on paper without sounding crazy. It will be great when you come to Toronto and we can talk in person. Do you know what you want to study? Art, I guess, because you're really, really good. I love the bracelet and *The Adventures of Squirrelyman* is brilliant. Leo's hair is a little longer in real life but, amazingly, you kind of nailed his face. My friend Isabelle is planning to become a chef but I don't know what it is I want to study.

The last few weeks we have had a new regular at the bakery. We call him Shakespeare Joe. He has a big, pale, moon-shaped face and it is difficult to tell how old he is. 24? 38? I don't know. He bikes through the snow on an old yellow three-speed, wearing giant lederhosen and a metal bowl for a hat. No joke! He comes in, and no matter how busy it is, he quizzes me on all sorts of odds and ends facts. What's the address of the prime minister? What was the name of the first dog sent up in space? What is the capital city of Bulgaria? (The answers are, 24 Sussex Drive, Laika and Sofia). If I can't answer right away he gives me clues that are baffling and then scolds me for being "dull-witted." This from a man in lederhosen and a metal bowl! He's always on a grift too, trying to convince us to "invest" money and/or food in his upcoming theatre production, or collection of poems, or Mozart-worthy opera libretto. He's an artist of many talents!

I hope you like the magazine. I found it at this flea market that's across the street from the St. Lawrence Market. It's full of treasures. We can go together when you're in Toronto. There are so many buttons there it will amaze you.

peace & love & holiday cheer!

Lou

I buy an envelope big enough to fit the magazine. It's hard to pick my favourites out but for Rufus I choose one called *True Gangster Crime*. On the cover is a picture of a woman, smoking and reading a magazine, the sleeve of her very full bodice falling tantalizingly off her shoulder. The articles inside include "Dope! Gateway Drug to Depravity and Delinquency!" and "A Swindler's Sweetheart: A Shady Lady Tells All." For Isabelle, I pick *Famous Crime Cases*, which features two stories: "Sex Road to Ruin" and "Daisy Davis: Fair! Fun-loving! Deadly!" The rest I'll give to Sal.

9

Wednesday is Christmas Eve day and because we are on school holidays, Isabelle and I work a full day as opposed to our regular afternoon shift. Leo and Anna are at the bakery when we arrive, frosting cakes, toasting almonds, and singing Christmas carols loudly and off key. Leo carries out tray after tray of goodies, strudel, shortbread, pecan squares, mincemeat tarts, until ten o'clock when he emerges with a tray of brightly frosted sugar cookies to give away to regular customers and kids: trees, bells, candy canes, gingerbread men and holiday wreaths.

"For the young," he says. "Or the young at heart."

Anna follows him, eating a sugar cookie dipped in chocolate, and tells us they are leaving for home to make their own Christmas preparations but will return at the end of the day to help with the bigger-than-usual closing routine. The bakery is closed until the weekend after New Year's and all the fridges need to be cleared out.

"Also," she says as she pulls on her winter coat, "we return for a little Christmas cheer." Leo winks at us and they leave.

"I hope what she means by 'Christmas cheer,'" Isabelle says, "is a cash bonus for the time we're off work."

I hope so too. Jonah pays off his last tuition instalment at the beginning of January and money is tight. We've been filling in the gaps between work shifts with peanut butter, rice and beans and noodle packs and the monotony is oppressive. There's no news on when Dad's money will be released and the realtor said the market in Linden is dead this time of year, which means no offers on the house until at least spring or summer. Money is coming, we just don't know when. But it's not that bad. You only have to watch TV for five minutes to know that people, small kids, are starving in Ethiopia. We might be totally broke but we're not starving, no distended bellies, no flies landing on our eyes. It's just, sometimes, I find myself day-dreaming about a full meal, complete with several different food groups: a cheese omelette with a big side salad, or a grilled breast of chicken with roasted potatoes and mixed veggies. I avoid talking to Isabelle about it. She's so aghast at the state of our fridge that talking to her always makes me feel a little more sorry for myself.

I flip a switch and the coffee grinder erupts in a jagged purr, the velvety smell of fresh beans filling the air. I grind enough beans to last the rest of the day as Isabelle takes a sponge and a bucket of soapy water to clean up the sticky remnants of an earlier spill of orange juice. Some bratty little squirt dumped his whole can of juice when his mom refused to buy him chocolate cake for breakfast. Isabelle is on her hands and knees, scrubbing, when Stella totters through the door, bags and bottle of Pepsi in hand.

"A-bell!" she yips. This is what she calls Isabelle, A-bell. Me she calls Whoo. "What's wrong?!"

"Nothing." Isabelle laughs. But Stella is transfixed, staring at the sticky puddle, the way the blackened soapy tentacles trickle toward Isabelle's knee.

"That bad. Hand." Stella points, then adds: "You look a little strange." She stretches out her fingers as if to pat Isabelle's head. "It's okay, it's okay, but you should get up. Now. Slowly."

"I'm fine." Isabelle grins. She huffs at the loose strands of hair dangling in front of her eyes. Golden wisps scatter up, then settle back down.

"Oh! What's wrong? You're very tired?" Stella's face purses with worry.

"Really, I'm fine. Someone spilled some orange juice and I'm cleaning up."

"Oh those bad boys," Stella says, clucking and pacing in tight, tiny circles. "They are so mean to you, I know, I know, dear, you don't like it. They put you in the ring until you're down."

I clear Stella's favourite table, pulling out a chair, and she sits with a weary sigh. "I have something for you, Stella." The baby-blue hat set has been stored under the register all day and I place it, unwrapped, silver bow barely sticking to the wool, on the table. "Merry Christmas!"

She stares at it before sticking the silver bow inside her coat. "My?" she asks, looking up at me and I nod. She shoves the scarf and hat and mitten inside her coat, maybe inside her shirt. It's hard to tell. Things disappear inside the folds of Stella's coat. Down on the floor Isabelle starts singing "You Are My Sunshine" in a showboat sort of voice.

Stella sings this song often, sitting at her spot by the window, with the pure and focussed attention of a child reciting a nursery rhyme. I sing along with Isabelle now and hold out my arms to Stella, blue dishrag dangling from my hand. Stella doesn't sing and she doesn't look directly at me but she keeps peeking. I put the dishrag down on a table and sway side to side, dancing with an invisible partner.

"Whoo, whoo," Stella says and pulls herself out of the chair. She holds her arms out to dance.

Her fingernails are scratchy, a thick yellow rind, and she smells like dirty concrete. We waltz a few steps in the middle of the room and Stella whoops and cackles and sings along, my sunshine, oh please, da de da, her brown crumbling teeth visible, her breath a thick paste blasting my face. She pulls away and sits down suddenly with a whoosh of rancid air. Her eyes, looking up at me, show sudden fear.

Isabelle is done cleaning the floor and as she carries the bucket behind the counter, I carry over a coffee for Stella, who is bent down, rummaging in one of her plastic bags. She emerges with Ruby, a small beanbag stuffed animal she talks to when she is rattled. Mottled white, blue and purple, Ruby most closely resembles a cartoonish vulture but Stella once told Isabelle and me that Ruby was a raven. Back behind the counter, I scrub my hands with soap and hot water, rubbing Leo's nail brush vigorously over my fingertips. Stella's mumbled words, repeating and rising in pitch, gradually start to take form. Isabelle arches her eyebrows at me. We both know we're in for a scene. Thankfully there are no other customers around.

"Oh and oh, oh that song, that's the hospital song with the dirty windows, somebody should clean the windows, let the sun in, it's not a hard job, if I had my own rag, not heavy blankets, good night! And lovey like the girl brings me sweet tea after I did that and you can't help it. You can't help it! When you're wet, like a baby. Whoo whoo missy." Stella's voice twists into a grotesque caricature, her *Exorcist* voice, Isabelle calls it, and she sizzles with accusation. "What are you trying to do? Bury me? Seize her! Seize her! Oh no sir oh no no no missy tick bells in my ears. I'll dig it out, dig it out."

Stella mumbles often and Stella mumbles with momentum, the small gravelly pebble of sound developing into an avalanche of discontent, the force of the rumble inevitably pushing her into motion. She scoops her bags into one hand, Ruby in the other, and bangs a path around the bakery, careening into tables and chairs, knocking several over, until, with a loud shout, she ricochets through the door, the echo of her outburst softening to a sudden hush. Isabelle flips the stereo on and Bing Crosby's "White Christmas" surrounds us.

"Berserker," Isabelle says as we right the fallen table and chairs. "Bee Zurrr Kur."

It is a busy day but, aside from the occasional run-in with a harried businesswoman doing last-minute Christmas shopping, it is a happy one. With every transaction the customers wish us a happy holiday, generally tipping more than usual. Stella returns to drop off a chipped Virgin Mary candle and a religious pamphlet, one with watery pastel pictures and thick Bible-black letters asking the question, *Who really rules the world?* by way of apology, but it's busy when she comes and she doesn't stay, leaving as soon as Shakespeare Joe arrives. Stella is not a fan. Joe, dressed in a relatively inconspicuous if oversized thrift store suit, orders a coffee in a takeout cup, drinks it, borrows a marker from Isabelle, writes TIPS surrounded by hearts and shooting stars on the cup and proceeds to sing all five verses of "Good King Wenceslas" in a deep baritone. He continues to sing four more verses with the same melody but different lyrics, and then proceeds to give a lecture on the history of the song. According to Joe's dubious authority, "Good King Wenceslas" is a rewrite of the thirteenth-century spring carol "*Tempus adest floridum.*" Translation: "The time is near for flowering." At four thirty Anna and Leo return. The bakery is empty except for Joe, who has continued non-stop to debate the merits of the competing versions of the carol. "Out!" Anna waves her hands as if she is shooing livestock from the front yard. Joe, with exaggerated dignity, pockets his quarters and then bows toward Isabelle, forearm circling with a courtly flourish: "All the world with beauty fills, gold the green enhancing." He turns to me and repeats the gesture. "Flowers make glee among the hills, set the meadows dancing."

"Out, you flim-flam!" Anna's voice is stern. "Time to be off."

"Madam." Joe bows one last time.

"Merry Christmas!" I shout, then Isabelle, then Anna, as Joe pushes through the door.

Once he's gone, Leo places a small bottle of Baileys Irish Cream on the counter and hands each of us an envelope. Inside is a Christmas card and a hundred-dollar cash bonus. Leo divvies the bottle into four coffee mugs, hands them out and, as we clink the china, toasts his lovely wife and charming employees. He then proceeds to bag up the contents of the fridge and the display cases. As Isabelle is leaving with her father to go to her grandparents' house in Thunder Bay tonight and won't be home until New Year's, she only takes an apple strudel. Anna and Leo take a few items, but the bulk goes to me. There's fresh produce: a cucumber, two red peppers, red onion, celery, cherry tomatoes and a basket of strawberries. There's a half-filled tub of cream cheese, a block of cheddar, a container of small shrimp, assorted containers of various leftover salads and four thick slices of ham. There's bread and bagels, cookies and muffins. A raspberry cheesecake, two-thirds of a chocolate ganache and a lemon meringue pie. I don't say no to anything.

"I'm buying eggs with the bonus money," I tell Leo. "We'll make an omelette tomorrow morning." A look of worry flashes over his face. He feels sorry for me. Now Anna is also shoving a carton of eggs into one of my bags, ignoring my protests.

"No, no, no," Leo says. "Eggs need to be fresh too. Plus, bonus money is for bonus items like lip gloss and shoes." He turns to Anna for help. She swats his arm with a dishrag and turns to me.

"It's for whatever you need or want it for, sweetheart."

I am embarrassed but it doesn't last long. Out on the wintry streets, walking home with Isabelle, I am all floaty and fine. Whether it's the Baileys, the pocket of money, the bounty of food or a combination of all three, it's a good feeling, one I didn't expect. It feels like Christmas. I can't wait to get back to the apartment and unpack the grocery bags for Jonah.

The apartment is empty but there's a new potted plant in the living room, placed atop a square of gold cloth, silver garland twisted through its leaves. Isabelle places two parcels beside it, one for me and one for Jonah. I want her to open her present before she leaves for her grandparents', but she won't have it.

"You only made the no-opening rule because you know there's no other presents for us Christmas morning," I complain. "You'll have tons of presents and mine will pale in comparison but if you open it now you will be both impressed and pleased."

"I'm waiting," she says, and tucks my gift, wrapped crudely in newspaper, into her knapsack. She blows me a kiss. "See you New Year's."

An omelette is such a good idea, it can't wait. I am pouring the beaten egg mixture in a warm skillet, when Jonah comes home. He watches as I add shrimp, cream cheese, onion and red pepper. "I was going to suggest we go out for all-you-can-eat Chinese, but this looks great," he says.

I cut the omelette in half and dish out Greek salad on the side and we take our plates into the living room. Jonah switches the TV on. *It's a Wonderful Life* is playing. Jimmy Stewart's suicide attempt has been thwarted by Clarence and now Jimmy, George Bailey in the movie, is about to witness what the world would have been like without him. George's extreme and selfish solution to his predicament always irritated me and tonight is no exception. Except tonight, for the first time, I wonder why Dad so loved this movie. Also, if some chubby amateur angel had intervened in Dad's death, would he be disturbed by the vision of the world without him? The vision of Jonah and me sitting on a couch, watching CBC and gobbling down shrimp omelette and Greek salad? Dad always told me not to fear change. Things change, he said, all the time. But sometimes what scares me is how little things change. I get up, I go to bed. I eat and drink and brush my teeth. My birthday, Christmas, come and go. I'll finish school and grow up and become somebody, all without Dad around. Once upon a time growing up and becoming somebody was important. I used to daydream about who I would be in the year 2000. At twenty-nine, that future self might have a profession, or a kid, or a great love affair. Now, it's hard to care. The year 2000 will come and go like all those other birthdays and Christmases and Easters, and in between I'll eat and drink and sleep and still, Dad won't be here.

Does Jonah feel the same? I don't know. Growing up it was easy to guess Jonah's mood — angry, excited, impatient — but he's much more contained now. Most of the time I have no idea what he is feeling and thinking. He gets up, takes both our plates back to the kitchen and toasts a bagel. "You want half?" He offers me the plate when he sits back down, a smudge of butter and crumb glistening his lower lip. I shake my head no and ask if he has ever tried magic mushrooms.

He has. Once before, during his first year of university when he was living in residence. "Would you be interested in trying them again?" I pull the tinfoil package out of Dad's sweatshirt pocket and unwrap it. Inside are two little wrinkled buttons: ugly, grey and smelling faintly of dead earth. "A guy at school gave them to me. They look like scraps of elephant skin."

Jonah picks one up and inspects it, turning it over, raising it to his nose and giving it a good sniff, as if he knows how to determine its quality, which I'm sure he does not. "I'd like to," I say. "Try. But I'm kinda scared."

"Magic mushrooms aren't any more toxic than Aspirin," Jonah says. "The problem is if someone gives you the wrong kind of mushroom. There was a girl at school who almost died from eating a poison mushroom."

"How can you tell the difference?"

Jonah shrugs. "Is the guy who gave it to you trustworthy?"

I think about Donnie, his cinnamon-cigarette lips. "No. Not particularly."

Jonah grunts, still turning the mushroom in his fingers, then says: "We could make a tea."

"Okay." How making a tea solves the issue of Donnie's trustworthiness is unclear but I'm willing to follow Jonah's lead.

It is the worst tea ever, about as appealing as squeezing rainwater out of a pile of rotting autumn leaves and warming it up in a mug. I gag down a first, then second, sip, turning to Jonah who is cautiously slurping.

"It's so gross."

"No pain, no gain," he says, raising his mug in a cheer. "To the long strange trip ahead." We clink cups and swallow it down, mouthful after mouthful, waiting to freak out. But nothing much happens. I put the Beatles' White Album on while Jonah grabs a stack of his computer paper and we attempt to fold the sheets into origami stars, to decorate our broadleaf Christmas plant. We are not successful and the closest we get to a star more accurately resembles a deformed snowball. We move on to animals but at this we are also staggeringly unsuccessful. We make a game of guessing the hybrid origins of our Frankenstein creatures: giraffe-airplane, boy-chair, tree-dog. The paper becomes slippery, the brilliant white atoms mobilize under my fingers to become something more fluid. Part of me knows it is a trick of the mushrooms but suddenly I am manipulating beams of light with my fingers. When Jonah gets up to flip the album over he leaves a silvery-blue trail in his wake.

"Whoa," I say.

"I know, right?" Jonah stands in the middle of the room, laughing.

We abandon our ill-fated origami and explore the apartment with new eyes. The striped shower curtain in the bathroom is a moving rainbow, and the floor, ordinarily a pea-green lino with a chaotic design of black squiggly lines, is alive. The lines emerge from their green backdrop, pulsing in a constant flux that is fascinating right up until the point it is horrifying, wiggle transforming into writhe, more a mass of struggling vicious worms than an animation of the universe. I drag Jonah to the kitchen where the tiled black-and-white chessboard countertops and the black, white and grey lino is safer. We sit on the kitchen floor, leaning into the cupboards, and compare the diamonds and stripes and cloudy grey bits in the floor pattern to rippled potato chips, TV static, bar codes, atomic structures and nimbus clouds. Who knew lino could be so interesting?

I draw a diagram to explain to Jonah how the kitchen is a small island in the sea of an immense black universe, an island in the void, but halfway through sketching it, I realize I have forgotten the initial, critical point, and start laughing.

"What's so funny?" Jonah asks, a question that makes me laugh even harder because I can't remember. "It was funny! It was important!" I shout, but realize I'm trying too hard to be stoned. I am always pretending: to be strong, to be asleep, to be awake. Am I pretending to be stoned too? "Jonah?" I say, and he giggles. He's tipped some coffee grounds on the floor and is making designs. "Remember how Dad would always say, 'Don't worry, just be yourself'? Well, do you ever worry that you're only *pretending* to be yourself?"

"You mean I'm-a-figment-of-my-own-imaginationaphobia?" He laughs and I laugh but this is serious. "Remember Dad's phobia card?" he asks, looking up from his trails of coffee grounds, and I nod. The phobia card was one we discovered when I was about ten or eleven. It stated the story of Phobus, a kind of ace-up-the-sleeve god to ancient Greek armies. If a battle was proving to be too tough, they could give Phobus a call and he would rise up and scare the bejesus out of an opposing army.

"Hippopotomonstrosesquippedaliophobia," Jonah and I say in unison. There had been a list of several phobias, fear of wind, fear of train travel, fear of peanut butter sticking to your mouth, but the two we spent days memorizing and practising how to say were paraskavedekatriaphobia, fear of Friday the thirteenth, and the best and cruellest one, hippopotomonstrosesquippedaliophobia, the fear of long words.

"I have the stack of Dad's cards. Reading them is a little like talking to him," I tell Jonah. The weight of this admission sobers me up and for a panicky moment I worry that Jonah will think I'm crazy.

"I forgot you had those," he says. "Can I see them?"

I stand, a little wobbly on my feet. Is Jonah aware he is asking me to leave the kitchen and enter the void? "Send a search party," I say, "if I don't make it back." Alone in my room, I am distracted momentarily by the beautiful blue of the walls, Isabelle's gift of paint, but I do not linger, returning to the safety of the kitchen, and Jonah, as quickly as possible. "Pick one." I hold the cards fanned out like a magician doing a trick and he chooses one from the centre of the pack.

"Art should cause violence to be set aside," he reads. "Tolstoy." He turns the card over in his hand, then says, "You know, the capital-A art people at school are really pretentious. They all dress in black and the only thing they listen to is the Smiths. I wonder — " he takes a long pause before finishing the sentence, turning the card over and over in his hand. "Last century they said they killed God. Maybe this century they'll kill Art."

I think about this for a moment. "*They* who?" I say. Jonah looks at me, his face blank, as if my question is too stupid for him to understand. "I have no idea," I say, "what you're talking about." For some reason this cracks Jonah up and he laughs so hard he rolls over onto the floor.

"My turn," I say and pick a card. "Alfred Hitchcock," I read, "had no belly button."

This really cracks Jonah up and for a few minutes he is lost to laughter. It's been a long time since I've seen him this happy. "I'm picking another." My new card is older than the rest, dog-eared and with a circle of coffee stain looping through the words. I read it aloud even though Jonah's laughing too hard to hear anything. "When you change the way you look at things, the things you look at change. Max Planck."

Jonah stops laughing, sits up and asks me to repeat it, which I do. He takes the card from my hand and turns it over, his dark, almost black eyes bright and focussed. His skin is so pale and translucent I swear I can see the blood moving underneath, thin veins congregating in the dark purple smudges beneath his eyes. "I remember talking to Dad about this one," he says. "Max Planck is a physicist." He gets up and leaves the room. I don't know if he is coming back.

He might not. This happens. This happens all the time. People are here one minute and the next they are gone and you never see them again. It is the most terrible and most true thing about being alive. It's enough to break your heart. If Jonah doesn't come back it will break my heart.

But he does. "What's wrong?" He drops down beside me, the heavy book he's holding slamming into the lino.

"Nothing," I lie.

"You're holding your heart, you're white as a ghost and your eyes are big as saucers. Hey? Are you crying?" He tugs my hands from my chest and holds them. His hands are chapped from dishwashing duties at the Falafel Hut, but the fingers are long and elegant. Artist's hands, Dad used to say.

"No, I'm not crying." I pull my hands back and sit up straight. "Sorry. I got thinking. That's all. Sal says I think too much."

"Sal's one to talk," Jonah says. He pushes the book, *Known Elements,* toward me. "He gave me this, one time when I was visiting with Dad." I flip through, happy for the distraction. Each page is a visual representation of every known atom in the universe, along with quirky facts and explanations to how each was discovered and named. My favourites are the colourful ones like bismuth, large crystals cooling in a shimmering rainbow, or the thick violet vapour of evaporating iodine. How long we are lost in the book I can't say but when I next look up it reads twenty after twelve on the clock.

"Santa's halfway through his rounds," I say.

"Oh my God," Jonah says. "I totally forgot your birthday."

"Yeah. You're going to have to double up next year."

"Oh my God. I suck."

"Yup. But it's okay." I punch him in the arm, but he doesn't retaliate. He buries his head in his hands, groaning.

"I can't believe I forgot," he says. "Dad would kill me."

"No, he wouldn't. Dad would understand. Plus, I didn't feel like celebrating anything. It's not a big deal. C'mon." I get to my feet, watching as Jonah massages his temples with his long-fingered artist hands.

"I'm tired," he says, "but I don't know if I can sleep."

"C'mon." I prod him with my toe and then grab a hand, pulling him to his feet. We return to the living room and turn on the radio. Q107 is taking requests. After a gazillion attempts, we finally get through and request they play T. Rex's "Mambo Sun," which they do. We turn the radio up loud and dance around and when it's over we go to bed.

I drift off immediately into a restless sleep. I dream I am trying to tell Jonah a story but the story won't co-operate: the plot lines are tangled, the characters, rebellious and dissenting. I struggle to unravel it, scattershot thoughts bumping back and forth through the hinged gate separating sleep and waking and finally, for one sweet moment, I succeed: the story is perfectly whole and complete. But then I am falling through the gate again, falling deeper into sleep. I hang onto the story so it's there when I wake in the morning, but only briefly, only an imprint in my mind, disappearing fast like one of those subatomic elements that decay the very instant they're created, leaving nothing but trace particles behind.

Trace particles that transform and reconfigure into the heavenly smell of fresh, hot coffee urging me down the hall to the kitchen. Jonah's already up and he's brewed an extra-big pot, arranged a plate of strawberries and treats from the bakery, and hung a string of small white Christmas lights around the perimeter of the living room. Christmas morning. Even though last night's high is gone, the presence of a vast and continuous void has remained. It is present in the extra-attentive way Jonah greets me, and the way I reciprocate; it's present in our hypervigilant focus on small details — a warming sip of coffee, a buttery crunch of cookie, the sunshine burst of fresh strawberry — as if by concentrating exclusively on each other and the present moment we can drown out the echoing silence of the ghost of Christmas past. Jonah refills our coffee cups as I carry the plate of cookies and fruit into the living room and we settle on the floor in front of our Christmas plant. There's a mystery box wrapped in a patchwork of newspaper and addressed to both of us, with love from Santa, but Jonah says I have to wait to open it last.

We take our time, fleshing out the thinness of the morning with an extravagant demonstration of pleasure for every small gesture or gift. Jonah loves his T-shirt, or at least he says he does, and he takes off his pyjama top and puts it on before opening the Paul Simon album, which he also loves. I make him play a few tracks, "Late in the Evening" and "Ace in the Hole," and we sing along before moving on to Isabelle's presents, which are gorgeously batiked T-shirts that she made in art class. Mine is a big grey elephant waving a party hat in his trunk. Jonah's is a monkey wearing specs and reading a fat book. Both are amazing. The small package from Jonah to me is an elegant black journal filled with beautiful unlined pages and a green pen, and the mystery box, which Jonah finally lets me open, is our skates. Jonah arranged for Mrs. Turner to go into the garage, pack up our skates and mail them. "I thought we could go skating," Jonah says. "We can play Shimminey."

"The dumbest game ever?" I say. "Awesome."

Shimminey is Jonah's age-seven version of shinny, a game he had heard about but never played. Basically you kick a rock around with your skate, sometimes to the other player, sometimes away. There are no rules and nobody ever scores or wins. It's not quite nine thirty when we leave the house wearing a double layer of clothes and carrying our skates, walking all the way to city hall. The air is icy but the sun is shining and the sky is such a bright colour of blue that you can't help but think of spring flowers. The city is so quiet it is easy to imagine Jonah and I are the only ones out on the street, part of the void, yes, but also in on a secret: Christmas is happening behind every closed door we pass. We lace up at city hall and spend an hour skating in fast circles. There are no rocks but Jonah practises speeding up and then stopping in a spray of ice and skating backwards across the rink, and I practise the tricks Julie and I once knew: spins, spirals, shoot the duck, but which now end with me sliding across the ice on my butt. When we leave, Jonah gives five bucks to a guy who looks like he has permanently settled into a park bench, a guy who, despite being cold and dirty, appears totally at home in the void, and who says, "Thanks! And Merry Christmas, you skating bunnies!" Jonah has enough money to buy hot chocolates but everything is closed, so we make cocoa and mix it with more coffee back at the apartment before we wrap up the raspberry cheesecake and make our way to Sal's cramped kitchen for Christmas dinner.

It's late enough in the afternoon that there are families out in the park when we pass through, parents holding hands while their kids scream and race around trying out bright new toboggans and magic carpets. There's even one kid, a fat little sparrow, wobbling around on snowshoes. The black-and-white mutt is weaving back and forth across the path ahead of us, thin icicles clumping the long hair around his tail and muzzle. "That dog is always here," I say to Jonah. "I don't think he has a home." I reach into the bag, scoop out a dollop of cheesecake and bend down on one knee. "Here boy. C'mon here. It's good, good to eat." The mutt looks at me over his shoulder, then moves to a garbage can, lifts a leg and pees for an exceptionally long time, a warm mist rising off the cold metal. He criss-crosses in front of us twice, nonchalant, coming a little closer each time. "C'mon boy. You'll like it." He lifts his nose in the air and sniffs and then reaches forward with his head, then tongue, to nimbly lick at my out-stretched fingers. "There's a boy," I croon. "Good boy."

"Easy, Lou," Jonah says. "He's not coming home with us."

The dog steps a little closer to finish the last smudges of cheesecake but pulls away when I reach out to pat his head, trotting off toward the tennis courts. "He seems like an *M* name to me. Marshall? Or maybe Merlin? Merlin the Mutt. I'd bring him home, if he'd come with me. Did you see his face? It's frozen. He shouldn't be out in this kind of weather."

Jonah smiles and sighs, both at the same time, and shakes his head at me. "You're right. He does look like a Merlin."

Christmas à la Sal is a lean and squalid affair. His apartment is over the bookstore, and is exactly how I imagined it, dirty and decrepit and crawling with cats. Courtney, his pocket kitten, is there, now a long-limbed adolescent jumping into my lap, her orange triangle of a face thinner but still sweet. Brazen and slinky, a tractor-sized purr rattling her thin bones, she climbs onto my shoulder and nuzzles into my hair. A platter of sliced deli turkey rolled into cylinders filled with canned cranberry sauce, a large bowl of warm mashed potatoes and a smaller bowl of cold peas are the centrepiece to Sal's kitchen table, set for three. It is obvious that Sal has taken some time to lay the food out but it is equally obvious that this is the first time he's ever done this. He usually showed up at our house over Christmas. I appreciate his effort but, honestly, I want to leave as soon as we get there. This is the kind of place where the cracks and fissures of the void lie near the surface and any moment they could open like the San Andreas fault and swallow us whole. Sal is weepy with Scotch, the bottle half gone, and one of his many cats, Snoopy, smells as if it is dying. Snoopy is a tumbleweed of matted toffee-coloured hair and Sal dotes on him, feeding him tiny bits of canned cat food with his pinky finger throughout the afternoon. It's heartbreaking, really, the set table, the turkey rolls, the beloved rotting cat. O sad and beautiful world.

I force myself to eat a big bowl of potatoes and a big slice of cheesecake and then make eyes at Jonah. He sees my look and nods. "Presents, Sal," I say. "And then we have to leave."

"Presents!" Sal is flustered. He lights a cigarette, mumbles, puts the cigarette in the ashtray, leaves the room, returns with three grocery bags, then lights a second cigarette.

"Two cigarettes, Sal? Are you crazy? Sit down and open this." I pass him his present, almost regretting getting him anything. It's brutal to witness his embarrassment. He alternates one cigarette with the other and fumbles with the tape, as if worried he might rip the paper. "It's newspaper, Sal. Just tear it open!" A prolonged silence falls as he unwraps the tea tray, creamer and sugar bowl, holding and turning each in his hands before placing them carefully on the table. He pulls the magazines out of the plastic bag and looks over each one, slowly reading the titles and flipping through the pages. It's only the mewling cats, Sal's ticking clock and distant sirens that fill the silence. Jonah looks at me, opening his eyes extra wide and I start to laugh.

"Sal!" Jonah passes him a second package and the agonizing unwrapping process begins all over again, finally revealing a biography of Jack Kerouac.

"Guys," Sal says, all choked up. It's horrible.

"We gotta get going, Sal," I say. "Thanks for dinner."

"Wait," he says. "These are for you. I didn't wrap them." He hands Jonah the *Collected Works of Pablo Neruda* and me, the *Collected Works of*

William Carlos Williams. Next he pulls out a VCR, a stack of movies and, from the last bag, a popcorn maker, a pound of butter and a bag of no-name popping corn. It is a weird selection of movies: *The Goodbye Girl* and *Jaws; Stand by Me* and *Close Encounters of the Third Kind.* Then I realize the common denominator.

"Richard Dreyfuss," I say. "Thanks, Sal."

He shrugs. "Someone dropped them off at the store and I knew I'd never sell them, so — " There is a catch in Sal's voice and for a moment I am scared he's going to cry but he rallies. "Merry Christmas, kids."

"Merry Christmas." Jonah hugs Sal, patting his shoulder with a forced heartiness. Then it's my turn, Sal stiffly wrapping his arms across my back. Up close, the smell of dying cat is even worse. Jonah gathers the VCR and movies and I grab the books and popcorn maker and then, thankfully, we are outside in the clean cold air.

Back at home I make popcorn and peppermint tea while Jonah sets up the VCR and we settle in to watch a marathon of movies. In between *Stand by Me* and *Jaws,* Jonah throws a handful of popcorn at my head.

"We made it," he says and I see he was as worried about Christmas as I was.

"Yes." I pick popcorn kernels out of my hair and return fire. "We made it."

Part 2

10

Zane's is practically empty. There are instruments set up on stage but no sign of Finn's band. Sal is at the bar and at the closest table are four old guys in army uniforms, one in an ancient wheelchair. Behind the bar Shelley darts around, polishing and lining up glasses, setting out clean ashtrays. She's wearing an orange jumper and one of those paper crowns you get from a Christmas cracker, a purple one, very royal, and by some holiday magic it remains glued to her head despite the flurry of activity. Jonah takes stock of the scene and then moves toward the table closest to the pool table, which also happens to be the one farthest away from Sal.

"He reaches a certain point of drunkenness," Jonah says, before either Isabelle or I comment on his rudeness. "And he starts crying and talking about Dad. I'm done dealing with it. At least for tonight."

"Fair enough," I say. Jonah fielded a weepy two a.m. call from Sal the day after Boxing Day. It woke both of us but only Jonah couldn't get back to sleep. Sal called to apologize the next morning but Jonah refused to talk to him. "I'll go over and say hi."

Sal is reading the year-in-review edition of the newspaper. He looks up and over his shoulder, noting Jonah's distance, as I slide onto the stool beside him.

"Jonah still mad?"

"Yep."

"I should never be left alone with a bottle of Scotch."

"Nope."

Sal grunts and turns back to his paper, handing me the section he's finished with, a roundup of the last year. I remember some of the top stories from Sunday-morning newspaper reads with Dad: Chet Baker, the jazz musician, fell out the window of his second-floor apartment in Amsterdam and died. The Oilers smashed Boston to win the Stanley Cup. Canadian Ben Johnson, fastest man alive, busted for steroid use. It wasn't so long ago that all that happened, and I was sitting around reading newspapers with Dad, but it feels like a lifetime ago.

The front-page news is monopolized by the details of a terrorist bombing that happened before Christmas. A 747 exploded in the air above a small town in Scotland, parts of the plane and parts of passengers scattering in the streets and in people's yards. One man found a dead boy on his front doorstep. Sal cradles his puffy head in his hands. "Most of the people were still strapped into their seats, alive, when they hit the ground."

I reach for the scattered sections of newsprint and refold them more or less into their original shape. "I'm confiscating this," I tell Sal. "It's not helping." I point to the tumbler full of amber liquid and melting ice cubes. "Neither is that, by the way."

Sal tips the glass back and swallows the contents in one long gulp. "You're right," he says, standing and pulling on his coat. "I'm going home."

I'm disappointed. Secretly, I was looking forward to him rambling on about past New Year's he spent cavorting with Dad. Did they ever spend a New Year's here at Zane's? Why did Dad never tell me about his secret girlfriend, Jillian Nash? I was going to wait until Sal was medium-drunk and make him give me a straight answer. I follow him toward the exit but before I can ask my questions he's stopped by the old, skinny, caesar-drinking cowboy and his lady friend.

"Sal!" The cowboy punches playfully at Sal's shoulder and Sal steps back, bumping into me. "Where you going, man? The evening is just getting started."

"Roger. Marie." Sal goes through the motions of introducing us. "This is my … Dan's kid … Lou. I'll see you all in the new year." Sal bulldozes past without even a backward glance or wave in Jonah's direction.

"He's not usually so upright going out that door," Marie says, laughing. She winks one of her spidery clumps of eyelashes at me, and I think about the graffiti in the women's washroom (*Marie L is a total cunt. Call her for a good time*) as several questions best left unasked pop unbidden into my mind. I smile, step back toward the stools, turn, and slam into someone's shoulder. It's Finn. He's knocked off balance too.

"Lou," he says, hand rubbing his shoulder. "That was some collision."

"Yeah," I say, dumbstruck. Finn's not much taller than me, not nearly as tall or as lean as Jonah. A compact, barely contained energy radiates from him. I want to reach up and touch his shoulder because, somehow, the contact has changed me. Finn and the bar around us shift into sharper focus as all my molecules rearrange themselves, vibrate at a higher, faster frequency, a flashback to Christmas Eve, to the mushroom high. Finn's lips are at my eye level. I could kiss him. Right now. Tractor beams pull me toward him, toward those kissable lips, but as I lean in, he steps a little to the left, revealing two girls standing with him. Both are wearing short skirts and high heels, their ankles thin and bare in the dressy shoes. Finn makes introductions: the girl with the shaved head and the dangly hoop earrings is Rebecca and the prettier one, the one with the long straight flaxen hair and pouty rose-petal lips, is Sophia, his girlfriend.

"Sophia," I say, leaning back into a stool. "Like the capital of Bulgaria." It's a joke but nobody laughs. Donnie slides onto the stool behind me so that, with no adjustment, I am leaning into the crook of his shoulder. "Hey," I say. He smells like cigarette smoke and aftershave and winter air and I am surprised by how pleased I am to see him.

"Hey," he says, and wraps his arm around my shoulder.

"You sticking around for the show?" Finn asks.

"Of course," I say, not bothering to introduce Donnie. Finn nods and then crosses the room to the door at the left of the stage, the girls following behind. In high heels, Rebecca's legs are wobbly as a foal's but Sophia's stride is easy and certain.

"So who's my competition?" Donnie asks.

I don't answer. Across the room, Jonah and Isabelle are deep in conversation, their knees angled toward one another, a feather's distance apart, so close they almost but not quite touch. A few tables away, Donnie's brother and his friend are sitting with a heavyset bearded man. "What are *they* doing here?"

"They have a line on some acid."

"I thought that was your domain."

"I'm a grunt, I just sell it. I don't broker the deals." Donnie angles himself to block my view, his mouth near my ear. "Don't worry about those guys. Let's get out of here. We'll have a smoke."

It's freezing outside. Donnie drapes his coat over my shoulders as we walk around the corner and lean against the side of the building. He gives me a cigarette and then holds up a lighter, the flame dancing. A tentative pull on the cigarette fills my mouth with the taste of ash and I talk quickly to cover the choking, spluttery sensation in my chest. "What's that guy's name? Your brother's friend?"

"Business partner. Kevin."

"Kevin what?"

Donnie takes a long drag and looks at me sideways before answering. "Morris. Kevin Morris. Why? You don't want anything to do with those guys."

"He told me his name was something else. That's all. I don't want to have anything to do with those guys." I take another little smoky puff. "I don't think you should have anything to do with those guys."

"Don't worry about me." He flicks his cigarette, the flurry of sparks fizzing out when it lands in the wet snow. He takes my cigarette and does the same. "It's painful watching you try to smoke that," he says and then kisses me. It starts more gently than the first kiss but quickly becomes less gentle, his hands sliding in opposite directions, down my jeans, up my shirt, cold fingers quickly heating up, my hands on his shoulders, then reaching for his sharp-boned hips. We are abruptly interrupted by a shout of "Hey! Dickwad!" and Donnie steps back, adjusting his sweatshirt. "That's me." Around the corner step his brother and Kevin Morris.

"C'mon!" Donnie's brother lifts both his hands in the air. "Bring your girlie with us."

"She's busy," Donnie says.

"I can't," I say, passing him his coat.

"Fucked if I care," Kevin Morris says, sliding into the driver's seat of his Nissan. "Get the fuck in. Now." Donnie waves but doesn't say anything. The car doors slam and they drive off.

Neither Jonah nor Isabelle noticed my absence. They both lean back in their chairs, away from each other, when I sit down. "Who were those girls with Finn?" Isabelle asks.

"Groupies," I say.

"Smart play, giving him space," Iz says. She turns to Jonah. "I call her play-it-cool Lou."

"You have never called me that," I say.

"Beer?" Jonah lifts the pitcher. "Here, I'll pour. So you like this guy?"

"Shut up," I say. "I can pour for myself."

"No you can't," Jonah says, handing me a glass. "Half of the pitcher always ends up on the table when you pour and we're broke. No beer wasting allowed."

"Did you see Sal left?" I say and take a sip. "You ran him out with your deafening silence."

"Good."

"Good? This is, like, the only place the guy goes for fun."

"That singer is a bit old for you, don't you think?"

"You're a bit old, don't you think?"

Silence. It rolls up like a thick fog, an isolating weather front that takes time to pass. Around us the bar has gotten busy. Shelley and her minions fly around the room taking orders and delivering drinks. More veterans have arrived. A crowd of them is concentrated at the table by the bar, men and women, all in uniforms, as if it's Remembrance Day. The old guy bangs his glass on the tray attached to the front of his ancient wheelchair and then holds it out to Shelley for a refill.

There's a more-than-usual number of people closer to my age here tonight, friends of the band, I'm guessing, but I spot several regulars in the crowd too. Red Randy Rocket is sitting at a crowded table near the back and Marie and Roger are prancing around in full New Year's regalia: he's wearing a baby-blue, wide-lapelled suit, the sort Jimmy Page used to wear, and she's wearing a frilly dress of salmon pink and cream and, I swear to God, there's an actual crinoline puffing out the skirt, all fancy milkmaid-meets-polka princess. They are as colourful as the frosting on a grocery store cake and both have caesars in hand, as per usual. Did Dad ever bring Jillian Nash to Zane's? It's apparent from the familiar way Sal introduces me as Dan's kid that Dad hung out here and knew these people: Shelley, Randy, Marie and Roger. They were a part of his life I knew nothing about.

Shelley, an unusually sour look on her face, comes by to ask if we want anything before the band begins to play. "If so, get it now, because those vets are running me off my feet. I'd like to turf those bastards out," she says. "This ain't no Legion."

"No," Jonah says. "It's the Lesion."

"Ha ha," Shelley says, tapping her foot.

"It's gangrenous," Iz says.

"We'll have another pitcher," I say. I'm buying. I still have more than half my bonus money left.

"Pus-y," Jonah says.

"Infectious."

"Suppurating." Jonah and Iz crack up, laughing. They must already be a little drunk.

"Hey Shelley, were you here the night Neil Young played?" Isabelle asks.

"Sure." Shelley places her hands on her hips and strikes a Wonder Woman pose, purple crown comically crooked. "Me and his drummer messed around in the band room."

"Messed around?" Isabelle is incredulous.

"Sure. Boffed, banged, monkeyed, messed around." Shelley winks at me and rolls her shoulders, an attempt at lasciviousness that is all wrong. "We had sex," she says with a calculated shrug implying no biggie, it happens all the time. She winks again before moving onto an adjacent table.

"Was she kidding?" Isabelle asks. "I mean, really, was she kidding?" In unison Jonah and I shrug our shoulders at the impossibility of answering her question, a gesture likely embedded in the DNA we received from Dad. He had a very distinct, expressive shrug.

Finn and his band have stepped onstage and are tweaking strings, flipping switches, their amps crackling into electric life, a power surge that extends out into the room and incites the buzz of conversation around us to rise in pitch and volume. Finn interrupts, and excites, the charged atmosphere by leaning into the mike and shouting: "Happy New Year's, Zane's!" The audience cheers in response as the drummer plays an extended, showy roll, ending with a toss and catch of his sticks, and then the three of them bust into their breakneck version of Dylan's "Subterranean Homesick Blues," the one I heard at sound check so long ago. The dance floor fills quickly, Jonah and Isabelle joining the crowd, neither of them glancing in my direction. I stay at the table, muttering the lyrics along with Finn and drinking my beer.

Finn doesn't make the mistake of trying to sing like Bob Dylan. His own voice is strong, distinct, and he sings with enough abandon the crowd on the dance floor goes a little wild. Marie and Roger do a crazy coordinated jitterbug in their corner. Jonah does a kind of restrained cool-guy sway but every now and then his elbows go all hee-haw and his knees and butt spaz out in opposite directions. Isabelle does a fast-stepping, skippy jumping-bean dance. Sophia, Finn's girlfriend, moves with a kind of insistent, hypnotic rhythm and after a few minutes of watching, it's easy to imagine that it's her, her curvy motion, that is setting the tempo, driving the beat. It's as if the music takes its cues from her. She dances awfully close to a tall, lean, soul-patched dude, which is interesting. I watch her and I watch Finn watching her. Very interesting.

The set is a good mix of originals and covers. Finn sings about someone being shipwrecked three storeys above ground, describing a heroin overdose, maybe, and I hear anguish in his voice, and love. Another song he dedicates to all the pigeons that die after slamming into the tall glass buildings of the city. The band rocks out a cover of the Stones' "Monkey Man" and then seamlessly transitions into an extended version of Jimi Hendrix's

"Manic Depression." It's intense and afterwards Finn drains a glass of water and announces that their friend Red is going to sing a few songs. He steps offstage as Red bumps through the crowded dance floor and I decide now would be a good time to get a glass of water at the bar.

I time it perfectly. I am just turning around as Finn arrives and orders a beer from Shelley. Onstage Red launches into his signature train song.

"Hey," I say.

"Hey," Finn says. "You're not up dancing?" He slides onto a bar stool and I do the same.

"I'm listening," I say. "I'll dance later."

"Yeah? How does it sound? Levels okay?"

"Yeah. Sure. I think. I liked the song about the pigeons."

Finn laughs. He sips his beer, his attention turning to the dance floor. Sophia and her soul-patched dancing partner are closer and curvier than before.

"She's mad at me," Finn says.

"Yeah?"

"She says I said someone else's name when we were fucking." Finn glances my way. "Sorry," he says.

"It's okay," I say. "Did you?"

"No. That's the crazy thing. I know for sure I didn't."

"That's weird."

"Tell me about it. I mean, she's dead certain, so one of us is delusional, right?"

"Or both of you," I say. "At exactly the same time."

Finn smiles. "She says she's not mad I said it, she's mad I'm denying it. But I know I didn't say anything."

"That is very, very weird."

"Yep. Well," Finn gulps down the rest of his beer, "back to the grind-stone."

Several questions arise in my mind after this conversation, none of which I am able to answer, but I am sufficiently energized by this exchange that come the second set I am ready, joints oiled with a little alcohol, to hit the dance floor with Jonah and Isabelle. I close my eyes and concentrate on the music. It is perhaps another leftover sensation from the Christmas mushroom buzz but in my mind's eye the music transforms into a silver thread that snakes up my spine so I am connected to both the steady rhythm of the drumbeat and the scaffold of notes that Finn builds, higher and higher, when he solos. I am tied to it all by a single, brilliant silver thread and for a moment everything makes perfect sense. Until Shelley storms the dance floor and hollers for everyone to shush up, effectively breaking the spell.

"It's time," she says, one knobbly finger jabbing at her watch. She leads the crowd in a New Year's countdown — ten, nine, eight — arms waving like a maestro, her purple crown radically askew but still, valiantly, holding on. As the clock strikes twelve and shouts of "happy new year" ring out, everyone reaches for someone to kiss. Roger grabs Marie. Finn steps off the stage and pulls Sophia into his arms. Isabelle and Jonah kiss for real. Only Shelley and I have no one to kiss. It's like a game of musical lips and we're both getting kicked out this round.

"Maybe next year, kiddo," she says and punches me in the shoulder on her way past. The crowd belches out a spontaneous and sloppy version of "Auld Lang Syne" as I back toward our table. One of the veterans over by the bar raises his glass for a toast.

"God save the Queen," he shouts.

"The Queen?" The shaky old guy in the wheelchair is agitated. The brakes must be locked down on his chair because he thrashes hard enough to send it spinning in every direction. "THE QUEEN?!" He's so mad he's spitting. "GOD SAVE THE QUEEN?!" The gnarled hand holding the mug punches the air with each word, liquid splashing everywhere. "*FUCK THE QUEEN!*" He crumples over the tray, sobbing, shoulders shaking, his mug tumbling to the floor.

But no one seems to notice buddy's breakdown. People are calling for drinks and still making toasts. Finn is back onstage and the band plays a slow song, "Time After Time," the Cyndi Lauper pop hit. Not one I would have imagined in the band's list of covers but it sounds beautiful the way Finn sings it. All the kissers sway-step, arms around one another. Roger and Marie, Jonah and Isabelle. Sophia is in the arms of the soul-patched dude but she's looking at Finn now. Roger and Marie expand their sway to a few well-executed steps. Marie lays back for a dip. All night long their moves have been getting riskier, more adventuresome, but neither of them ever cracks a smile. Dancing is serious business, their bodies say. It strikes me that they are wearing the clothes they will be buried in. I wish Sal were here so I could tell him that, make him see the picture the way I do. He's the only one I could say it to who would understand. To anyone else I'm sure it would sound morbid, and not at all as happy, or at least less unhappy, as it makes me feel. I'm ready, for what I don't know, but ready at least. I throw back the last of my beer, put on my coat and leave.

I head east on Queen toward the park. The street is quiet but in the far-off distance car horns honk and music spills from open windows. Somewhere in the city is a circle of bright, loud light but here, on this deserted strip of street, I am far outside of it. So. Jonah and Isabelle are officially an item. I have been expecting this to happen since I moved to the city, so why am I now so shocked and appalled? Preoccupied with itemizing all the reasons why this is a terrible turn of events, I almost trip over an indistinct crumpled bulk blocking the sidewalk. It's Stella; she's lying on her back, staring up at the stars. When she sees me she starts singing.

"You were standing by the bus stop, you were a good girl and it felt so good to have your body close to mine because I'm on a jet plane, root-toot-tootsie goodbye! Everybody sing along! Everybody join the music — "

"Stella?" She stops singing but otherwise doesn't seem to register my voice. "Stella? It isn't safe to stay here, Stella. What can I do?"

She doesn't answer, slowly uncrumpling herself from the cement and sitting up. A small stone stays pressed in the skin above her left temple and she raises her hand to brush it away.

"Should I call an ambulance?"

Her eyes focus for a moment on my face and then drift away, scanning the road and the buildings beside her. A tremor rattles her head and shoulders and she moves her torso counter-clockwise in a taut, jerking loop. Her hand reaches to her mouth, smearing a trail of blood that has trickled over her lips from her nose. Then she points at me. "Are you a hunter?"

"No," I say.

"You've got the whole world," she says, "in your hands." She sneezes and droplets of blood and phlegm spray in an arc around her, the nosebleed flowing, large splotches of blood staining her dirty blue coat. Movement rustles the shadows along the corner of the building as Merlin the Mutt emerges and trots across the street, ignoring both of us. "There's soap," Stella says, "that smells like oranges."

She means at the bakery. Anna bought hand dispensers and filled them with a sweet orange-scented soap. Stella's bottom lip is swelling. A fat lip, the kind you'd get from a punch in the face. "Stella? Did somebody hurt you?"

"Those bad boys, seize her, seize her," she says.

"Who was it? What did they look like?"

"Oh, them. Double double." She's placing an order for a coffee. Maybe she thinks she's at the bakery.

"I'll be right back." I run as fast as I can to Legacy Variety. The big Friar Tuck guy, Desmond, is working. I pour two coffees and grab a handful of cream, sugar and napkins. At the counter I add ten chocolate icy squares.

"Happy," Desmond says, as he punches the prices into the till, peeking out at me, "New Year's."

"Yeah," I say. Dude's so shy he's making me embarrassed. Plus, I'm in a rush. I grab my change and sprint back down the sidewalk. Stella is still sitting by the curb. I hand her a coffee and she carefully stirs in four packs of sugar and then opens a creamer, a fleck of blood immediately splotting the surface of the thick white liquid. I pass her a wad of napkins. "This is for your nose. It's bleeding."

Stella ignores my statement of the obvious and drinks her coffee. When it's done, she reaches for her grocery bags and the few items that have spilled out and then hands them to me.

"Do you want to go to the hospital?" I stand up with her bags. "Do you want me to call an ambulance?" No answer, just a grunting noise as she struggles to find her balance, finally managing to get up on all fours. When I reach my hand down she grabs it, almost pulling me back to the curb with the effort of hauling herself upright.

"Come on," she says, and waves like royalty, as if I'm a bellboy at a hotel carting luggage to her room.

"Where we going?"

"Queenston," she says and trundles down the street.

I trail behind with the bags. We head east on Queen and on the block past the hospital Stella weaves across the road to the south side of the street. We pass the deserted candy factory, a huge, spooky, boarded-up building. Isabelle and I often joke about the Oompa Loompas that live there and how one day we'll get the golden ticket that will allow us to visit the fabulous inside where we will sip from a river of chocolate and eat licorice that grows on trees.

Stella marches on at a steady pace, passing a smashed storefront window, a red ribbon sign, Liquidation Sale, dangling from the pane. Broken glass litters both sides of the window frame like a carpet of dirty, crunchy diamonds. Inside, a snoring man wrapped in a sleeping bag lies in a large cardboard box, the ends of his dark matted hair a-twinkle with slivers of glass. A half a block farther and Stella stops under a sign that reads Queenston Arms Furnished Rooms. We're out front of a crappy old building, the dark brown paint of the window frames peeling in long slivered strips, and even though the neon sign in the window blinks OPEN, the front door is locked. Stella mumbles something about a shrubby hedge and a maze, an amazing maze. I decide to bang on the door. It takes about three minutes of straight banging before a woman dressed in turquoise stretch pants and matching top answers the door. "Stella!" she says. "It's late!"

"It's New Year's Eve," I say, only because it's the first thing that comes into my mind. "Is there some kind of curfew?" Stella pushes past the woman into a narrow hallway and I follow.

"Stella!" the woman says, ignoring me, her lips stiff, dog-teeth bared. "Who is this?" Stella mentions the hedge again and the amazing maze.

"I'm her niece. Lou."

"Stella! I didn't know you had any family." This woman talks in the condescending tones of nurse to naughty child and I don't like her at all.

"I just moved to town," I say, trying to sound tough. "I'll be around a lot more."

A door halfway down the hallway opens into a small room with a rickety desk, a filing cabinet, an old brown plaid couch and a TV, volume blasting, tuned to celebrations in Times Square. The top half of the door is a shuttered window with a large ledge, which must serve as a kind of check-in counter when it's closed. Stella walks past to a metal door at the back of the hallway that opens onto a steep, poorly lit flight of stairs, the stark light from a bare bulb casting odd-angled shadows. Moving slowly, she lifts one foot and then the other, both joining at each step. At the top of the stairs she turns down a hallway painted a dull dirt colour, an exact and flooding shade of despair. The walls breathe out a stinging vinegary whiff of urine, which mingles with several other competing bad smells: dirty shoes and stale smoke and the evil creamy scent of vegetables about to ferment. There is an oily black trail down the hall, the path made, I imagine, by the scurrying, faithless feet of rats. We pass the open door of a communal bathroom. Water drips from rusty pipes. Damp, chipped and mouldy, it is a bathroom designed with suicide in mind. Behind the walls, rats chirp and squeak and scratch like a hidden, grounded flock of birds.

Stella's room is painted the same terminal beige of the hallway only it's darker and dirtier, and the room is crammed full of her treasure. Aside from a small army cot, the space is filled with papers, purses with broken clasps, string. Stacks of coupons for grocery store items and slices of pizzas and pamphlets for diaper delivery services and mutual fund investments line the walls along with towers of business cards and empty pop bottles. The surface of a small desk is covered with books, torn and water-stained, album covers and a radio, missing the volume dial and the cover to keep the batteries in place. And finally, on Stella's neatly made-up cot, there's an oversized bear bleeding white stuffing from an inch-long gash in his side, wearing the baby-blue hat, mitten and scarf set I gave her for Christmas.

"Home," Stella says. She sits on the floor to pull off her boots, one leg bent toward her body and the other, now free of its boot, splayed open. She isn't wearing socks and her pants bunch up toward her knee, exposing the skin of her foot, ankle and calf. There are several deep ulcers that look raw, pulpy and infected. The dark purple of her veins swells and bruises the pale white skin, splits the skin. It is horrifying. I want to close my eyes, look away. I want to not have seen it.

I breathe in and there is a new smell of something rotting, sweet and corrupt. A sickly smell. I put the plastic bags on the floor.

"Well," I say, looking up. The dried clot of blood on her upper lip looks like some malignant blister or a feeding insect, its shell dark and cracked. I am exhausted. "Well, I better be going."

"Here," she says, and hands me a spool of thread.

The turquoise woman is back on the plaid couch, TV blaring. "Happy new year," I say, stomping past. "You old cow," I add, at the door, but not so loud that she could hear me over the TV, chickenshit that I am.

Outside, I take a moment to orient myself. Across the street lies the park, the dark corner shadows an inky absence of light, soft and dark and violent. I don't know where to go. Back to Zane's? Downtown? The apartment? It is a pointless line of questioning as I have been unequivocally defeated by this night. The only place I am fit to go is back to bed, to wait for another, hopefully better day than this one. Across the street, a pure-white squirrel darts out of the shadows and into the beam of the street lamp. He's difficult to see against the white of the snow and afterwards, on the long walk to the apartment, I'm not sure if my eyes deceived me.

At home, I pull on my pyjamas and Dad's sweatshirt and crawl into bed but I'm still awake when Jonah and Isabelle come home. "Her boots are here. She's here," Jonah says, and then they stop speaking. The strain to make sense of their shuffling, whispery, giggling noises soon shifts into the strain of *not* making sense as they move from the hallway to Jonah's bedroom.

I cover my head with a pillow, switch on my Walkman and listen to Rufus' tape. It's at the beginning, so it's Bowie singing "Five Years." Where was Rufus tonight? Who did he kiss at midnight? I have a few guesses — either Jenn or Rochelle would love the chance to kiss Rufus — but I don't want to think about that and I don't want to think about Finn or Donnie either. I distract myself by thinking about the squirrel. Do white squirrels even exist? Could it have been a ghost of a squirrel? Maybe it was an albino squirrel, a freak of nature. Or maybe it was just a bushy-tailed rat.

New Year's Day I wake with a raw, sharp-edged throat, achy bones and a headache that turns into a fever by the late afternoon. I make a brief attempt to rise but quickly abandon the wavy pain of real life to return to bed and my jumbled world of dreams. There, Dad is trying to visit. He calls on the phone to tell me something important but I can't make out what it is. Isabelle and Jonah and Rufus and Sal and Stella and Anna and Leo are all making too much noise. Mrs. Turner is there, and the cop that came to the house after Dad died. Officer Wood, or is it Detective Phillips, the one that came to Zane's? I tell them to be quiet but they won't listen. I try to find a quiet room but the house won't stay battened down. Doors do not reliably lead to the same room each time they are opened, balconies are built off bathrooms, attics are built, impossibly, over balconies. Thick jungle vines grow in through the hole in the ceiling, and tables, ornately set, are surrounded by crumbling brick walls. Outside is the void. Inside, the crowd of people finds me wherever I go. What? I shout into the phone to Dad. What did you say? I can't hear you.

And then he is there, in my dream, and then here, in my room, standing by my desk and looking for his notebook. I call out but he doesn't hear me. Jonah leaves water and a bottle of Tylenol by my bed but I don't take them, worried if my fever disappears, so will Dad.

On the second night, Indium joins me. We are looking for something and we must hurry because he might be burned at the stake. He sings David Bowie's "Modern Love" but I can't sing along because I can't swallow, my throat is filled with scalding knives, slicing, and it wakes me, whimpering, in the dark middle of the night. I cry and drift and Dad returns. He is back at my desk but this time he is holding his notebook. I found it, he says. I press my eyes closed for a long second and when I open them he is still there. I didn't believe you were dead, I tell him. I knew you were coming back.

Oh, I'm dead, he says. I'm teaching a class on it.

On being dead? I ask.

Of course, he says. It's not like we're born knowing how to do any of this. You make it up as you go, he says, clutching at his chest as if feeling a deep and pressing pain.

It's your heart, I say. What's wrong with your heart?

Oh, he says, you know. I know you know.

But I don't know. I close my eyes again and this time when I open them, he's closer to my bed. Ghost warning, he says, then adds: It's a wool coat, a wool coat being eaten by moths. And then he starts disintegrating, whoofed out of existence by little patchy holes, and I'm screaming and Jonah is there, holding me up, handing me a Tylenol, holding out the glass of water.

"This is nuts, Lou. I'm taking you to the ER."

"It'll be okay," I say, curling back into sweat-drenched sheets. Dad's sent his message, whatever it means, and won't be back tonight. "I'll be fine." Dreamless sleep descends, a tidal wave pulling me under, and when I wake, late in the afternoon, the fever has broken.

11

Isabelle and Jonah are falling in love and it's disgusting. I stay sick for as long as I possibly can but eventually have to leave my bedroom and face the goo-goo eyes, the neck sniffing, the hand pawing. The way they seem to tumble into corners and land on top of each other. They jump in the shower, laughing and knocking things down, then leave a trail of clothes and wet towels from Jonah's bedroom to the bathroom door for me to trip over. It's brutal. The two of them are sucking all the joy out of the air, so there is none left for anyone else, and the more exuberant and connected they are, the more alone I am. It's January and the world outside has hardened into a black-and-white drawing of itself, a picture sketched in cold, thin lines. No beauty, just sadness. Sadness and going through the motions and making do. I complete my homework, plod through work shifts and fill out university applications without having any idea of where I want to go, what I want to do, who I want to be. Time snails along, leaving a slimy trail in its wake.

All month long, I wrestle with the impossible situation of how to alert Detective Phillips to Mike Hunter and Kevin Morris' drug business without snitching on Donnie but, after another beating is reported, I abandon my dilemma and call. It goes straight to his answering machine, so I leave him a message: "Detective Phillips. Hi. I, uh, have some information that might be useful. About the guys that live at 1407 Walker Street? Their names are Mike Hunter and Kevin Morris? A reliable source says that they are buying and selling drugs. So, maybe that's something you could use, you know, to launch an investigation. Okay. Well. Happy new year. Oh, this is Lou, by the way. Lou James." The answering machine beeps and stops me from rambling on about how the reliable source is perhaps somewhat involved, but is not all that bad, just an innocent kid caught up in his brother's bullshit. I consider calling back and leaving a second message but don't. I'd likely make it worse, plus, I'm not sure how innocent Donnie is.

I don't know what I will say when I see him. How angry will he be if I tell him the truth? Various scenarios ranging from relieved-angry to out-of-his-mind rage all seem equally possible. Given this unpredictability the bare truth seems ill-advised, and over the next month, I spend many mental hours concocting a plausible lie about how the detective approached me about Mike and Keith and their drug business, so Donnie will at least have a heads-up that he needs to be careful. But I don't get the opportunity to tell either the truth or my lie because Donnie's not at school and he's not at Zane's and he's not roaming around the neighbourhood with his long, loping strides. I have no idea how to contact him. His disappearance is unsettling but also a relief. If he's not around, I don't have to choose truth or lying. I don't have to kiss him.

The memory of the New Year's Eve kiss is a constant source of aggravation. I regret going outside with Donnie, agreeing to and participating in something that for all its heat and urgency, was also distant, impersonal and rough. It was nothing like the night Rufus and I danced to the Waterboys, the fire smoke ghosting our hair and wool sweaters, and the utter sense of certainty, and dreamy uncertainty, when we pressed lips over my bike's handlebars. That is the time I want to return to but the longer I stay in the city, and the more things happen, the less likely that seems. I don't think I'll ever get that moment back. When Rufus' next letter arrives, I carry it, folded up in a tiny square in my back jean pocket, for days.

Lou!
I have a confession to make: I have been hanging out with alternate reality Lou. It's the final stretch of high school and I can't wait to be done so I can move out of Linden and into the city. Really, waiting is such a colossal drag. It would all be way more fun if you were still here. But alternate reality Lou and I have been making plans about all the things we're going to do when I get to the city. I hope you don't mind, but I have a busy schedule planned for us.

The magazine was the bomb and the market sounds great. It's on the top of the to-do list. Sorry for such a short note, but I want to get this in the mail, and I have an essay to write on gender roles in *A Midsummer Night's Dream*, which may or may not be done on time. It's hard to care. I photocopied the cartoon I sent you and am considering handing that in. It doesn't address gender roles or conform to proper essay structure but Ms. Davids might pass me for creative effort alone. She's good like that.

I can't wait to be done with high school.
Love,
Rufus

The accompanying comic is entitled *Shakespeare Joe Puts on an Extravaganza*. Rufus has captured Shakespeare Joe's moony face and nailed the lederhosen, metal bowl hat and daffodil yellow of the bike. In the comic, Joe lives in a travelling caravan parked in the middle of a busy city street. One side of the caravan advertises Dr. Shakespeare's Nostrums, Curatives and Potent Elixirs of Medicinal Quackery and the other side folds out into a travelling theatre. Dr. Shakespeare, a sojourner and man of infinite knowledge, is raising money for his alter ego, Shakespeare Joe, a thespian of international renown. Shakespeare Joe is planning his pinnacle production, but his endeavours are sabotaged by a lack of funds and the unfortunate consequences of Dr. Shakespeare's potions. A remedy for heartburn turns out to be a laxative. A sleep aid causes hair to grow all over the body of a synchronized swimmer. An auctioneer requests a cure for warts, but instead leaves with permanent hiccups. The unsatisfied customers swell to an angry mob and swarm the caravan. Things are dire, but Shakespeare Joe saves the day. Although disorganized and unrehearsed, he is fuelled by croissants supplied by the charming WildFlour bakery girls, croissants acting on the imagination the way spinach supercharges the muscles. Armed with a lute and a metal bowl, Shakespeare Joe tames the crowd by enacting, in its entirety, act 2, scene 1 of *A Midsummer Night's Dream*. "How now, spirit! Whither wander you?" he begins and then proceeds to play all parts, both male and female: Fairy, Puck, Oberon, Titania and even the mismatched lovers, Helena and Demetrius. The scene, bookended by Puck's final proclamation, "Fear not, my lord, your servant shall do so," is punctuated with a deep bow and a masterful "Exeunt: end scene." The crowd goes wild.

It's even harder to answer this letter. My first reply is more of a confession.

> Dear Rufus,
> Why is it that I feel heartbroken reading your letters? Things are shitty here. I wish I was back at home in Linden, and not just an alternate reality version of me. I miss all sorts of things that I never thought I would miss, like the way Rochelle laughs like a horse and if you make her laugh at lunch at precisely the right time, she'll laugh milk out of her nose. I miss my locker in the grad hall. Because I came late in the year, my locker here is on the top floor with all the grade nine students, like a big loser. And I don't know anyone that well, not enough to be involved in all the stupid, fun,

gloriously demeaning things that happen in the months before graduating. It wouldn't be so bad, except that Isabelle has started dating my brother and they are so preoccupied with each other, I don't fit in anywhere. And I miss my dad. The longer he's gone, the less likely this whole thing is a big mistake.

There's lots of cool things happening in the city but most places ask for ID and anyways I don't have enough money to pay for the cool stuff. Mostly I walk around looking in windows at places I can't go and things I can't buy. I saw someone burning alive the day my dad was cremated. When it happened, it felt too pointed and personal to be a coincidence. Like my dad, the burning man is inside my head all the time and it's exhausting trying not to think about them both.

I have a hunch who might be responsible, although even as I write that, it feels too crazy. How could someone be responsible for setting someone else on fire? My guess is that it's these two guys, Mike Hunter and Kevin Morris, but ... could they actually do that? If they did, it would make them real-life monsters. They are awful but it's hard to believe that monsters like that really do exist. It makes me feel as if I am living in a new world, one that requires new eyes and new, tougher skin. Sometimes I wonder if you'll even recognize me when you move to the city. I practically don't recognize myself.

I've been smoking random cigarettes and drinking lots of beer and I took mushrooms at Christmas and I have a bag of stinky weed in my underwear and sock drawer. And I kissed this guy Donnie, Mike Hunter's younger brother, or more precisely, he kissed me and I didn't punch him in the nuts. In fact, I mostly enjoyed it. I don't know what that means? For us? Are we a thing? Are there rules? Did I break them?

I don't send it of course. I tear it up and write another.

Rufus!
Here's to the home stretch! I can't wait to be done school too. I've sent in my uni applications. I don't have any special skills or clear focus so I've applied for a regular bachelor of arts degree, which seems like it could be a colossal waste of time, but my brother says

it's all about the process. He says you figure it out as you go along. He's finishing up this interdisciplinary degree, which means he's been studying pretty much everything. He says he might teach, but what he'd really like to do is make documentaries. He's started dating my friend Isabelle, which honestly is a big drag. She is over at our place all the time. She wants to go to cooking school next year, so she is always trying out different recipes in our kitchen. This is a good thing because she brings over supplies from her house and our diet has transformed from eating mostly white food — rice and noodles with the occasional day-old muffin for a little dash of colour — to eating all sorts of fancy dishes. The last few weeks she has been testing Indian food recipes: split pea dal, butter chicken, a spicy ground beef dish called Keema. A few weeks ago, it was all French cuisine: boeuf bourguignon and French onion soup. But this is also NOT a good thing because I relied on hanging out with either her or Jonah and now that they are a couple, I am the perpetual third wheel. When we sit down to eat one of her special meals, they both go out of their way to be extra nice to me. It is infuriating.

Your comics are really, really good. You could make them into whole books, like *Watchmen*. I'll take you to Sal's when you get here. Sal is an old friend of my dad's and he drinks and smokes too much, compulsively rescues cats and owns a second-hand bookstore close to the bakery called Black Cat Books. The best thing about it is that it has a secret passageway that runs around the perimeter where he keeps his rare and expensive books. He has a whole shelf dedicated to *Catcher in the Rye*, out-of-print editions and copies owned by various famous people. He told me he put a bid on both John Lennon's and Mark David Chapman's copy but they were too expensive.

New Year's Eve was a weird night here. We went to this bar by the bakery called Zane's to see a band but I ended up leaving by myself just after midnight. Outside, I almost tripped over one of our crazy regulars, Stella, who looked like someone had punched her in the face. She also has epilepsy, or at least seizures of some kind, and sometimes they drag her down and knock her out wherever she is on the street. She has a small stuffed bird that she calls Ruby which she hides in her shirt, in her bra, I think, and lately she's started wearing this big Don't Worry Be Happy button on her winter coat. She sits on the side steps of the church across the street like a boulder-shouldered stone demon, muttering curses at people passing by, but when she comes into the bakery for hot coffee, she always brings something for Isabelle and me: a drawing of us as birds or cupcakes or as ourselves holding red guitars or bouquets of balloons. Over the past few months she has also brought gummy bears, pigeon feathers, various pamphlets and an SPCA fridge magnet. I don't know what happened in her life but you can tell it wasn't easy or kind. You can't imagine someone more beaten up by existence. It has stormed and wrenched and torn her apart, struck her with bolts of lightning over and over again, and yet, still, she manages to exist. Sometimes she seems kind of afraid but mostly gritty and tenacious, like even a nuclear bomb wouldn't faze her that much, and somehow, despite life's shitkicking, she still has enough generosity of spirit to draw kooky pictures and bring sweet gifts to two spoiled girls who have the outrageous good fortune to work in a bakery. We've speculated that perhaps she is an eccentric with a big bank account hidden away and the whole bag lady getup is an extravagant artistic tic, but that's the lie we tell so that we feel better about the life she must lead.

Enough for now. Time to study. I have a physics test. And I, too, am finding it hard to care.

Love,

Lou

A couple of weeks after New Year's, I brought out the bag of dope Donnie gave me and put it on the kitchen table, hoping that a little dope smoking might make things less tense around the house. Isabelle scoffed a pack of her mom's rolling papers and rolled the whole bag into nine little joints, each fitted with a small cardboard filter on one end and, on the other, a professional twist of paper for easy lighting. Isabelle is good at rolling, unlike Jonah and me who are hopeless, but she's terrible at smoking. The first time we lit one of the joints, she only took a few small puffs before it made her queasy, and she stumbled to the bathroom to puke. I didn't like it either. The sense of estrangement from couple Jonah-and-Isabelle was worse stoned and while dope is supposedly all about being laid back, I've

152 — ghost warning

found the gauzy, floating sensation makes me anxious. And angry and impatient. Still, we persisted. The fog of smoke did help to dull the edges, and after a few tokes, no matter how weird and uncomfortable the interlude of hanging out with Jonah-and-Isabelle, I could crawl into bed and fall asleep as soon as my head hit the pillow. But the dope is all gone now and there is no more buffer between the three of us. I haven't decided whether I'll get more. That is, if I ever see Donnie again.

I avoid the apartment by spending more time at Sal's bookstore. It's a good place to do homework and Sal is surprisingly good company. After a couple of weeks of me showing up every school night that I wasn't at the bakery, Sal presented me with my own key and asked if I would mind the store for a few hours on Tuesdays and Thursdays. It's top secret, I've sworn not to tell Jonah, but Sal's going to group therapy for people who survived life in the mental hospital and, because he's also trying to cut down on his drinking and smoking, he's swimming a few laps in the pool at the YMCA afterward.

Sal insists that the radio stay tuned to CBC, classical music playing softly. Time, especially when I am alone in the bookstore, slows down so pleasantly and completely that I forget, as I do my homework or read Sal's newspaper, to look at the clock and am aware of the hours passing only because the grey light outside dims and darkens. Sal has a new mascot, a wild flash of black, neither kitten nor full-grown cat, who Sal let me name Bagheera. He hates the cold, Bagheera, and any time a customer opens the front door, he races behind the counter and presses against my ankles. Courtney is there too, but she's more mellow; she likes to settle into a lap or a corner or onto a stack of books, humming in the back of her throat and licking her elegant little paws. The rest of the cats stay upstairs during the day. They're quiet until the sun goes down and then they start mewling in various cat harmonies, waiting for Sal to feed them dinner.

Tonight there's another warning for women in the newspaper. When Sal comes in, cheeks flushed and hair still damp and curling at the ends, I ask if he thinks the rapes and the disappeared people are connected. "I think Dad did. There was something he said, or something in his notes. I can't remember."

Sal lights a cigarette and opens a can of Pepsi as I move out of his swivel chair to the less comfortable stool, so he can sit down. Sal is the only one who takes my theory of Mike Hunter and Kevin Morris as possible suspects seriously. Jonah chides me for playing Nancy Drew, Isabelle thinks it's too far-fetched, and Detective Phillips has never returned my call. But Sal, who knows a large network of people who live in and around Parkdale, has been canvassing for information. There are a few outlandish theories — people are disappearing or bursting into flames because of an alien presence in our midst, is one. Another, from a man who goes by the name Corporal, is that the disappearances are engineered by the CIA. Corporal fought in Vietnam and returned with a missing leg and a latticework of scar tissue from his lip to his right ear and down, under the collar of his shirt. The scars mottle his black skin pink and grey and make his face rigid and his speaking voice formal. After the war, he was so disgusted by his birth nation, he left Detroit and moved to Toronto. He's a bookstore regular, squeezing his wheelchair down the narrow aisles to spend hours bullshitting with Sal. His favourite topic: how every evil in the world can be traced back to the CIA.

"Homelessness, Third World nations, the great huddled masses, this is the biggest threat to so-called American democracy," he says, and Sal wholeheartedly agrees. "Democracy, ha! It's more like a corporate oligarchy!" It's hard for me to take Corporal seriously. He will condemn the CIA in exactly the same tone in which he asserts that he survived Vietnam because he learned to breathe underwater and that soon he will learn how to grow his missing leg back. At night, he is visited by an angel, with glimmering halo and gold-tipped wings, who plays the trumpet so he can get a few hours of sleep, and his cat, unlike Sal's dumb beasts, can read his mind. However, his theory that the CIA is the puppet master behind the disappearances isn't any more outlandish than the story Sal stitches together. Sal's claim, based on a few central facts that have gained plausibility through sheer gossipy repetition, is that there's a group of guys that all meet up at a warehouse, a kind of gentlemen's club, by invite only, to bet. At first they would fight dogs, or roosters. ("Cockfights," Sal said. "How's that for a metaphor?") But then someone had the grand idea to get bums to fight. Jake the Fish told Sal he was approached by a couple of guys who offered him money to fight and when he said no, they got threatening. Jake thought it could have gone bad but a cop car pulled up, asked if everything was okay and Jake asked for a ride to the shelter, and the guys made themselves scarce. Jake told Sal the cop didn't seem too surprised when he explained what happened. It is outlandish and horrifying, yes, but Sal's theory is also remotely possible. Donnie did tell me his older brother killed his Rottweiler in a dogfight.

"I don't know if the rapes are related. Could be," Sal says and lets loose a long stream of smoke. He appears to enjoy his cigarettes far more after a little exercise.

"So you really think the cops know about it but are doing nothing?"

"Not nothing. They're doing the best they can, like the rest of us. But cops are just cops, they're part of the system too." Sal takes a haul from the can of Pepsi as Bagheera jumps up on the counter and leans into his shoulder, purring like a hive of bees. "Point is, it's some sick shit. And it's not a solitary guy, it's a group of people making it happen. It doesn't seem impossible that one of those sickos might also be up for a little sexual assault."

"Some crazed fucker."

"Yeah. Some crazed fucker. Exactly." He stubs out his cigarette. "On that note, it's time to close up shop." I pack up my school books and follow him to the door. From the vantage point of inside, the darkness outside is complete, as if it has laid claim to the whole world. Stepping out into it from the bookstore, I am an intruder. The door hasn't quite closed behind me when I remember something.

"Hey! Sal! Did you get my hot dogs?"

"Oh yeah." He moves back behind the counter and grabs a Legacy Variety store bag. There's a pack of twelve hot dogs inside.

"Thanks. I'll see you tomorrow."

"Good night, kid. Get home safe."

When I get to the park, I don't even have to whistle. Merlin the Mutt is waiting for me. He trots over as I tear open the package of hot dogs. His tail never commits to a full wag but he's started grinning when he sees me and occasionally he lets me pet the top of his head before pulling away. I've been trying to coax him home with the hot dogs but no matter what, I can't get him that far north. As soon as I approach Dundas, he skedaddles. But at least now he is my chaperone across the spooky park. We walk together, me talking and tossing hot dogs, him gulping them out of the air. "Hey Merlin. How was your day, boy? Cold and wet, I bet. And how is your tummy? I'm hoping the hot dogs won't give you worms. But you probably have worms. And fleas. But you're a good boy, aren't you, Merlin? Such a good boy. And so smart and handsome. You look like a dog made out of chocolate chip ice cream. If you come home with me, I'll give you a bath and feed you kibble and steak. Kibble and steak for the rest of your days. What do you say, Merlin? How about today? You could do it, boy.

Dundas Street isn't that bad." But he's gone, trotting into the dark corners of the park, half a hot dog hanging from his mouth.

The days are wet and snow lies in dirty, granulated deposits edging the sidewalks but at night, when the temperature drops, it slicks over into a sheet of ice. Mr. Baptiste is walking down his driveway holding a big bag of salt when I hit Rosalind. He holds up his hand in a halt gesture and I stop at the edge of his yard. He pours salt liberally across the cement and then, with a flourish of his arm, urges me to continue. "Thank you, kind sir," I say. It's clear even before I open our front door that, surprise, surprise, Isabelle is over and she's been cooking. The smell of cumin and fried onions drifts into the vestibule. "Hello!" I say at the bottom of the stairs. It's become necessary to announce my arrival so I don't walk in on any crazy sex games. "It's me! I'm home."

"C'mon upstairs! We're about to eat." In the kitchen, Jonah is setting out plates and cutlery for three as Isabelle removes a large serving dish from the oven and places it next to three others in the middle of the table. Her mom must be getting suspicious, with all the cookware and food supplies that have migrated over to our house. "Chickpea masala," she says. "Tandoori chicken, spiced cauliflower and lemon rice."

"It smells great," I say, sliding into a chair.

"Isabelle's marinated the chicken overnight." The way Jonah says this, it sounds comparable to climbing Everest or winning a Pulitzer.

"And taste this." Isabelle holds out a piece of roasted cauliflower, which Jonah eats, licking the spices off her fingers.

"Ew," I say and pile some food on my plate. "I've got to study. I'm going to eat in my room." They protest, but not that much, as I carry my plate and a glass of water down the hall, loudly closing my door. I lied. My homework is done and there are no tests to study for. Headphones on, I turn up Rufus' tape and pull out the heart book from under my bed. I've been meaning to re-check out the section on endocarditis since New Year's.

You know, Dad said when he appeared in my fever dream. *I know you know.* It's been driving me crazy, because I don't know. I have no idea what I am supposed to know. Am I supposed to know that Dad was depressed and wanted to die? Or am I supposed to know that his cardiac arrest was a sudden, unpredictable event and he would never have willingly left me or Jonah alone? I don't know.

Dad once told me that most stories begin with a great deal of educated guesswork. Since there was no autopsy we will never know exactly why

Dad went into cardiac arrest, but what I *think* I know is that endocarditis is the name of the infection that Dad nearly died from when he was a kid. He likely contracted it after his horrible experience that left him with a crooked smile, because endocarditis is more likely to occur after invasive dental work. It is also more likely to occur if he already had a slight abnormality in one or more of his heart valves, and the infection likely made this pre-existing condition worse. And then, for the rest of his life, Dad's heart had to work extra hard to pump blood through his body.

The list of endocarditis symptoms is horrifyingly familiar — fever, chills, achy muscles, night sweats, a persistent cough. How are you supposed to know if your heart is infected or if you have the flu?

The flu. Dad had the flu. It is an aha moment so big, I pull off my headphones and shout for Jonah before I know what I'm doing. In the kitchen he and Isabelle are laughing. A chair squeaks back and Jonah hollers down the hallway: "Lou?! Did you say something?"

"Nothing," I holler back. "Forget about it."

Endocarditis occurs when bacteria enter the bloodstream and then settle around the damaged heart valve, creating a site of infection. If you've had it before, you are more likely to have it again. And when the heart is infected, clumps of settled bacteria can break free and travel in the blood to the brain, or lungs, or other organs and cause a stroke or organ damage. If left untreated, endocarditis usually results in heart failure. Heart failure as in cardiac arrest.

For a moment, this is what I know: Dad had endocarditis, not the flu. He wasn't depressed, he was literally sick at heart. His cardiac arrest was not planned, but it was preventable. Relief, then sadness, knocks me down, sends me crawling into bed under my covers. Relief, then sadness, then anger, shaking my shoulders, knotting my stomach, burning my eyes. But what possible good does it do to glimpse inside the secret workings of Dad's heart, if I can no longer do anything about it? All of this — the billowing relief, the annihilating sadness, the corkscrewing rage — all of it frenzied, pointless, and stupid.

On Easter weekend, Isabelle snags the keys to her mom's car and the three of us and Sal go on a road trip to Lake Huron. Dad had an uncle who had a vacation house in Grand Bend, and he used to spend his summers there. Then, when we were kids, he'd take us camping every year and we would swim and hike and read. Dad would store his watch in the car glove compartment and we'd eat when we were hungry and sleep when we were tired and get lost for hours in activities like fishing or searching for arrowheads or learning how to skip stones. It was the happiest place that Jonah and I could think of and so we're taking his ashes to throw in the lake. Jonah drives Allen Road to the 401 but at Kitchener he exits the big highway and we head west through Stratford and Exeter, driving on flat narrow roads past white-fenced pastures and long-laned farmhouses. The sky is the colour of light shining through a robin's egg, a glassy, luminous blue, and big droopy boughs of wild lilac and small white and yellow flowers crowd the ditches along the side of the road. This is spring, the unfurling wet-earthed blooming birth of colour. This isn't happening in the city. There, save for a few brave daffodils and stuttering tulips, spring is a drippy continuation of the cold grey monochrome of winter.

Isabelle sits up front with Jonah and I am in the back with Sal. Dad is in the urn on my lap. The car is noisy, as if excessive cheer can balance out the mournfulness of our mission. "What is a shark's favourite illegal substance?" I shout over the radio station playing John Cougar Mellencamp's "Jack & Diane."

"Easy!" Jonah shouts back. "Reefer! How does the man on the moon cut his hair?" No one has a guess. "'Eclipse it!" I can't see his face but I imagine him grinning violently as Isabelle and I both groan.

"Okay, I got one." Isabelle has prepared for the day. She pulls a piece of paper from her purse and reads the question and answer of the joke out in one big exhale. "Why was the sand wet? Because the sea weed!"

"Okay," Sal says, tentative. Telling jokes stresses him out. "Did you hear about the fire at the circus tents? It was — wait. Oh shit. Let me start over. Did you hear about the fire at the circus?" We all wait for his punchline but when it doesn't come I prompt him. "No, Sal, I didn't hear about the fire at the circus."

"It was in-tents," he says, turning a look so dour on me I have to respond. "What, Sal? It's not my fault you can't tell a joke to save your life."

"Okay, I got another," Isabelle says. "What was Beethoven's favourite fruit?" Jonah and I both know this one and we shout the answer together: "Banananaaaaa!"

It's a long ride, about three hours, but when we turn into the entrance of the provincial park, I experience the same rippling anticipation I felt as a kid. The road is narrow and curving and canopied by pine and beech and maple trees, a transitional passage between everyday life and summer holidays. At the camp store we turn south, and the forest turns to low-lying mounds of dogwood, the bright green leaves starred with clumps of small white flowers. The road inclines upward and as we crest the tops of the gently sloping hills, flashes of blue water shine in the distance and the ripple of anticipation turns into a familiar tidal wave of excitement. The hills alongside the road become increasingly sparse, sand dunes patched with scraggly long grass and a dark green spreading weed that Jonah and I had long ago christened the "spit plant," due to the frothy gobs of spit that lie hidden under the bright yellow flowers. We crest a final hill and pull into the parking lot. The sky has washed out to a troubled grey, a bank of muddy storm clouds rolling in. When I step out of the car, a steady spring breeze lifts and ruffles my hair, snaking across the back of my neck like a warm hand. We march in single file up and across the boardwalk that protects the vulnerable sand dunes from too much foot traffic. At the top, as we step over onto the water side of the dunes, the temperature drops dramatically and the steady spring breeze becomes a whistling, bullying wind, strong enough to whip words right out of our mouths. We walk sideways down to the shore and the whitecapped waves, sand blasting our faces. I clutch the lid of the urn so it doesn't blow off. Jonah and I move away from Isabelle and Sal, who wait by a lone piece of driftwood.

We stand at the water's edge and I ask Jonah if he wants to say anything, shouting so he can hear me. He shrugs, his face unreadable.

"Do you?" he shouts back.

"I guess — " I hold the urn up and speak directly to it. "Dad. I don't want you to be gone." There are other things I want to say but the stormy weather has me drawing a blank. The wind rearranges Jonah's face, contorting his lips and cheeks and eyes into a Picasso version of himself. He's crying and I'm crying too, although the wind makes off with our tears as fast as they fall. I lean into Jonah and he leans into me, the urn pressed between us. It's like the night on the snowy street, when I was convinced that all I had to do was find him and everything would be all right. It physically hurts, this sensation of the wind ripping our sadness out of us, but it is also familiar and reassuring to be in a place, even for a moment, where it's wholly me and him again.

Jonah takes the urn and opens the lid, throwing a handful of ash into the choppy water, but it is a disaster, and the ash blows back into our eyes and mouths. We make a block of our bodies, facing away from the water, and Jonah turns the urn upside down and the ash sails away on the wind.

"I think Dad had endocarditis," I say. "It's an infection of the heart."

"What?" Jonah asks, leaning into me.

"An infection," I say, thumping my fist against my chest, marking the rhythm of a heartbeat. "An infection caused the cardiac arrest."

Jonah nods but I'm not certain he heard me. He takes my hand and we move away from the water, Sal and Isabelle following. None of us say anything until we reach the lee of the dunes.

"That was exhausting," Sal says. "Five minutes and six of my seven layers of skin have been scoured away."

"Yep," I say. The sand is everywhere, folded in the creases of my clothes, settled in my hair, coiled in the whorls of my ears. A dirty grit scuffs my eyes and I keep blinking back tears.

"Let's go to Grand Bend and get something to eat," Jonah says, taking Isabelle's hand.

We eat burgers at Dad's favourite restaurant and buy chocolate pecan fudge at his favourite candy store and then the rain starts coming down, hard drops like thrown stones. We dash across the parking lot as the thunder and lightning start, soggy by the time we reach the car. Jonah and Isabelle settle up front, bending their heads over the opened road map, while Sal and me, the two of us equally wet and gloomy, huddle in the back. The raindrops fall with such force and volume they sound like eggs splatting on the roof.

"Jonah! Turn on the heat. I'm freezing." I pull Dad's empty urn onto my lap as if it will keep me warm. We drive for about an hour into the storm, the sound of the radio barely audible over the rain and the thunder, the wind so strong it buffets the car from side to side, the hypnotic swirling and gnashing outside the window a singular, monotonous shade of darkening grey. "Shit!" Jonah says, and brakes to a full stop. Up ahead a tree has fallen into the ditch, taking down a power line with it, and now it lies, a giant black snake, across the road, blocking our way.

"We'll have to backtrack," Jonah says, turning to Isabelle. "Is there another route?"

"I don't know, I don't know." Isabelle's voice contains an unfamiliar note of hysteria. "Oh my God. We have to have this car home by seven. My mom will kill me if she finds out we took it."

"What?" Jonah says.

"You didn't tell your mom we were taking the car?" I say.

"No!" Isabelle wails. "I'm dead. I'm so dead."

"Hold on," Jonah says. "The car tires are rubber."

"I can't believe you didn't tell your mother we were taking the car," I say.

"Oh my God," Isabelle moans.

"Hold on," Jonah says again. He sucks his lips and clucks his tongue, something he does when he's thinking hard. "I don't see why we can't just drive over."

"What?" Sal says. "Are you crazy? We'll fry like sardines in a can."

"You think?" Isabelle says, ignoring Sal.

"I don't see why not," Jonah says. "Especially if we go fast enough."

"Let's do it."

"Are you kidding me?" Sal leans forward in his seat. "Jonah, this is madness."

"Hold on, Sal." Jonah puts the car in reverse, backs up and then accelerates toward the power line.

"Jonah!" Sal bellows like a bear. "Stop, STOP!" But he doesn't. I shut my eyes tight, holding Dad's urn close. Time and space clatter in my ears like an unstoppable train and I'm tied to the track. Jonah and Isabelle cheer as we sail over. "Hallelujah," Isabelle says. "We made it."

"See, Sal?" Jonah says. "We're not dead yet."

Sal grunts as I twist in my seat to watch the power line disappear but the turning back makes me carsick and I have to get Jonah to stop the car so I can puke in the rain by the side of the road. It's a little better after I've thrown up, but the carsickness lingers for the rest of the ride and even after we've reached the city.

Back at home, I place Dad's urn on my desk beside the two framed pictures of Jonah and me and Jonah and my mom. I pull a blue card from the middle of the stack. It's one I've had before, about the Zen archer firing his arrow over the ocean, and somehow hitting his Bull's Eye, and so I put it back and pick another. *Gertrude Stein defined love as "the skillful audacity required to share an inner life."* This card does not seem to pertain to me. I mean, I'm all for attempting to share an inner life with somebody, if they're interested, but I haven't had a letter from Rufus or seen Donnie in months. Finn visits the bakery semi-regularly and is still as flirty as ever but, obviously, with him, that doesn't mean anything. I pick one more card, and it's the Zen archer hitting the Bull's Eye again. All right, Dad. What is it, exactly, that you're trying to tell me?

The days get warmer and longer, and after I'm done at the bakery or the bookstore, I stay out later and later. Walking helps clear my mind. I enjoy learning the city all over again. Spring city is different from winter city, mostly for the better, except for the neighbourhood directly around Zane's. The snow covered up a general squalor that is clearly visible now. The park too is different in the spring, less spooky and more tragic, the anemic grass littered with condoms and beer bottles and the occasional needle. Stella has started following me to the park to watch Merlin's training sessions. Tempted by my packs of no-name hot dogs, he has agreed with only a hint of disdain to sit when I ask him and to walk at my left side, keeping eye contact with me as we move in small circles. He races to greet me when I enter the park, his scraggly tail thumping a half wag, a janky, jolting motion that only goes to the left. He's still too cool and tough and noncommittal for a full wag, and nothing I do will persuade him past the Dundas Street boundary, but we're making progress. Stella insists on calling him Scrubs and she sits on a park bench, squawking and trilling, "Go Whoo! Go Scrubs! Go Whoo!" a derelict, geriatric cheerleader, while I run Merlin through his paces. She is happier here, and more animated, and a little wild too. Her face opens and becomes more transparent and inscrutable, both at the same time. Behind her startled eyes lies a trapped bird, its wings flapping and beating against the inside bony wall of her skull.

It's almost seven o'clock, still warm, and I am zigzagging through the park looking for either one of them when I see Donnie sitting on the top edge of a bench. Even though the temperature is at a record high for the end of May, Donnie is wearing a blue Roots jacket, a bright red ribbed cuff around his hips and wrists. He must be boiling. I've cut my last decent pair of jeans into knee-length shorts and am wearing the batik T-shirt Isabelle made for Christmas, and I'm still sweating. His inappropriate clothing strikes me as odd and infuriating.

"The last time I saw you, you were wearing a hoodie in the middle of winter," I say, walking toward him. "Now a wool jacket for spring? What gives?"

"Hey," he says. "Lou." He doesn't look too good. His skin is the colour of a raw oyster, his eyelids heavy as if not able to support the weight of his thick lashes, and he is breathing rapidly. Sick, maybe, or stoned.

"Where have you been? Are you okay?"

"I've been working for my brother."

"Oh," I say, and when he gestures to the bench, I sit down on the far edge, keeping some distance between us. "Dealing?"

"Yeah, that. And other stuff. Mike and Kevin have been running stuff since Kingston. That's where I've been. Kingston."

"Kingston, Jamaica?" I ask. I'm stuck on the weed angle.

"No, no, no," Donnie says. "They went to school at Queens. Business school — " and he laughs wildly.

"And they started a business — " I prompt.

"Yeah. Business, right. Smuggling, stealing, dealing. Fights. I broke into a Roots delivery truck last week." His smile is sentimental as if the memory of the Roots truck was ancient but fond. "Did you ever watch *Star Wars*?"

"Sure," I say. "Everyone watched *Star Wars*."

"Did you want to be Princess Leia?"

"Well, no. Not really. If I wanted to be anyone, it was probably Han Solo."

"I wanted to be Luke. I wanted to be the good brother. The good son." As he talks Donnie's eyes cloud over, lose focus. He seems paler, whiter even than moments ago.

"Donnie? Are you high? Did you take something?"

"No," he says. Smiles. "Not really. I'm fine now. I'm glad you're here."

"You don't look so good."

"I'm not so good. I'm bad. I don't know how — " A kind of whispered, ragged howl escapes from him and he puts one clenched hand to his mouth. "I don't know how to be good."

"Donnie? Maybe you should see a doctor."

He laughs a little, teetering from side to side, and then grips the bench with both hands. Something drips from the edge of the wood to the grass below. Blood. I watch as a large drop rolls from under the cuff of Donnie's jacket, dripping onto the wood and rolling onto the ground. And another.

"You're bleeding," I say, as he topples, then slides, then bumps down from his perch onto the bench seat and then all the way to the ground. He mumbles incoherently as I check his wrists. There are horizontal slash marks across the pale underside of each arm, about an inch wide, and two jetting streams of blood. Blood soaks the interior of the jacket, so much that when I tug the zipper open, it spills like a warm waterfall onto the grass beside him, pooling and darkening. I scream for help, for an ambulance, for someone to help us, as I try to figure out what to do with his wrists. Should I lower them? Should I raise them? I straddle his stomach, lift his wrists over his heart and hold them as tightly as I can, pressing them together, the blood, viscous as honey and warm as bathwater, running down my forearms and dripping off my elbows onto Donnie, who is not Donnie anymore, but a body, growing cold and unconscious, his skin a translucent tint of blue, as a crowd of people gather. My head swims with the nauseatingly rich smell of blood clogging my throat and nose and eyes, so that my vision narrows and all I see is blood, flecks of blood, pools of blood, geysers of blood, blood flowing between my fingers.

There's noise, and lights, a confusion of people, an ambulance. I surrender to the anonymous authority of the paramedics and move aside to sit on a patch of unbloodied grass, wiping my hands in the spiky green over and over again. The police arrive and ask questions I have no answers to. "I know him from school," I say. "I was walking through the park and he was sitting here. I stopped to say hi." I don't tell them that he was dealing drugs, or that his brother might be part of an evil network of abusive and murdering fascists who count the poor and the homeless as disposable people, or that he kissed me twice on side streets and his breath tasted like cigarettes and cinnamon gum.

When the crowd disperses and the ambulance drives off with Donnie I realize I'm angry. Furious. There are long rusty stains on my jean shorts, my only pair, and there is blood caked on my hands and forearms. I walk to the nearest doughnut shop where I throw up and then wash my hands, rinsing the smell of blood and taste of vomit away with cold splashes of tap water. When I leave, the clerk shouts at me that the bathrooms are for customers only.

I walk east, away from the apartment but with no clear destination in mind. It's late, but still hot. Above me a bird flies into a building and drops, a dark, rushing form, onto the sidewalk. A black-and-brown brindled cat investigates cautiously, slow, soft-padded steps over tacky asphalt, doubtful perhaps of his sudden bounty. He pulls the bird, a plump green and gold-flecked pigeon, one wing splayed open, into an untidy corner where he can lick and rip and tear to his cat-heart's content, green eyes trained on the parade of feet beating by. I'm not looking where I'm going and walk smack into Finn.

"Hey," he says. "It's always hit and run with you."

"I just saw a pigeon," I say. "It smashed into an apartment building."

"Oh." He looks confused.

"Like in your song?" I am compelled to explain what strikes me as an extraordinary coincidence. "It's weird, you know, that I'd see that and then you. Bird falls. Boom. Then you." I falter. Finn's face is unreadable. "Sorry. I don't know what I'm talking about. It's been a strange afternoon." I gesture at my clothes. The stains are barely visible on the navy cotton of my shirt but my jean shorts are ruined and despite my vigorous hand washing, dark rings of dried blood have settled in my cuticles. Finn raises a thick black eyebrow.

"You okay?"

"Yeah. Just. Strange. Surreal."

"It's been a weird day for me too." His face, still distant, suddenly brightens. "Can I buy you dinner? I know a great Mexican place."

"Sure," I say. Why not? Yesterday, the idea of a dinner date with Finn would have put me in a tailspin, flailing in an orgy of pre-date anxiety, wrestling with deep questions such as, what to wear? How to fix my unfixable hair? Makeup, or no? But today, I don't care. Bloodstained hands stuck into bloodstained pockets, I keep pace with Finn's brisk walk. Anything might happen this evening and right now that is okay with me.

The restaurant is called Las Margaritas. It's small, with terracotta tiled walls and large tropical plants encircling the room, small white candles flickering on the tabletops. We take a seat closest to a fan and open the oversized menus. Finn recommends the fajitas for two, which we order along with a pitcher of sangria, and then Finn asks why my afternoon was strange.

"It's not only this afternoon," I say. "It's my whole life. Strange things keep happening all the time." For a moment, I smell Donnie's blood again and my head swims, surfing a wave of nausea, but I will it back down. I won't throw up, here, in this nice restaurant, sitting across from a gorgeous boy. I don't want to talk about Donnie. I don't want to think about Donnie. I want to look at Finn. He has a small birthmark below his left ear and dimples when his face creases into a smile.

"Well, this is the neighbourhood for strange things," he says. The waitress delivers the pitcher of sangria and Finn stirs the cut-up pieces of strawberry, grape, lemon and lime floating in the pitcher, then pours out two glasses. "Cheers."

The sweet wine-and-brandy smell pushes the tide of blood away. Three long gulps of the cool liquid and I am finished, fishing out the pieces of fruit with my bloodstained fingers, spooning them into my mouth, drops of sangria tie-dying the white tablecloth a pretty shade of purple. Finn must think I am an uncouth, no-table-manners barbarian. I don't care. I have never been so thirsty or hungry in my life. "More?" he asks, laughing. He refills my glass as the platter of fajitas is served — green and red peppers, onions and zucchini sizzling in a hot skillet — surrounded by several small colourful bowls filled with grilled chicken, refried beans, guacamole, sour cream, grated lettuce and pico de gallo, and we spoon a little of each into the centre of a warm flour tortilla. "Pico de gallo," I say, heaping the fresh, diced tomatoes and onions on top of my fajita creation. "Rooster's beak."

"It looks like salsa to me," Finn says. "Restaurants are always giving fancy names to everyday food. It drives me crazy."

When the fajitas are finished, we order another pitcher of sangria and a dish of chocolate mousse, another moniker Finn finds contentious. "What's wrong with calling it pudding?" Finn asks the waitress but I forgive his contrariness when he dips a strawberry in the chocolate and leans over, lowering it to my mouth. I am drunk and I like it, the alcohol sufficiently blurring the rest of the fucked-up world so I can focus solely on Finn.

"Let's get out of here," he says. "We can go back to my place."

"Won't your girlfriend mind?" I don't dare say her name.

"We're not together. She's visiting family in Germany." He pays the bill and takes my arm, leading me out onto the street where the sun has gone down but it is still humid and warm, a few resolute stars shining in the smoggy sky. "Finn," I say and lean in to kiss him, his lips dry and pillowy, his hands already on the back of my neck, in my hair, pulling me close. We press into the alcove of the blue door adjacent to the restaurant and the clamouring city disappears or is distilled into the long, firm lines of his chest and shoulders, his urgent mouth, his thigh against my thigh. Up close his skin is fragrant with a spicy aftershave oil I can't identify but would like to, and I burrow into his neck and chest, breathing deeply.

"Screw you!" someone shouts behind us. We both turn to look as a man who is either drunk or stoned, or in the middle of a mental break-down, or some combination of the three, sways on the sidewalk behind us. He doesn't meet our gaze but boxes the air with a sharp jab, sucker-punching a nearby ghost. My heart thumps wildly as I check to see if he's holding a knife, or some other weapon.

"Take it easy, buddy," Finn says, reaching for my hand.

"Screw you, motherfucker!" The man says, the anxiety in his voice escalating even as he turns and weaves away, muttering and swatting his invisible companions.

"C'mon," Finn says, and I stumble after, a little breathless, uncertain of how far I can go without kissing him again. I am too soft and warm to stay on my feet long. Like the garlic bulbs Anna roasts at the bakery, when they emerge from the oven, ready to ooze and pull apart, plump section by plump section, at the slightest touch. We kiss again across from the park and when we separate I see a prone huddled shape in the shadows of the trees. I turn away, burying my head in Finn's shoulder, and we move on.

He lives in one of the closed storefronts, sheets of newsprint taped to the front windows. The drummer, Dylan, and his father, a sculptor, live in the front half of the building and Finn has the small room at the back.

In the sober light from a single bulb the room is spartan, unadorned. There's a mattress on the floor, three guitars, one amp, a boom box on a milk crate, a desk lamp on another crate beside the bed and two posters advertising gigs crookedly pinned to the walls. There's an alarm clock and a much-rumpled and folded collection of lined paper on the milk crate with the lamp. A letter, maybe. From Sophia? There's also a box of condoms, which is a relief because not ever having done it before I wasn't quite sure how to bring condoms up in, like, a sexy way. The condoms, and my lack of experience with them, fill me with a sudden swell of doubt, doubt that, disturbingly, smells vaguely of fresh blood. Am I really doing this? The face of Freddy Fender, my science lab partner in Linden, flashes through my thoughts, and behind that face, with its squidgy, lascivious smile and halo of crotch hair, are all the dirty, perverse, squidgy, icky, intriguing things he said, as if they've been lying in wait like some X-rated monster under the bed ready to pounce. I don't know how to do any of them. I have no idea what I am doing. But then Finn turns out the light and kisses me again and I slide his T-shirt over his muscled arms, and my hands find his belt buckle, no fumbling, as if they have a mind of their own. As I move closer his skin releases a musky odour, a distant cousin to skunk, familiar and pungent and fine, and as we settle down into the bed, I press into the scent, wanting it to stain my hair and lips and fingertips, and everything in me that is tired and sad and worried and afraid slides away and, no more questions, no more imagining. No more words. I'm ready.

Over Finn's shoulder the alarm clock reads 4:07 and I am, without ever having fallen into true sleep, suddenly, acutely, wired, wide awake. Unbearably uncomfortable. I am wedged into Finn's shoulder, our sticky legs intertwined, my right arm pinned beneath him, our bodies and faces so close in the narrow bed that his soft nasal snore ruffles my hair, breezes over my face. The sweaty musk of his body is strong, pressed as I am into his armpit, and though still not unpleasant, it is less compelling than a few hours ago. His heartbeat is strong and sounds exactly how the heart book describes it — lub-DUBB, lub-DUBB, lub-DUBB. No swooshing sounds. Despite my discomfort it feels impossible to move, to extricate my limbs from his. *Making the beast with two backs.* That's how Iago describes sex in *Othello*. It's not a bad description. I wasn't going to tell Finn it was my first time but there was a moment when he caught my earlobe with his teeth and whispered *you're beautiful* and then, I'm not sure why, I told him. All he said was *oh,* but after, we slowed down and he made me wait to touch him, holding my wrists, and kissing and pressing and kneading and nipping and licking until there was not a single thought in my mind except *yes.* It was such a relief to stop thinking for a little while. Sex, I'm happy to discover, is like a perfect little holiday from yourself. But now there are pins and needles in my right arm and I'm thirsty, bad-breath ugly, and I have to pee.

Slowly, with the precision of playing a game of Jenga, I remove one limb at a time and slide backwards out of Finn's bed, dressing blind in the pitch dark, stubbing my toe on a guitar case. I don't know where the bathroom is and so I follow the route we came in, back out to Queen. The pre-dawn air is light and cool as I move quickly down the street, still desperately needing to pee. Leo and Anna will be at the bakery, kneading bread, baking cookies, roasting chickens — I could use the bathroom there. But I turn north, opting instead for the shadows of the alley, pulling down my jean shorts and squatting by a concrete block. It's not ideal, or sanitary, and Sal would have volumes to say about my unladylike behaviour, but it is surprisingly satisfying. Liberating. It's not like I'm going to start squatting and peeing everywhere I go, I argue with the Sal inside my head, but I'm also not going to apologize. If you have to pee, you have to pee. Plus, guys do it all the time.

12

Monday is a day of tutorials, prep for our final exams. There is a buzz in the grad hallway but I am excluded from it. Neither Isabelle nor I have attended the series of grad parties that have been building toward this moment all spring, Isabelle because she is so preoccupied with Jonah, and me because without Isabelle I don't fit in anywhere. Occasionally I wonder what is happening at my old school, what Rufus is doing, but it all seems distant as a dream now. No, the only thing I'm abuzz about is the lingering memory of last Friday night. On Saturday, Finn showed up at the bakery with a single iris for me. Isabelle raised her eyebrows but didn't ask any questions and it was busy, so Finn and I didn't talk. Sunday, I studied all day, not allowing myself to even think about visiting him. But today I'm giving in. I manage to avoid Isabelle at the end of classes and I leave, my last official day of high school complete, hightailing it down to Finn's.

The front door is locked but Dylan opens it and leads me back to Finn's room.

"Finn," he calls out, rapping on the door. "You decent? You have a visitor."

"Send 'em in," Finn says. He's lying on the bed when I enter and Sophia, pretty-as-a-picture Sophia, is sitting on a milk crate, leaning forward as if in the middle of an intense conversation. She doesn't look pleased at the interruption.

"Lou," Finn says. Casual.

"Hey," I say, raising a hand in a quick wave. What's going on? Maybe they're breaking up?

"You remember my girlfriend, Sophia?"

No. They're not breaking up. "Hi," I say. She smiles but doesn't say anything.

"We're heading out for pizza," Finn says. "You want to come along?"

Is he kidding? Is he crazy? Something distorted and explosive pops inside my mind, makes me want to moan out loud, and it takes all my effort to fix my face in a neutral expression. "No, that's okay." I force my voice to match his casual tone. "I don't want to interrupt." I edge back to the door. "We'll hang some other time," I say and turn and go.

Speed-walking down the street, I try to put as much distance between them and me as possible, my throat aching with the stopped-up moan, the fireworks behind my forehead transforming into a blinding headache, hot pools of tears sizzling in the corners of my eyes, refusing to fall, as I retreat to the apartment. Inside the front door, Isabelle's sandals lie haphazardly next to Jonah's sneakers and I kick them both out of the way. The two of them are in Jonah's bedroom, music thankfully turned up loud enough so they can't hear me and I can't hear them. I make a ridiculous show of attempting to study but fail miserably, crawling into bed even before it's dark, not able to stop the cascading reel of images: what I did with Finn, what he's doing with Sophia right now. When he touched me, kissed me, I trusted him. I thought it was true. Foolish. I could tear my hair out with the foolishness of it all. How could something that meant so much to me mean so little to him? I'm still awake when Jonah calls my name through the bedroom door, says we need to talk, but I don't answer.

Two days later, acceptance letters arrive for all my university applications as well as a thinner-than-usual envelope from Rufus. There isn't a comic book included this time, only a portrait of Stella, sitting on church steps. He's used all the details I gave him: Stella is wearing her Don't Worry Be Happy button, and Ruby is poking out from the mysterious folds on her chest. Her shoulders round forward and she is drawing in a sketchbook with a red crayon. Still, her face isn't quite right. He's drawn her with a stony blankness that isn't Stella at all. Moods and emotions flit over her face, cagey and sly one moment and full of wonder the next, as if she was inhabited by a whole cast of characters, some cruel, some kind, all of them locked in a perpetual battle to take possession of her soul. But even though he hasn't totally captured her, I love it, and I hang the picture up on my bedroom wall before I read his letter.

Lou!
Don't hate me for taking so long to write back. Things have been both busy and weird here. Every day it seems there is some kind of grad-related event or party and everybody has been hit with the "This will be the last time ..." Insert anything you can think of: the cross-country ski team meets, there is a Valentine's Day home-room Hershey's Kiss delivery, Rob Cheech and Chris Chong get caught smoking in the shop hall bathroom. Everyday normal stupid things are weighted with importance because, apparently, it's

the last time any of this will occur. Like next year none of us can buy Hershey's Kisses or all of a sudden Rob and Chris are going to turn into engineers or doctors. I admit though, while cynical, I am also caught up in the drama as much as anyone else. I went to the grad formal with Jenny and it was a pretty fun night. Also, I won an award for top arts student, which was unexpected and very cool. Rochelle won the award for best all round student, which everyone agreed, even Rochelle, would have gone to you if you were here.

Generally things have been super busy at school and not as boring as usual, so that's been okay. But I've been distracted. I think my parents are going to get a divorce. I don't know why because neither of them will tell me anything. It might be because my mom wants to see someone else, or it might be because my dad had a one-night stand last year. I'm not sure there even is a reason. I think they both just want a change. Which is messed up considering I'm pretty sure they still love each other, so I don't understand why the fuck they can't grow up and work it out.

Anyways, enough about me. How are you? Classes end the middle of next week and then we have exams. Is that the same for you? I'll be all done with everything in three weeks. I wanted to come into the city and look at schools and rooms in residence versus trying to get an apartment. When I'm there, I'd like to take you out for an official unbirthday date. What do you think?

xo

Rufus

What do I think? I have no idea what I think, or more precisely I find myself thinking several things all at once. I hate the fact that Rufus went to grad with stupid Jenny Abrahms and I wish it had been me and I wish I was the one who had been awarded best all round student. But I'm not the same person I was when I lived in Linden. Maybe Rufus will come and I won't be at all who he is expecting to take out on a date. And do I want to go out on date with him? I'm not sure I ever want to go on a date again. Finn has ruined me.

Donnie has ruined me. Sometimes when I close my eyes, his face pops into my mind, cold and bloodless and dying. He didn't die, though. Through Isabelle's network of childhood friends, we found out he had been taken to Toronto General Hospital. The two of us went to visit but he was in the ICU in critical condition, and only family was allowed. "That's ironic," I said to the clerk. "Since it's his family who put him here in the first place."

"That's not my place to say." The clerk was prim and stubborn and wouldn't budge but she did say we could try again in a few days.

On Saturday morning, when Isabelle and I arrive at work to open, Leo asks if we've seen Stella. Anna is off sick, so Leo has had to do double the work and it shows in the chaotic Jackson Pollock food smear on his apron, the dusting of flour down one side of his face, and the large oval grease stain that has soaked through his apron to his Blue Jays jersey. Apparently, no one has seen Stella all week. A dizzying clutch of worry grips me as I remember the dark shape lying prone in the park the night Finn and I passed by.

"We'll keep an eye out," Isabelle says.

"Last week of school, hey girls?" Leo asks as he pulls off his apron, shaking his head as he notices the impressive grease stain. "Shall we talk next Monday about summer schedules?"

Isabelle agrees for both of us, my mind still stuck on Stella. Sal comes in as Leo leaves and settles into the table closest to the cash register.

"Tea," he says "Danish. Please."

"I got it." Isabelle pulls out an extra-large mug for Sal.

"Do you know what excoriate means?" I ask both of them as I brush beaten egg on the limp uncooked dough of one of Leo's baguettes. "It means — it's a verb — to remove part of your skin. To strip it off. Like if you have skinned your knee you have actually excoriated it."

"I wish I'd known that when I was ten." Isabelle laughs. "My scabs would have been much better represented."

Over at his table Sal grunts and folds the newspaper into a rectangle, drawing his fingers along the lines of an article that has caught his interest. The timer for the wall oven jangles and Sal looks up as Isabelle pulls out a tray of oatmeal cookies.

"Hey," he says. "You two better come read this."

He passes me the paper, one stubby finger pointing where to read: *Body Found in Trinity Bellwoods Park.*

According to the article, a man out on an early-morning dog walk last Sunday spotted what he thought was a pile of damp burning leaves at the base of a tree. Upon closer inspection it was revealed to be, in fact, the

charred remains of a human body. The body, which was yet to be iden-
tified, was believed to be the remains of a woman, possibly a transient. It
was the fourth burned body found over the past year in the vicinity. In this
particular case, the article concluded, police suspected foul play.

I read it over line by line, and then again. Isabelle rests her hand on my
shoulder.

"Foul play?" I say. "*Foul play*? What kind of stupid fucking phrase is *foul
play*?"

"It doesn't mean it's Stella, right?" Isabelle says. "I mean, it could be
anybody."

"It could be anybody," Sal agrees, as he packs up his paper and leaves.

Stella knows how to take care of herself. Stella is fine. She's fine. I repeat
this over and over again, as if through sheer repetition it will be made ac-
curate and true. The timeline doesn't add up — I saw the huddled shape
Friday night and the body was found Sunday morning. I wash dishes and
tell myself that Stella is fine. I open my textbooks to study and tell myself
that Stella is fine. I lie in bed and tell myself that Stella is fine. I make deals.
If Stella walks into the bakery next Saturday I will take her home and
clean her up. Run a bubble bath and make her tea and honey toast. I will
squirt pearls of antibiotic cream on her sore skin until it grows coherent
and whole again. Why hadn't I already done that? It's not enough to worry
about Stella's brown teeth and sore skin and the way her back curves as
though bowed under an unseen weight, not enough to worry about that
wild bird caught behind her eyes, as if worrying alone ever changed anything. But I don't have to worry. Stella knows how to take care of herself.
Stella is fine. She's fine.

My math exam is Tuesday morning. Proofs of trigonometric identities. The
ordered process of solving a problem from the inside out doesn't save me
from my circling thoughts, and I stare at the exam question book, drawing
a blank. I wonder briefly what would happen if I failed my exam. I used
to imagine that if I did for some reason fail, the world would be over, the
future finished. Stupid. The world won't stop, the world won't care. My
future is coming whether I like it or not. I flip back and forth through the
stapled pages, looking for a question that will restore the calm and confidence math usually provides, but the magic is gone and I waste a ridiculous
amount of time so that when the exam is over I haven't finished the full

booklet. I've only answered about three-quarters of the questions and at least half of those weren't even real answers, only my best guess.

After the exam, I head to Isabelle's to study for history. Isabelle and her mom live in a three-and-a-half-storey house, tall and narrow. I climb two steep staircases to reach her bedroom, an entire half-storey attic that creaks in the wind, a large chaotic space full of abandoned clothes and painted in varying shades of rosy pink. There are many, many pillows and a wide bay window that we climb out of onto a patch of roof to study and sunbathe. I unpack my history text as Isabelle climbs back inside.

"One minute," she says. "We need supplies."

The spot on the roof is flat, safe, but very, very high. Below, the steep slope of the lower roof slides down to the stony yard, and beyond, over the sweaty, sooty top of the city to the far-off edge of Lake Ontario. The sun's rays glint off the water with a sluggish brilliance.

"Here," Isabelle says and passes a plate of chocolate chip cookies through the window, then a pitcher of iced tea and two green blown-glass tumblers.

We make a valiant attempt at studying but the heat, the steady hum of traffic and the noise of children shouting are distracting. Not even the dramatic ups and downs and reversals of fortunes of the French Revolution can compete. The shrill whine of a mosquito buzzes in the empty space between Isabelle and me, and a sudden siren, coming closer, blisters the hot thick air. Isabelle puts her book down, sits up straight and starts talking.

She talks a lot. She talks about Donnie. What was he thinking? How could he do that? Why was he down on Queen Street and not farther north at his mom's place? Maybe he moved in with his brother? Was he crazy? He must be crazy, mustn't he? Did I think he was crazy? After Donnie she moves on to her plans for next year: chef school at George Brown College. What should she specialize in? Baking? French cuisine? Restaurant management? Did I know that for one of the courses you actually went to Paris for two weeks? Next she starts making silly suggestions for how we can make extra money over the summer by running a dog dating service. Her voice deepens into an adman's pitch as she suggests a business that caters to an elite group of pooches who don't have time to setup important social and procreative connections. We could throw dog parties. With themes: Bitches' Night Out. "What do you say, Lou. You in?"

"I have to see Donnie," I say. I don't know why. The whole time she was rambling on I was thinking about Finn. About how I'd like to tell Isa-belle everything. But the whole thing is so humiliating. Better not to talk, or think, about it. Better to erase it from my mind. "I need to ask Donnie some questions."

"About what?"

"About his brother and his brother's friend, Kevin." I clear my throat. "About Stella."

"Lou?" Isabelle's voice is kind but patronizing. No matter what I tell her she thinks the theory that Sal and I have cooked up is too far-fetched. No way Donnie, his brother or Kevin Morris are involved in anything as evil as a murderous network of people who stage fights between dogs or homeless people. And I'll give her that, when I explained it to her, it sounded ludicrous. Totally insane. "Stella's probably at the hospital like be-fore," she says. "I'm sure she's fine. She'll be back in a week."

The image of the huddled shape lying in the shadows, an image that has started to look more and more like the crumpled shape of Stella, flashes in my mind. If she had a seizure in the park she would be helpless, vulner-able to whatever monster passed by. I clear my throat again. "Sometimes there are things so bad we can't look them straight in the face. It's too terrifying to see it for what it really is."

"I don't really know what that means, Lou."

I can't help but sigh. "Me either, I guess. This is the kind of thing my dad knew how to investigate. Get to the truth." I lie back on the hot roof. "Forget it." Isabelle lies back beside me but doesn't say anything. In the far-off distance a large white cruise ship sails away from the water's shoreline. On it, I imagine, are men wearing bright-coloured polo shirts and women wearing sundresses. There is a live band, dressed in white suits, playing *Copacabana*. The men's faces are an overstuffed red and the women smell of expensive perfume, of chemicals and exotic flowers. Everybody drinks too much. *Sink*, I think. *Sink*.

"Lou?" Isabelle says. Her voice is low. "You know, I really like Jonah. A lot. You know I do. I liked him way before I even met you."

Pause.

"Things don't have to be so different."

"Yeah, yeah," I say. "I know." I'm lying. Things are totally different and they will never be the way they were before. I close my books and finish the last of my iced tea. "I got stuff to do. I'll see you tomorrow."

"I'll be at your place later today."

"Of course you will," I say as I climb back through the window, but softly, so Isabelle can't hear.

I don't have anything to do. I just wanted to move, so after dumping my knapsack in our hallway, I start walking. I don't have a destination in mind at first but as I walk along University toward Queen's Park, I realize I'm headed to the hospital. This time the clerk at the front desk gives me a room number and when I check in at the nurses' station, the nurse smiles and says it's good I came today, as Donnie is being transferred tomorrow.

Donnie is alone, the room's second occupant temporarily absent. The acrid smell of bleach is stronger than out in the hallway, and under the outrageously bright fluorescent lights his pale skin has a greenish hue. The TV is tuned to *Jeopardy*, and Donnie appears to be asleep, his bandaged wrists resting on top of the blue blanket, but his eyes flick open when I settle into the chair beside his bed.

"Lou," he says, heavily, as if the word weighs more than his mouth can handle.

"Donnie," I say. "Hey."

"I wanted out." He says this slowly, his tongue thick, his words rounded, his heavy eyelids threatening to crash closed any moment. He must be heavily sedated, although not sedated enough to be happy to see me. "You're an asshole."

"You're welcome. You don't go to a park to die, you go to a park precisely so some chump like me will save you." His eyes lose the fight and close and for a moment I've lost him, but then the heavy lids drag back open and he smiles a little and flips me the bird. "There's other ways for you to get out, Donnie. You can talk to the police."

"There's only one way out." This time his eyes close and stay shut. I lean over his bed.

"I know someone, Donnie. Detective Phillips. I've got his number. I really think you should talk to him."

"Who do you know?" A strong hand clamps over my upper arm and pulls me to standing. I am face to face with Kevin Morris. His bloodshot eyes draw close and he sniffs the hair tucked behind my ear, the stinging bleach of the room replaced by the equally abrasive smell of cologne and rum and a sour body odour. Behind him is Donnie's brother. "Who do you know, you little cunt? Who should our dear Donnie be talking to?"

"Let go of me." I pull away but he only squeezes harder, a hot shearing twist of my arm, and I squeak with pain. He smiles and runs his tongue over his top lip, circling, and then bites down on his bottom lip. "I think it's time you come for a visit to our apartment. See our playrooms. Don't say no."

I glance down at Donnie but his eyes stay closed and his face turned away. I force myself to look up at Kevin's face and at Mike, both staring with hard, fixed smiles. Behind Mike's shoulder, a nurse steps into the room. "Only two visitors at a time," she says.

"I'll go," I say, and Kevin drops my arm. I angle away, as the nurse asks Mike if he will be around to assist with Donnie's transfer tomorrow. I don't wait to hear his answer. When I reach the hall, I sprint to the elevators.

Out on the street I move in the opposite direction they would expect me to, running to College and heading east. When I am out of breath I duck into a Second Cup and order a coffee. Settling into a corner seat, I pretend to read *NOW* while covertly watching the street outside. After an hour of nothing, I head home, staying on side streets and checking each approaching car, darting into driveways or hiding behind bushes, if it looks anything like a black Nissan.

My heart continues to pound late into the night, making it difficult to properly study. My heart pounds so hard I worry that, like Dad's, my heart is poorly formed, vulnerable to the sicknesses of the world, and that worry makes it difficult to sleep. Still, even without sleep or study, the history exam is straightforward and I'm fairly certain I ace it. Isabelle and I go out for coffee afterward but we are both tired and conversation is stilted. I sketch out the events of last night but she is so wiped out and stressed about her final French exam she barely responds. My last exam is biology, so studying together is pointless and we part ways on Rosalind. Back at the apartment, I call Detective Phillips and this time he picks up on the third ring. I explain that Stella is missing and that Donnie is in the hospital and that Kevin and Mike continue to be aggressive and weird and threatening. I tell him about Jake the Fish's story and Sal's hypothesis of the warehouse fight club. "You might want to talk to Donnie today," I say. I've given up worrying that Donnie will think I snitched on him. "He might have some important information."

"Lou. We are building a case." He speaks ponderously, as if reflecting on each word and weighing its consequences before saying it out loud. "There are some dangerous people out there. You need to steer clear."

"It's my neighbourhood. It's where I work. I'm only going about my life," I say. "I'm not meddling in an investigation."

"No, no. I'm not saying that."

"Well, Stella is missing. She's hasn't been at the bakery in over a week. She lives at some crappy single-room-to-rent place called the Queenston Arms. Have you heard anything about her? Maybe she got taken to the hospital?"

"No, I haven't heard anything. Not specifically." He pauses. "But we did find a body in the park. We haven't been able to identify the victim yet."

"How will you — " I start but have to stop. If I keep speaking I'll cry.

"I'm sorry about your friend, Lou," he says, his no-nonsense policeman's voice softening. "Listen. I'll let you know if I hear anything."

Jonah comes into the living room as I hang up the phone. I've been avoiding him since my night at Finn's. Jonah couldn't prove I was out all night but he was suspicious, and when I outright lied to his face, he was quietly furious. I don't even know why I lied. I could have just as easily told him the truth. "Hungry?" he asks, holding up a brown paper bag. "I've got some grub."

"No gourmet Isabelle meal tonight?"

"She's studying, as you know. What about you?" he asks as we sit down at the kitchen table. He pulls two oversized pita breads wrapped around crunchy deep fried balls of falafel from the bag and passes one to me. Expert fingers roll down the wax paper into a cone shape and he takes an extra-large bite, yogurt sauce dripping from the corner of his mouth. "What do you have left?"

"Biology tomorrow. Then I'm done."

"Then what? Have you decided on your university?"

Jonah wants me to go to U of T; he thinks it's the only possible choice I can make. I have no idea. There is way too much on my mind to decide the whole rest of my future. I have a sudden memory of last September: Dad and I had taken Jonah out for Chinese food and were heading back home to Linden. At the corner of University and College we passed a flock of girls, "U of T" smeared across their foreheads in red grease paint. They were waiting for the light to change, laughing and tugging one another's wrists, all of them in matching green shirts the colour of ripe limes with black lettering across their various chests: FRESH FROSH MEAT. I watched them for as long I could, until they were nothing but thin green wicks in the distance, thinking, next year that could be me. I could be them. "I don't know if I want to go to university," I say. "I've been thinking about taking a year off. Maybe travel a bit." I haven't, really, but it doesn't sound like a bad idea when I say it out loud. To me at least. Jonah, on the other hand, goes ballistic.

"What?" Jonah says. "What do you mean?"

"I could get a bus pass," I say, improvising. There are ads posted all over the city for a Ride Anywhere $99 Greyhound bus pass. "I've got enough bakery money saved to travel for a month or so before I'd need to find work. It would be cheaper than school."

"No," Jonah says. "Don't be an idiot. That's not a plan."

"It is. It's my plan," I say. "I want to go away for a bit."

"That's not going away," Jonah spits. "That's running away."

I have no answer to this and so I stomp down the hall to my room, leaving my falafel behind, and when Jonah tries to talk to me through the closed door, I yell at him for making it impossible to concentrate on my studying.

Despite the fact that I have memorized every nook and cranny of the human heart, biology is the most difficult exam to get through. As I label the various components of a cell or describe the difference between systolic and diastolic pressure in the heart, I am overcome with a sense of the body's frailty that threatens to make me weep, right there, in the middle of the exam. Biting my lower lip hard enough to draw blood, I stay focussed long enough to finish the last of the long-answer questions, hand over the exam booklet and walk out the door, high school officially behind me.

On Saturday Isabelle and I ask all the regulars if anyone has seen Stella but nobody has. At the end of the day, Irene, the skinny clerk from Legacy Variety, comes in for her usual macaroni salad and yogurt and tells us she saw Stella's stuffed bird, Ruby, lying in the grass at the park earlier that week. "Dat raggedy ting?" she says. "The one she hold inside her shirt?"

"We know it," I say.

"She could have dropped it," Isabelle says when Irene leaves.

"Sure," I say. "And she's probably not missing, she's probably moved back to her mansion next door to Casa Loma." My sarcasm sets a tone for the rest of the day and at the end of our work shift Isabelle and I argue. I want to go to the park and find Ruby. Isabelle says it's a waste of time.

"Jonah and I are going to the Bloor to see *Blade Runner*," she says. "Come with us."

"I'm going to find Ruby," I say.

"It won't do any good," Isabelle says. "You're driving yourself crazy." She sighs extravagantly when I answer with a shrug of my shoulders. Aside from a terse exchange of goodbyes at the end of the shift, neither of us says anything else.

I do feel a little crazy twenty minutes later as I comb the grass of Trinity Bellwoods for the carcass of a stuffed raven disguised as a vulture. Other than finding a spot where the ground looks scorched, I don't find Ruby or anything else that could be considered a clue. Merlin shows up even though I have forgotten his hot dogs. He trots around after me and I coax him to come home but he won't. "Please," I beg, my voice breaking. "It's not safe here." A mother with two kids holding matching blue and white kites passes by, watching me as if I am one of the crazy ones, but I don't care. If Merlin won't leave, I won't leave. I find a spot of decent-looking grass, lie down and close my eyes. The grass against the bare skin of my arms is a thin quiver, the tiny tread of ants ticking over me. Every now and then I peek my eyes open and Merlin is still there, sniffing and peeing and checking out the bushes and the ground beneath the garbage pails. The sun presses white gold against my closed lids and from the direction of the playground comes the sound of mothers corralling unbroken children, who, answering the call of dinnertime, stampede past on their way home. I don't move. I muddle in the warm air, soft and sleepy. I sense Merlin and then Stella next to me as I drift, and she whispers the secret history of the park in my ear. She marches me over hill and dale, skirting swing sets, crouching beneath slides, chipping at the cracks in the concrete. She picks up discarded Popsicle wrappers, broken lockets, beer bottle caps and condoms and stuffs them in empty shopping bags, and she leads me into deep, deep sleep.

In my dream, the park fills with uniformed men. They are concerned. The fire is out but one small fire, a finger of fire, a thread of fire, has escaped. It has tunnelled underground, wormed inside tree roots, steamed through hidden pipes. The men are determined. I am implicated by both my confusion and my lack of concern, and so I help them look. I paw through weedy tufts of grass, kick up chalky clouds of gravel, until I realize, with a sudden squirt of shame and fear, that the fire has found me. The fire is in me. A thin, molten vein pulses along the length of my throat. The men notice. I have nowhere to hide.

When I wake the sun has cooled and settled, a pilot light turned down in the western corner of the sky, a blanket of smoggy blue piled up overhead and the shadows of the trees no longer divisible from the darkness. Stiff and cramped, I creak into a sitting position, surprised to hear someone calling my name. It's Finn cutting across the grass toward me. Merlin is gone.

"Lou, you're pretty solid for not busting me the other day," he says. His thin-lipped smile verges on abashed but doesn't even come close to apologetic or ashamed. "You played it cool."

"Thanks," I say. Ridiculously. It's not exactly the fuck off motherfucker I had been planning to say the next time I ran into him. He holds out his hand and I let him pull me to my feet. He continues to hold onto my arm, pulling me a half-step closer.

"You busy?" he says. "I'm going home to make spaghetti. We could get a bottle of wine and I'll cook you dinner."

The skin of his hand is warm and dry and I catch a whiff of both his aftershave oil and musky body odour. I love this touch, this closeness, want to lean into it, but there's a distance. A disconnect. He touches me like that and I want to say, Hello, maybe I'm falling in love, and he's saying, Let's fuck.

"Can't," I say. "I'm busy." He doesn't insist or ask a second time, which is good, because I don't know if I would say no again. We walk back toward Queen together and I tell him I saw a white squirrel in the park once.

"Really?! That's supposed to be good luck."

At Queen he turns right and so I turn left. Across the street is the Queenston Arms. I decide to see if Broom Hilda at the front desk knows anything about Stella.

She's there and wearing, amazingly, the same turquoise stretch pants and matching top she had on at New Year's. She's seated on the brown plaid couch watching *Dallas* on TV. The room smells strongly of corn chips.

"I'm here to see Stella," I say.

"Stella's not in." She barely glances away from the flickering screen.

"Have you seen her at all this week?"

"Well, no, I haven't. But she's paid up to the end of the month." Turquoise shoulders rise and fall in an oceanic shrug.

"I want to check her room," I say with all the firm authority I can muster.

"Well, dear, I can't let you in without Stella, can I?"

"She could be up there, sick or something." I take a deep breath and make my voice as hard and as tough as I possibly can. "I'm family and if you don't let me in, I'm calling the cops. And I don't think you want me doing that."

She breathes a heavy sigh, looking longingly at her TV. J.R. Ewing is walking around, drunk and waving a gun. She doesn't seem too worried by my threat, only harassed. The show switches to a commercial. "Oh, all right. If it's so important, c'mon then."

Stella's room is empty, the air stagnant and undisturbed. Mould grows on a half-eaten pizza bagel by the bed. I poke aimlessly through a few of the many piles of stuff that clutter her room, following the same half-formed notion I had in the park of finding a clue as to where she might be. But there is nothing.

In one of the piles I find a stubby white candle, wax melted into a tinfoil plate. I pull out Dad's lighter and Swiss Army knife from my purse, sit in the middle of the tiny floor space, the least dirty spot, and shave off strips of wax so that the wick is exposed enough to light. I pass my fingers back and forth through the flame, picturing Stella out on the streets, picturing her coming home. This is the place, this room, with its thin gauze of safety that Stella would reach, would try to reach, each night after the bakery closed. I picture Stella walking in the muffled starlight, picture her reaching the metal door of the Queenston Arms. She is climbing the stairs. She will be so surprised and so irritated when she finds me sitting here. I picture this over and over again, and because there is nothing else I can do, I bargain with the universe: if I stay all night weaving my spell, by morning Stella will be here. Over and over again, Stella is coming in the metal door, climbing the stairs, one foot and then another, any minute her room door will swing open. When the picture dims, I tip the candle, wax splashing on my skin, and bring it back into focus.

Rats are crepuscular creatures, meaning they are most active at dusk and dawn. It is the exact right-sounding word — crepuscular — to describe a rat. They stay with me, the rats, through the long night. I hear them bumping and skittering through the walls. Toward dawn, there is a scratching in the ceiling above me and through the loose particleboard a piece of rat shit falls like a single drop of hard black rain.

I say goodbye to Stella and let myself out.

Outside the street is still and silent, stars dimming amidst the rustle and coo of bird sounds, as if only the stars and birds know dawn is coming. The rest of the city is still asleep. But not me. I am so awake, I might never sleep again. Jonah was right when he said I was running away. I am running. I've been running since I left Dad and our house in Linden. Behind me is a multi-headed Horror — part rat, part rapist, part Grim Reaper, along with all the other things I'm too cowardly to look at. Horror is a malicious, sinewy weed of an emotion that attaches to the central nervous system, twists its roots around the spinal cord and spreads out long, choking tendrils. It's got me right now. Horror that Stella could disappear that quickly, that easily. That she could slip out of daily life with barely a ripple. That I could have helped her that night, but didn't, burying my head in Finn's fickle, trust-less shoulder instead. That someone found her when she was weakest and chose to hurt her. And horror now, at the dawning of another indifferent day. The streetcars will roll by and the people will rush to work. One more day in the city. I don't know what to do with all the horror twisting itself inside me until the moment a black Nissan glides by and then slams on its brakes twenty feet away. Then I know. I run.

Behind me a car door opens and slams shut, followed by heavy footsteps and then a scuffle and shouted curses. I veer onto the road, empty of traffic in either direction aside from the Nissan, which is making an illegal turn, and cross over onto the opposite side of Queen. I run east, turning down Euclid, hazarding a look over my shoulder. Someone — I can't see his face but guess by his size and stockiness that it's Mike — stumbles to his feet on the other side of the road and lunges forward. I turn down into the shadows of the back alley, pressing into a door when I hear the running beat of his footsteps, the continuing litany of fuck, fucking fuck. I hold my breath, leaning into a rough stone wall and breathing in the smell of urine, as Mike moves past the mouth of the alley. A rat, bigger than Sal's Bagheera, scales the edge of a dumpster, ignoring me as I move on. The shadowy edge of the alley is a minefield of refuse, forcing me to move more slowly, dark shapes shifting and transfiguring. A body prone in a sleeping bag turns out to be a black garbage bag stuffed full of rotting meat, a putrid stench rising when my foot knocks the damp bottom edge. Slinky shape of cat turns out to be another rat and the stealthy patter of a rat is a tailless cat. A bucket that smells of shit turns out to be exactly that, a bucket of shit. As I move, I open my purse and pull out Dad's knife and Sal's keys to the bookstore. I have almost reached Palmerston when, behind me, headlights turn down the alley, trained like spotlights on the back of my head. The engine guns, the car accelerating, as I sprint the last few feet to the end of the alley and double back a half block onto Queen, sliding, breathless, into the doorway of Black Cat Books. I have never used the keys before and the lock is clunky, not easy to open, and then once it's open, it's impossible to get my keys back out. I twist and wiggle them left, then right, the key unmoving when I pull back. It won't come out. The Nissan turns onto Queen, that new song "Funky Cold Medina" spilling out from the open car windows. I take a deep breath and twist hard to the right and the keys pull free and I slip into the store, pulling and locking the door shut behind me. I am certain they didn't see me enter but as I reach the back counter the lights of the car pull up out front and blink off, Tone Loc's rap abruptly silent. I crouch beneath the cash register as the banging begins and a voice that neither shouts nor whispers recites a long list of obscenities and threats in a piercing tone. "I saw you, you stupid fucking bitch. You're not getting away. I am coming in there if I have to break every last window and when I find you I will rape every hole in your body with those shards of glass until you are bleeding from your eyes and your mouth and your ugly fucking cunt."

There is a pause. I look up at the *Chat Noir* poster above me, wondering if Sal's awake yet, and have an idea.

"She's in here. Yeah, that's it." There is a tremendous shatter of glass as I ease inside the secret passage and pull the hidden door closed behind me. I crouch in the darkness, certain that my pumping heart, my ragged breath and chattering teeth are all loud enough to be heard out on the street. It is so dark I could be floating in outer space, unmoored, exempt from gravity. I fumble with Dad's knife, trying to open it, but almost drop it instead, and so clutch it to my chest, uselessly, breathing in through my nose and out through my mouth, trying to slow everything down. Be a smart animal, I tell myself. Don't give your hiding spot away.

When they first enter, they are quiet, Kevin cooing softly, "Puss, puss, puss, come on out to play." But when I am not immediately visible, he goes into an ape-shit, feral rage, smashing glass cases, knocking down bookshelves as he outlines the ways I've messed with Donnie and endangered his plans. He explains, in graphic detail, the multiple ways he will violate me. He promises to kill me several times over and then burn this whole fucking dog-shit ghetto place to the ground.

Footsteps start banging around upstairs. "I've called the cops. They're on the way. You better get the fuck out of here." It's Sal and he sounds convincingly tough but I am terrified he will come down. Don't be a dumb animal, Sal. Stay where you are. What feels like thirty agonizing years —

184 — ghost warning

but is likely only three minutes — passes, Kevin's threats interrupted by the familiar sound of sirens drawing closer.

"C'mon, man. We got to get out of here." It's Mike's voice, speaking for the first time. "C'mon."

"Fuck! Fuck you, you dirty cunt. This isn't over."

Car doors slam and the engine revs as Tone Loc picks up mid-verse, the music fading as they pull away. Then, silence. Outside a streetcar rumbles past and the broken panes of the windows thrum with the rattling vibration. I know they are gone but I don't move until I hear Sal crunching over the broken glass, calling my name.

Detective Phillips arrives about an hour after the cops, stepping over the yellow-and-black crime scene tape that flutters in the early-morning breeze. The bookstore has been destroyed, everything glass is smashed. Everything breakable busted. Books lie all over the floor, their pages bent and creasing under flayed-open spines.

"Lou," Detective Phillips says, sitting on Sal's stool while I remain in the better, more comfortable swivel chair, one of Sal's tobacco-scented blankets wrapped around my shoulders. He's different in real life from the detective I imagined on the other end of my phone line. He's younger than I remember and skinnier and taller, and his hair is fine, with only a hint of a curl, a nondescript light brown that must lighten to white blond in the sunshine. I remember his eyes as being kind but they are just steady and serious. Sal hands me a cup of tea but my hand is shaking so badly that after a moment Detective Phillips reaches over and takes it, the floral saucer and cup looking childish in his large hands. I remember suddenly his first name is Rory. It's an uncommon name but it suits him. The counter is smashed so he sets the cup and saucer on the floor and pulls out a small notepad and pen. I repeat what happened for the third time, the detective interrupting every few minutes to ask a question or clarify a direction. "It was them," I tell him. "It was Kevin Morris and Mike Hunter."

"Did you get a good look at them both?"

"No." I run back through my memory. I never saw either of their faces once. "But it was their car. And I heard them, clearly. It was them. It was their voices."

"Okay." He makes a note in his pad, visibly disappointed with my answer, and for a moment I am willing to recant and lie wildly, telling him whatever he needs me to say. Yes, I saw their faces, their ugly monster-man faces. Yes, those faces are seared permanently into my brain. It's not even a stretch. But Detective Phillips is handing me a card. "This is the number for Victim Services. You give them a call if you need to talk to someone." He moves to the front of the store where Sal is sweeping up glass.

Victim. I am a victim. A Victim. It's an odd word if you repeat it several times, losing its meaning rapidly, hard consonants more like knife jabs than a description of a state of being. I don't want to be a victim. Bagheera jumps onto my lap, undisturbed by the chaos, and allows me to stroke his back once, twice, three times before he leaps again, landing on the floor and padding carefully around the broken glass. *Victimvictimvictim*. It's just a word. Like evict. Or vitamin. It doesn't mean anything.

My loopy thoughts are interrupted by the rising pitch in Sal's voice at the front of the room. "What are you saying?" He leans the broom against the wall but it slides to the floor with a loud clatter, which he ignores. "Does she have to get raped, or worse, before you can do anything?" Detective Phillips looks to the counter, to where I sit huddled in Sal's blanket, pointedly, and Sal's eyes follow. Sal lowers his voice and angles his back away from me but his hands continue to move in angry sweeps and exclamations. I go to the bathroom and run cold water, splashing my face and practising deep breaths. When I return, it's only Sal in the bookstore and he's brewing a fresh pot of tea.

"Sal, I'm so sorry." I gaze out on the disorder and violence of the room. Can the bookstore survive this kind of destruction? Can Sal? Can anyone?

"This? Pfff!" Sal's sweeping gesture takes in the whole room. "I have insurance. I'll be able to renovate now. Don't worry about that." I sit down and he hands me a new cup of tea. The deep breathing must have worked because the cup and saucer don't clatter in my hand.

"I'll help you clean up."

"No. I'm going to get a claim started and get professionals in to do the cleaning. You are going to drink this cup of tea and then you are going home to get some rest." He reaches up and rubs my head, an unnatural gesture that embarrasses us both. The silence that follows is awkward too. I can't help but think of Dad. I wonder if Sal is thinking about him too.

"Sal? Why didn't Dad ever tell me about his secret girlfriend? That Jillian Nash lady?"

Sal puts a fist to his mouth and harrumphs into his hand. "She wasn't his girlfriend."

"Well, whatever. Lady friend. Fuck buddy."

"Lou!" Sal manages to look as scandalized as an old blue-haired church lady but I stare him down, no apologies. He clears his throat, says, "It wasn't ever that serious. He would have had to really love her to bring her home to meet you. And he didn't."

"Why didn't he take better care of his health? He knew his heart was weak, but he smoked and drank. He liked butter and eggs and ice cream." The last syllable of ice cream rises to a tremulous pitch as I run out of air, but I can't stop now. "He was always telling me to be a smart animal but he didn't even exercise. He *never* exercised, Sal, and that's just dumb. Dumb and hypocritical and — " There's no end to my sentence. I take a deep breath, start again. "Why did he do that?" I ask, and this time, I can't help it, I start to cry. Sal stands up and hugs me, a move more awkward than the head pat. And then I can't help it, I start to laugh.

Sal sits back down. "You're a mess."

"Yup."

"Look, Lou, I don't have any good answers for you. Your dad loved you and Jonah more than you can ever know. And for a long time he took exceptionally good care of his health; your mom made him do it. But when she died it was hard. Losing her broke his already broken heart. But he pushed through. He fought it. For you and Jonah." Sal sweeps the mass of black bangs off his forehead and pushes his glasses up his nose. "Losing your mom was a shock. She was the strong one. Determined and fierce and unrelenting. Like you."

"She died giving birth to me. It's my fault," I say, not able to look Sal in the eyes. "Sometimes I feel like it is all my fault."

"Right." Sal harrumphs again, the sarcasm in his voice sharp-edged and pointed. "Because you're the centre of the universe." I don't have anything to say to this and for a moment we are quiet, watching a streetcar rumble by. "Lou — " he tries again, his voice softening. "It's not your fault. How could any of it be your fault? You just think that 'cause you're young and young people are stupid and selfish and egotistical."

"Thanks. That makes me feel so much better, Sal." Now I'm the one being sarcastic but also truthful. It does kind of make me feel better.

"Stop thinking, kid," he says, a smile creasing his face.

"Right. 'Cause I'm not very good at it." I return his smile. "Hey Sal? I've been thinking about taking a year off from school to travel. Maybe take a bus out west."

"Hmm. The old Grey Dog." Sal takes a long slurp, finishing his cup of tea. "That's not a bad idea." He opens the locked cash box and from underneath the tray of bills he pulls out an envelope and hands it to me. Inside are a few fifties and a stack of twenties. "There's over $700 in there. It's payment for all the hours you worked here this winter. I was going to save it for when school started, you know, for your books, or whatever. But maybe you could use it now."

"I can't take it, Sal. Use it to help clean up all the mess."

"I told you, I have insurance. This is all covered."

With $700, I could get on a bus tomorrow. I could leave all this behind. "You're like my fairy godfather, Sal."

"I am, you know." Sal ducks his head, long brown bangs hanging over his face. "Your godfather? Your dad insisted. I told him it was a crazy idea but he wouldn't listen. Stubborn. Also a lot like you."

I want to leave so badly it makes me dizzy. But really, truly, leaving is a prospect that is also terrifying. My heart starts to pound like a pumping fist in my chest. "Sal," I say. "I might be going a little crazy."

"Well enjoy it while it lasts, kiddo." He smiles. "Then you better get back to work."

Despite the hammering of my heart, the more I think about boarding a bus, the more impatient I am to do it. "I could leave today," I say. "Will you tell Jonah for me?"

"No," he says. "That you have to do yourself."

Before I head home, I stop at the bakery. Leo is whistling and rolling out pie dough in the back room and Anna is serving a customer. They both drop what they are doing and rush over. News has travelled fast down the block.

"Lou," Anna says. "Darling girl. Are you okay? We heard there was a break-in at the bookstore. Irene saw you there. We've been worried sick."

"I'm okay," I say. Unconvincingly, apparently, because while Anna finishes putting the customer's order together, Leo pours me a coffee and leads me to the little staff table with the same kind, conciliatory body language he uses when some particularly kooky kook gets out of hand.

I cut right to the point. "I'm sorry for the short notice but I need some time off."

"Okay," he says.

"I'm not sure for how long."

"Okay," he says.

"I want you to know," I say, "that I really love working here." And then, embarrassingly, I start to cry.

"I know, I know," Leo says. He places one hand over mine. Anna comes to stand behind me and strokes my hair, the way I imagine a mother would, and this makes me cry even harder. "There's always work for you here, Lou."

"Yes, darling girl," Anna adds. "You take the time you need. Come back when you're ready. You know where to find us."

I wipe my eyes and rein in my hiccuping breath. "I might take a trip out west."

"That's a grand idea," Leo says, and they each in turn hug me goodbye, Leo kissing the top of my head. "Wait," he says, and pulls out a stack of twenties from the till. "Last week's pay." He counts out $160. It's more than he owes me. "Take it," he says, waving the bills. "No argument."

"Thanks, Leo, Anna." They both hug me, again, and I almost start to cry. Again. But Anna says, "Go, go," and shepherds me out the door, like I'm a loony or a grifter like Shakespeare Joe.

The walk home is long and I am unbelievably weary but not afraid. The streets are busy with people ecstatic to have shed their winter clothes and bare their faces to the bright shining sun. There is no room on these streets for monsters. On Rosalind, Mr. Baptiste is trimming a tree covered in tumbling white blossoms. "What kind of tree is it?" I ask. "Peach," he says, and it is the first time I hear his speaking voice. It is low and smooth, thick with a Spanish accent. "Later, you bring a basket and we will fill it with peaches for you." Back at home, the apartment is empty. Jonah must be at work. I strip my clothes off down to my underwear, pull on Dad's sweatshirt and pick out a blue card. It's a quote from Nietzsche: *I overcame myself, the sufferer; I carried my own ashes to the mountains; I invented a brighter flame for myself. And behold, then this ghost fled from me.* I crawl into bed with it, pressing it against my cheek, my mind made up.

It's dark when Jonah wakes me, pounding on my bedroom door.

"Go away," I say. "I'm sleeping."

"That's two nights, Lou! Two nights you've stayed out all night. We need to set some ground rules here."

He hasn't talked to Sal then. He doesn't know what happened. "I'm sorry, Jonah. It won't happen again. We'll talk tomorrow, okay?"

"Jesus, Lou. I was worried sick!"

"I'm fine, Jonah. I'm sorry you were worried."

"Tomorrow. You and me. It's time to clear the air."

"Okay, I promise."

I sleep for a few more hours and get out of bed around three to quietly make a pot of coffee. I take a cup into my room and attempt to write a letter to Jonah. Each attempt is worse than the last. The more I try to explain or tell him how I'm feeling, the less and less I believe myself. On an impulse, I pour out the last slim finger of Dad's Scotch into my emptied coffee cup, then, pretending to be someone else, someone bolder and more courageous, I swallow it in two burning gulps. This new frame of mind makes the letter easier to write. A brief note that is straight to the point will be best. *I'm off. I'm taking a bus out west. Don't worry, I'll call from the road. Ask Sal what happened at the bookstore and you'll understand at least part of the reason why. I don't know if I'm going to school in the fall or not and I didn't tell you all this in person because I knew you would try and change my mind. Don't be too mad. Love, Lou.* I pack, filling my knapsack with some clothes, the black journal and green pen that Jonah gave me for Christmas, my Walkman and Rufus' tape. In my purse are Dad's lighter and knife, and the single card with the Nietzsche quote, along with the envelope of money from Sal and Leo. I leave the note for Jonah on the kitchen table underneath the stack of blue cards. It's his turn to spend some time with them.

At sunrise, I start walking, determined, but a block away from the bus station I stall, stopping at a burnt-out corner lot where an old foundation has been torn up, leaving a crater-sized hole in the cement. I slide the heavy knapsack straps off my shoulder and rest it on my feet. A green chain-link fence blocks off the hole, bent and tugged so it hangs like a garland from pole to rusty pole. Inside the pit: nails, pizza box, thistle bushes; crystal wineglass, broken; old couch, dirty blue and cushion-less. A small maple stands between me and the fence, pigeon shit dropping off a broad green leaf. The exposed concrete foundation of the brick building next door is covered in graffiti. A black and yellow punching fist. A space invader shooting a Mr. Pac-Man. Some undecipherable tags and, like on the side of the Legacy Variety, a big black scrawl reading ILL KID.

An old man limps toward me. Even in the heat he's wearing thick track pants and a bright red fleecy vest. The track pants are too short and his sweat socks are tugged up over the elastics. As he passes, two women also sweep by, all business in dark suits, black nylons, shoes with thin straps and wedge heels. "She eats like a pig," one says, "even though she is so frigging skinny." I pick up the knapsack and walk in their wake and a few minutes later I am boarding the bus. I stumble to a seat on the right almost at the back. The windows are tinted a grey shade against the city's heat, and the air conditioning verges on cold. I grab Dad's hoodie out of my knapsack and put it on, pulling up the hood and balling my hands inside the sleeves. It's been a long time since it smelled like Dad but the faint whiff of Pears soap in the fabric is reassuring. It also smells like falafel and sweat, which makes me think of Jonah. I look out the window, half expecting him to be there, ready to drag me off the bus, or at least wave goodbye. An old lady stands with a younger woman pushing a baby stroller filled with a large bag of dog food. A skinny guy in a baseball cap horks onto the sidewalk, then picks his nose. A man in a bad suit shakes hands with a bigger man in a better suit. But no Jonah.

The bad-suit man, the final passenger, slips into the seat beside me as the bus groans into motion. We head north and the city slides away like a dirty postcard. Curry house, aging laundromat, adult movie store, XXX blinking its incomplete equation of love. I curve my body to the window, away from my seatmate. I thought I might feel bad, leaving, but I don't. All I am is relieved.

Part 3

13

I didn't plan it. But when the bus pulls into the Becker's parking lot where I boarded, what seven? eight? months ago, I know this is where I was headed all along. "This is me," I say to the bus driver, who, despite the air conditioning, is sweating profusely, damp skin glowing an unhealthy, jaundiced yellow. "I'm debarking." Under his brown cap, the driver's bushy brows lift and his eyes widen.

"Debarking?" I repeat. "Is that the right word? Or is it disembarking?"

Now he frowns and his forehead quizzes into deep folds. He thinks I am a raving lunatic.

"Or, whatever, getting off," I say. "I'm getting off."

Now he smiles, all sleazy-man, and the door opens with a low whooshing exhale. He says something as I turn down the stairs but my face is too red and my ears too hot to hear. Sometimes I have no idea why I say the things I do. Maybe Jonah is right: I should not be out in the world all alone.

I sit on my knapsack in the middle of the parking lot and watch the bus weave its way back to the highway. The sun is bright and the sky daubed with fat little clouds, flakes of white in a wash of reassuring blue. After purchasing a loaf of bread and extravagantly priced jars of peanut butter and raspberry jam at the Becker's, I head down the back route, along a dirt trail that skirts the perimeter of a scrubby pine forest. It is the route we always took as kids because, even though it is longer, there are no major streets to cross. When I was very young, I was afraid of the pine forest. Jonah convinced me that not only was it haunted, it was also heavily patrolled by police and trespassers would be executed. Not prosecuted. Executed. Later, Julie and I played bike tag there, a fun game made more fun by the lingering possibility of encountering ghosts or heavily armed forces or some extreme combination of the two. Past the forest, the back route winds through a dry weedy field that cuts behind the elementary school. This is where Julie and I used to set off caps and firecrackers and build bike jumps and where, notoriously, in the sixties, a teenager murdered his best friend and the girl they had fought over. There is a new dump of large boulders blocking the path and I clamber over with a tippy sense of balance, weighted by my getting-heavier-by-the-minute knapsack. On the other side a cricket careens into my ankle. I startle and almost fall on my sorry ass. It's hot as hell too.

Past the field, the path narrows and pits into the shape of a dried-out riverbed. It is twisty and narrow here, runnelled with the now parched and dusty trails of heavy rainfall. The calf-high grass surrounding the trail is scratchy and sparse, full of squashed-up pop cans, brightly coloured chip bags and glossy black crickets that continue to knock into my ankles. And spit bushes studded with buttercup flowers. I still don't know if the spit bombs come from the plant itself or from a bug that makes its home there. But they litter the field too, a neat and nasty combo: bright yellow blooms, big gobs of spit.

It takes almost ten minutes to reach the water tower. Someone has added a giant red *WAR PIGS* to the circle of graffiti at the bottom but otherwise things look exactly the way they always did. Same dirty white tower, surrounded by the same ineffectual chain-link fence, the narrow metal ladder leading to the top, three, maybe four, storeys high, still as enticing as ever. But I pass by. There is one final incline and I dig in, hamstrings straining, sweat dripping, to make it to the top. There, in the middle of the path, lies half a mouse, his squandered insides spilling out, bright red and wet, a cheery and terrible reminder of something once alive. I make a left at the mouse onto a stretch of sidewalk, turning my gaze down to the concrete with the childish hope that if I don't see anyone, they won't see me. Then I'm at the house.

HOUSE FOR SALE: The red, white and blue Re/Max sign is crooked and squat as if someone had come during a windstorm and hammered it in, extra hard and deep, at an angle. I know this shouldn't bother me, but it does, and I fight the urge to get down on my knees, tear it out and replant, so it stands straight. But someone, the Turners, would spot me for sure if I started monkeying with the sign so I give it a fierce tug as I pass, accomplishing nothing, and keep moving. The front door is locked with a realtor's box but a window at the side of the house is easy to open and I slide in with the skill of a cat burglar, landing on the old Maytag washing machine. Dad and I loved those stupid commercials with the Maytag repair guy who is lonely and bored because Maytag machines never break down.

There are a few lights on in the house. Smart, I think, to have a few lights on in case any of us come home, which, I realize, is a dumb thought even before I've finished thinking it. The realtor's left a few lights on to give the impression that someone still lives here. That the house belongs to someone. That it is not empty or abandoned or haunted. That at any moment somebody inside could laugh or yell or fart or make a sandwich.

The invisible and magical hand of cleaning lady Nancy, Dad's one extravagance, is evident in the orderliness of the house. A lingering whiff of Pine-Sol perfumes the air and the stacks of newspapers have been cleared away. In its quiet cleanliness, the house exudes a patient anticipation, as if waiting for us all to return from a very long vacation. When I was a kid, a movie about nuclear war played on prime-time TV. Dad refused to watch it — brazen fear mongering, he said — but basically everyone else in North America did. Except maybe if you were a Mennonite. Dad and the Mennonites missed it, but everyone else saw. The movie glossed over the initial explosion, which I imagined as biblical and blinding, and focussed more on the inevitable slow death of the survivors from radiation fallout. Afterwards, all I could think about was an abandoned world full of houses and fully stocked stores, a world empty of people but full of stuff. Pots, pans, tins of soup and peaches, TVs, hair dryers and record collections. A world full of things, unused for the rest of eternity. That's sort of how the house feels right now.

In the bathroom, the hairbrush, toothbrushes and razor are all neatly aligned on the counter. Even the desk in Dad's office has been tidied, his notebooks and torn-out sheets of paper squared into a pile. A horrible neat little pile. How am I supposed to retrace Dad's thoughts when they have been tidied away? I reach down and muss the papers, a gesture so futile and ineffective it is both pathetic and laughable. I retreat down the hall to my room — there on the table beside the bed is my book, *Indium's Ark* — before returning to the kitchen to peruse the fridge, half expecting to see a mountain of casseroles, untouched and mouldering, but it is empty inside and sparkling clean, cleaner than it's ever been. There is a box of orange pekoe in the cupboard and an unopened jar of Dad's favourite mango chutney but otherwise the cupboards, too, are empty and wiped clean. I make a peanut butter sandwich, relaxing in the familiar space of the kitchen, then return upstairs to crawl into my crisply made bed and read my book. Just like old times.

Things are bad for Indium, the half-human, half-cyborg hero of the story. Devastated after the death of Sera, his seventeenth-century mortal lover, Indium is consumed by a bleak and unending depression. During this depression, Indium investigates some of the more unethical practices by his futuristic employers, Biolight, the corporation that has taken control over time itself. When Indium comes precariously close to discovering Biolight's nefarious secrets, he is suddenly reassigned some two hundred years into the future to Victorian England, where he encounters a woman who appears to be the living incarnation of Sera. Indium is a swirl of enhanced mortal emotions: he delights, he despairs, he falls in love all over again. This new woman, Rachel, is an amateur naturalist who is exposed to a virulent strain of flu shortly after meeting Indium. Afraid he will lose the love of his life all over again, Indium exposes this new lover to a type of nanovirus that will grant her a similar type of immunity to his, but when she learns who he truly is and what he has done, she conflates futuristic technology with soul-stealing devilry and fills her pockets with heavy rocks, drowning herself in a lake. The book ends with Indium in custody awaiting punishment for his various indiscretions and misdeeds, to be continued in the next instalment of the series. I put the book down, pull the covers up and fall asleep.

It is dark outside when I wake up. Maybe ten or eleven at night. The light is on in my bedroom, cozy and familiar, and for a brief flash, in the mushy moment of waking, I wonder if Dad is home yet. He never kept normal work hours and this would be about the right time for him to be getting in.

This is the time I should have gone to check if he was home. And if I had, I would have found him in time to call an ambulance and get him to a hospital where they would pump him full of Aspirin and nitroglycerin or defibrillate or whatever doctors really do when they aren't on a TV show. And I would be a hero and he would be alive and we would both be so inspired and full of gratitude that I would become a doctor, a heart surgeon, and he would be so proud of me. If this were an episode of *Twilight Zone*, this would be my do-over. This would be the moment when I get up, go downstairs and open the door to the garage —

There's a loud bang on the front door. "Lou! Lou! Are you in there, Lou?!" It's Mrs. Turner. I don't move. I barely breathe. "Hello, Lou? Are you there? Jonah's worried about you." The bangs eventually fade to a few half-hearted knocks and then silence. I wait ten minutes before I return to the kitchen to make another sandwich, which I put on a plate and carry up to Dad's office. His notebook, the one he searched for in my fever dreams, is on the bottom of the pile, and I open it to the page of point-form notes I skimmed over the day he died. This is what I have come for. *Parkdale area, significant increase in multiple assaults. Nine? Ten? Rapes, beatings, immolation. And then it is right there. Kingston 1984-87. Similar pattern. Alert out for Black Nissan w Licence 271 SEN. Police receive several tips and ... abrupt halt. A year later starts up in Toronto. Connection?*

I knew Dad could figure it out.

Quietly, so I don't alert Mrs. Turner, I unlock the back sliding door and step out onto the patio. It must be around midnight, not so late in the city but late in Linden. The sky is high and salted with stars and the darkness has a luminous underwater quality, as if it fell over this small town in gentle waves and ripples, lapping at the edges of a bigger, darker night. Dad could be out there, enjoying the darkness, on his way home. It's easy to imagine, easier than the thought that he is never coming home. Easier to imagine that all things that have perished cannot be lost forever, and all things that are lost must once again come home. *Come home, come home, come home.* It is a kind of a mantra, a meditation in the darkness, except the word meditation implies a kind of clarity and I have no clarity inside me. More like a black hole.

I want so desperately to find Dad and there is one place I haven't gone yet. The garage. It's cold in there, colder than the night air outside, and there is a clear rectangle of whiter concrete where Dad parked the car but nothing to mark the spot where he fell. I know the spot, though. I know exactly where it is.

I don't know what I expect when I sit on the cold concrete but nothing happens. He doesn't talk to me and, despite the familiarity of medical terms learned from the heart book — cardiac arrest, arrhythmia, endocarditis — I still don't understand what happened. It is as confusing and unimaginable as the day I walked downstairs and found him here. If I had got there a little earlier, he still might have died, but maybe he would have had a chance to say something before he left. "Don't forget Lou: garbage day." That's the last thing Dad ever said to me. I lie down, arranging my arms and legs inside the imprint he left behind, and close my eyes.

"Hello? Is someone here?" An unfamiliar voice rattles me into consciousness. Not Mrs. Turner. A man. Sounds like he's in the kitchen, or maybe the hall. I am confused. And cold and stiff on the garage floor. I must have fallen asleep.

"Hello?"

Is it the police? No. Why would the police be here?

"It smells faintly of smoke." Another voice. A woman. "Are they smokers here?"

"Not that I know of. Hmm. Looks like someone dropped by." Purposeful footsteps pass by the garage door and back again, stop, then the man's voice, brighter this time: "Well. Let me show you the upstairs. Three bedrooms and a fourth room, an office, which could easily — "

Ah, a realtor. He's showing our house. My house. So why do I feel so caught? So guilty?

As the voices float upward, I dash into the kitchen, grab my knapsack and slip into the backyard, hopping the fence and knocking on the Turners' back door. Mrs. Turner, dressed in a matching shift and pant set of swirly blues and greens, her own orbiting planet, is putting a kettle on the stove. "Lou! You crazy girl! I knew you were there." She opens the back door, releasing a powerful blast of lemon-scented furniture polish. "Come in, come in. I'm making tea." A new hutch between the back door and the kitchen table forces me to slip in sideways. "I want to hear all about your new life in the city. Look at you. You're a little on the thin side but, that smile!" She crushes me into a bear hug, pressing my face into her shoulder and the flowing folds of her linen blouse, the smell of rose lotion and onions mingling with the furniture polish

"I can't stay long," I say, accepting a cup of tea. "I have to catch a bus in an hour. But I was wondering if I could make a phone call. Long distance to Toronto. It won't be long and it's really important."

"Of course, sweetheart. You know where the phone is."

I take my tea into the living room and dial Detective Phillips. It goes straight to his answering machine. "Uh, hi. It's Lou James. I have some new information. Remember I told you my dad was investigating the assault story? Well, I went back through his notes and he said from 1984 to 1987 there was a similar pattern of violence in Kingston. The suspects drove a black Nissan with the licence plate 271 SEN. That's not the licence plate of the black Nissan now; I can't remember what it is but there's a nine in it and an eight maybe, and the letter K. But they could have changed the plates, and Donnie told me both Kevin and Mike were in Kingston for business school at that time. It can't be a coincidence. Right? Anyway, I hope that helps. I'm not going to be at home for you to call. I'm going on a trip out west. On the bus. So. You won't be able to reach me. Okay, well. Bye."

After draining my teacup, eating two muffins and submitting to two more bone-crushing hugs, I leave the Turners' and retrace my steps onto the dirt path, past the dead mouse, the water tower and the haunted forest all the way back to the Becker's parking lot, arriving fifteen minutes before the next scheduled bus. I dig in my purse for a quarter and retrieve Rufus' mixed tape out of my knapsack, pulling the cardboard sleeve with his scribbled phone number out as I step into the phone booth, avoiding half of a Creamsicle melting into a sticky puddle on the cement. I pick up the phone but don't dial, realizing I have no idea what to say.

There is a kind of milky warble to the glass at the back of the booth so the world outside distorts, rounding and softening. Beyond the weedy edge of the parking lot is a large manicured yard with a brand-new-looking house, its vinyl siding painted white and grey. They don't call it white and grey though, the people that live in that house, they say *ivory* and *heather*. A pretty flowering vine climbs a trellis at the side of the house, newly in bloom. Morning glory, maybe? Or clematis? I can never keep the names of flowers straight. An above-ground pool sits in the centre of the backyard and the swing set beside it is the deluxe kind: slide, tee-ter-totter, double-seated swings. On the front steps beside an assortment of potted plants lies a bright green plastic watering can with a white spout, tipped on its side. Power lines intersect the newly repaved road at a right angle, a row of giant crosses that lead to the dark pines. It's not visible from here but I know there are train tracks that run parallel to that tree line. In the distance the trees look agitated and the crows that dot the garlands of black wire are unreal, make-believe. I blink my eyes and the house and hidden railway tracks and trees and power lines and blue-black crows all blend together into a watercolour image in the milky glass. It's hard to understand how the world can look so plastic and cheap. So holy and so strange.

The bus is pulling off the highway and so I hang up the rattling phone receiver and go out to meet it, standing behind two other people getting on board. As I pull out my bus pass, a car drives by and I see the face in the open window of the passenger seat: Rufus. His eyes meet mine, surprised, then hurt. I don't have time to wave before I hop on board.

We drive all day. I am a restless, fidgety passenger while, in sharp contrast, my seatmate appears to have preternatural powers of sitting still. He never moves. He wears camouflage cargo pants and a black T-shirt, and he has a moustache, droopy and lush as a cat tail, the kind of moustache I abhor. I bet he combs that moustache. I could never trust a person who combed his moustache. He was reading a book a while back, not in English. Russian, maybe. He's asleep now and his head dangles at an awkward, disconcerting angle and he nose-breathes, loud. A glistening line of drool leaks from under the moustache, which, as I study it, looks less like a cat tail and more like a small woodland creature hunched over his lip.

I don't know if I can make it all the way across the country. Outside my window it's rock, tree, sky; it's barn, cow, power line. All the houses look lonely and far away. Inside, when I consider all the lives the speeding bus passes, a panic feeling drops right through me. A stone thrown in deep water, rippling down to the bottom of my belly. My head is full of mad-dog thoughts, the kind that chase their tails in circles and bite the hand that feeds them; they combine with the static countryside to create a kind of violent, apocalyptic state of boredom. One of those cranky existentialists should have written a play about riding the bus.

Passenger One: Is this your stop?

Passenger Two: Yes, I … I don't know.

Passenger One: (Nervously) Excuse me.

Passenger Two: Yes, of course.

Passenger One: Were you sleeping?

Passenger Two: I don't think so. You?

Passenger One: I don't know. Where are we?

Passenger Two: (Sighing, looking out the window. Wondering.) It could be anywhere.

And so on. Except that scene is more interesting than life on the bus right now. I should have taken the train. Everyone knows trains are better than buses. That's why there are so many train songs with distant towns gliding by and brown-bagged bottles of whisky and the chugga chugga sounds of never returning home. Everyone is sad and beautiful on a train.

Not so on the bus. Feeling melancholy here is about as poetic as stubbing your toe. If I wrote a bus song it would chronicle the accumulation of leg cramps and the awareness of a neighbour's nicotine stains and the drinking of many Styrofoam cups of bad coffee. Where a train song smells like a far-off wind, diesel smoke and pine trees, a bus song would smell like a potpourri of doughnut eaters' farts. This I can now say from first-hand experience.

At dusk the bus pulls off the highway at a truck stop in the middle of a Christmas tree forest. Stepping out of the bus I realize how far away from Toronto we have come. The grass and gravel are paisleyed with frost and the air is glorious and tightly cold. I breathe baby clouds into the blue evening air, the cold tingling my teeth, tasting like crisp apples.

The truck stop tilts, its sea-foam green paint peeling. One good gust of wind could carry it aloft, set it spinning like Dorothy's house in *The Wizard of Oz*. There is a big marquee-style billboard that reads: Goody's Goodies Homestyle. It's made of tin, the edges so thin and rusty I'm in danger of getting lockjaw looking at it. The place should likely be condemned. I love it.

Inside, behind the counter, a short woman with pouffy bright bottle-blond hair flings her arms like a circus ringmaster. Must be Goody. Doughnuts fall from the glazing rack. Flapjacks flip. The kitchen thrums and bangs and glows and all the crazy action emanates from Goody's fingertips. She is the star of the show.

"Darling," she says when I reach the front of the line, "what can I get you?"

"Talk to me," I say, "about flapjack versus fritter."

"Well." She runs a hand over her ruffled blue apron, polka-dotted with grease stains. "A fritter is naught but a fried wad of dough shellacked in sugar. My flapjacks, on the other hand, are something special."

"Sold, and a big coffee too." She punches my order into the till as I dig into my purse for money. "You must be Goody?"

"My real name," she winks, "is Judy."

I scan the dining area looking for an empty seat. There is none of the kitchen's energy in this section of the diner. The tables are old and flimsy, relics from the 1960s, with metal legs and orange tops. The walls are flimsy too, entire sections of drywall warped, puckered and buckled. Someone has attempted to cover the cracks by taping up hundreds of postcards. Postcards of places someone has been, I wonder, or places they want to go? The only empty seat is beside the mustachioed Russian Zombie. I turn back to the counter.

Goody is wiping off a small statuette. It's one of those pseudoawards, the kind with robust little people smiling over cheesy inscriptions. Best Dad Ever. #1 Bowler. The kind of thing kids insist on buying their parents until they are old enough to acquire good taste. Scrubbed clean, Goody places him back on top of the till. His arms are spread wide and the inscription reads: I Love You This Much.

"Can I get the flapjacks to go?" I ask.

"Darling," Goody says, "your wish is my command."

Outside the sky is softly purple, night-smudged, although daylight isn't en-tirely lost yet. I follow a dirt road that winds away from the diner and the highway to a small oval lake, passing by tall spruce trees, their ragged arms moving in the soft wind as if animated by something big and strangely human inside. The purple of the sky deepens and beyond the lake there is a twinkling of lights. A small solitary rock town, I imagine, buried deep in the trees beyond Goody's restaurant. The inhabitants have leathery skin and slow smiles and they live in simple houses. It is either winter or almost al-ways autumn in this town. The mornings are sunny and nipped with frost, the air glassy and absolute, a fine time to walk about. But late afternoons the wind tends to get edgy and if you are unlucky enough to be out in the elements when it rouses, your heart will grow uneasy and your mouth will fill with dust and when you return home your clothes will be the colour of the road. It is a town waiting for a stranger to arrive. I could be that stranger. The idea hits with such force I spin around, half certain the bus has left without me.

I jog up the dirt road, backpack bouncing, coffee splashing over my fingers and, sure enough, there is no bus in the parking lot. I run faster, as if that will make a difference, and by the time I pound up into the empty parking lot I am breathless, my heart and lungs bobbing away into a wide-open void.

"Oh, honey. Did you miss the bus?"

It's Goody herself. She's sitting at the picnic table halfway between the diner and where the bus is supposed to be, smoking an extra-long cigarette.

"That would appear to sum up my situation. I missed the bus."

Goody laughs, not unkindly, and inhales on her cigarette with a slight sucking noise. Even in my panic I have to admit her hair is truly spectacular: the shape of a cotton-candy swirl and the colour of runny egg yolks.

"You in a rush to get where you're going?"

"Not particularly," I say.

"Where are you going?"

I shrug. "Haven't figured that out either."

The back door of the diner opens and someone yells that the Welton's distributor, that bastard, is on the phone.

"Well, in that case, there's a bus coming by in about forty minutes," Goody says. "But I'm not sure which direction it's headed. Maybe back the way you came."

"Figures," I say.

"There's a complete schedule inside," she says, dropping her cigarette butt to the ground, the toe of her penny loafer pirouetting it into the dust. "I have to go but you come on in if you need anything."

I sit outside on the park bench with no idea of what my next move should be. Wait in the parking lot for the next bus heading west? Stay here, forever? Turn around and go back the way I came? Call Rufus and apologize? Tell him I really do want to go on a date? Or call Jonah, ask him what the hell I should do? All options seem equally ludicrous and pointless.

Daylight disappears and I sit in the dark. Country dark is different from city dark. Above me the sky is impossibly high, thick scuds of blue-black clouds lie like spooky continents across the silver of the moon. A flitting cloud of bats tangle in the peripheries of my vision, skeletal butterflies drained of all thought of colour, their squeaky nightsong similar to the rats' song in Stella's room. After everything that has happened, it's silly to fall apart because I missed the bus but when the tears start to come, I let them. It's as if a dam has burst loose, and there is a spring-fed well burbling inside of me with an endless supply of tears. I have turned into water and the flowing stream blurs the black edges of the night and the bats and the memory of the rats and Goody's diner all disappear.

Everything happens for a reason. It will all work out in the end. Lame, right? Those are the kinds of cheesy useless sentiments people say when they don't want to deal. What they are really saying is take the path of least resistance, but dress it up with rainbows and unicorns and baby *i*'s dotted with fat little hearts. So, it is a mark of my defeat that this is what I say to myself when the bus pulls up and, with barely a conscious thought, I wipe my tears away with the sleeve of Dad's sweatshirt, flash my pass and climb aboard. Everything happens for a reason. It will all work out in the end.

What end?

Whose end?

What bullshit.

The only empty seat is near the back. As I tuck my knapsack into the overhead compartment I ask the old man seated by the window where the bus is headed.

"Winnipeg," he says.

Winnipeg? As I slide into my seat and the bus pulls out of Goody's parking lot I realize I have made a terrible, terrible mistake.

14

"I got fizzy pop."

My bus buddy, the old man in the window seat, is being friendly. I blow my nose on the last of Goody's napkins and take a good look at him. Do I want to ask what a fizzy pop is? He registers my look and reaches into a canvas duffel bag at his feet and pulls out a twelve-pack of Molson.

"It's not a good idea to drink when you're sad," I say, taking a beer. The top is all dewy and the snap open sounds extra loud in the quiet bus.

"No," my new neighbour says. "It isn't. Are you sad?"

I shrug. Yes. "More like lost at sea," I say.

He smiles and nods. "I can see the sailor in you."

It's hard to say how old he is. Somewhere roughly between forty-five and seventy-two. Stinky. Imagine a cologne that captures the exact morning-after smell of a tinfoil plate full of ground-out butts doused with the dregs of many beers. Imagine a nervous man, newly washed but starting to sweat, preparing for a first date with a woman named Beulah (who answered his personal in *The Banner* or *The Local* or *The Gazette*) by splashing himself with said cologne. Imagine he laces up boots, ripe with the smell of fresh shoe polish and caked cow shit, pressed eternally into the bottom treads. Imagine as he leaves for his date he hastily checks the oil in his almost-antique Ford pickup (truck has a goddamned leak, gets worse in the cold weather). Oil stains his newly manicured nails and provides the top note in his overall bouquet. That's my neighbour. He's nice, though.

"Frank Dinesen," he says, holding out his hand.

"Louise James. Lou," I say, and shake. "You know, practically everyone I know is an alcoholic."

"Everyone?" he says, leaning back in his seat and chugging half a beer.

"Well, no. Sal. Just Sal. But he's got problems. He's self-medicating."

I know I'm being an asshole, acting like a little kid who thinks because she knows someone the rest of the world does too. But Frank doesn't seem to mind. Apparently he's self-medicating too. He's nervous because this is the first time in forty years that he's left his family's farm. Three weeks ago, the barn burnt down. He grew up there but after the fire he knew it was time for a change. He sold what he could and left the rest at the dump. Now he's on his way to Winnipeg to visit his cousin and then he's going to

Nevada to get a blackjack licence. According to Frank there's good money in dealing cards.

"It's for the best," he says, taking a long slurpy drink, "no matter how I look at it. If the barn hadn't burnt down I would have been there till the day I died."

I feel sorry for him but he doesn't want my sympathy. He opens another beer and grins at me.

"In the casino, it's going to be showgirls and buffets, night and day. Showgirls and lobster buffets!" He raises his can in a salute. "Yes ma'am, when a barn burns down it's hard but it's for the best."

We clink cans and drink.

"And you," Frank says. "Where are you headed?"

"I don't know," I say and start to cry again. The kind of plump, hopeless tears shed by an overtired child. It's stupid, really. Frank nods his head up and down as if he's agreeing with me and after a good minute of my bawling he passes me an old-fashioned handkerchief, wrinkled and piped with embroidered cherries. "My dad died ..." I say, "in the garage." As if that explains everything. Frank keeps nodding. "Sorry," I say, patting my eyes dry.

"No need to apologize for tears. Myself, I cry at the drop of a doll." Frank opens a third beer and takes a long hissing sip. "So ... you're setting off in the world? That's brave. You're doing it decades ahead of me."

"Yeah, well," I say. "I don't have any idea where I'm going."

"Maybe that's for the best."

I fold the cherry handkerchief into a rectangle and pass it back.

"Keep it," he says, waving my hand away. "I'm practising non-attachment."

The word non-attachment evokes an image of Merlin the Mutt, the way he cocked his head at me and half wagged his greasy, ragged flag of a tail, and fresh tears swell into my eyes. Now that they've started falling, they might not stop. Frank doesn't seem to notice though. He's on a roll. "Listen, I'll tell you this. I had an old tin box full of teeth back at the house. Every tooth that fell from the mouths of my family, young and old, with cavities and cracks and tea stains and what have you. Out of all the stuff I got rid of, that box was the one thing I didn't think I could leave behind. The teeth. I packed them into my bag to carry with me. And then I thought, this is crazy. I'm going to start a new life with luggage full of dirty old teeth."

"Did you bring them?"

"Nope. I figure a pocketful of teeth ain't worth a pitcher full of spit. I flushed them down the can." In return, I tell him the story about the Zen archer firing his arrow into the sea. He nods his head emphatically when I reach the punchline. "Yes! That's you and me, we're loosed arrows and wherever we land — " he winks a watery bloodshot eye. "Bull's Eye. Hey, do you want a doughnut?" He reaches into the duffel bag and pulls out a box of Timbits.

"Did you know that Canada has more doughnut shops per capita than any other country in the world?"

"Is that true?" Frank eats a honey-coloured doughnut hole in one bite, washing it down with a swig of beer.

"Yeah. I think." Sal told me that to backup one of his crazy theories about Canadian identity and it may, or may not, be true. "I don't know. I could be making it up."

"Of course you are, honey," Frank says, passing me the box. "Of course you are. We all are."

I told Sal once that drinking beer made me feel like crap. He got all prissy, saying it pained him to hear a young girl being so crass. My new friend Frank, future King of Blackjack, informed me as we exited the bus in Winnipeg that there was a legitimate word, *crapulous*, that refers specifically to the bloated, seasick, icky sensation caused by too much alcohol. Derived, Frank said, from the ancient Greek word *crapula*. The opposite feeling, perhaps, to *fabula*? To keep up with modern times the word might have to be amended to include the day-after feeling of grossness when one indulges in both drink and doughnut. Crapdoughnulous? Crapdapulous?

Crapdapulous: that pretty much sums up the state of my body. My mind is a little lighter though. I only had a few moments to make my connection heading west after I said goodbye to Frank in Winnipeg. I'm back on the bus now. Next stop: Calgary.

I miss the moment when we cross into Saskatchewan but there is no doubt that's where the bus is now. The sun rises behind us, lightening the charcoal sky to reveal an endless blue above and, below, a tide of faded grass as far as my eye can see. Every so often we pass a frail vanguard of trees soldiering against the wind, thin shadows trailing like ribbons twisting in a breeze. My eyes are red and sore watching for horses. It seems to me they should be everywhere, here on the prairies, herds of tough brown horses, but I've been watching for hours and I haven't seen one yet. The only consistently visible signs of life are birds, big black crows that throw themselves into the sky, bobbing on the currents like string-less kites.

There's an owl perched on the spindly arm of a tree by the side of the road, his black saucer eyes alert, although now that day has dawned, it must be near his bedtime. Julie and I did a project on owls in grade eight. A group of owls is a parliament. They are extremely far-sighted. To the Greeks they symbolized wisdom but to most everyone else, the Aztec, the Maya, certain African tribes, they symbolized death. A family of barn owls can eat up to three thousand rats in a single season. They are efficient, stealthy predators. This one tracks me as long as it takes to pass. I mean, I *know* he's tracking the bus but it *feels* like he's tracking me. He's round and feathery, a grey, fluffy smudge with slight tufted ear horns, wide-open eyes so silky black and bottomless it's easy to believe he's a bearer of messages from the underworld and for one clear moment those bottomless eyes are looking inside me.

It bugs me that Jonah thinks I'm running away. Why can't he see that sometimes running away is a legitimate option? I mentally argue the case with him, a one-sided argument I am in danger of winning except for the fact I can't stop seeing the hurt look in Rufus' eyes and I can't stop worrying about all the strays I've left behind. Who is going to bring Merlin hot dogs? What if Stella is somewhere, hurt, and in need of somebody to find her? And what about Sal, who has to deal with the fallout of Kevin's bookstore destruction all alone? And who will help him mind the store so he can go to his therapy sessions and get some exercise in the pool? Sal played it cool, but those were big steps for him. He's a person who has a hard time letting go. I'd love to tell him the story of Frank's family's teeth. It would slay him. In fact, I wish I could teleport Frank to Zane's, right onto the bar seat next to Sal. Those two, they'd hit it off. They're two of a kind, like peas in a pod, or bull rushes in ditchwater.

I hope Frank's loosed arrow lands him a job in Reno or Vegas or wherever he ends up but there are so many outside forces that can knock an arrow off its path, and, I have to admit, it is easier for me to imagine him sleeping on a park bench than wearing a suit and dealing out hands of blackjack. He seemed to be about two drunken benders and one unfortunate mugging away from a life sleeping on the streets.

But it's bad mojo, all my worrying. Frank deserves better than the picture I've created in my head and so I refocus the image into one where everything goes according to plan. Frank is inside, in an enormous, well-lit room, his shoes and hair are slick black and he's smiling. Around him people shout out bets to the steady rhythm of money being made, money being lost. He's at a buffet and there's lobster and prawns, thick slices of steak, chocolate mousse, strawberries and champagne. To his left and right are dolled-up girls with feathery headpieces, shiny hair, kohl-lined eyes big as hard-boiled eggs, pouty lips, big rumps and sparkly tassels hanging from ten-gallon tits. Frank is smiling and pinching soft, plump places and helping himself to a second, a third, a fourth helping. The only sadness that tugs at his heart, the only unanswered longing, is for a fridge full of good strong Canadian beer.

"Amen," I whisper to the passing fields, the thin shadows and the black birds bobbing across the sky. I send good thoughts out to the rest: Dad, Sal, Isabelle, Jonah, Rufus, Stella, Merlin, unhappy Donnie, even that jackass Finn, and then I try and banish them, along with all my worry, to the past tense. It doesn't work. I am as flat and as lonely as the prairies and I miss them all.

15

There's a three-hour layover in Calgary. In Toronto, Jonah has finished up his evening shift and is walking home right now. If I call quick, I can leave a message and not have to talk to him in person. It's a rambler, my message, full of long descriptions of the Russian Zombie, Goody's Goodies and Frank, King of the Blackjack table. I talk a lot and say nothing. Jonah will be furious. "Listen," I say to the empty air. "I'm sorry for running away. But I couldn't catch my breath. It's like I was drowning. And I want to be diving in, you know? Not drowning — "The machine beeps. There's no more space and I hang up the line.

I settle into a booth at a diner and order the soup of the day, creamy tomato, with a grilled cheese sandwich that comes with a side of potato chips, requesting both ketchup and raspberry jam as condiments. This was something Dad showed Jonah and me: the first triangle of sandwich is dipped in ketchup (your vegetable) for dinner, the second half is smeared with raspberry jam (your fruit) for dessert. Jam on grilled cheese was an overlooked culinary delight, according to Dad. Better than cheesecake, he'd say. My sandwich is so good I order a second and a cup of tea, and pull out my black journal and green pen.

It is thrilling, the unsullied blankness of the first page, an empty space waiting to be written, and in that anticipation, before that first mark is made, it is both nothing and everything, its very emptiness allowing for infinite, endless possibility. I can't bring myself to write anything on it yet but I tear a page out from the back of the book to write to Rufus.

I'm sorry I didn't call when I was in Linden and I'm sorry I won't be in Toronto when you go apartment hunting. I left because one of my dad's blue cards told me to go to the mountains. And I left because Toronto exploded into a violence that was so ugly and terrifying and everyday that I could not understand and did not have the courage to face. And I left because I slept with this musician — a guitar player! — and it was awesome and awful and I have no idea if I should tell you or if it has ruined things between us. And I also left because I felt like if I stayed my future would roll along, would just happen, regardless of what I choose or want.

And I don't know what I want yet. Jonah says I'm not leaving, I'm running away, and this is true. If I could run away to a time instead of a place it would be the moment my dad came home and his heart stopped. I would be waiting for him and I would call an ambulance and then he wouldn't have died on cold concrete all alone. If I could go back to a second moment it would be the night at the bonfire, when we danced to the Waterboys, because that's the last time I remember being truly happy.

My scribbles cover both the back and front of the page and when I am done I tear it all into thin strips and throw it in the garbage before boarding the bus to Vancouver, scoring a double seat all to myself. I press my face against the window, waiting for the mountains, but outside the night is pitchy black, and all I can see is my face reflected in a dark mirror, looking watery and vaguely familiar. The darkness is a heavy blanket, dragging the weight of the past few sleepless nights over me, thoughts like heavy ballast thrown overboard, dragging me down, dragging me under into the deep waters of sleep, and I don't stir until someone from the next seat over tugs at my shirt sleeve. I open my eyes to bright bedazzling sunshine. We are in a large bus station parking lot, a salty breeze stirring the air.

"We're here," the shirt tugger — a middle-aged mom — says, smiling at me.

"Here?" I say.

"Vancouver. Is this your stop?"

"Vancouver! I missed the mountains?"

"You can't really miss them here." She smiles. "They're everywhere. The bus to Victoria leaves in about twenty minutes," she says, pulling a small luggage bag and a green Teenage Mutant Ninja Turtles knapsack from the overhead compartment. She hands the knapsack to her daughter, who is about three or four and has two uneven ponytails on either side of her head. "Vancouver Island. That's where we're going."

"We're riding the ferry, right, Momma? The really big one?" The little girl bounces down the aisle, springs in her feet. One last smile in my direction and the woman follows her daughter. I trail behind, eavesdropping. Whales, the little girl wants to know. Will she see whales and dolphins on the ferry ride this time? "Maybe," her mother says. "Maybe seals. Definitely seagulls. Tugboats too. And waffles. We'll have ferry waffles for breakfast."

"Waffles! Whales!" The spring in the girl's step gets higher and higher. They turn to the back of the bus station where a line is already forming for the Victoria bus and I drift toward the main terminal. Now that I'm here I have no idea what I am going to do. Something to eat, first. Waffles would be nice. Whales too. Without making a real, conscious decision I morph my drift into a large loop that tags onto the end of the lineup to Victoria and board the bus. I take the seat across the aisle from the mom and daughter. Mom smiles at me and then turns back to their game of I spy. "I spy," the girl says pointing out the window, "something deeee-licious."

Even through the tinted windows the sun is bright. The streets look dusty, sleepy, as if the city isn't quite awake yet. We pass a woman carrying an extra-large coffee cup, walk-running toward a bus shelter, and an old guy pushing a caravan of shopping carts ahead of him. Three carts, precisely, linked together and piled monstrously high. Buddy looks like he crawled out from behind a dumpster but he moves with vigour and purpose, combing through garbage pails. We pass blocks of pawnshops, Money Marts and skeevy-looking hotels. Coffee shops. Mountain Co-ops. Florists. Takeout sushi. In less than an hour we reach the ocean. "I spy," the little girl next to me shrieks, "I spy something blue. Something blue, Momma, and something wet!"

"The ocean," I say. Mom and daughter look over at me: mom with a questioning smile, daughter with a wary frown. "It's my first time," I say. "I've never seen the ocean before."

The driver parks in the ferry lineup and opens the bus door. "You can stretch your legs," he shouts back to the bus, pulling a pack of cigarettes from his shirt pocket, "but don't go far."

The terminal is on a long narrow spit of land, water on both sides. The sky is higher here than it is in Ontario, I'm sure of it. It has to be to accommodate the giant trees. The air is less dense, cooler, and the sunlight shimmers with invisible colours: ocean blues, leafy greens, silver linings. Offshore, in the distance, are red metal cranes that remind me of aquatic versions of the giant snow walkers from *The Empire Strikes Back,* the best movie, Jonah and I both agreed, in the Star Wars trilogy. Rising out of the gilded surface of the water is a mountain ringed with a dark swath of forest, rosy in the blue morning light, so exquisitely beautiful and incomprehensibly grand it is impossible it belongs to this world. It is Avalon, Middle Earth, Heaven.

"Heron." The mom from the bus steps beside me and points to the rocky beach. A large bird with a long neck balances on stilt-like legs at the edge of the water, still as a statue.

"Whoa," I say.

"Where you travelling from?"

"Toronto."

"That's where I'm from." She smiles again, sweeping curly hair that at one time must have been dark brown or black but is now a salt-and-pepper grey into a long ponytail. Her face is youthful, her dark brown eyes inquisitive, and she is short, shorter than me by a few inches, giving an overall impression of an ancient but vigorous child. "Originally Toronto," she adds. "Now, Wolf Bay. That's home." She checks to her left where her daughter is down on all fours playing puppy with a tiny, drooling black Lab and then extends a hand to me. "Marie," she says, "and that's Hannah."

"Lou." We shake and smile. I'm smiling too much, a big goofy grin, which I can't turn off. Too much oxygen, maybe. "Is Wolf Bay near Victoria?" I ask. It sounds picturesque, Wolf Bay, the kind of place I'd like to go. I'm tired of cities.

"About an hour and a half outside of the city proper," Marie explains. She gives me a brief overview of Vancouver Island's geography and, as we make our way back to the bus and board the ferry, climbing three long flights of stairs to the passenger deck, I inquire about cheap places to stay and good places to find work. I am amazed at the size of the ferry, and tell her so while we wait in the lineup for waffles, and as the three of us eat at one of the cafeteria-style tables, she asks me questions about Toronto. Bit by bit, between bites of fluffy, syrupy waffle, I piece together the events of the last year in the city and my random, cowardly flight away from it all.

"That's quite a story," she says as we return our food trays piled with sticky plates and dirty cutlery to a cleaning station and head outside to watch for whales.

"There!" Hannah shrieks as soon as we go outside. She rushes to the guardrail and points. Sure enough there is something bobbing in the placid, sun-stippled surface of the sea. A seal? Hannah thinks it's a seal. I think it's a seal. But no, Marie points out, it is only a waterlogged piece of wood. After about half an hour of sea watching we head back inside and Marie asks if I mind watching Hannah at the play area while she makes a phone call.

Hannah climbs aboard a hard plastic bright yellow duck and grips the handles on either side of the duck's head so tight her knuckles turn white.

I sit down in front of the duck.

"This is *my* duck," Hannah says. I nod. She purses her lips, then continues: "My duck's name is Val."

"As in Valerie?" I ask. "Or Valentine?"

"No." She kicks her heels in the duck's side.

"Faster, Val," I say. "Faster."

She smiles, says, "Frosting is my favourite food."

"I like it too."

"But I can't have it. I like salmon though."

"Oh, me too," I say.

She smiles, slides off the duck and sidles over to me, leaning a hip into my elbow. "I can sing 'O Canada.'"

"Hit me," I say.

"O Canada," she trills, her voice high and squeaky in my ear. "True pasted love in all the sons to man … O Canada … the laaaaaaaaand."

"Beautiful," I say, and she sits down on my lap.

"Let's play house. You can be the mom. He," she points at Val, the yellow duck, "can be the dad and I'll be the dog. And oh! It's nap time! Go to sleep!" She barks a few times while I, eyes closed, pretend to snore. Several of the busily playing kids in the vicinity stop to check out our ruckus and when I wake up I see Marie standing at the edge of the play area, smiling at us. An announcement comes over the loudspeaker instructing all passengers to return to their vehicles. On the way downstairs Marie asks me if I would be interested in being a nanny for the month of July. I could stay with them in Wolf Bay and look after Hannah while she and Howard, her husband, are working. I could help with the cooking and the cleaning.

"Howard and I take August off for family time," Marie says, "but we're crazy busy for July. We could use help."

And *I* could use help, obviously, but she is too polite to say that. The overoxygenated smile is back on my face. I nod: Yes. Desperate, giddy, hound-dog grin all over my face. "Sure. That would be awesome." We shake on it and reboard the bus, riding past Victoria and on to Wolf Bay.

The bus drops us off at the juncture of the highway and Bell Road. A few cars whistle by while I wrestle my knapsack onto my back but otherwise there are no signs of life. Human life, that is. Animal life, yes, and vegetable. The birdsong is loud and varied. The sides of the road are crowded with brambles and weeds and beyond are trees. Big trees! Huge monstrous gargantuan poking-the-bums-of-angels skyscraper trees. I take three steps and stop.

"Holy," I say. "What kind of tree is that?"

"Cedar," Marie says. She points her finger in a wide arc. "That's a Douglas fir and that's a hemlock. And this — " she draws me across the road to a slight clearing. Beyond a steep decline of rock lies the ocean. "This is an arbutus." A thin gnarly tree grows on a slant from the rock, its upper branches twisting in an oddly shaped crown of thick green leaves. Fibrous, tan strips of bark peel away revealing a smooth cinnamon-red skin.

"Beautiful," I say. And it is. Dad would love it.

"Only native broadleaf evergreen in Canada. It only grows here, on the coastline."

The brambles on the side of the road are loaded with fat jewelled berries the shape of a large raspberry and the colour of pale apricots. Hannah plucks and pops them into her mouth at an alarming rate.

"Edible?" I ask, just to be sure.

"Yes, edible. They're salmonberries. Edible, but not really flavourful. Hannah loves them though." Hannah nods, pale cheeks puffed with berries, a greedy little chipmunk.

"So," I say, spreading my hands wide, "Wolf Bay?" We have yet to see a house, a car or another person.

Marie smiles. "There's not much to it. There is a general store — "

"With ice cream," Hannah adds, a few beads of berries escaping the corner of her mouth. A large German shepherd trots up beside us. He has a limp but his manner is certain, as if he had been waiting for Marie and Hannah all day.

"Yours?" I ask.

"Never seen him before," Marie says.

"His name is Serious," Hannah announces.

"Sirius?" I say, and he looks directly at me, black eyes blinking, thick tail a-wag. "Sirius is the name of the Dog Star."

"That's right," Hannah says. "He is a dog star."

Marie turns up a long lane, Sirius still trotting at our heels.

We pass a cherry tree loaded with nearly ripe fruit, four raised garden beds with pale green shoots poking through black soil and a chicken coop. Empty, Marie explains, because while she likes the *idea* of chickens and fresh eggs, she's not so sure of the reality.

"They're stinky," she says. "And they attract coons. And bears."

"Bears?" I say, as I scratch the ruff around Sirius' neck.

"And cougars," Hannah says. "The cougars are the worstest."

"Cougars? Bears?" I say. "For real?" The dog thumps his tail reassuringly against my leg. We're at the house now, a wide rectangular rancher painted white and green, a second storey over only half of the first, and I bend down to say goodbye to Sirius. For my attention, I receive a dry nose prod to the cheek and a few more tail thumps.

The family bedrooms are upstairs but I will be sleeping downstairs. Marie leads me along a narrow hallway off the kitchen into a small sitting room that separates a bathroom from a bedroom. The hallway and sitting room are unfinished: bare drywall in some places and in others, just wooden frame. The bedroom and bathroom are finished and painted a soft lemon-on-drop yellow and trimmed in white. The large window has lace curtains on the bottom half and outside is another cherry tree, drooping branches pressed against the glass. She and Howard built this extension, Marie explains, for his parents, who live in Edmonton and are getting older.

"Well, I'll let you get settled in. You probably want a bath or a shower. There are clean towels in the bathroom. Let me know if you need anything."

The water is hot and there is a bottle of peppermint body wash. I rinse away a lifetime of dirt — it is glorious — and emerge from the hot water clean as a candy cane to crawl onto the cool sheets of the bed. My plan is to rejoin Marie and Hannah in the kitchen momentarily but sleep slams into me once again, hard and fast, and I fall so deeply that when I wake I am unsure where I am and whether hours, or days, have passed.

"Daddy! Daddy!" Hannah shrieks outside. I hear the low rumble of a man's voice and then Hannah, shouting, excited, explaining who Sirius is. "He is a *star*, Daddy, a dog star."

I get up, pull on some fresh clothes and make my way down the unfinished hall to join the family.

Dinner is salmon, asparagus and new potatoes, the whole affair drizzled in a tart lemon butter. Delicious. Howard could pass for a skinny Santa Claus, his snow-white locks falling into amiable twists and curls, his broad smile and rosy cheeks belying a personality that is less jolly and more whip smart. He asks a few pointed questions, his interest piqued only when I explain Dad was a journalist. He is familiar with Dad's name and says he remembers an article published in *Newsweek* on South African apartheid.

The remaining dinner conversation consists of Hannah's animated descriptions of the bus ride and visit with her aunt and various cousins in Nelson. After the dinner dishes are cleared, Howard carries Hannah on his shoulders upstairs for a story and bedtime. While Marie washes, I dry, and we discuss the details of my stay.

Howard and Marie are busy. They operate a small publishing company, Red Pyjama Press, which also produces a quarterly literary and art journal due out at the end of the month. And they are behind. What they could use is someone to be with Hannah twenty-four-seven while they work crazy-long hours. At the end of the month, over the long weekend, they would like to go away for three days to a friend's wedding on the other side of the Island. When they return, I'll be free to go. They can either pay me in cash or in an old '82 Honda Civic Howard has been fixing up for Marie. "I can't use the car. I'm the old lady loser who still doesn't have her licence," Marie says, leaning closer as Howard comes down the stairs. "Which is good. I don't really want to drive."

"Do you drive?" Howard asks as he comes into the kitchen and switches the kettle on.

"I have my licence," I say. "A car would be great. A car would be awesome."

I say a lot of things like this: awesome, like, for sure, no doubt. Like, a car? That's awesome, for sure. Marie and Howard are both smart and very articulate and often, when we speak, I am impressed with my dumbness, the way it settles like a lump on my tongue. Occasionally they ask my opinion about a piece of art or a poem they are considering for the journal. I'm not sure why because I never have anything interesting to say, only, yes, I like it, or, no, I do not. Thumbs up, or thumbs down.

But we don't speak much. Marie wasn't kidding when she said they would be busy. I barely see them. They have a business office in a nearby town called Nanaimo and when they aren't there, they are holed up in their home office upstairs. Marie tries to appear at dinner, although the effort it costs her is obvious. She emerges from the office, reminding me of Jonah: mole-ish, blinking in the light, clothes rumpled, energy level always extreme, either feverish or exhausted. They work around the clock while Hannah, Sirius (who, it appears, has no intention of ever leaving) and I slide into an easy routine of long, luxurious days at the beach.

Birds wake me every morning around four thirty. There's a hush that swells just before sunrise, the climactic quiet of the night, and then the birds begin, all together, as if God, the holy conductor, has given the signal to announce the imminent arrival of daylight. The first symphonic over-ture contains melody and harmonies, but as the sun rises the birds begin to improvise, and the notes stutter and dive-bomb and crash into the most unholy early-morning racket imaginable: unhinged, raucous, unrelenting. A pair of doves nest in the upper arms of a cedar in the front yard and, with the first rays of sunlight, they begin to *coo coo coo* with all the romance of a drill bit boring through a skull. So I get up, me and Sirius, early, before the rest of the house. After filling his bowl with kibble, I make coffee and go out onto the porch where I read or write in my journal. My journal writing started as an open letter to Rufus, trying to explain everything that happened last year, but I realize I needed to explain it as much to myself as to him. It's not a letter I'll ever send, but I'm also not going to tear this one up. When I finish writing, I do some stretches. Dad once told me my mother stretched every morning, claiming it improved one's general out-look. This, I think, is a worthy goal: to improve one's general outlook.

Hannah wakes around seven thirty and patters out to the porch in a sky-blue nightie, her hair a-muss. She likes to snuggle in the morning and tell me her dreams, which occasionally involve being chased by a witch but most often feature an adventure with multiple animal mounts — whales, eagles, elk — and resolve in arriving home in time for a dinner of fruit and chocolate. She is never hungry for breakfast until the moment she is and then she is starving, teary, desperate for a bite of boiled egg and toast. After breakfast we pack her Ninja Turtles knapsack with water, zip-lock bags full of almonds and carrot sticks and a Tupperware container full of juicy cherries and head down to the beach.

The beach access is across the road from the house. Difficult to climb up and bordering on treacherous to climb down, our descent almost al-ways includes a scraped, bumped or bruised something and a flurry of Hannah's angry, bereft tears. At times like these the only thing that will distract her is an instalment of the Sirius Dog Star story I have been telling. The basic story is always the same: Sirius is out one day exploring a crayon factory where he falls into a vat of silver colour and emerges, glittering. The animals of the forest, from the smallest frog to the shrewdest wolf, are awed by the vision of silver Sirius and believe him to be an animal god, the Dog Star, fallen to earth. The only animal unconvinced is Sirius' old friend Rocky, a cranky black Lab who steals from his owner's dinner table and likes to sniff other dogs' butts. Rocky devises several methods to expose Sirius as a regular old dog: he howls at the moon, coaxing Sirius to join him; he purposely infests Sirius with fleas, forcing Sirius into fits of uncontrolled scratching; he orchestrates a stick being thrown so that Sirius, in the midst of speaking to his forest followers, will dart off to fetch, thus publicly humiliating himself. Whatever the method of exposure, the result is always the same: despite learning his true identity the animals of the forest still love silvery Sirius, the Dog Star. Hannah could hear that story fifty times a day.

The beach is covered with barnacle-encrusted rocks so sharp that, if you are not careful, they will slice through the bottoms of your feet. Hannah has a pair of black swim shoes and she skips over these rocks with the ease of a mountain goat but I move more slowly. When the tide rolls out, it leaves the most outrageous and fantastic sea things in its wake, and a sandbar that stretches for miles. Sirius, Hannah and I splash and explore for hours every day. A large rock formation dominates the south end of the beach and during our first week together, Hannah and I carried stray pieces of driftwood up to the highest point and built a rickety lean-to. Hannah calls it Home Rock. We've heard seals barking from there, seen a mama and a baby deer, watched a pair of eagles fishing and, once, two killer whales arcing in and out of the water. It never gets boring on the beach.

In the afternoons we return home and water the garden, read story-books and make dinner. Or ready dinner. Usually Marie has something prepared or at least planned out. With Sirius watching from the corner of the kitchen, Hannah and I warm up stews, or cook premade pizzas or grill chicken breasts dabbed with olive oil, garlic and rosemary. After dinner is Hannah's bath time and she takes her turn telling stories, long run-on sentences about funny ghosts and houses made of potatoes and people with bells for heads that ring, ring, ring. Towelled off and back in her sky-blue nightie, Hannah disappears with Howard or Marie for bedtime and I am free. There is a large library in the living room full of novels and non-fiction, books about the spice trade in the 1600s and Tibetan Buddhism and urban planning and theories of modern art. I make a pot of peppermint tea and take one of the library treasures to the front porch, where Sirius and I sit, reading (me) and farting (Sirius), until the light fades and the giant cedars loom large in the gathering dark. Sometimes I continue to read in bed but mostly by the time the sun has set, I'm ready to sleep.

I called Jonah when I first got here and left another brief message on the answering machine and I wrote one postcard but I'm not too anxious to talk to him in person. If I did, I'd have to be honest and say I love it here and I never want to leave.

And then suddenly the month is over. The journal is finished on time. The oil is changed, the brake pads replaced on the Honda, and Marie and I drive into town where I sign transfer-of-ownership papers and put insurance on it. We have what Marie calls a family dinner with fresh prawns and white wine and spicy leafy greens and raspberries from the garden and the next day Howard and Marie pack and leave, off to someplace called Sooke, for their friend's wedding.

Hannah is outraged to be left behind. She storms around the house in her nightie and cowboy boots, a small wet fury, kicking books and yelling at Sirius to get out of her way. Even the Dog Star story won't distract her. When she is all cried out she glumly allows me to help her into her bathing suit. I ask if she is ready to go to the beach: she chews her lip and refuses to speak but eventually accepts my outstretched hand.

We are almost at the end of the laneway when a passing black pickup squeals to a stop in front of us and the driver shouts through his open window.

"Ripper! Hey, Ripper! Hey, that's my dog!"

Slowly, decidedly, Sirius turns away, crosses the road and pees on a bush.

Hannah squeezes my hand and speaks loudly, her little girl voice fierce and firm. "His name's not Ripper. It's Sirius and he's *my* dog." She looks up at me for the first time that day. "Right, Lou? He's mine, right?"

"Hannah, I — " The kid in the truck is about my age. Acne-blotched skin, muscle shirt. Easily twice my size. As he snaps his fingers and whistles, he flushes a deeper red. Sirius, preoccupied with sniffing the ditchwater, does not even glance in the truck's direction. "If he is, in fact, your dog," I say, "he sure isn't happy to see you."

His hands lift in disgust and he yells again. "Ripper, c'mon boy, c'mon Ripper." Sirius' sad quizzical eyes arch for a moment before he turns and walks toward the beach access, his limp pronounced.

"I'm telling my dad," the kid says, gunning his motor and pulling away.

Down the path to the beach a blackberry bramble leaps out and tangles around Hannah's ankle. It pulled her down *by purpose,* she says, it tripped her, *by purpose,* another maelstrom of tears raining down.

"I ... don't ... want ... him ... to ... take ... Sirius," she cries into my shoulder.

"Me either, kiddo." I un-snare sock from thorn and ask if she wants to hear the story of the day the Dog Star fell into the vat of rainbow colours.

"Not that one." The sobs subside, her voice less shrill. "I want a new one."

"Well," I say as we start walking. "I have been thinking about a story with a little girl in it. A little girl with almost-black hair."

"Almost-black hair, just like you and just like me?" Hannah says as we reach the beach. "And, I know, her name could be Hannah. And she could be four years old."

"That *is* you!"

"No! Just *like* me."

"Well, this girl's name is Stella," I say as we reach the end of the rocks and the start of the sand. "And she's actually almost six years old, but she could be a lot like you. Except she has two older sisters."

"And they're mean?" Hannah asks as she bends and unties her shoes.

"No," I say. "They are about the nicest sisters ever, which is good because they are very poor and live in a garbage bin. They don't have any neighbours except for gigantic rats and they don't have good food or nice clothes. All they have is each other and a piece of chalk and a skipping rope and for fun they play hopscotch and skipping games."

"Hop Stoched?" Hannah says. "What's Hop Stoched?"

"It's a game," I say.

"Where are their mom and dad?"

"They don't know," I say. "They never knew."

"Oh." Hannah wrinkles her nose, unsure of whether she likes this story.

Sirius, a few feet ahead of us, sneezes when a water snake slithers through a deep puddle in a rocky indent and surprises him. Hannah darts away to find a piece of driftwood.

"It's okay, Sirius," she shouts. "Don't worry! I've got a wiggle stick." She splashes then stirs the puddle with her driftwood, splashes then stirs again.

"Wiggle stick?" I say.

"Yeah," Hannah says. "It takes all the bad stuff away."

Hannah is out of the bath and in her blue nightie when the woman arrives. I have been half expecting, wholly dreading, the knock on the door. Hannah spies from the top of the stairs while the woman and I talk in the front hallway.

"I'm sorry." The woman speaks and sighs at the same time. She watches my face when I answer but looks away whenever she has something to say.

"We didn't force him to stay here. He wants to stay. And … he is welcome to stay. We want him to stay."

"I'm sorry." Speak-sigh. "My husband wants him home tonight."

"He's happy here." I scratch the dry skin at the back of Sirius' neck and he pushes back against my hand and into my leg, looking up at me with a wide grin. "Hannah really loves him."

"I'm sorry," the woman sighs again as she reaches for Sirius' collar. "I'm really very sorry."

"So you said," I say as they walk away. Sirius doesn't strain away from the woman but when she lets go of his collar to open the door he stops moving. She reaches back down and leads him to her car. I close the door as they drive off, afraid to face Hannah.

"Don't worry," she calls from the top step. "He'll be back."

And he is back the next morning, in time for breakfast.

Hannah executes an impromptu dance around the house. She throws her hands above her head as if she's shaking off water drops. She leaps in the air with a buoyant side-to-side skip. Sirius' black eyes follow her around the room with dubious bemusement, oversized tongue lolling pinkly through his doggy grin. Hannah twirls till she falls to the floor. Placing one hand in front of the other in a dizzy line, she crawls to where Sirius lies.

"Sirius," she sings, cupping his jaw with one tiny hand. "Oh Sirius, we really, really missed you, oh beautiful Sirius, we really, really love you, and my dear Sirius we never want you to go awaaaaaaaaaaay." She ends on a high note, shrill but sustained. Sirius blinks and tucks the white tip of a paw under his black and tan chest. Hannah gives an encore performance on our hike down to the beach, variations on her central theme, but when we arrive she stops singing and asks me casually about the girls in the garbage bin. "Did Stella and the Hop Stoch girls ever wonder about their mom and dad?"

"They did," I tell her. "They wondered all the time. But they were also very busy with many different jobs. Life in the dumpster wasn't easy."

"Because they were alone?" Hannah asks as she sits on the wet sand, replacing her sneakers with swim shoes.

"Exactly," I say. We walk along the shoreline, Hannah skipping over foamy trails of surf, Sirius, in the rear, sniffing and peeing on pieces of driftwood.

"What kind of jobs?"

"Well, in the morning Stella and her sisters would go to an abandoned field and pick dandelions and stinging nettle and collect stones to make a soup for breakfast."

"And what did they eat for lunch?"

"The stone soup. And they ate it for dinner too. It was a terrible soup but they had to eat it to stay strong. In the afternoon they searched the streets for pieces of string to mend their clothes and in the evening they searched for sticks to build a fire to keep them warm through — "

"Jellyfish!" Hannah shouts. Sirius rushes over to inspect.

"Don't!" Hannah screams with real horror and throws herself in front of him. "It's a jellyfish, Sirius! It stings like a thousand stings."

The jellyfish is platter-sized, rubbery looking and transparent, save for the four iris-coloured petal shapes that form a rough centre. I prod it with a stick and it feels exactly as it looks: rubbery goo.

We stay at the beach longer than usual hoping to avoid a repeat visit by Sirius' supposed owner. When we return, we are so hungry and tired we eat cereal and banana for dinner. Hannah bathes and climbs into bed. I rub my fingers in small halfmoons behind her ear, a trick to make her fall asleep faster, and continue our story, Sirius listening from the doorway.

"One day Stella was out filling her basket. She had found lots of precious stones for her soup but there were barely any dandelions or stinging nettles left. She walked farther down into a neighbouring field and into a little forest, and still she couldn't find any dandelion patches or beds of stinging nettles. She walked farther and farther. Still nothing. She was so hungry and tired she sat down on a big tree stump, wondering what she should do next. As soon as she sat down she realized the stump was surrounded by a pretty green bush, covered in bright red flowers and tiny, translucent berries. She was so hungry, she wanted to pick and eat them all. But what if they were poisonous — "

A single knock on the door. Sirius rouses himself and trots downstairs with me. Hannah is asleep.

"That dog!" the woman says when I open the door. She smiles and sighs and tries to laugh all at the same time. "That dog! I guess he gets lonely during the day. We are all out at work."

"Tea?" I ask and hold the door open wide. I've decided to change my approach.

The woman hesitates before crossing the threshold. "I can't stay long," she says as we enter the kitchen. I scoop up the cereal bowls in one hand and pull out a chair for her with the other.

"I don't mean to be disrespectful," I begin as I switch the kettle on and stuff two peppermint tea bags in the pot. "But it seems to me that Sir — Ripper — prefers to be here."

"Well," the woman says.

"I thought, I mean I was wondering if, maybe, I could buy him from you."

There is a slight whistle in the woman's sigh. I fill the teapot with boiling water and carry it, along with two cups, to the table. I pour us each a cup, holding my breath.

The woman looks at her tea, hands in her lap, and says: "My husband has decided to put him down. Because of his hip." She looks up and blushes. "I wonder if that's why he left?"

It takes me a second to fully grasp what she is saying. "Are you … do you mean … why? If he's happy here and we … we want him … why? Why would you?" I am explosive. Still standing, I trip on the leg of my chair, knock the table and send tea sploshing over the sides of the cups. In the corner of the kitchen Sirius raises his head. Looks at me. Blinks. I take a deep breath.

"His hip's not that bad, really, is it? It's stiff and stuff but what's wrong with it exactly?"

"It's a bone condition, common enough, especially with big dogs like German shepherds." She stands. "My husband, I guess, wants to remember him how he was before. He doesn't want to see him crippled." She purses her lips in a pathetic half smile. "I don't suppose you'd understand."

"No. No, I don't understand. Adults are supposed to make sense," I say, which I know, even before I finish saying it, is childish but I don't care. It's good Hannah is asleep so she's not hearing this shit. The woman snaps her fingers to get Sirius' attention. I've never had a fight with someone but I prepare myself to wrestle this woman. I'm not letting her take Sirius. "Look," I say. "I'll give you money. I'm sure we can work something out."

"Yes," she says, surprising me. But she grabs hold of Sirius' collar.

"Leave Sirius here." I move to block the door.

"You don't understand," she says.

"I think I do," I say. But I don't. "Just … please … leave Sirius here." My voice cracks. Weak, and the bitch presses her advantage.

"I have to bring him home now." She moves to the door and this time she needs to tug to get Sirius moving. "My husband wants him home. But it's a good idea. We'll discuss it."

I hold my ground in front of the door as they approach.

"I need to take him," she says, soft, as she reaches my side. "Even if it is only to say goodbye."

I move aside. Sirius balks at the door but she gives an extra tug and they're gone.

I check on Hannah. In the dim glow of her night light she sleeps, open-mouthed, rosy-cheeked, damp sweat curls framing her face. The air in the room expands and contracts with each of her breaths, deep but rapid. She moves her lips, makes a smacking noise, as if she's testing for traces of sugar in the air. When Sirius sleeps he dreams of chasing rabbits and deer. His feet paddle the air, he woofles and yips and twitches, and when he first wakes up he looks around the room as if he's returning from some place far, far away.

The phone rings. I pick up in the kitchen. It's Marie, wanting to know how everything is going. The whole story comes out in a gulp. "I should have tackled her," I finish. "I shouldn't have let her take him."

"Oh, honey," Marie laughs. "You're a lover, not a fighter. You did exactly the right thing." In the background Howard is asking questions and Marie mutes the mouthpiece to talk to him for a moment, then comes back on the line. "Our plan was to be home midday, day after tomorrow. Do you think you can hang in?"

"Yes," I say, lying. "Of course."

Sirius doesn't show up until almost lunch, meeting us down on the beach where the tide is extra low. Hannah is inspecting stones and, according to some mysterious criterion, either throwing them back to the sea or placing them in a plastic orange bucket. She rejects a smooth grey stone and when it hits the water with a heavy plop Sirius is there, ears flicking up. He barely says hello before racing into the water to rescue the drowning stone, long disappeared.

I take pity and throw him a piece of driftwood. He paddles in a circle, solemn, stick poking out the sides of his mouth, before returning and dropping it on the shoreline when two gulls sweep by. He races after, zigzagging to follow their flight pattern. His lame back leg doesn't impede his speed much, and when he needs to make a quick change in direction he drops his haunches and pivots.

"Sirius is full of beans today," Hannah remarks.

"What about this one?" I hand over a black stone, brindled with orange, very pretty.

"Nope, not special." Hannah tosses it to sea. "Let's go to Home Rock."

The three of us shelter from the sun in our little driftwood lean-to. Hannah builds a pretend fire and makes a pretend dandelion stew that everyone must eat and then she asks me to continue the story about Stella and the Hop Stoch Sisters.

I explain Stella was still very lost in the forest, and very hungry, not knowing whether she could eat the translucent berries or not, and her sisters were very worried when she didn't come home in time for dinner.

"Everything is terribly wrong," Hannah says solemnly.

"Yup," I say.

"Uh oh."

"Uh-oh is right," I say. "Let's head back. I'm hungry."

"So, Stella's all lonely?" Hannah asks as we start the long climb back to the house.

"Lonely, yes. And hungry, like me. She doesn't know what to do. She doesn't know how to get back home."

"Is Stella scared?" Hannah asks as we reach the house.

"Sure," I say.

"I know, I know," Hannah says as I unpack our knapsack and pull a carton of eggs out for dinner. "Sirius, sit down. I am Stella and you are Sirius the Dog Star and I am the hair salon. The hairdresser. You are going to the beauty shop and I will do your hair." She races away and returns with an array of tools: comb, brush, barrettes and a lavender can of styling mousse.

I scramble eggs as Hannah primps and fluffs the coarse ruffle of fur encircling Sirius' neck. My stomach is in knots anticipating the inevitable knock at the door. In the corner Hannah explodes with a deep-chested cackling laugh.

"What's so funny?"

"You won't believe!" Hannah gulps air in an exaggerated attempt to catch her breath. "Sirius just FARTED!" She laughs on and on.

"So, Stella is alone and lost and hungry," I tell Hannah. She's bathed and in her nightie. We're drinking cocoa in the living room and she wants to know the end of the story. It's hard to concentrate. I keep listening for the knock on the door, but I'm happy to be distracted and so I dive in: "Guess what happens next? Sirius, the silvery Dog Star, trots right into the meadow and comes over to the tree stump to say hi.

'Sirius,' Stella says, because she recognizes him immediately. 'I'm very hungry but I don't know whether these berries are poisonous or not.'

'Those are jellyberries,' Sirius says. 'They are not poisonous, but they are magical. You may eat only three berries. No more.'

Stella is so hungry she grabs three berries and eats them in one gulp. They are delicious. The best thing she has ever had. She wants to eat lots more and when Sirius darts off to chase a squirrel she reaches down to grab another handful — "

There is a loud bang on the door. From the living room window a black pickup is visible in the driveway. Sirius limps over to the sofa to stand beside Hannah. He stays standing, watching me. I decide not to answer the door. After a brief pause the banging resumes, this time without stopping.

"Lou," Hannah says, worried. "There's somebody here."

"I don't think I'm going to answer the door."

But the door isn't locked. And suddenly he's there, standing in the hallway, staring into the living room. A tall, narrow man with receding hair, skin flushed a vivid red. "I've come for my dog."

"No. I — "

"I'm taking my damn dog." He strides toward Sirius and Hannah, who has wrapped her thin arms around the dog's neck.

"No," I say, moving to block them but he closes one massive hand around my upper arm and pushes me against the wall. I crumple to the floor with all the resistance of a bird hitting a windowpane. Hannah begins to sob and a low growl rumbles in the back of Sirius' throat. The man brings his hand down like a hammer on Sirius' nose, grabs his collar and drags him toward the door. Hannah is on the floor, the air full of her wet cries.

"Stop it. You're hurting him … you're hurting him … stop!"

I crawl over to where she lies and cradle her body with my own. At the door, Sirius drops to his haunches, his body a heavy, dead weight, but the man manages to jerk him through the door.

When Hannah is settled in bed, still snuffling but exhausted, I call the RCMP detachment. The officer is sympathetic but apparently there is not much I can do if Sirius doesn't belong to me. He will alert the SPCA and asks if I want an officer to drop by. No, I say, that's okay.

I hang up and dial Jonah's apartment. Isabelle answers. She sounds embarrassed when she explains Jonah is at work. "So where the hell are you?" she asks, her voice suddenly less awkward. "What the hell have you been doing?"

"Nannying," I say.

"Like Mary Poppins?"

"Yeah. Mary Poppins, that's me." I tell her bits of things, about salmonberries and jellyfish and killer whales.

"Give me your number. We'll call back when Jonah comes home. We can call late, right? Because of the time change?"

It's ridiculous, but I don't know the phone number at Marie's. "Don't call," I say, scrabbling through the list of emergency contacts to see if it is written down anywhere.

"Oh."

"I mean, I'll call you guys. When I figure out what I'm doing."

"Oh. Okay." Quick inhale and exhale of breath. A dainty bull snort. Something Isabelle does when she is nervous. "Did you see the news?"

"No. What?" I haven't read a newspaper or listened to a news report since I arrived.

"They arrested Kevin Morris and Mike Hunter. You were right, it looks like there is some connection between the rapes and the fires and the people beaten up and missing. I don't know if the cops figured it out because of your tips. Most likely, I think, but the newspapers said they got a search warrant because a neighbour came home one day to find his dog — one of those little shish kebab chihuahuas — had been soaked in water, stuffed in his freezer and frozen to death. The neighbour figured it was them and when the police were investigating they found all this other incriminating shit. It's all over the news."

"Oh. What about Donnie?"

"I don't know. I haven't heard anything about him. The news is all about Kevin and Mike, weird bits and pieces, like Mike lost his job at an accounting firm in Kingston because he got caught kicking a homeless guy and that's like, the *reason*. And with Kevin, the police found all these tapes. A library of tapes. Sex tapes and shit — ”

“Did they, I mean, is there anything about Stella?”

“No, nothing. No sign of her.”

“I saw her, Isabelle. In the park, on the night before she went missing. I was with Finn, on the other side of the road. I didn't stop. I just passed by.”

“Lou, hey — ”

But I don't wait to hear the end of her sentence. “Look, Iz, I got to go. I'll call back soon.” Click and disconnect, the nerve-racked sound of the dial tone unspooling in my ear, and then I dial a number I have memorized but never called before. The phone rings twice before he picks up.

“Hello?”

“Rufus? It's me, Lou — ”

“Hello?” A third person picks up.

“It's okay, Mom. It's for me.”

“All right. What time is it?”

“Mom! It's not that late. Get off the phone, go back to bed.”

“Fine.” The phone clicks.

“I'm sorry,” I say, into the silence. “I shouldn't have called so late. I'm on the West Coast. Vancouver Island. It's three hours behind.”

“What the hell are you doing in BC?”

“I don't know.”

“It's a long way to go to avoid a date.”

“It wasn't our date that made me go. It was everything else.”

“Tell me,” he says, “about everything else.” And so I do, or try to. I tell him about the burning man and the fighting club and Stella disappearing. I describe the frenzied run down the alley and hiding in the dark at Sal's. I explain that, like a coward, I thought I could outrun violence and for a little while, down on the beach, it felt like I had, but then it showed up on the doorstep tonight, a red-faced furious man, determined to exert his right to kill a dog.

“What are you going to do, Lou?”

“I get a car tomorrow. A Honda Civic. I thought I might drive across the country and pick you up in Linden. And we could go on our date. After that, I don't know. I might sign up for some science classes at U of T. Biology. Anatomy. That kind of thing.”

Rufus laughs. “Okay. Well, you have my address. I'll see you when you get here.”

"Goodnight, Rufus."

"Goodnight, Lou. Sweet dreams."

Sweet dreams. I hang up the phone and move to the front porch, worrying over the strangeness and foolishness of that phrase. Outside, the cool air smells of cedar and the crickets and frogs resound a happy chorus, the darkness curving like the domed ceiling of a cathedral painted with the silvery bright diagram of stars. From the porch, you can't see the water but you can sense it, the salt in the air and the slight smell of sulphur and seaweed, the deep fluid movement that both fills and empties all westward space. I want to call Rufus back and say sweet dreams are for children, like Hannah, or for idiots, and I am neither. I want to call him back and say that if falling in love involves the skilled ability to share an inner self, well, I might be lousy at it. My inner self is riddled with guilty secrets and the truth of those secrets is amorphous and inchoate, depending on the weather, or my mood, or the time of day, an inner self more fabula than fact. How can I share that? I want to call him back and confess that I hold as much dread as hope in my heart when I imagine what our date might be like. For a long time, I sit, numb, wishing Sirius was in his usual place, the place he favours right beside me, positioned precisely so that when I drop my hand over the side of the chair it settles on the back of his neck and when I scratch his ruff, he pushes his head back into my hand and his black eyes look back over his shoulder and up at me, as if to say, What a pleasure it is to find myself sitting here beside you. When I eventually climb into bed the birds are already beginning their cacophonous morning wake-up call.

Hannah refuses to go to the beach after breakfast even though it's our last morning alone together. Instead she stands vigil by the front window in case Sirius returns. Howard and Marie arrive home just before lunch.

Amidst the chaos of kisses and unloading bags, Howard pulls a large cardboard box from the back seat. A caramel-coloured puppy peeks over the edge. Hannah shrieks and pirouettes and drops to her knees beside the box.

"I'm going to call him Tango." She looks up at me. "Or maybe Rocky."

Now, I think, Sirius will never return.

I decide to leave that afternoon. Marie invites me to stay for a few more days but I can't. They are ready to start their family time and it's better to rip the Band-Aid off than to linger. Hannah is outraged when I tell her it's time for me to go and over lunch she cycles between crying, pouting and not talking, but afterward she follows me to my sunny yellow room and watches me pack my knapsack from the unmade bed.

"Help me," I say when I finish packing. I straighten the sheet on the bed and she rolls to the other side and begins to straighten too.

"The Hop Stoch sisters were very worried and Stella was lost in the forest," she says. "She ate the jellyberries? You never finished."

"Hmm, that's right." I fold down the top of the sheet and move to her side of the bed to help her tuck the edges. "Just in time, before she gobbles down all the berries, Stella reminds herself that Sirius told her to only eat three berries and no more. And it's a good thing she remembered, because the berries were magical."

"Magical?" Hannah tugs her right ponytail.

"Magical. If you ate only three, then three wishes would come true." I float the comforter over the bed, let it settle and pick the pillows up off the floor.

"And Stella wishes she was home with her sisters and her parents were there too?" Hannah mimics me, plumping the second pillow at the head-board.

"Right," I say. "And with that wish Stella is reunited with her parents and her sisters, and they all live in a palace and eat plums and moon cake all day long and the girls have boxes of chalk and a skipping rope each and colouring books and crayons and as many dolls as they want and they are very happy." I pause. Hannah is leaning into me, still and breathless.

"The end?" she whispers.

"The end," I say.

"But what about the Dog Star?" she asks.

"Oh," I say. "That's her third wish. He's fine. He's there too."

"Call," Marie says and hands me their contact info. "Write. Come back any time."

Hannah plays shy when I bend to hug her. She won't look me in the eye.

"Let 'er warm up a few minutes in the morning," Howard says and bangs the Honda's hood.

A map of Vancouver Island, open, sits on the seat beside me and beneath it, a map of the country. Pulling away, I wave to Hannah through the open window. I don't go far, driving down the lane and parking alongside the road for the beach access. I pick my way down the brambly path, hearing the hoarse chorus of sea lions, and as I make my way over to Home Rock I scan the whitecapped, sunlit blue, but can't see a single bobbing black sea lion head. One of the books in Howard and Marie's library stated that out on the water the human eye can see fourteen miles before the curve of earth claims the view and the horizon disappears. Hannah thought she disappeared when she closed her eyes. I settle back into our driftwood shelter and pull out Dad's sweatshirt and my journal. I'm going to wait awhile, in case Sirius comes looking for me.

16

I wake from an uneasy sleep to a deep darkness. My head has rolled off the makeshift pillow of Dad's sweatshirt and a small sharp stone presses painfully into my temple, and my head and hands and wrists and shins are itchy, bitten, likely by sand fleas. The sky is high, silver studded, and the ocean shimmers with a blue-green phosphorescence but I am in a pocket of blackness, the surrounding trees locking me into a deep unseen space, making it impossible to navigate the steep path back to the road. I feel for my purse and pull out Dad's Zippo but the flaring light does nothing to disperse the darkness; if anything it makes it worse, the darkness all the more absolute beyond the singular bright wick of flame. I cannot guess what time it is. The cricket and frog sounds are far away, overshadowed by the voice of the ocean, with its lisps and laps, its patters and airy exhales.

The breeze is cool enough to raise my skin in goosebumps as I smooth out Dad's sweatshirt, a rain of beach sand falling in my hair as I pull it on. The woods behind me creak and shift and titter, as unseen animals break twigs and push through undergrowth on their way down to the water. There are deer in the woods, and raccoons and elk, but also wolves and coyotes, bears and cougars, any number of hungry beasts with claws and teeth that might pass by as I sit, blind and unprotected. Be a smart animal, Dad's no-nonsense tone echoes inside my head. I tap the ground, feeling for rocks, which I gather in a pile on my lap, ready to throw if anything should come too close, and then I sing all the songs I know. I cover most of the songs off Rufus' tape, "Five Years" and "Fisherman's Blues," and then some of our favourite bakery songs like "Goodnight, Irene" and "You Are My Sunshine," and then the Presley song that Red Randy covered, "That's All Right Mama," as if by sound alone I can preserve a boundary that cannot be overrun by the wildness and darkness of the night. I sing loudly, out of tune, accompanying myself with hand claps until my voice tires and the night falls silent, but the quiet is only momentary, filled suddenly with a great rushing of beating wings nearby as an eagle — I think — sweeps out of the trees. He circles, a dark form against the sky, and then dives into the undergrowth below, the air fracturing with the screams of an animal, climbing higher and higher, feral and terrified, only to abruptly stop. In the silence, my heart beating, I restart my set list but falter after a few songs, too weary to run them all again. After a second round of "You Are My Sunshine," which has surprisingly sorrowful lyrics, I pull Dad's hoodie up around my face and lie back into the driftwood shelter, softening my body against the cold rock and closing my eyes. It's impossible to keep them closed for long, though. The night is too noisy, full of imagined padded, prowling feet and sharp-toothed growls. My eyes pop open at every creak of branch and every rustle of leaves, straining to scan the boundless black space. But it doesn't matter. Eyes open, eyes closed — the world inside is as dark as the world outside. This kind of impenetrable darkness is terrifying, a kind of prison or death, but it is exhilarating too: I am a small part of the bigness of the ocean and the sky and the forest and the night. It makes me think of the last blue card that Dad wrote: *Death hath its seat close to the entrance of delight*. I thought that card meant he wanted to die, that he wanted to leave me and Jonah, but now I see it might mean something else. That night two days before he died, Dad lay on the couch, sick with what I thought was the flu, all the lights in the house turned off. "What are you doing?" I asked, switching on the lights. "Enjoying the darkness," he said.

Can I enjoy this darkness? It would be easier if Sirius were here. Or Jonah, or Dad. If they were here, it wouldn't be darkness, it would be camping, and it would be fun. An adventure that would include proper supplies. Things would be much more enjoyable with a blanket and pillow. Maybe even a sleeping mattress. The stone is cold and somehow, no matter which way I turn, my head is lower than my feet. Patting the textured surface of Home Rock with blind fingers, I ignore the grit and small stones until I find a smooth piece of driftwood that can serve as a pillow. It's not great, but it's better than nothing, and after a while I drift into the fluid space that is neither fully asleep nor fully awake and I dream, or imagine, that the ocean, which is so close, is a wide river and it is flowing very fast and Dad is lying on the couch, his face flushed and feverish, a crumpled tissue in his hand, and he says, *It is a delight*.

A shift in the darkness wakes me from my half sleep. It deepens and intensifies, the darkest night coiling in on itself, becoming even darker. This happens, this deepening, only because, on the edge of the horizon, the sun is gathering itself to rise. And in this moment, as my eyes finally acclimatize to the shadowless night, I understand something my father would want me to know. Death is both darkness and bright light. It is an immense hallway with cathedral ceilings, the long lines of the walls disturbed in the distance by the subtlest of detours. A billowing distance off to the left. And he's there. If I could join him, if I could lie down on the couch beside him and press my head against his chest, his swooshing heartbeat, he would say, *It's okay. Life is difficult, Lou. It's violent and treacherous and heartbreaking. You can hardly blame someone for occasionally giving up or running away. But you'll figure it out, kiddo.*

Morning is coming. Morning is almost here. Although the darkness is no less impenetrable now, it is also comforting. Enjoyable. If I breathe deeply I can taste morning in the air. This great sea of darkness will recede, only to return once again. No one can escape it and we all must choose: Do we drown? Or do we dive in?

The woods behind me rush, filled with the waking cries of the birds, and when it is light enough to see the outline of my hands and feet, I carefully pick my way along the beach and up the brambled hill. The sun crests the horizon and the sky lightens to a watery blue, streaked and feathered with long bands of pink and apricot and gold, a rosy glow spreading over the dimpled surface of the ocean. By the time I reach the car, I have come up with a plan.

Bell Road is narrow and hilly, hemmed in between ocean and thick forest, forcing me to drive slowly as I look for the black pickup. It doesn't take long to find it and when I do, I park down the road, inconspicuously, at a beach lookout. Huddled in my car like a cop on a stakeout, I have a pretty good view of their house. Dad and pimply teen son leave in the pickup around seven thirty and Mom leaves in a white Tercel about an hour later. I turn the Honda over, let the engine warm up and ten minutes later I park right in the driveway. I leave the car running and walk around to the backyard gate. It's fastened with a twisted piece of wire and bicycle lock, an arrangement whose purpose is more likely to keep Sirius in than strangers out. The wire is easy enough to cut with the scissors in Dad's Swiss Army knife. I open an unlocked glass sliding door, and Sirius is there, waiting patiently, wagging his tail, following me to the car, dry nose knocking my fingers. He settles into the passenger seat as I lock the car doors and we drive straight to the ferry in Nanaimo. On the boat, I finally remember to breathe.

We dock on the mainland and Sirius and I head east. We're on the run again, both of us, Sirius and me. Now it could be said that not only am I a coward, I am also a dog thief. But that's okay. When the forces you are up against are bigger, stronger and more malicious, sometimes the best you can do is be a smart animal and out-think them, even if it is a little sneaky. It's not too bad, being on the run with Sirius in our Honda Civic. Outside, the world zooms past. Inside, I am lean and muscular and my eyes are open wide.

Sirius barks when I sing along to Rufus' tape in the cassette player, a chatty bark, different from the short sharp warning he gave the coyote we passed on the side of the road outside of Hope. Like me, his favourite travelling food is grapes and his favourite places are provincial parks. He inspects the various picnic tables, sniffs and pees, sniffs and pees, reading a complex history of urine while I stare at the pleated and rippled ridges of the mountains and the hieroglyphic swirls of clouds written in the big blue sky and repeat the Nietzsche quote from Dad's index card. *I overcame myself, the sufferer; I carried my own ashes to the mountains; I invented a brighter flame for myself. And behold, then this ghost fled from me.*

The faces of the mountains are stoic, undeterred by erosion, and their timeless presence brings to mind a summer afternoon about a year ago. It was warm, but rainy, a Saturday, and Dad and I were both home — me in the kitchen, him at his phone desk sorting bills — when there was an unexpected knock. Dad answered the door, but a minute later he hollered for me: "Lou, come here. They have yo-yos." Standing on the porch, clutching Bibles, were two skinny, well-scrubbed boys. Older than me, maybe in their early twenties, but still, boys.

"Look," Dad pointed at their belts. "Holstered yo-yos. I've never seen anything like it."

"Sir, if we could have a minute — "

"Here's the deal. You show my daughter and me a few tricks and I'll give you — " Dad looked at his watch. "Five minutes. Exactly. Out here on the porch. I'm not inviting you in."

Heads bobbing, the boys agreed, eagerness a bright sheen across their skin. They unholstered the yo-yos and performed a series of tricks with descriptive names: Man on the Flying Trapeze, Pinwheel, Brain Scrambler, Seasick. Dad and I clapped and cheered and they both blushed a deep red and then Dad looked at his watch and said, "Your five minutes starts ... now."

They spoke in a jumbled rush, each finishing the other's sentences, trying to get as much preaching done in five minutes as possible. Their story was confusing but inventive. Apparently Satan has been running a world government here on earth in opposition to the government in heaven, both of which were established in 1914. When Satan is finally overthrown, then the earth will transform into a paradise. I wanted to ask, Why 1914? But Dad interjected mid-sentence: "Time's up."

"But, sir — "

"Sorry boys, but no amount of talking is going to make me believe. I'm an atheist. I believe we live and we die. I don't need supernatural beings to provide my moral compass on that ride."

The boy on the left nodded his head and turned away but the boy on the right was crushed by Dad's easy dismissal. "But, sir? If you aren't resurrected to a paradise where there is no crime or sickness or death or poverty, then — " he stretched both arms wide, Bible held aloft. "Then what's the point in dying?"

Dad laughed out loud, a big belly laugh, but, seeing the pained look on the boy's face, quickly toned it down. He smiled and patted the boy's shoulder, said, "It's a good question, son."

"You were bullshitting him, right?" I asked when the door was closed and the boys had moved over to the Turners' doorstep. "It's not a good question."

"Ah, Lou. Who am I to say what's a good question, or not? We all have questions. We all tell stories. Some stories are more appealing to me than others. But they are all just stories. So yes, I guess I was bullshitting him. As a general rule, I think people make too much out of the 'point' of living, let alone the 'point' of dying. Maybe there is no point in living or dying, other than the overarching point that we are biological organisms trying to propagate our species. The rest is just stories."

"I like stories," I said.

"Me too, kiddo," he said, razzing my hair. "And I know you'll make yours a good one."

I drive until my eyelids grow dangerously heavy and then pull into a hotel parking lot in a small mountain town, leaning both our seats back as far as they will go and falling asleep immediately. When I wake, the sun toasty across my cheek, Sirius has bridged the two seats, his left foreleg wrapped around my shoulder like we're teenagers on a movie date in an episode of *Happy Days*. I unravel my seat-shaped body and step out of the car, Sirius stiffly following, and we investigate the main street, walking out our kinks and creaks. It is a picturesque town, and we stroll like we are the moving parts of a pretty postcard, the wooden storefronts painted in bright colours and the broad shoulders of mountains in the background whatever direction we turn. Merchants have placed metal water bowls for dogs outside their stores and Sirius laps noisily from every one we pass. I buy him beef jerky and kibble and a travelling food and water bowl at a pet-food store, spending fifty dollars from Sal's envelope. With the change, I buy a Danish and coffee at a bakery called The Bakery, chatting with the long-haired girl behind the counter. She gives me directions to a campground on the east side of town that has showers and a lake. Tonight, she says, there will be fireworks down by the water, not for any reason except that after a long winter and spring it is finally summer.

The temperature climbs steadily until the heat is visible, rising off the road around the steady pulse of cars in shimmery, undulating bands, and glinting a jewelled blue across the surface of the lake, so bright it tires the eyes. Sirius and I hike the grassy perimeter, finding a quiet spot surrounded by clumps of daisies, where I strip to my underwear and we both slide into the surprisingly cool water. Sirius dog-paddles in slow circles and I float on my back, buoyant. The shifting prisms of light twinkle and bounce across the water's surface and when I close my eyes, the backs of my lids burn with a hidden sun. An arrow arcs from the mountaintops and lands in the lake, disappearing without leaving a ripple. Bull's Eye. It's lovely here. We'll stay a day or two, before we move on.

Acknowledgements

In its earliest drafts, this novel was entitled *Gut Bucket Thunder*, a name I loved but which was only nominally related to the story I was trying to tell. I was, in fact, guilty of linguistic and narrative contortions trying to work it into the story, and when my husband asked if he could also use the title as a band name I was forced into an unpleasant confrontation with the truth: the name, so perfect for Simon's band, no longer worked for my manuscript. And so the story floated in the ether, nameless, until I began a final revision under the working title *Ghost Warning*. This was the name suggested by my good friends Amy Bespflug and Joe Denham, for Joe's new band. Ultimately Joe went with another name and okayed my use for the title. The musical symmetry of this story both giving and receiving a band name is one I find pleasing, and I think Lou would too. And I want to thank Amy and Joe for allowing me to swoop in, magpie-like, and re-fashion those evocative words into something entirely different from their original vision.

Also, a big thank you to Carolyn Swayze, Kris Rothstein and Vici Johnstone for believing in this story, and to Jane Silcott for her editorial insight and generosity.

I am grateful to Alison Acheson, for guidance through the earliest drafts of this novel; to Amanda Lamarche, for her eagle eye on the final draft; and to Rachel Rose, for critical encouragement over the years.

The genesis of this story owes much to Anna Withrow, co-writer of the original Fart Song and my dear friend. I love you, Anna! And to Rob, for the intellectual, emotional and material support you offer. To Eli, for your unwavering faith — your confidence and love sustain me. And to Simon, for everything. You are my Ideal Reader.

Notes

16, 31, 233. "Death hath its seat … " This is an excerpt from *The Rule of Saint Benedict,* written in approximately AD 535, and translated by D. Oswald Hunter Blair, M.A., Abbot of Fort Augustus, and appears in Chapter VII. Webpage: http://www.liturgialatina.org/benedictine/holyrule.htm#ch7

44, 53, 60. "The only people for me …" Jack Kerouac, *On the Road* (New York: Penguin Books, 1976), 18.

55. "No ideas but in things!" This is Sal's paraphrase from a line in the poem "Paterson." William Carlos Williams, *The Collected Poems of William Carlos Williams Volume 1 1909-1939* (New York: New Directions, 1986), 263.

119. The lyrics to "Good King Wenceslas" were written in 1853 by John Mason Neale and set to the music of *"Tempus adest floridum,"* a hymn written in the 13th century, author unknown. *"Tempus adest floridum"* was included in Theodoricus Petri's compilation of hymns, *Piae Cantiones,* 1582. Webpage: http://hymnary.org/tune/tempus_adest_floridum

123. "Art should cause violence to be set aside … " Leo Tolstoy, *What Is Art?* translated by Aylmer Maude, 1899.

188, 235. "I overcame myself … " Friedrich Nietzsche, *The Portable Nietzsche* (New York: Penguin Books).

Author

PHOTO CREDIT SIMON PARADIS

A graduate of UBC's MFA program in creative writing, Kara Stanley lives, works and plays on the Sunshine Coast with her musician husband, Simon Paradis. Her writing has been published in *Fugue*, *HipMama* and *Paste* and she is a contributing songwriter to the 2013 Stanton Paradis CD *Good Road Home* and the 2015 Simon Paradis CD *Mouth Full Of Stars*. Her non-fiction book *Fallen: A Trauma, A Marriage, and The Transformative Power Of Music* was included on CBC's Best Books of 2015 list.